The Ironwood Staff by James E. Hamilton

Dear Monika,

Thanks so much for your support.

Hope you enjoy it!

Best wishes,

J. Hamilton

THE IRONWOOD STAFF

By J.E. Hamilton

To my father, Doug Hamilton – whose fantasy collection started it all;

To Sarah the Bard, for cheerleading;

To Patricia, whose encouragement was essential;

To Jacinta – for her long-suffering patience!

MAP OF THE SOUTHLANDS

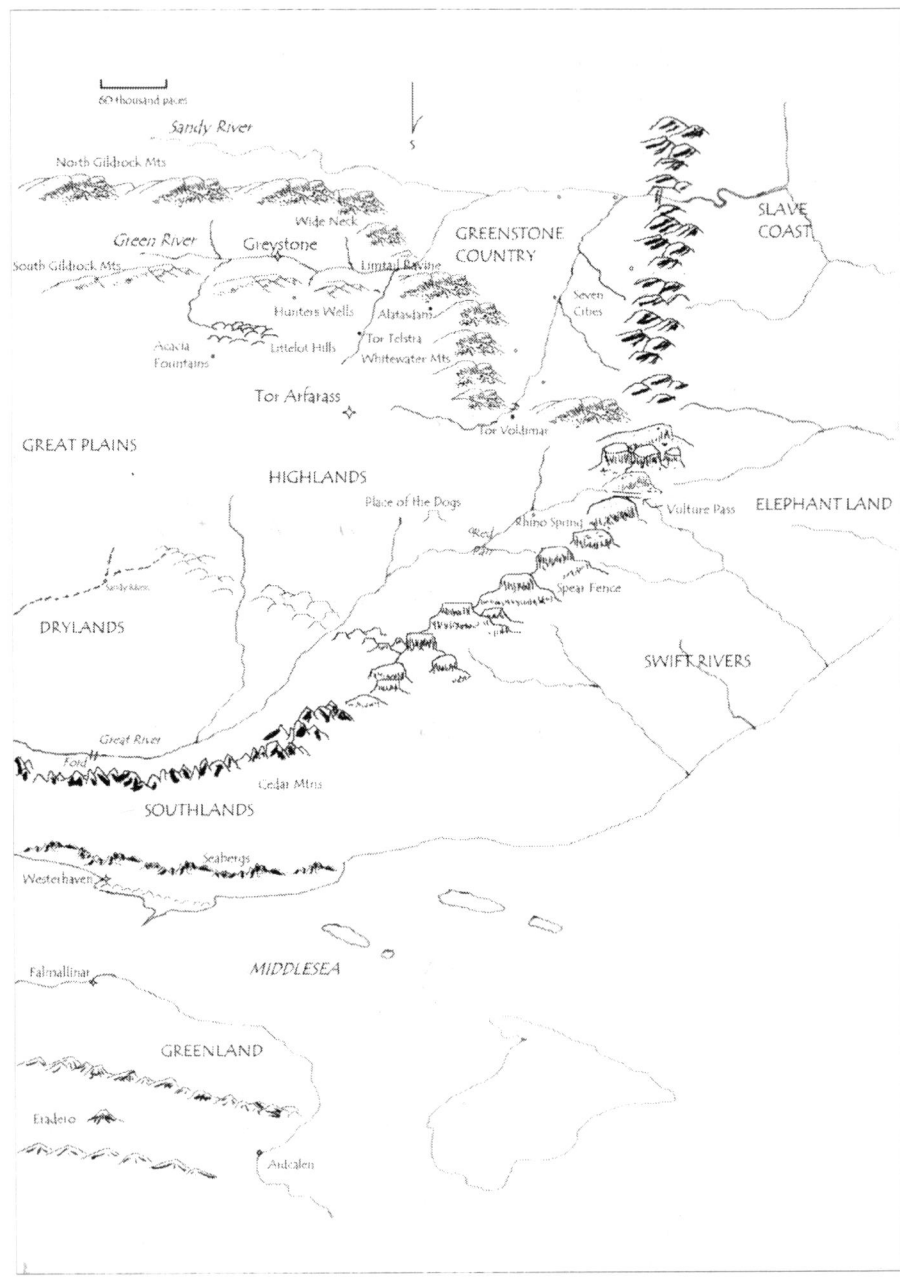

CHAPTER I

Tomas entered the gatehouse of the hallowed place, the haildom. His sandaled feet felt the chill in the south-facing archway, though it was only the fourth month of the year. He heard the sound of hooves clattering outside on the hard-packed dust, and someone dismounting. Turning, he saw a courier come in, wearing riding gear, leather hose and travel-worn tunic. He carried a bamboo tube, of the kind used to carry messages. Seeing Tomas, he called: 'Hi, brother! Where can I find the Archmagister?'

'I'm going to his chambers now,' said Tomas.

'I need to give this to him personally.'

'Walk with me, sir.'

Tomas led the courier through the gatehouse, into the courtyard on the other side. Autumn sunlight bathed the peach and apricot trees with the wistful tint of remembered summers. The trees showed yellow-spangled green, the grass about them sprinkled with flecks of red and gold. Before long, the grass itself would yellow with winter's drought, and the trees would be bare; but for just a few weeks, autumn mellowed the courtyard.

The courier seemed to be in a hurry, so Tomas picked up his pace. On the other side of the courtyard, up a short, wide flight of steps, to a high-roofed hall in a grand set of rooms over the offices, there lived the Archmagister of Hunter's Wells with his family. At the wide, sparely-decorated door of the copy room, the two stopped. Tomas rang the bell.

'Enter!' called a large, confident voice.

Tomas pushed the door open, bowing to the Archmagister. The courier followed, doing likewise.

'Ah! Tomas, welcome!' the big man boomed, striding out from his own room, all business and large grey toga. He stopped short, looking at the messenger: 'Are you from Alatasdam?'

'Yes, my lord.'

'Come in to my office,' said the Archmagister. Looking back at Tomas, he said, 'Wait here, Tomas, I'll be with you shortly,' and he closed the heavy door behind him.

The copy room of the haildom was large and rectangular, with tall, mullioned windows facing north to catch the sunlight. The steeply-sloping thatched roof was supported by tarred beams, blackened by lifetimes of candle-smoke. Tapestries hung on the white-plastered walls, and rugs with faded patterns covered the shiny, hard clay floor. There were several tall writing desks along one side, and a long table where ponderous books lay open. The tools of writing, ink pots and brushes, were scattered all around. Tomas wandered about for some time, until someone else came in: he wore hose and a long, loose tunic as Tomas did, and a knee-length poncho, a *tulme*. He had obviously decided it was winter already.

'Are you the new lad?' he asked, taking off his hood.

'Yes, I'm Tomas.'

'I see you, I'm Stefanos, the treasurer.' He put his bag down in the corner. 'Well,' he said, 'If his lordship's busy, I'll show you about.'

Some time later, the courier left and the Archmagister called Tomas into the office, and bade him sit down. 'Now, Tomas,' he began, slumping into his high-backed chair, 'you come here on recommendation from your Docent, Tolemeo. I know him quite well, in fact we studied together in the old days, when we were just Mythtellers. He took up his post in the Scribal School a few years after I took over the chair from my father, the twelfth Archmagister. That was a long time ago, now,' he waved his hand, 'and things have changed in these lands since.

'Now,' the big man shifted in his chair, 'I know that Tolemeo's Scribal School had a certain, shall we say, old-fashioned attitude in its teaching.' Tomas noted he was being watched closely, 'but in this town, in this haildom, we have a more – modern approach.' He stopped, waiting for Tomas' reaction.

'Yes... I am aware of that, my lord,' Tomas replied cautiously. 'I know that loremen today are less likely to be found in traditional roles, and times have changed.' He heard that a lot.

The Archmagister smiled. 'Well, a loreman remains a custodian of inherited wisdom, and of course your profession is the only one to preserve, copy and distribute the High Histories. That still holds, even here, but there are always more loremen than there are positions for them in haildoms and houses of learning.'

Tomas knew that by painful experience. He kept his face neutral.

'So, I am sure that you appreciate the benefits that Awakened Law has brought to this town. You have heard of the Awakening, have you not?'

Tomas said, 'I have, but know little about it.'

'Well,' said the Archmagister, 'the Law of the Kings has been around for a very long time, and some of its teachings need updating. I know that there are some who say that the town should not allow trading on the rest day, and we shouldn't favour the elders against the guilds; but if we didn't where would we be now? We would not now be living in such comfort, would we?'

'No, my lord,' said Tomas. 'I realise where my good fortune comes from.' It was a platitude, but the big man swelled as if complimented.

'Well,' beamed the Archmagister. 'I'm sure you do; I know you might have heard of the debates between the Awakened and the Traditionalists.'

Tomas, however, had decided to avoid the debate as far as possible. He had seen what happened to unwary young scribes who had too many strong opinions.He simply said, 'I am, my lord. And I am glad of the opportunity to work here, thank you very much.'

'Now, we're all brothers here, in the copy room,' the Archmagister said. 'Each loreman here has his place, and I expect you to fit in with established practice. Stefanos has shown you around?' Tomas nodded. 'Your duties will include taking dictation, and if we can't find a runner for a local message, to take it yourself. If your colleagues are complaining for any reason, I want to hear about it.' There was quite a lot else the big man said, but Tomas could never remember any of it later.

Once back in the copy room, Tomas met with the other loremen. After the Chief had left, Stefanos said quietly, 'Tomas has just had the chief's "We're All Brothers Here" speech.' The others all chuckled. The tension Tomas had felt in the Archmagister's office evaporated. Working here wasn't going to be too bad at all, he thought.

Thus did Tomas the Loreman begin his new duties. One morning, he had occasion to go into the Archmagister's office. He was in search of a seal, but the big man was not there. Tomas went to the large desk, but he made a deliberate detour past the bookshelves in his search. Here, he thought, must be a wonderful library, with scrolls old and rare. He divided his attention, looking for the stamp but distracted by the books on the shelves. All too soon it seemed, he found the stamp. On his way out, he cast one last look along the shelves – and his gaze was arrested.

His glance had passed over a carving, half-hidden behind some old scrolls. A feeling of unease crept up his spine.

The statue was only about as long as his forearm from wrist to elbow, its head poking out at a strange angle, as if the surface it rested on was uneven. The head was only vaguely human, with large simian ears and sweeping horns like a sable antelope. It was jet black, seeming to gather shadow about itself. The eyes under the horns were picked out in white quartz, with slit, black pupils. It was a carving of a *gochfeya*, a death-spirit, the haunter of places where magic had been practiced – but its eyes seemed not dead. They stared at Tomas with malevolent expectation.

What on earth was it doing here?

Back in the copy room, Tomas said to Stefanos, 'Have you seen that statue in the chief's office?'

'What statue?' Stefanos looked up briefly.

Tomas said quietly, 'The *gochfeya*.' It wasn't a word for polite conversation.

Stefanos gave a mocking half-laugh. 'Oh, that. What about it?'

'Isn't it a little –' Tomas sought for the right word '– inappropriate?'

'You don't believe in that nonsense, do you?' Stefanos said with a mocking snort. 'Next you'll be saying you only pass to the right of memorials, and bless yourself frantically when passing a graveyard at night!'

Tomas made an exasperated sound. 'I'm not superstitious!'

'Well then,' said Stefanos, 'you know there's no such thing as a *gochfeya*.' He put down his brush. 'That statue was given to the chief by some visitor. It's rather creepy,' he shrugged, 'but it's just a statue, made by the superstitious to scare the stupid.' He took up his brush again, saying, 'We don't worry about that rubbish around here. We have been Awakened.'

Tomas returned to his desk. While not consciously superstitious, he maintained a healthy fear of dark spirits. His upbringing, not to mention his studies, had included historical accounts of their existence. As for the thing being a 'gift', he knew of only one kind of visitor that would make a gift of something like that: a kchaban shaman or human sorcerer. While Wizards were mostly quacks or charlatans, they were harmless. Shamans and sorcerers were another thing altogether.

Tomas could not shake his unease. The disbelief of others could not change the darkness he felt from that statue, every time he saw it.

Outside of the Haildom in the wide world, there were darker things stirring. The western border of the Highlands was a shifting, uncertain thing. Tomas had seen maps, the western edges of which bore the simple name, 'Drylands'. Beyond a certain point, the rain simply became too erratic to support Free Farmsteads, the self-sufficient hamlets which supported and fed most Southlanders. In dry years, those farmsteads furthest west suffered, and it had not been unheard of for them to be abandoned if a dry spell lasted more than a few years.

If a Southlander farmstead was abandoned, it seldom remained so for long. The Drylands were home to a nomadic people, Riders they were called, who spoke a dialect of the Southlander tongue. The Riders simply moved in, used up all the trees, and moved on after their goats had eaten all the grass to the roots.

Riders were of mixed racial stock, living in groups of related families. Heads of clans were addressed as 'Captain', but their authority extended only to their own clan. The clans were constantly bickering and feuding. At times, an exceptional leader would gain control of several clans, and style himself 'Lord' in the fashion of the Southlanders.

When Tomas was a boy, there had been a terrible dry spell that lasted several years. Many Free Farmsteads in the west Highlands had been abandoned, their people dispersed among the walled towns and villages of the west Highlands. Two Rider clans took over the territory, and they raided far and wide in the days when the Highlands were weak, striking even as far as Hunters' Wells.

The year Tomas turned twelve, the Duke of the Highlands had sent a force from his seat at Tor Arfarass. Many displaced Farmsteaders had joined the Commando at Hunters' Wells, and the Highlanders struck hard and fast, driving the Riders out of all the abandoned Farmsteads. The summers since had been rich and quiet, and the Highlanders had re-established themselves since – but the Riders were an ever-present threat to the west of the high, dusty plains.

In the green years that followed, the Riders had fought amongst themselves, but just lately one clan had emerged victorious. Their Captain now styled himself Lord Vloch.There had been raids recently; but the Farmsteads were well-populated and well-supplied, and resisted.

One of Tomas' jobs as the office junior was sorting correspondence for the Haildom. Once there was a letter headed, 'From Lord Vloch'.

'What's this?' he said incredulously.

'What's what?' came the reply from one of the others.

'There's a letter here saying it's from Lord Vloch!'

To Tomas' astonishment, no-one even looked up. He stood dumbfounded for a few breaths. Finally, Stefanos looked up and said, with exaggerated patience, 'Lord Vloch is all right. It's Telstra we have to watch out for.'

Tomas was amazed at his colleagues. Lord Telstra was ruler of Gildrocks province. It dawned on him that his colleagues were not only dissenters, but rebels as well. 'But – I thought Vloch was using kchabani?'

Stefanos shrugged. 'The Archmagister is on good terms with him. His power is growing, and we have to stay on his good side - especially with the trouble in Tor Telstra.'

'You mean the strife between the families?'

Stefanos nodded. 'Lord Telstra is Universalist. That's what all the trouble is about. He's persecuting the Awakened in his city.'

Tomas said no more. He shook his head. He knew now he was on shaky ground. Better not to say too much, he thought. He didn't want to be sent back to his family in Sweetwaters with the indignity of a dismissal hanging over him.

It was a day of late autumn, when the sky was dark blue and crystal clear, and dark shadows stretched long in the copy-room, when a message came. Tomas and Stefanos were the last people in the office. Tomas saw no courier, but an acolyte, one of the clerics of the haildom, came into the office, looking like someone who has trodden in something unpleasant. He came directly to Tomas' desk, and handed him a thick bamboo message-tube.

'Kindly give this to the Archmagister,' he grumped, and left the room quickly, wiping his hands absently on his brown habit as he left.

Tomas got up, taking the roll to the door of the Chief's chambers, and knocked. There was no answer.

Stefanos called, 'He's out,' without looking up from his work. 'Just leave it on his desk.'

Tomas opened the door. At the large, beautifully-carved desk, he lightly tossed the roll onto a pile of parchment. The roll bounced off and onto the floor, on the other side of the desk.

With a sigh of exasperation, Tomas walked around the desk. The bamboo roll had come unsealed on one end, and the parchment had fallen out onto the carpet. It was lying open on the floor, a strangely floppy, discoloured sheet. Tomas picked it up, politely trying not to read it, but his curiosity was piqued. It was written in the tongue of the Southlands, but Tomas had never seen a script like this, and he knew two alphabets and three languages. Examining the short scroll, he read and understood with utter disbelief.

Lord Vloch to Archmagister Andrias

I will assume control of your domain in the next two days. You have done well to cooperate. Others did not, and their skulls adorn my tent. My own men will not harm you, nor any of the town elders. Your people however, and everything in the town are hereby made over to the possession of the Lord Kroghnash Skullbreaker, son of Smulbuggu. His esteemed counsellor, the Shaman Fegga, will visit tomorrow to ensure your compliance with my will.

Please be aware of the blessing of the primal spirits that have been invoked over this message. As the addressee of this scroll, you are now under their protection.Do not undertake any spiritual offices until the visit of the Shaman.

Be submissive.

The signature on the bottom was in heavy, black runes, and Tomas' mind shuddered at the sight of them. Darkness fluttered in his peripheral vision, and he had a horrible, fleeting vision of gaunt, hollow-eyed *gochfeya* with too many teeth. The vision passed quickly, but it left a sour, dry smell like old urine.

Suddenly Tomas heard a movement in the room outside, bringing him back to his senses. Quickly, he rolled up the parchment, but noticed as he did so the similarity of the parchment to his own skin. His nerves jangled with a horrible suspicion. Replacing the seal on the end with shaking hands, he placed the roll on the desk, and left the office as quickly as he could. He felt the eyes of that statue on him.

Stefanos was gone. Tomas could hear him in the records room, on the other side. Tomas closed the door, and walked to his desk, where he stood holding the slanted sides. His soul was shaken. Stefanos bustled out of the Records room, saying, 'Don't look at it now lad, the light's failing. Leave it for now, or you'll ruin your eyesight.' He hadn't seen Tomas' ashen face. Picking up his cloak from the wall, Stefanos said, 'Peace! See you in the morning,' and bustled off.

Tomas left as soon as he could.

Dead leaves blew over the dust of the road as Tomas made his way to his boarding-house. Again, the shock fluttered at the corners of his mind. The long evening shadows threw grim grey fear on his heart, and he tried to make sense of it all. Why had the Archmagister adopted the Awakening? Was it just politics, or did he think the Raiders were going to win, and he should be in their good books?

The magnitude of the betrayal was shocking. How could he turn out to be a kchaban-friend? He was an Archmagister, and the son of an Archmagister! The kchaban hordes did terrible things to people, even ate them!

Tomas picked his feet up and started moving again. Then he jumped as a familiar voice shouted behind him: 'Hey, baboon-brain!'

He turned round to see his friend Tadeos, wearing his habitual smith's apron under his cloak, and a kilt as usual. Tadeos wore a kilt even when there was ice on the ground.

'What's wrong?' Tadeos grinned, pushing Tomas ahead of him along the road. 'Don't get in people's way! You look like a dog that's just had its bone stolen.'

Tomas managed a weak smile. 'Can you talk?

'Yes, I'm fine thanks,' Tadeos sarcastically reminded him of his manners.

'Sorry, I see you. Are you going to Simon's tonight?'

'I was thinking of it.'

'Straight after work?'

'Right. See you after dark, then,' said Tadeos, hurrying on down the road.

Simon's House was a nicer pub off the town square. Its clientele was mostly junior loremen and journeyman craftsmen. In a small town like Hunters' Wells, there were few enough of them to know each other. Tomas and Tadeos had met there years ago, when they were in the same gaming team.

In a small booth screened off by grass mats over wooden frames, Tomas and Tadeos sat down on low couches, drinking their usual beer from leather cups. After making small-talk for a few minutes, Tadeos said, 'So - who is she, and where is her husband?'

Tomas got up and closed the blinds.

'Oh-ho, a local man, is he?' Tadeos quipped.

Tomas sat down. After a moment trying to muster his thoughts, he blurted, 'The Archmagister is making an alliance with a kchaban king.'

There was a silence. Tadeos stuttered for a few moments, then managed to say, 'How, what - how do you know?'

'I happened to see a message sent to him. He doesn't know I saw it. Or I hope not. It was -' but Tadeos interrupted him:

'But he's the third in a line of Archmagisters! His father, and grandfather -'

Tomas interrupted in turn: 'It was written in our language, on -' he swallowed '- human skin!'

Tadeos put his leather cup down gingerly. 'We're cursed,' he said, swallowing.

'We're going to roast,' agreed Tomas.

'What are you going to do?'

'I don't know,' Tomas sighed. 'If he realises I saw the message, he'd have my gizzard for lunch.'

'Have you told anyone else?'

'No! Are you mad?'

Tadeos sat quietly, thinking for a moment. 'I just don't believe it. But somehow this is almost expected. He's been getting more and more fruity for a while, now. But, you'll have to keep it to yourself for now -'

'There's nothing else I can do!' Tomas interrupted. 'There are no more Universalist Eldermen, and they were the ones who would have called the Duke's Men here! But get packed in the meantime, in case we have to leave in a hurry.'

'What do you mean, "We"?'

'You know as well, Tadeos. Sorry.'

Tadeos made a grunt of disgust. 'Maybe we should run off and join a society of wizards.'

Tomas managed a weak smile. 'Professional fakes? I think I've a bit more self-respect than that.'

Sometime during the night, the wind woke up. It moaned under the eaves of the boarding-house, rattling the shutters. Tomas woke early, feeling cold and uneasy. The moon shone pale and silvery out of a pitiless, lightening sky. Winter had come.

When he got to the haildom, there were two tough, wiry ponies tethered by the gatehouse. One had a strange harness of barbarically splendid make, all silver studs and tooled black leather. The other was kitted out with the same rough gear that Tomas had seen on the horses of the strange messengers. To Tomas the ponies seemed dejected, and he stopped briefly to talk to them; they stared at him with dull disinterest. Then, remembering his own troubles, Tomas went carefully up the steps up to the hall, and quietly across the courtyard. There was no-one to be seen. The sky was dark winter blue, and an icy wind wafted dead leaves around the gardens, mocking the pale sun's ability to warm. The haildom, once such a quiet place of peace and wisdom, had become cold and dark. The silence seemed to mask an unseen threat.

Walking along the gloomy corridor with his sandaled feet getting colder, Tomas heard the Archmagister's booming voice: 'I want to know when he comes in!'

Tomas' heart skipped a beat. He felt like a naughty child caught out in an indiscretion. But, he thought to himself, he can't know – can he? He walked quietly to the door of the office, and peeped in. Stefanos was busy with something on a desk, his back to the door. Tomas was about to sneak in quietly, and ask the loreman what was going on, but something held him back. As he watched through the crack of the door, Stefanos left the room with a tray of empty ink-pots, heading for the storerooms.

As he stood in the corridor wondering what to do, Tomas became aware of someone watching him. His heart in his mouth, he jumped round to see the acolyte from the night before. He looked as if he hadn't slept in a week, his habit rumpled, and the front of his head silver-speckled with stubble. In a haggard whisper, he said, 'It's that message, isn't it?'

Tomas felt the blood drain from his face. The old acolyte's eyes were bloodshot and staring. 'I've been handling holy writings for most of my life. I've been awake all night with the worst nightmares I've ever faced. It all started as night fell, and it was only as dawn broke that my mind cleared enough to think: the only thing I can think of that was different was my touching that message. Come,' he beckoned, and Tomas followed him further along the corridor. 'The messenger was probably told to give it straight to the Archmagister, but he was lazy, and wanted to go to the pub. He gave it to me instead, and I've been up all night, battling the rot in my mind. Thank the Powers I don't follow that Awakening rubbish, so I can still shake the thing off. Did you open it? Did you touch the scroll?'

'It fell open as I dropped it on the desk in his office,' Tomas pointed to the Archmagister's office. 'I picked it up, and saw the writing.'

'And?' the acolyte stopped in front of the garderobes. They slipped into the doorway, out of sight of the corridor. The acolyte was looking intently at Tomas' face. 'What did it look like?'

Tomas swallowed. 'It was written in a style of runes I could only just read, and it was written on human skin!'

It was the acolyte's turn to blanch. His voice rose to a hoarse whisper. 'You read it! I don't know how you're not a jabbering idiot already! What in the name of all the Heavens are you doing here still?'

'I don't know anything about magic!' Tomas hissed. 'There are kchabani coming to our lands. The Archmagister and the Eldermen have arranged it all to suit themselves, and I don't believe for an instant that the kchabani have taken up trade.'

'I don't understand it! Are you eladan, that you haven't been affected? Do you think he doesn't know? Get out! Now!'

Tomas' legs stiffened with the beginnings of panic. 'Where should I go?'

'As far as possible - out of the country, if you can. Just go! But hold on a bit -' the acolyte came up to Tomas, marking a blessing on his forehead. '"I bless you in the name of the One,"' he intoned quietly, '"May you be blessed in all your ways, may evil be confounded around you, may your paths be straight and blessed."' And may you always be protected from those who seek you with evil,' he added. He slapped

Tomas' face gently. 'I can at least give you that much.'

Tomas felt a calm come over him, for the first time since he'd seen the scroll. 'What about you?'

'Don't worry about me. My place is here. I'm too old and tired to go running around...'

There was a tense moment, and then came was a sound that both had dreaded: the Archmagister's voice. As they stood, not daring to move, there came the sound of heavy steps. All of a sudden, a pair of watchmen, in their leather armour and helmets, appeared from the opposite direction. Seeing Tomas, they turned and seized him, twisting his arm behind his back. One of them called out, and they were quickly surrounded by other watchmen, including the Chief of the Watch. The officer said to the acolyte, 'You'd better come with us, too, Acolyte Timaeos.'

Tomas was frog-marched back up the corridor to the Office. There, the Archmagister stood speaking to Stefanos, who stood ashen-faced in front of the chief's door. The Archmagister looked at Tomas, then at the old acolyte. His face was inscrutable. He said to the chief of the watch, 'Good, he hadn't got far; but you'd better take him too, officer,' he pointed to the acolyte.

The acolyte said 'On what charge?' But the Archmagister said nothing. His face seemed strangely different, as if distracted.

Tomas noticed something in the Archmagister's office, just inside the door. It seemed to be muttering. The atmosphere suddenly became dead and cold, a burden on the mind. Tomas saw the acolyte saying something under his breath. The muttering from behind the door of the office increased in volume. Tomas could see a tall, rank shadow in there, through the crack of the door. His heart seemed to labour, and he felt dizzy. As he swayed, the acolyte bellowed in a voice shockingly loud: 'Be still!'

The shadow in the office convulsed and fell out of sight. There was a crack, as of wood splitting. Tomas' head and heart suddenly cleared. In a rush of clarity, he heard the Archmagister say to the officer, 'That does it, lock them up! And be careful, don't let them say anything, they could put a spell on you!'

While Stefanos looked on in shock, they were taken away.

It was cold in the cellars. For most of that day, Timaeos and Tomas sat in the gloom, silver winter light coming from a tiny grille high up on the wall, which looked out at street-level from the cellar. They were the only ones there. Tomas wondered what people were saying in the town. He wondered what his parents in Sweetwaters would think if they heard about this. Around sunset, when it became too dark to see in the cellar, there was a racket at the door, and they were escorted into the presence of the Archmagister.

As in any human settlement, there was a judge in the town court to hear cases. He was normally a respected figure, so Tomas and Timaeos hoped for a fair hearing.

In the windy cold of the evening, a large crowd had gathered outside the courtroom. There was a lot of shouting and jeering as the prisoners were taken from the cellars to the courtroom. 'Go to hell, witches!' 'Been having fun together in the cells, have you?' 'String 'em up!' Tomas noted that there was a heavy watch presence outside the courtroom. He had never seen so many in one place before; but they stood guard without their usual hardware, carrying only truncheons. Inside the courtroom there were more, perhaps the rest of the force. The tension in court was palpable. It occurred to Tomas fleetingly that there couldn't have been many men on rounds if so many of the Watch were here; but then he had enough to worry about.

The courtroom was full. Not only were the Archmagister and the Eldermen present, but so were most of the craftsmen Tomas knew, practically all the community of the haildom, and the entire staff of the Scribal School. Anyone who was anyone in Hunters' Wells was there. Tomas looked at the crowd, seeking a friendly face: There were grim faces, contemptuous faces, thoughtful faces - none friendly. Scanning the left of the courtroom, he found one face looking downright worried: it was Tadeos. Tomas tried to catch his eye, but he looked away quickly.

The Sergeant-at-arms bellowed out, 'All be upstanding!', and the judge swept in to the room. He wore the usual black robes and blue headdress draped down over the shoulders. He had a huge, bushy beard, which made his face look dark and threatening.

Taking his place in the high chair, he made a few announcements and called, 'Who are the accused, and what are the charges?'

'The accused are Tomas the Loreman and Acolyte Timaeos, a member of this Haildom,' boomed the officer. 'The charges, your Excellency, are gross indecency with respect to minors, and conspiracy in witchcraft!'

There was a vicious mutter from the crowd, and Tomas and Timaeos were subjected to curled lips and disgusted sneers.

'Have the defendants pleaded against them?'

'No, your Excellency.'

'Call your witnesses. Let's hear this out, at least.' The judge appeared to have already made up his mind. Tomas felt his stomach drop, and glanced at Timaeos. The acolyte was strangely calm, his lips moving slightly.

The officer called out, 'The Law calls My Lord Archmagister Andrias!'

From his place at the front of the courtroom, the Archmagister swept to the witness-circle. He bore his badges of office, a polished staff of black ironwood and a leopard-skin cloak. Facing the judge, he began his oration: 'My Friends, Sons and Daughters! My own son, aged twelve, has accused this man in my presence,' he shook his staff at Tomas, 'of plying him with drink, attempting to seduce him!'

The crowd's muttering became a muted roar.

'Not only that,' the Archmagister intoned, 'but when arrested, these despicable fiends cast a spell on a good man from the Thornlands, rendering him an imbecile!'

The crowd's tone changed from angry to fearful.

'My people,' the Archmagister continued, 'The Law given to us by the kings of old, and guarded yet by his descendant the duke, is clear on this - such vile, unnatural deeds are punishable by death!' There was a surge of sound from the crowd. 'A death, good people, as dishonourable as any can know - that of being hung from a tree!'

The angry muttering became louder. The judge banged his desk with his orb, shouting 'Order! Who speaks for the defence?'

The Archmagister turned round, addressing the judge with some impatience. 'Since all parties are of ecclesial rank, it has been decided that both prosecution and defence can speak for themselves!' Pressing on with his oration, he continued, 'These two unspeakable fiends have not even pleaded in their own defence! When accused by the arresting officer, they had nothing to say! Your Excellency should find them both guilty, and send them to the Abyss where they belong!' There was another wave of sound from the crowd.

'Do the accused have anything to say?' The judge cut the Archmagister short.

'Yes, your Excellency!' declared Acolyte Timaeos with sudden energy, surprising everyone. 'I find it strange that My Lord wants Your Excellency to send us to the Abyss, when he himself is manifestly of the opinion that there is no such place!'

The courtroom became deadly silent. Timaeos had raised the stakes, effectively declaring himself the Duke's Man. 'According to his Awakened teachings,' the acolyte went on, 'there is neither good nor evil, so how can pederasty be a crime? We must all follow our own hearts, after all!' His turn of phrase was deliberately ironic, thought Tomas. 'We both deny all charges. We were not even accused by the arresting officer! I further submit, Your Excellency that these charges are nothing but a smokescreen for a real evil, uncovered by this loreman and myself – the crowd suddenly became noisy – the making of an alliance with kchabani!'

There was deathly silence for a second – then the courtroom erupted in shouting. The Archmagister bawled, 'Liars! You won't get out of it that easily!'

Tomas was suddenly aware that there was more shouting from outside the courtroom than within. There was some disturbance outside. With a shocking crash, a rock was thrown through one of the tall windows, and flames danced on a roof visible to one side. There was a fire in the square! With a slam, the doors were thrown open. A freezing darkness blew in and every single lamp was extinguished. A tall, dark, hooded figure stood in the doorway. Holding its arms aloft, it mouthed a few hideous words, and a dread gloom descended on the room. No-one moved. It was as if a suffocating blanket of despair had fallen. Everyone stood or sat where they were, faces drawn, their eyes staring hopelessly in the dark. The Archmagister remained still, as one turned to stone. While Tomas watched, the room filled with dark-cloaked figures. Some were men, but others were not: tall and blocky or short and squat, and every shape in between, mostly shorter and even darker than men, with huge ears pointing out at weird angles from their heads; their legs were bowed, and many had huge hands; there was a clink of armour under the cloaks, and the flickering light glinted on metal-bound helms; but it was the eyes of the non-humans which Tomas noticed most - all glaring big and red with reflected firelight, slanted, almost reptilian. Thus did Tomas make his first acquaintance with kchabani.

When the courtroom was ringed by the grim, silent figures, the horror that had cast the spell over the courtroom walked in, and a number of big, heavily-armed kchabani in identical suits of armour followed. They took places on either side of the door, standing like a guard of honour. The human who came in was tall, bearded and wiry, brown-cloaked with his legs in leathers in the fashion of the Riders, and carried a broad-bladed cutlass. Steel rings jingled on the upper edge of its blade. He looked around at the crowd: 'Well? Where are the heroes of the hour? Is anyone going to stand against the Lord Vloch?' He looked around at the grey faces of the people still under the dark spell. 'I didn't think so.' As he paced forward, he stopped, as if remembering something, and said, 'Are there any half-eladi here?' The question met with a room full of blank, dreary looks. He clicked his tongue in irritation.

Walking up to the Archmagister, he said, 'Well, now! Thank you so much, Andrias. We couldn't have done it without you!' He cuffed the big man on the back of the head, and looked around. Seeing Tomas and Timaeos, he swaggered over. 'So, what's going on here? A trial of some kind? Well, any lawbreaker among you Southlanders is a friend to me!' Laughing derisively, he ordered, 'You are free to go!'

As they made to go, the tall, dark spell-caster rasped, 'No, lord!' and he indicated the acolyte. 'Not this one! He is deep in the Nameless One's service!' The shaman's face was invisible under his hood, but he stank. Tomas could smell him from several paces.

The human turned to Timaeos, his face smouldering hate. 'You must be the dirt that ruined my best magician! Aren't you? Just when he'd gained control of the Archmagister, you had to cast your own spell! He hasn't spoken since! He's a wreck! Do they know that you cast spells in a haildom? Answer me, you filth!' He punched Timaeos in the face and the acolyte fell to the floor.

Stung even in his repression, Tomas made a move towards Timaeos. The attacker swung his sword up, hitting Tomas' face with the flat of the blade. 'You stay out of this, dung,' he snarled. Tomas staggered back.

In a rage, the man turned to Timaeos and stabbed him as he tried to rise. The rings on the blade dragged out gobbets of flesh as he ripped it out. The acolyte gave a hoarse scream as he died. Tomas looked on numbly, his face smarting from the blow, his nose bloodied; but his senses were deadened by the spell of despair. As the man stood up, he bellowed, 'Move them out!' The humans were rounded up and taken outside.

In the cold square a huge fire had been lit, fed by furniture from nearby buildings, and by the truncheons of the Watch, now dead or captive. There were some kchabani dancing around the fire, beating drums and chanting in their horrible language. The humans had the clothing cut off their backs, and were tied in shivering rows, hand to foot. However, no-one seemed to notice Tomas. Once, he was seized by a kchaban, but another stopped him. They gabbled at each other, something in which the name of Vloch featured prominently, and Tomas was allowed to walk away. The leader's half-joking judgement of him seemed to count for something. Tomas trudged to the edge of the square, keeping to the shadows. He moved towards a side street, but turned back at the sight of raiders and kchabani looting houses and shops. Feeling the effect of the spell beginning to wear off, Tomas stood still. His mind slowly woke up to the danger he was in. Taking his chance, he walked as slowly and carelessly as he dared back towards the side porch of the courtroom, which was now completely dark, having been well looted. He thought of nothing beyond finding somewhere to hide.

As he mounted the stairs, the spell wore off completely. Fear, no longer suppressed, came in waves. His mind reeling, he slid down the dark side of one of the pillars, listening to the talk in the Square. The spell had obviously started to wear off the others, too. A voice was raised in protest: one of the Eldermen was complaining. 'But, my lord, you promised that you would spare us when you took over!'

'I promised no such thing!' It was the voice of the man who had killed Timaeos. That must be Lord Vloch, thought Tomas. 'It was the Lord Kroghnash who made those promises – and promises made to Highlander men count for nothing!' The man's voice took on a gloating tone. 'Now, you asked what is to happen to you - your women are to be mothers to arkchabani. Do you know what those are?' He waited, apparently enjoying the anguished wails and screams of outrage. 'Yes, quite right! Halfmen! Kchabani that can endure the light of the sun! They will probably enjoy it!' He laughed unpleasantly, saying, 'The men might be used in a similar way, those that aren't for the pot, I couldn't possibly care less! You people have lorded it over us for far too long, in your fat little towns and villages. I'm not running from you filth ever again!' He stopped short as a sound came over the beating of the drums. It was a horn, harsh and braying. It came from the east side of town. 'Rot!' shouted Vloch. 'It must be those blasted Dukesmen already! Thragga! Get after that horn, go help your people on the east side!' Most of the kchabani and raiders made off in the direction of the horn. Lord Vloch's bodyguard remained. The raiders continued with the binding of the prisoners. Sounds of fighting came from the east. Hunter's Wells was a town with only ruins of walls, since the Awakened never fought. Then a high, clear bugle began to sound from the east side of the town, like a signal. It rang out three times. A few heartbeats later came a new sound, this time from the west side of the square.

Tomas listened, not daring to hope. It was horses! Without a fanfare, without even slowing down, a commando of Dukesmen charged into the square. The firelight flickered on their long, straight swords, as they swung and hacked at the Riders. Some fired arrows at the kchabani of Vloch's bodyguard. Vloch swore and ran for the Courtroom, the nearest shelter. He was running straight for Tomas, slumped in the shadows. As he drew level, Tomas threw one leg up, tripping him. Vloch fell face-first onto the stone floor in front of the door.

'Over here! He's down!' Tomas yelled at the top of his voice.

Vloch pushed himself up, shaking his head. 'You little slime!' he snarled, his face a mask of blood and hate. He drew his sword, raising it for a killing blow. Tomas was too slow, he just couldn't move his legs in time. Just as Tomas thought it was all over, an arrow sailed into Vloch's side, and he staggered and fell with a hoarse cry.

Tomas looked into the square, hoping to see the person who had shot the arrow. What he saw was a scene of absolute chaos. The kchaban bodyguard had managed to regroup. With their night-vision, they were fighting too well against the men on horseback. As he watched, a shadow detached itself from a pillar nearby. With a start, he saw the Shaman. It moaned as it came at him, its hood falling back to reveal a nightmare of grey skin and matted hair, its eyes fitful red in the firelight. It was too much. Tomas jumped up, leaped down the stairs and made a frantic dash towards the fire. An arrow narrowly missed his head as he ran, and another smashed into the stone at his feet, cutting the sole of his sandal. By now, some prisoners were free, having been cut loose by the Dukesmen. Others fled in their bonds, not waiting to be cut loose. Tomas found himself surrounded by frantic, coffee-coloured, wobbling, rank humanity.

'Hey! You with the clothes on!' It was one of the Dukesmen on foot. 'Get out of here!' He indicated the direction the other prisoners had fled. Tomas needed no further prompting: he ran as fast as he could.

Some distance up the road, he heard screaming behind him: a mounted Dukesman came galloping out of the square, shouting, 'Scatter! Run for your lives!'

With sinking heart, Tomas realised something must have gone wrong. He took off to the right, through someone's kitchen garden. Weaving his way through the vegetable plots and fruit trees behind the houses to the edge of town, he soon found himself in open pastureland. There was nowhere to hide. In a nightmare of fear, he ran on.

The moon rose huge and gibbous, low in a pitilessly cold sky, as Tomas trudged north and west from Hunter's Wells. He had run and walked for some time, and there was no sound of pursuit. He reached the ridge north of the town, a line of golden quartzite boulders at the top of a sudden, dramatic drop in the land to the north. The grass here was short, the soil thin, with tiny aloes and small-leafed herbs not found anywhere else, standing silvered in the moonlight. Following landmarks known only recently, Tomas picked his way down the slopes.He hid in a patch of bush at the bottom of a watercourse, not quite dry at this time of year. There, he wrapped his cloak around himself, and fell into an exhausted sleep.

CHAPTER II

'Well, look at this!' The voice was loud and aggressive.

An unintelligible grunt came from further off. Tomas tried to shake sleep off. His body protested, stiff and cramped. He groaned.

'I found one already, fast asleep in the donga.' The abusive voice came from a huge, heavily muscled individual, who was looking down at Tomas with an extremely unpleasant leer on his face. 'C'mere, you!' He pulled Tomas up by the tunic with one vast arm. In the cold glare of the winter sun, Tomas found himself looking into a rank, gap-toothed mouth, partly hidden by a large, straggly, black beard. The small, close-set eyes reminded Tomas of a baboon. Dropping the water-can he was carrying, the huge man used both hands to hurl Tomas onto the lip of the gully. Tomas was still trying to right himself when the man kicked him in the stomach, and he collapsed, gasping. Then, two pairs of hands grasped him by the shoulders and pulled him upright. The pain in his midriff lessened. 'First takings of the trip!' This came from a smaller, though still dangerous-looking, man. Tomas was half-dragged to a wagon. They took a pair of manacles on a long chain, passing the chain through a rail on the bodywork of the wagon. The manacles were clamped around his wrists, leaving him some freedom to use his hands, as long as he didn't move too far. They then left him there, and he slumped onto the spiky-dry grass, glad of his long winter hose. All around him, a band of ill-favoured thugs was rising, peering out from sleeping-blankets and cloaks around the remains of last night's fires, all scattered in the long, yellow grass. Another wagon stood further off. The men wore an odd assortment of old Highland army gear, Pedlar leather, and Thornlands hides. There were no more than thirty of them, all armed. Tomas' heart quailed. They were slavers, human-scavenging wherever there were people fleeing from war. They must have pitched camp only a few paces from him last night, and he hadn't heard a thing. They must have followed the invaders, he thought.

Slaving for profit was illegal under the Universal Law, though slavery was a penalty for serious crimes. According to the Law, a slave had to be freed on the Rest Year, which was not due to occur for some time still. The terrible events of the day and night before suddenly seemed remote, in the immediate horror of Tomas' situation. Not for the first time in the past two days, he tried to find solace in prayers. Again, it seemed as if they were not being heard.

For that entire day, Tomas was left chained to that wagon. The sun had little warmth to it, shining from the north, pale in a dark blue sky.

The wind blew all day, cutting mercilessly. The slavers moved out in small groups, and from time to time during the day would return over the lip of the shallow valley with fresh captives, some still naked from their attempted escape from Hunter's Wells. They reported little that Tomas could hear, but it seemed that the Dukesmen had been few in number, and had been driven off. Most of the captured humans had escaped from the town, but the slavers were hoping to pick up as many as possible this day, while the raiders and kchabani were distracted by the sacking of the town. They brought in men and women, moving quickly and quietly so as not to attract kchaban attention. The men were chained to the same side of the wagon as Tomas, the women on the other. As despairing as he was, Tomas' heart went out to those captives who had first been caught and stripped the previous night. They were continually shivering, wincing from the sharp touch of dry grass on bare feet and legs. All day long, he heard the frightened weeping of human beings; the sound burned into his heart. In the evening they were all given food, dry road-bread and hot water. If anyone needed to relieve themselves, they went under the wagon. Around sunset, when the shadows were long and blue and the light dull orange, someone came round with tattered blankets, which doubled as garments for some in the days that followed.

After a night of deepest misery and cold, Tomas saw a crisp morning, sneezing and coughing. He doubted he'd slept at all. The wind had lessened and there was a fine dusting of frost on the grass. A hot bowl of thin sorghum-meal was given to each captive, and they moved out soon afterwards. Though kchaban groups sometimes wandered by at a distance, none seemed to pay the slavers any mind.

For two days, the slavers and their stock moved north by west, towards the distant cuesta ridge of the Gildrock Mountains, and the Thornlands beyond. There were no human settlements on the way they took; any runaways would be alone in the wild with no water. The wind had blown itself out and the air became warmer as the little-used road they were on followed the land down. Small, scraggy, evergreen thorn-trees and springy, waxy-leaved bushes grew in the long, golden grass on either side. At the end of the second day, after trudging alongside the ox-wagon on short rations, the captives were in a sorry state. Everyone was coughing, and many had red noses and bleary eyes. The women on the other side of the wagon had been subject to long abuse, and no longer cried themselves to sleep. They walked numbly, no longer caring. A few of the men had been subjected to the same treatment. Anyone who had tried to intervene on another's behalf, would do so no longer –

those who had survived the beating now walked with swollen faces and broken bones, and looked as hopeless as the women.

At the end of the third day they came to a stop in a narrow pass flanked by sandstone cliffs, bronzed by sunset. Above the cliffs on the right, an ancient, tumbledown tower brooded against the darkening eastern sky. Tomas knew that it and the others along this ridge had been built by the oreladi in remotest times, and had been rebuilt and used again and again, by eladi or men, during the three Foul Wars that had taken place over the centuries. Now, its windows gaped empty. There was no salvation there.

He wondered what would happen to them the next day. Suddenly, with an inexplicable certainty, he knew that his captivity would come to an end very soon. Where did that come from, he wondered. Maybe it means I'll be dead, he thought, mildly surprised at the relief that came with the thought.

The small hours of the morning found him in a restless dream. He felt sure that the cold would kill him, if he didn't find more warmth; but he couldn't seem to rouse himself. Under the light of the moon, now waning from the full, he dreamed that some of the thickly clustered trees at the foot of the cliffs had started to move. He watched with growing alarm as they slowly crept closer to the camp, where the sentry sat slumped, sleeping by the last livid coals of the fire. Tomas jumped awake - but the trees didn't stop. They came closer. Tomas saw they were people, clothed in a shade like the trees. In their hands were alien, long-handled swords, glinting bitterly in the moonlight. Some carried long bows, others bore spears with long, elegant heads. He shook his head and blinked his eyes and the armed figures became distinct. Dressed in strange, rigid sheets of some kind of armour, and hooded, they were almost invisible in the moonlight. They seemed human, or at least they were not kchabani. He looked to the sentry, but the man would never wake – a long-shafted arrow was buried in his chest. Looking around, he realised that the entire camp was surrounded by mute, deathly silent, dull figures. Without a word, they kicked some of the sleeping slavers awake. There were several short, ugly scuffles, but the slavers were overpowered quickly. Those who fought were slaughtered without mercy. The strange, grey fighters spoke little. They moved with quick efficiency, gathering the surviving slavers around one of the fires – but didn't put any wood on it to make some more light, as Tomas expected. The moonlight seemed to be enough for them.

One of them, a rangy figure with a long sword slung across his back, said something to the slavers in a strange, lyrical language. Another, armed with a long-bladed spear, translated: 'You are slavers. You have trespassed upon the soil of Greystone with human traffic. Such is punishable by slavery in turn. Your fellow humans, whom you have taken captive, will be allowed the protection of the Lord Engolaran.'

Then the senior fighter with the long sword gave an order. A pair of foot soldiers made their way to the slave-wagon. Without a word, they opened the manacles of the slaves, who responded with tearful gratitude. Tomas noted that they all wore helms under their hoods, and their armour was strange, made of metal bands embedded in heavy fabric. There seemed to be a fragrance, or a glimmer beyond sense, about them. It made Tomas think of white flowers on a starlit summer night. When the captives were all released, the slavers in their turn were chained to the wagon. A ragged cheer and scattered applause went up from the former slaves. Some of them kicked or spat at their former captives, but the grey fighters separated them.

The officer then addressed them through the translator: 'Pay attention, Men! Ye are now free to go whither ye will. However, if ye wish to be protected people, ye must accompany us and do as ordered by our Commander. Those who will not so do, must leave now and make their way to their homes.' Their language was rich, rhythmic and very beautiful, but with a sharpness to it at the same time. The translator's accent had an ennobling effect on the Highlander dialect. Tomas recognised some of the words as being eladan - but if these were eladi, their language was quite different from the antique form learnt by all loremen in their studies.

None of the former captives moved. Home was a ruin, or worse, two waterless days away through hostile territory. There was nothing for them to go home to.

After a long pause, the leader gave some more orders. The dead slavers were quickly and efficiently buried, and clothes were found for most of the blanket-clad captives. In the last few cold hours before dawn, the oxen were spanned in and the group moved off, grey warriors, captives and refugees. Their rescuers moved silently, scarcely rustling the grass as they went.

Passing along the narrow gorge in the still, cold light, they left the dirt road they had been following and struck off north through the bush. Although Tomas and the other captives could see no path and little open space, the heavy ox-wagons had little trouble following the course the strange warriors traced. The land beyond the pass rolled gently down, and the country opened out. They walked through wide, flat lands between two cuesta ridges as the sky began to lighten in the east.

Somewhere on the flat, open floodplain, they joined a road of hard-packed earth, dark and damp underfoot with dew. The sky in the east was bright, and Tomas heard fowl calling far off on the plain. He tried to engage some of the alien fighters in conversation, but while they were not unfriendly, none of those at the back of the column spoke his language. Nor did they seem to speak any Tsuna, which Tomas had learnt in his childhood. Tsuna was the tongue of the dark men of the Thornlands, north of the Highlands.

As the sky brightened they came to a stop, and Tomas saw that the leader was speaking to a mounted figure, riding – a zebra? He wore similar gear to that of their rescuers, his head covered in a steel-bound helm and a long headdress. He sat on a saddle that bore a large quiver on one side, a heavy bow on the other, but used neither bridle nor reins. His armour was more recognisable as such, with breastplate and shoulder pads of what looked some lacquered hide, and steel forearm and calf guards. Tomas noticed that his mount had stripes on its neck and forequarters, butwas dun brown otherwise. After speaking with the footmen for some time, he turned and galloped off the way he had come. The column travelled on.

The sun rose in a stab of orange over distant trees as they went. The fighters greeted it with a song, many-voiced and of piercing clarity in the crisp morning. Their voices were clear and beautiful. Tomas remembered that first morning of new freedom for the rest of his life.

That whole day, the refugees trailed the slave-wagon along the same dusty, red-brown road, travelling north, then eastwards. The air became warm and very dry as the sun rose. They stopped regularly to drink from the slave-wagon's tank, and at mid-day the fighters gave them dried fruit and bread. Winter bit less in this northern country, leaving a land mild and dusty. They stopped for the night in a circle of thorny acacia trees, where the soldiers built a large fire and tended it all night. The humans were grateful to spend a night in warmth for a change.

The next day, rising before the sun, they continued north. During the morning they were passed by a column of mounted troops, their lances keen and bright in the winter sun, their mounts' flanks coated in dust. Around noon the road ran onto an elegant bridge, spanning a deep river course with one slender, golden stone arch. The water here was flowing strongly despite the season, rushing loud over black stones. Someone told Tomas that the translator had called this the Green River. That information wandered through Tomas' mind before it connected with something. Then, just as he stepped off the bridge on the other side, he remembered some geography. 'Hey!' He shouted, 'We're in Eladan country! It's Greystone! We're safe!'

'Eladi?' said a bitter-mouthed old man in a blanket. 'But they're witches!'

Tomas didn't feel like talking philosophy at this time of day. 'They have powers, yes, but natural ones. They didn't get them from the Abyss, like that shaman.'

The old man humphed. 'Same difference, as far as I can see.'

Tomas left him to clutch his bitterness. He had enough of his own, but he could ignore it when he was walking toward freedom.

Eladi were known to keep to themselves, and were seldom welcoming to strangers; but they were deadly foes of all Foul Folk. The eladi of Greystone were on their side! The mood of the company lifted. As they came out of the trees on the far side of the bridge, the sun was at its zenith. It was mild, like an autumn day in the Highlands. The road turned due east, as they walked behind the eladan company, who sang a strange, wild song as they took the last road home.

Late afternoon of that same day found the refugees still on the same dry, dusty road. They were now quite close to the northern of the two cuesta ranges of the Gildrocks, and they walked below steep, south-facing slopes, shaded somewhat at this time of year. Tall trees, mostly stinkwoods and ironwoods, crowded thickly on either side. The dusty dull sunlight traced shade-echoes of their bare branches on the grass and the road. Tomas looked in wonder at the trees – he had lived all his life on the grassy Highlands, where trees of such size were rare. They were watched for some time by a group of giraffes, peering snootily over the trees from the south. As they went along, Tomas struck up a conversation with the translator, whose name was Tenvardo. Tomas told him what had happened in Hunters' Wells in the tongue of the Southlands as they walked.

The column approached a pair of tall, four-sided obelisks, one on either side of the road. They looked extremely old, standing taller than the trees, as if marking a gateway. Devices were graven on them, thrown into relief by the afternoon sun: the one on the left showed an orchid in a rhombus, the other a heptagram in a circle. Tomas and Tenvardo moved between the obelisks while still talking. All at once, Tomas experienced a sudden recognition, as if someone had called his name. The feeling was so strong that he looked around, looking for the source of the greeting. He caught the eye of Tenvardo, who was looking at him very intently, as if he had done something unexpected. The column halted, and the officer spoke to Tenvardo. The translator then turned round, and announced to the humans: 'This is the entry to the Heartland of Greystone. Ye may enter as friends in need.' He then watched as the humans came through the gate.

Beyond the gate, they moved into thick forest. The trees were mostly evergreen ironwoods, but others were bare with winter. Large, strange birds with unfamiliar calls moved through the trees, high above their heads. A troop of pale grey monkeys watched them warily. After some time, the road passed close by a long, low building. The roof was of dark slate, the thick walls of dressed grey stone. The windows were narrow slits, and there were eladi there in the same dusty-coloured headdresses and light armour as the humans' rescuers wore. There, all received more water and dried fruit to eat, and the former slavers were taken into custody. The oxen were outspanned, and the refugees were escorted onwards by the guards.

The road beyond the guardroom was paved with slabs of brown slate. It took them on through the trees and suddenly went past a garden, where bare branches traced shadows on short grass, yellowed by winter's drought. In the midst of the garden was an elegant, domed building with thick walls of rough-dressed golden stone and tall windows filled with coloured glass. The east side of the building consisted of three tall arches, framing complex patterns of intricately woven stonework, all filled in with coloured glass. Tenvardo told Tomas that it was a Hallows, dedicated to the memory of eladon fighters who fell in the First Foul War. After the gardens, the road descended in wide, shallow steps, down through the steeply-sloping forest in a series of hairpin bends. At the bottom it crossed a gully on a simple wooden bridge, and wound gracefully back up among the trees. The trees there were especially large and ancient. At the top of the slope, the road ran under winter sun branches for some distance, until it suddenly opened out onto a wide square of very fine, close-cropped grass. There were grassy terraces on three sides, all edged with strange plants and bright, unfamiliar flowers. The group crossed to the un-terraced side. All was growing and healthy, even now, in the first half of winter. It seemed as if time did not touch this place, or at least touched it without destruction. In the middle of the open side of the lawn stood a large stone archway, wound with by climbing roses. The pathway beyond that arch was lined by solemn, silver-leafed ironwood trees which shaded it, deep and cold. They looked ancient. Straight as an arrow the path ran for the distance of a long sprint, gloomy and chill in the late afternoon. The refugees moved along in reverent silence. This was a fine, a glorious place, and they keenly felt their own littleness and poverty.

In all this time, they had met no-one, but at the end of the straight pathway they came on a common, cobblestoned road. There, for the first time, they saw workaday eladi: eladi moving around their daily business with unconscious grace, as if they knew exactly their place in the universe, and were quite content to be there. Some looked at the refugees with astonishment and pity; most were completely inscrutable. Eladan children, small and beautiful in bright-coloured ponchos, watched them with eyes too old for their solemn little faces. The people here were golden-skinned, with unearthly light green, grey or even blue eyes, and hair ranging from black through red-brown to gold. Their ears when visible were neat and pointed, as Tomas had been led to expect; but theirs were discreetly close to their heads, which only emphasised the ugliness of kchabani, made from warped eladan stock.

Most of the buildings of Greystone were similar to human houses. Houses were thatched and circular, with wattle-and-daub or brick walls, all plastered white and timber-framed; some consisted of a set of such buildings set about a courtyard. Grander buildings could be square, with grey stone walls, tiled roofs and wide eaves for shade. The eaves were supported by graceful arborescent pillars of wood or stone, carved at the top with fronds, birds and monkeys. Live trees closely surrounded many buildings, often growing around or over them, the buildings accommodating the landscape. Houses had wide windows open to the breeze, which could be closed off by screens or blinds of bamboo or wooden slats, all painted with animal figures, or trees, or vines. Balconies had railings with simple branching patterns, all in wood or stone. Stone buildings had arched windows with patterned casements, filled by fine-woven netting to keep out mosquitoes, or by glass, which seemed luxurious to the humans.

The streets were lined with still more trees, forming shaded avenues and sheltered ascents, with broad, shallow, slated steps painted white on the edges. The humans walked along like country bumpkins, gawking at everything. The eladi and their town were all so alive, so bright and sparkling in the evening. There was life in abundance in Greystone, even though the land outside was dead and dry with winter in the fifth month of the year.

The refugees were taken to a compound by the river, consisting of a few score simple, circular houses gathered around several small market squares. There was a large boma, a communal area under a roof with no walls, with a large hearth and communal cooking area. It seemed to have been made for a large number of people. Tenvardo told Tomas that it had been built some time ago, for humans who came to the market, sometimes in large numbers; but the trade had dried up since. It was a run-down part of town, and cold by the river, but the humans were all too glad to have food, shelter and clothing. It was the Camp by the River, or as the eladi came to call it, the Man-camp.

Life in the Man-camp was not too bad, all things considered, and as the weeks went by the humans counted themselves lucky. News came from eladi who had been south, and from other refugees who began to trickle in to the eladan country - and it was all bad. Tomas heard of the rape of towns, the pillage of food and farm stock, and the disunity of men, who were at first slow to come to the aid of other humans on the opposite side in the civil strife. The movement called the Awakening had taken root in the western half of the Highlands, and wherever there was disaffection with the rule of the Duke. The enemies of the Highlanders had been quick to take advantage of any divisions. Always, the Evil Alliance was at work: the kchaban hordes of Kroghnash the Skullbreaker would march in by night and take over, and then raiders would occupy and loot the towns by day. Towns were betrayed as Hunter's Wells had been, or resisted, but if they fell, the walls were made hideous with stakes and crosses. Cruel executions were the least of the evils recounted. The atrocities of kchabani had been legend for centuries, but were only confirmed by reports. There were tales of leaders being skinned alive and vultures set on them; of people nailed to the ground and left for hyenas; and of burnings, blindings and blastings with acrid salts and strange arts. Again and again, people asked for loved ones by name.

Such were not the only tales. Tomas found to his dismay that tales of his trial in Hunter's Wells had come to the camp as well. With the usual embellishment that goes with word of mouth, the stories bore little to no resemblance to the truth; and he was mistrusted. No-one would confront him, so he never had an opportunity to put the record straight with anyone. As time went by, even those who had been present at the event, came to listen to the more lurid versions. There was never any open confrontation – just a suspicious look, a knowing nod of the head, a sudden silence when he appeared at the cooking-fires – and it didn't improve as time went by.

On the other hand, he was one of the few humans consulted regularly by the eladi, mostly thanks to his skill in languages. Tenvardo came often to offer him a job somewhere in the Town itself, along with any others who knew anything of the local language, Celadi. Over the course of several weeks, his fluency increased, and it was a joy to speak, even though he came to live as an alien to both men and eladi.

When Tomas had been in the camp for several weeks, a new group of refugees appeared. It was a chilly night, and he found the new arrivals around the fires in the communal area. Tomas went up to a fire and addressed no-one in particular, 'Hello, everyone. Is there anyone here who speaks Celadi?'

Most simply looked at him blankly before resuming their conversations. One man asked, 'Why do you want people who speak – that language?'

'Celadi,' Tomas repeated. 'It's the local language here. There aren't enough who speak it, and there's always work for anyone who does. The Eladi pay money.'

The man shook his head. 'Don't know. Hey, did you hear there's a magus here tonight?' Some of the others around the fire looked round, agreeing. The magus was obviously already quite popular.

'A Magus?' Tomas asked. 'Is he real, or just crazy?' The only time Tomas had met a wizard, it had been a tipsy old quack who had regularly come to his home town of Sweetwaters. The old man had said that Tomas was to become a wizard himself, which had led to no end of ribbing from his friends.

The man didn't smile. 'He's all right. He's over there,' he pointed to another fire.

Tomas moved over to the hearth and repeated his question. Sitting among the group of new people was a stocky, salt-and-pepper-bearded man in his sixties or so. A staff rested against his shoulder. He wore rough home-made tunic and hose such as was worn by labourers, and a plain, dark green mohair cloak. He had his hood up against the cold. He looked up at Tomas' question and said, '*Hei quen Celadi,*' I speak Celadi.

Tomas answered in the same language, 'The eladi will pay you to translate in dealing with us.' The old man excused himself and stood up. He and Tomas left the fireside, and went a short distance away, past the huts and down to the riverbank. It was very cold and dank. The days were warmer here than in the Highlands, but nights by the river were really cold. The three-quarter moon reflected in the still waters of the river, shining strangely on the reeds on the far side.

'How are you known, father?' Tomas asked as politely as he could.

'My name is Bethnero, people call me Master Ben.'

'I am Tomas the Loreman,' said Tomas, bowing.

'I, um –' the old man watched Tomas closely. 'I suppose you've heard about the wizard that's supposed to be with the new people here?'

'Yes,' Tomas replied guardedly.

'Well, I'm the one they're talking about,' he said, watching for Tomas' reaction. Tomas noted he had very light eyes, rare among Men. He could think of nothing to say, so he said simply that.

'I knew today that I would meet someone,' the old man went on, 'who would be looking for people who spoke Celadi, and that that person...' he hesitated, still watching for Tomas' reaction, '... was to undertake instruction to become a magus.'

Tomas felt strange. It was as if someone had told him the most wonderful news in all the world, but the message had been delivered by a jester. 'I am to be a wizard? I'm sorry, father, I have no idea...' He stopped, but the old man said nothing. 'I'm sorry. I don't think I'm the person you're –' Tomas stopped.

'No?' smiled Ben. 'Well, please listen carefully: tomorrow, someone will mention a journey to the Middlesea. You must follow that person to wherever they are staying, and they will ask you to accompany them.'

'If you say so, father.' Tomas really wanted to get to a fire, now. The situation had just changed from tiresome to eerie, especially down here by the misty, cold river. This old man seemed a bit too eccentric for his liking. Just then he was rescued from further awkwardness by some people looking for 'The Wizard', so he made his excuses and left.

The following day he was kept busy enough to forget the strange conversation of the previous night. He had a hectic time, since there was now more work than ever, translating for eladi organising the refugees. At the midday break, when people were settling down for a rest after lunch, Tomas met a stranger, a human merchant named Kobos, who ran a caravan that usually ran from the Thornlands over the Cedar Mountains to the South coast. He and his people had just left the western Highlands before the raiders had come, and were now stranded by the war.

'I'm thinking of going all the way to Westerhaven, next time - that is, when things quieten down again. I brought a caravan up, but I need one to go back again, if I'm to live. We may meet eladi in the Cedar Mountains, and I'll need someone to translate,' the merchant said.

'I speak Celadi,' Tomas said. 'I've read about the eladi in the Cedar Mountains,' he added. 'They are among the oldest peoples in the world, related to some of the eladi here.' He stopped, realising he sounded a bit egg-headed.

Kobos looked interested. 'You know a bit about these people, do you?'

'Only what they taught me in Scribal School.'

'Scribal School? So you can keep accounts, as well?'

'Well, yes.' Tomas decided not to mention that he had seldom managed to balance the books.

'Tell you what,' Kobos made as if to leave, 'I've got to go now; but come to my house near the Singing Gate of the city in half an hour – mine is the place with the green door – and I might have a job for you. I think I can pay you better than the Fair Folk here,' he added with a grin.

'Very well, then,' said Tomas, and they bade each other farewell. Tomas never even thought that Westerhaven was on the Middlesea coast.

However, on the way to the Singing Gate of Greystone City, Tomas was called back to the hospital. By the time everything was sorted out, it was a lot more than half an hour since he'd left Kobos the Merchant - so naturally, by the time he got to the house near the Singing Gate, the man was gone, and Tomas had no idea where to find him.

That night in the man-camp, old Ben found him on his way to the hut he slept in, and asked him how things had gone. Tomas replied with some asperity, 'No, it didn't happen as you said it would.'

The old man was surprised. 'Some ill will must be against you, Tomas.' He looked around, saying, 'Do you live here? Can we talk in private?'

None of the other regular occupants of the hut were there, so in they went. It was cold and smelly, as usual for a space occupied by single men, but Ben made no comment and sank down on Tomas' pallet. Tomas lit an oil-lamp.

'I came across other ill-will against you,' said Ben. Tomas thought he knew what was coming. He sat down on his clothing bundle as the old man continued, 'Tell me your story. I want to know about Hunters' Wells.'

Though wary, Tomas was glad of the chance to tell the truth of the matter. He began, 'It all started when a treasonous old fool, an Archmagister no less, tried to shut me up with a false accusation.' Tomas told the tale of that autumn afternoon, and Ben asked what happened when the Riders attacked. Tomas found some parts of the tale difficult to tell, with a history of opprobrium weighing on them.

Old Ben remained neutral throughout, with complete understanding. At the end, he said, simply said quietly, 'I see. You've had a bad time, at least as bad as the rest of us.' He sighed, gathering his faded green mohair cloak closer about himself in the lamplight. 'Tomas, I know you don't trust me much. You probably think I'm a complete charlatan.' He humphed, 'I can understand why: people have a lot of strange ideas. But, I am the genuine article, whatever your experience may have been. And I can tell you, that people such as us –' Tomas looked up at him sharply '– sometimes have troubles like this – people don't trust us from the start, and so they look for a reason.'

'Like us?'

'Yes. You are meant to be a magus, and evil will try to stop you. You will be eventually, I can tell.It would be better for you in the end if you just stopped fighting it. You can't argue with the One.'

'Why should I drop everything to follow you? And, what's the One got to do with it? He isn't doing anything for me!'

'The ground of all existence doesn't make bargains. Even the gods don't do it often. All this is happening, just to burn the evil out of you, so to speak.'

Typical, thought Tomas. As soon as he starts losing the argument, he turns it on its head to suit himself. His resentment hardened. 'Sorry, Father, I'm not interested. All I have left is revenge.' His jaw clenched as he rose, saying, 'I'm not going to be a victim anymore. I'm going to make them pay!' He stopped for breath. Why was the old man looking at him like that?

'Such is not your path, O Tomas,' Ben said simply. He stood up in the awkward silence. 'There is much danger for you, and little glory, on the road of revenge.'

'It's a path I have chosen, at least. If you want a disciple, you'll have to find someone more free from hate.' Ben left, and Tomas didn't see him again for some time.

The next week was Midwinter's Night, at the end of the sixth month, and in the man-camp there was quite a party. The customary bonfire was huge, and some eladi came down too, bearing food and season's greetings from the city. Tomas took part in the ceremonies and the singing, but the festival only emphasised his alienation from the other humans. It was a bad time of year to be alone.

After Midwinter there was a sudden flood of refugees. A Highlander city, Tor Aradan, had fallen to the Evil Alliance. While the news was very bad, Tomas was glad that the city was nowhere near Sweetwaters, where he'd grown up.

Then, after two weeks of madness, the flow of refugees suddenly stopped, as the hordes of Kroghnash the Skullbreaker started probing the borders of the land of Greystone itself. They were strong and numerous, attacking from staging-grounds in parts of the Highlands under their control, and always at night.

By that time there were a few more fluent Celadi-speakers among the humans. The Lord Engolaran of Greystone announced the formation of a human militia, to improve the defences. There was no shortage of volunteers eager for revenge. For the first time in his life, Tomas was eager to learn the craft of war. He wanted to strike at something. Every time he missed home, he cursed Lord Vloch; whenever he worried about his family in Sweetwaters, he felt like killing a kchaban; every time he caught someone giving him that knowing, suspicious look, he wanted to bash in the head of Archmagister Andrias. The day that Tenvardo told him about the Militia, Tomas went to the Watch headquarters just above the man-camp to volunteer. It looked as if a good part of the male population of the man-camp had decided to do likewise.

The hard-eyed elado who came out of the main building gave them a keen look, and addressed them fluently in their own language, but in the archaic mode of several centuries ago: 'So! Wish ye to fight against the Fouls?'

There was a rumble of assent from the humans.

The eladan held his hand up to his ear, as if he couldn't hear.

'YES!' the men shouted in unison.

'That is well!' the eladan shouted back, 'for so do we! Now, the measure of a fighter is not merely in the weapons he bears. The measure of a speaking-being in armed service is his loyalty,' he counted off on his fingers, 'his readiness to obey, and his endurance! An ye are prepared to undergo training for war, I shall teach ye these things. An ye will not learn them,' he paused, 'ye will not be trusted with arms.' He stopped and looked around at them. 'Those of ye who will yet submit to the Lord Engolaran's authority, must be at the Singing Gate of the City ere I come there!' And he took off at a jog.

The humans took a moment to work out what he was on about. Then someone bellowed, 'COME ON!' And took off at a flat sprint. The next moment, every last man was running up the hill after the eladan, tulmes flapping and sandals slapping. Fortunately, the eladan wasn't running very hard, and they all reached the Singing Gate before him – just.

Such was Tomas' introduction to military life. It was the beginning of the hardest twelve weeks of Tomas' life, with boring food (though there was always plenty of it), chronic fatigue and being shouted at in two languages, all day and every day. As new recruits, they were not allowed to walk anywhere: they had to run whenever they were outside a building, or there was hell to pay. It was easier not to think, and in many ways that was a blessing. The friends Tomas made during that time were still friends when he met them years later. They shared a common fund of experience, jokes and a language that was a strange mixture of Celadi and Southlandish: '*trin, doel, trin, doel,* halt, *doel dui*', right, left, right, left, halt, left turn; 'This kit is *raca*, lousy'. Any rule-breaking was punished by hours of punishing training on the parade-ground. Standard individual punishment exercise was a head-stand, which was supposed to build shoulder strength and balance. To the heavily-set men, it was a sore trial. If the group was at fault, they didn't bother with acrobatics – they ran, and they ran... and then they ran some more.

For three months, they lived in an isolated camp a full half-hour's walk to the north and east of the city in the forest. They wore uniforms of dusty-drab tunic and hose, and went barefoot. Their clothes had to be kept clean, as did the elongated rondavels where they slept. The barrack-rooms had to have their hardened-mud floors polished; the pallets they slept on had to be precisely lined up and ludicrously neat. Personal hygiene was enforced – regardless of how cold the water was. Everyone was issued with an iron-shod wooden staff and an *equet*, a single-edged sword with a short, gently curved blade, which had to be kept sharp and rust-free. Everyone was given a smooth nicking stone, rust and notches for the removal of, and there was a grindstone in the middle of each rondavel. Such was not a life Tomas would have chosen for himself, among his own people; but having to stay one step ahead of the *Tinceldo*, the leader-of-twelve, every day kept his mind off his own troubles and built camaraderie among the muckers.

Over the course of the first six weeks, the recruits had regular practice with javelin, bow and *encti*, the eladon glaive that comprised a sword-blade on the end of an assegai-wood spear-shaft. Each man's ability with each kind of weapon was assessed, and halfway through the training, they were drilled individually and issued with the weapon in which they had scored the most points. Most men were given *enctii*, but Tomas was glad to be issued with a longbow: he was simply not brawny enough for hand-to-hand action, but he knew he was a good shot. Also at the half-way point of their training, everyone was issued with suits of armour, which Tomas had first seen on the eladi who rescued him from the slavers. The helmet was standard iron and leather, with a sun-veil over all that hung down over the neck, and hid the metal from view so that it didn't glint in the sun. The body-armour was made of heavy canvas which had bands of iron woven into it. It was light and flexible but hard, and could even be repaired in the field. Tomas had never seen anything like it. They were also allowed to wear sandals again, which was an improvement.

The second half of their training was spent mostly camping in one of the more remote corners of the Green River valley. Here they learnt to survive in the wild, living partly off the land, even in the dead of winter.

Tomas often found himself wondering if he had made the right decision – he didn't take orders well – but he strengthened himself with the memory of Acolyte Timaeos in Hunter's Wells, gritted his teeth and carried on. In later life, he was to look back on this time with amazement, wondering how he could have lived, expecting to die fighting; but if he learnt anything in that time, it was to disregard his personal feelings in favour of a greater good.

After those grim twelve weeks their introduction to the Greystone Human Militia was complete. They left the training camp for special quarters in the city, to make space for the next batch of men to come in for training.

It was springtime, at the end of the ninth month, when Tomas first saw action. In the small hours of morning, they were roused from their thin pallets by the strangely melodious shouts of *Ethenceldo* Cordun, the leader-of-120. Men came tumbling out of their huts, some still tying up sandals, or with cloaks in hand. The Ethenceldo just sighed and shook his head. When all were gathered together, they were given a briefing: the regular guards had had to go to take part in operations up the river, and the Militia was required to set up a perimeter at the west end of the settled forest, in case any enemy units got through.

'This is your chance for some strokes against the Fouls, O Men!' bellowed the Ethenceldo, looking far too young and refined to be the martinet that the humans knew him to be. A hard elado he was, but scrupulously fair. 'Perform this task well, and ye shall be trusted with greater things!'

He struck the right note with that, thought Tomas. There was cheering and a clashing of staves on shields. Tomas felt his stomach twist with tension, but reminded himself of Hunter's Wells and checked his bowstring. He had twenty-four arrows, and each one had a kchaban name on it. He loosened his short, elegant *equet* in its sheath. This was it!

In short order, the humans had formed up into their deployment groups, the largest of *enctostari* or spearmen, one of *econstari* or javelin-throwers, another of *quenstari* or bowmen. There were around a hundred all together. In the moonless, dead cold of early morning, with no-one to mark their passing, the tawny-cloaked figures jogged along the high road eastwards, a bloodthirsty eladon song rising in the steam of their breath as they went. They passed a hallows in the dark, and moved out of the settled forest and down into a shallow, wooded valley. Here during summer ran a tributary of the Green River, but at this time of year the stream was little more than a muddy gully. At the crest of the rise above the watercourse, they were separated into groups of four to six, each with at least two spearmen and one bowman. Then they took a long run in a wide arc, and one group was left at regular points along it, each within shouting distance of the next. The forest was thick in places.

Tomas' group consisted of himself, two *enctostari* who he knew only as Ben and Andy, and an *econstar* from Hunter's Wells called Simon. Their station was at a place where a faint track led down the short, steep slope to the gully, passing through thick undergrowth on the near side, but not crossing the watercourse. The far side was much more open, with a gentler slope.

After the Ethenceldo had left, taking the torch with him, Tomas could at first see little. After a minute or less, his eyes grew accustomed to the darkness, and he found himself able to see surprisingly well. The budding stinkwood trees formed eerie, scrag-fingered shapes against the starlit sky. Time dragged on, and Tomas began to feel cold, as the heat of his run began to dissipate through his cloak. For some time, the men crouched quiet and alert in the shadows. Eventually though, the two *enctostari*, who were old friends, started talking to each other in quiet whispers. Their voices gradually became louder, and Tomas shushed them as he sat shivering in the cluster of stinkwood trunks where he hid. From their positions below him on the track, they looked up at him, then at each other, and started talking again, only not quite as loud. Tomas looked back at Simon. He sat quietly in the dry leaf-litter further up the track, his three javelins leaning against a tree-trunk.

Tomas was surprised by a strange feeling of being watched: he could see only vague shapes across the gully, but there was a faint rustle in the darkness ahead. He gave a quiet hiss, and nocked an arrow on his bow, looking for the source of the sound.

The men below him jumped to the alert, readying weapons. They adopted combat poses without even thinking. For a time they all stood still, as the tension grew, then slowly dissipated. Then, as the men started to relax, Tomas' sense of threat suddenly increased. One of the spearmen said quietly, 'Must be a bird,' but as he said that, there was a crackling and a thumping in the dead undergrowth on the far side, and a party of kchabani moved out into the gully, bristling weaponry.

Time seemed to slow down for Tomas, but he just couldn't seem to move fast enough. Gritting his teeth in concentration, he drew the bow, sighted and loosed an arrow at the nearest kchaban. The missile whooshed lethally as it flew, then clanged as it ricocheted off the thing's helmet. The kchaban reaction was frighteningly fast: they ducked, bounding like monkeys back towards the sparse cover of the trees. Tomas loosed another arrow after the last of them, and was rewarded by a short, sharp scream. He was just nocking a third, when an arrow, shorter than his, thudded into one of his sheltering tree-trunks, just in front of him. He jerked back, slamming into another trunk. There wasn't enough space to dodge in here, he thought.

'How many are there?' called one of the spearmen in a hoarse whisper.

'More than us!' Tomas replied. Another arrow thwacked into another tree-trunk, spraying wood-splinters. There was a whiff of the tree's pungent bark. He peeped out quickly. He couldn't see a thing. 'They can see in the dark!'

'*To me, Militia!*' bellowed the other spearman. There was no response, but Tomas knew the other groups must have heard. There was a hoarse shout from the other side, and about ten kchabani charged down into the watercourse, pelting for the track where the humans were. Tomas saw a javelin from Simon soar down the track, transfixing the hide shield of the biggest kchaban in front. Disregarding it completely, the big one came on and engaged one of the enctostari. Tomas readied another arrow, and fired it neatly into the crotch of another kchaban. The target collapsed with an incredibly high-pitched shriek. Tomas, exulting at finding his mark, exposed himself too much: an arrow, fired by a night-eyed kchaban, found its way between the trunks, hitting him in his left hip. Bellowing with pain like a bull, Tomas was knocked back. He saw the archer-kchaban break cover across the gully, moving to fire at him again, but it was a fatal mistake: Simon's last javelin arced over, embedding itself in the kchaban's ribcage.

As Tomas battled in agony to right himself, the *enctostari* were overrun. Ben fell, slashed by kchaban machetes. Andy, realising he was alone, made a break for it, but was shot in the lower back by another arrow which found its way past the panels of his armour as he ran. Simon, to his everlasting credit, stood his ground. Standing over Andy, he drew his *equet* and put it through the face of the big kchaban, before he too was beaten down. Tomas managed to nock another arrow, but he panicked. His shot went wide, as three kchabani came at him in his hiding place at once. Tomas drew his *equet*, but as he did so, there was the whipping sound of eladon arrows, and most of the remaining kchabani fell. Reinforcements had arrived! Tomas' assailants knew nothing of it though, and one lunged at him with a great spear. The heavy head hit him below his right collarbone, punching right through his armour, and he reeled in shock. He fell screaming, waiting for the death blow – but it never came. Instead, he was seized by friendly hands. The kchabani attacking him were killed or taken. Human and eladon figures whirled in the dark above him, and he heard the words, '... stuck like a pig, but still alive!' For some minutes he lay sobbing in agony, coughing up blood, until some eladi came. One held him still, while the other deliberately broke the arrow in his hip. Tomas was engulfed in a wave of pain, and he fell into darkness.

CHAPTER III

Golden light streamed in the window. There were thin curtains of misty fabric hanging gently in front of the glass. The ceiling was plastered, moulded with vines on the edges and crossed by heavy wooden beams. His mind was blank. For a moment, he lay there remembering who he was; where he was, was another matter.

Conscious of a terrible thirst, he tried to move. As he did so, pain screamed at him from his left hip and his right shoulder, and he gasped. Memory flooded back, in all its gory horror: steel and blood, bone and pain; in the dark; the fear; those kchaban eyes.

'Hey, he's awake!' came a voice from his left.

'About time, too!' came another.

'Call the Healer-lady.' The voices came from other men in beds. He was in a sick-room.

A figure in white moved into view. It looked like an eladan woman, but one somehow earthier than most. Her glossy brown hair was gathered in a veil at the back of her head, in the fashion of married Southlander women, and her dress was cool and light, allowing free movement. Her eyes were large, deep, exquisitely tilted and dark blue. Her face was perfect, thought Tomas - just perfect. After a quick look at him, she turned and called. A human woman appeared seconds later with a cup. The human woman somehow tilted one end of his bed up, putting him in a reclining position, and helped him to drink. It was cool, deliciously pure water. When that was finished, they brought him the same again. Then again, a third time, but this time the draught was cold, sweet and tingled with vitality. It seemed to work its way into all the corners inside him, making friends with all the sore parts. As the human nurse left, he sank back onto the rough sheets with a sigh of satisfaction. 'Bless you, mother,' he said to the 'Healer-lady'. She smiled at him, and he thought he saw a glimpse of heaven.

For the next two days, his greatest ambition was to be able to get to the latrine, instead of having to wait for a bedpan. He was told by an eladan surgeon that he had been lucky: there was no rot or poison in the wounds, and his shoulder would eventually be as good as ever; but he might not ever walk again without a stick. His soldiering days were over.

'Well, I wasn't much of a soldier to start with,' Tomas smiled. 'I'm a loreman, I was just trying to make myself useful. I wanted to kill kchabani.'

'If thou art a loreman, thou'rt less "use" as a soldier,' said the surgeon, one eyebrow arched in disapproval, 'unless in the gravest need

– which may yet come. On that day, we must all take up arms.' He sat down on the end of Tomas' bed. 'Knowest thou thou'rt a good part elado?'

Tomas took a moment to translate the question from the archaic idiom into common Southlandish. Then he blurted, 'No! I know there were eladi on both sides of my family. But how did that come about?'

'By some quirk of inheritance or intervention, thou hast inherited nigh-equal portions of the Elder and the Younger people. The Seafarer Men once mixed freely with eladi. Thou'rt somehow almost as eladan as the Healer yonder,' he nodded towards the elada who had given Tomas a drink when he had first awoken. 'She too is *araneladon.*'

'But I don't look as eladon as her, do I?' Tomas followed her around with his eyes.

'Thou hast the colouring of the *oreladi,* who dwelt here long before us.' The surgeon paused, until Tomas took his eyes off the woman. 'Their cities, their ruins, are found all over the lands of the South, in the Thornlands, and the Elephant Country. I myself am of the Searovers, eladi from the sea, who were paler. Thou hast many markers of my kind. Thy ears sit high on thy head, and thy eyes art pale and wide-set. I would also guess that thou hast greater gifts in music, words or form than thy fellows?'

'I have some ability with words, and with the ancient scripts,' Tomas said.

The surgeon smiled, and Tomas felt all was well. 'Well, thou art welcome as amongst distant kindred. We hath known thy ancestry since the Healers, Liriel amongst them –' he looked towards the "Healer-lady" '– trained their art upon thee. Thy spirit didst respond in a familiar way. Alas, 'twas not enough to completely heal thy joint, I know not why. Hadst not the belief, perhaps, or grew hard among men.' He changed over to his own language. 'Can you understand me?'

'I can,' Tomas replied, in the same language.

'Excellent. As you recover, I shall need you as a translator in this hospital, if you will. I would have allowed you to return to your own people, but perhaps, in some ways, you already have.'

Tomas sat while translating in his head. Then as the message sunk in, he laughed. His alienation gone, his lifelong sense of 'otherness' suddenly made sense. It was like coming home. That whole day had a flavour of newness and rightness.

One day whilst still in bed, he had a visitor. Old Ben came late in the afternoon, when the spring-dusted branches of the trees outside etched chill grey shadows on the mist-curtains.

'I've heard all manner of stories about that night on the eastern boundary,' he said, settling himself on Tomas' bed. 'Most of them have it that you all died, killing scores of kchabani.'

Tomas laughed. 'Most of them?'

'Well, one said that the loreman had shot his comrades and run off with the enemy!' Ben laughed grimly. 'No-one takes that drunk seriously, though. I wouldn't worry about it.'

Tomas suddenly felt very good about changing his species.

'The surviving *enctostar* from your group will back you up. I've just come from visiting him. He took an arrow in the spine, and I fear he will not walk again - but he will live, with honour in this place. Not all of us respond to the eladon Healings as well as you *araneladi*,' Ben grinned. 'At least I can tell people that you're up and about.'

'Not quite up yet. I may only ever walk with a stick, the Surgeon said. The arrow went into my hip-joint.'

'Oh. I see. Well, when you're a magus, you can use your staff to support yourself!'

Tomas had a sinking feeling. The old man wasn't letting this strange obsession go.

'Don't look so fed-up,' Ben laughed. 'Do you think you would have been allowed to die out there? There's work for you to do, yet! If you can't walk without a stick, you can't be a soldier, and that just means one door has closed for you. Now you need to find a door that's open. You should not have tried to be something you're not.' He pushed himself up. 'Please learn the lesson – or something worse might befall you.'

Tomas was silent as the old man left. It was hard to argue against him, and Tomas didn't think he wanted to anymore.

It was springtime, the tenth month of the year. The forest was bright with the young green of budding stinkwoods, and there were hard green fruits on the peach and apricot trees. The day-long rains of spring had arrived, turning the slated pathways of Greystone black and slick. In clearings the grass grew thick and green again, and the evenings were loud with the song of crickets. In the Highlands, it would have been time for spring planting, wherever the lands were free of the kchaban scourge. Refugees had begun to make their way to the eladi again, after the Evil Alliance had been turned back at the passes of the South Gildrocks during the winter. The fugitives bore grim tales of lands laid waste, unploughed, livestock slaughtered or strayed. Kchabani had no time for honest farming, believing that the strongest had a right to whatever they could take.

Despite the horrors of that time, Tomas remembered that spring with nostalgia. In the midst of all the loss he had suffered, he experienced the acceptance of the Elder People, translating for human patients in the infirmaries.

With the rain and cloudy weather of springtime, the kchabani were more able to move around in daylight. On an overcast or misty day, the skirmishes could be continuous. Men came in during the day, eladi at night.

Tomas' new post was busy, although the work was not physically demanding. When he could, he asked about the Healers, one in particular. Liriel, the Healer who had been Tomas' first sight on awaking, was the daughter of an Animal Magus, one who could control animals by thinking with them. Her mother had been human, one of a family of landowning Southlanders from the north Highlands, three hundred years ago.

Despite the veil, Liriel was not married – all eladi women in the hospital wore head-scarves, to prevent contagion, she said, and to keep cool. Tomas realised he probably didn't stand a chance with a woman who had seen a few centuries, but that didn't stop him trying. She didn't seem to mind having him around, and they talked sometimes.

As spring bloomed into summer, Liriel introduced Tomas to someone who worked for her father, Celevrau. He was an *orelado*, one of the first eladi, and his name was Limlot. He was so old that he had a light, tawny beard, and had served the family faithfully as a tutor, chaperone and secretary for over a thousand years. His face was like light brown leather, tough but smooth, and his keen green eyes could read anyone. He was working on a comparison of human and eladon versions of the Classics, known among humans as the Elder Writings. Tomas, a loreman who could speak both languages, was the ideal assistant. Tomas' introduction to Limlot seemed merely lucky at the time.

It was late in the eleventh month of the year, and the forest was in luxuriant leaf. The mulberry trees had dripped the last of their purple fruit onto the slated pathways. Tomas was called from the Healer Hall to the house of Celevrau in the late morning. He made his way along the dapple-shaded avenues of the town to the house, sweating already. The sun beat down on his head-dress, much hotter than it was in the Highlands. His new walking-stick clunked steadily along the paving stones. Beetles, bees and butterflies danced among the waving flowers of Celevrau's gardens, a blaze of light and colour in the sun.

The house of Celevrau was one of the finer ones, built of the grey volcanic stone that gave the town its name. Like most eladan houses, it consisted of several rooms about a common living-area, and this one had two storeys. The house stood like a graceful outcrop among mulberry and bushwillow trees. It had a brown-tiled roof with wide eaves supported by slim, straight columns of golden sandstone.

Tomas knocked on the side door of the house. It would not do to go in the front door, since he had not been invited by the master of the house. He looked at the latch, and saw an eldastone, a tigers-eye, in its setting by the side of the door. Somehow, the eladi did something to semi-precious stones, which made them open a door in response to a touch. Tomas touched the stone, but unsurprisingly nothing happened. Limlot came and welcomed him in; he left his sandals by the door and politely washed his feet in the little pool by the side of the door, wiping them on the fat rug beyond. Inside it was pleasantly cool and dim, with a small fountain playing in the bright light of the courtyard. The musical plinking of falling water was cool and very restful. Limlot guided him through to the garden, where stood another orelado, short and barefooted, wearing a faded dark green robe. He was even older than Limlot, or he was more wizened by the sun. There was something extremely beautiful about him, even more so than the average elado. He seemed to twinkle in the shade, as if overflowing with life and energy. He carried a staff in his left hand, apparently unworked, but smooth with age.

'This is Helder,' Limlot introduced him. 'He is a Loremaster, who travels widely, and has only recently come here from the Elephant Land. Master Helder, this is Tomas, the *aranelado* of whom I spoke. He may have some Abilities that interest you.'

Tomas blinked at Limlot. What abilities?

Helder nodded slowly, looking at Tomas. 'He is less human than I feared; and yet more so.' His voice was mellow and unhurried.

Tomas bowed from the waist, as he had seen eladi do to superiors. Helder gave a knowing smile, appreciating Tomas' efforts. 'I believe you know an old student of mine, by the name of Bethnero?'

Tomas was surprised. He could feel himself blushing, but the eladi chuckled at his reaction.

'Are you so surprised that "Old Ben" is a true magus?' chuckled Limlot. 'Dear, dear – one so young should not be so cynical.'

'Such unloving thoughts could form an obstacle to your growth,' Helder said. 'Wouldn't you like to give them up?'

Tomas thought for some moments, recognising a test. His searched for a fitting word and remembered the teaching that if one was not a master of one's heart, one was a slave to one's passions. Choosing his words, he said in his own language, 'My head is willing, but my heart argues.'

The eladi nodded slowly in understanding. Helder looked politely at Limlot, who said, 'Yes, please come this way,' and led them to the study, where he and Tomas had lately been absorbed in ancient writings. They sat at the long, low table on large cushions.

'Now, Tomas,' Helder rubbed his hands together. 'Tell me, what do you do?'

'I'm a loreman.'

'You write for a living?'

'I was a secretary in Hunter's Wells.'

'Do you have training in the styles of writing?'

'I mastered the old scripts - including both kinds of runes.'

Helder nodded. 'Any artistic abilities?'

Tomas thought for a moment. 'Not that I can think right now.'

'Do you play music? Dance? Sing?'

Tomas smiled. 'No.'

'Ah. Is there anyone in your family who does such things?'

'Well, my sister is keen on dancing, but so are most ladies,' Tomas smiled wanly. He felt a stab of homesickness.

'Hmm... do you or anyone in your family have special abilities with plants, or animals, or in making things?'

'Well, my father is a Farrier, but not a Master. He is very good with horses. My mother and I have green fingers.'

'Green fingers?' the eladi looked blankly at him.

'We're good at cultivating vegetables, potted plants, and so on. If my mother squeezes a tomato along a furrow, every seed will sprout - but I'm not that good.'

'Ah! Interesting expression,' the eladi were amused. 'Are there any water diviners, or prospectors in your family?'

'Most of my ancestors were prospectors – that's what brought them to the Highlands.'

Helder looked unimpressed. 'We know. We were there.' The gold rushes of antiquity did not sit well with the oreladi. 'But no-one does it now?'

'No.' I need to watch my words, Tomas thought.

'Very well. Limlot, may I have some skin or paper, and a pen?'

Limlot brought out a sheet of paper, and a charcoal stick. Helder said, 'Thank you, that should do. Tomas, Master Limlot has told me you have some unusual skill with writing: would you be so kind as to write out some lyrical verse for me, please?'

'Lyrical verse?' Tomas didn't know the Celadi term. Limlot translated.

'Write as beautifully as you can. Put your heart into it.'

Tomas looked dubiously at the stump of charcoal, but started to write out a song he remembered, about a summer thunderstorm:

'Darkling clouds in a summer sky
Lightning flashes, the end of the dry...'

'All right,' said Helder. 'Now write something else, in another alphabet.'

In short order, Tomas had produced three specimens of rough calligraphy. Helder ran his fingers very delicately over the writing. Tomas felt a strange lightness, a tension in the air. Limlot looked between the two of them, his cool green eyes intent.

'Wonderful,' Helder said at last. He looked keenly at Tomas. 'Tomas, I think you have some small, but genuine ability with Arcane Writing. I think you should try to develop it.' Gathering the papers together, he said, 'Your father is a Farrier, you said. Have you any doings with animals?'

Tomas looked around for some of the resident animals. In most eladan houses, there were a few chameleons and geckoes kept as pets, for the control of crawlers. In the summer when it rained, insects were a problem, and the little reptiles grew fat and sleek. In Celevrau's house there was also a serval, kept in case of rodents, and a hand-reared lourie called Lotu, who hated the servalbut followed Liriel around whenever she was at home. Lotu had liked Tomas at first sight. 'Well,' Tomas said, 'before I met the lourie here, I used to help my father at work with the horses. We also had a cat in our house. I was the only one who could get her to come when I called.'

'Did the cat seem to like you, then?'

'Yes, it did.'

Helder said, 'Could I prevail upon you once more...?'

Tomas turned round on his cushion, calling, 'Lotu!'

There was a flapping of wings which stopped just outside the door, and the family lourie walked into the room. The bird was plain grey, crested and about crow-size, with a tail of stiff quills standing out about his own bodylength.

'Lotu! Here, boy!' Tomas held out his arm.

The bird cocked its head at Tomas, and raised its long tail-quills. Then, with clumsy flapping, it launched itself onto Tomas' arm, its long tail dipping up and down to steady itself. Tomas patted his head and stroked his wings.

'Tell him to come to me,' said Helder.

Tomas looked at Lotu, and said, 'Go to the nice elado, Lotu.'

Lotu obligingly hopped onto the table and walked click-clack over to Helder. He looked up at the elado, crest down, and looked closely at his closed left hand with one eye. Then he pecked at the paper with his short, hooked beak, but there was nothing of interest there either. Raising his head, he looked back at Tomas with the other eye.

'I wonder if he's hungry,' mused Limlot.

'That flying bin is always hungry,' laughed Tomas, 'but now, he's just bored. He'll take any food that's offered.

Lotu wandered over the table, back towards Tomas.

'Well, I see that you have very strong Animal Sympathy,' Helder grinned. 'I really think you should accept instruction in these abilities of yours, O Tomas. In fact, Bethnero has prophesied about you, which is very encouraging. I realise you might still have some misgivings – so I want you to think about it over the weekend, and we can talk again on Firstday. Are you willing to do that?'

'I am,' Tomas replied. His lingering doubts now just seemed silly. Whatever his previous experience, these people were the real thing. He owed Ben an apology. Lotu stalked over to Tomas and climbed onto his shoulder, where he turned around and started preening.

It was in the hot, sticky Greystone summer that Tomas attended his first Magus Lectures with Limlot, Liriel and Ben. Once a month, on the New Moon, Master Helder would give public lectures to practising magi in the gardens about the Hallows. Tomas attended as a prospective student.

After the first talk, Tomas was keen for an argument. Helder had been talking about ethics, and using the stories told by the refugees to illustrate differences between good and evil.

'I thought the reason that kchabani were evil was because they reject the Rule of Universal Law,' Tomas opined. 'Surely that's the simplest distinction.' They were walking back to town along the slated pathways. Large moths fluttered around the golden lamps.

'It is, but too simple,' said Liriel, taking up the challenge. She was out of her working clothes, and wore a cool, plain green dress with loose sleeves down to her forearms. Her long, dark hair was done up in a plait that curved round the back of her head, exposing her neat, pointed ears and exquisite neck. 'There was a time before the Universal Law, but the kchabani in that time were still evil, or of evil. And, imposing law on the lawless might make them law-abiding, but can't make them good: goodness comes from inside.' She looked to Limlot for confirmation, but he was walking along with his eyes on the ground ahead of him, lost in his own thoughts.

Tomas thought for a moment, and said 'But, how else do we know what's good or bad, except by comparison to Natural Law?'

'What's the one thing all your laws produce?' Liriel asked, as one preparing an argument.

'Justice,' said Tomas automatically.

'Well, in a perfectly just city, what would be the one thing that everyone should show to their fellows?'

'Well,' Tomas had to admit he hadn't thought that much about it before, 'I can't think of just one: consideration, fairness, generosity... all good things.' He thought for a bit, and said, 'I suppose laws only really tell you what not to do. Goodness –' he trailed off.

Ben stepped in. '– boils down to,' he said, 'what?'

Tomas wondered where this was going. 'Doing good?' he offered.

Liriel shook her fine head, smiling. 'You can do good for self-seeking reasons.'

'What, then?' Tomas gave up.

Ben looked between Tomas and Liriel, his eyes crinkling in a knowing grin. Liriel didn't notice.

She said to Tomas, 'Love.'

Tomas felt himself colouring. 'Oh. Of course,' he admitted.

'Now, to get back to the point,' Ben continued, 'can a set of laws, even if given by all the Powers and the One in council, make anyone love his fellows?'

'Well, yes,' said Tomas confidently, 'they can act with love to each other.'

'Yes, they can act. But will they really love others?'

Tomas thought that was a trivial point. 'Does it matter?'

'Well, now,' said Ben, 'I'm sure you've met, or at least heard of, some men who were upright as far as the Law was concerned – they never did anything illegal – but in private, they could be greedy, malicious, womanisers; and then, they might have retained good lawyers, or were powerful in their own right, so if anyone dared make a complaint about them, they would never be found in the wrong.'

Tomas grunted. He could think of one at least.

'Now, we know they were bad men,' Ben continued, 'though the Law said they weren't.' He spread his hand out. 'How can that be?'

Tomas nodded. 'I see. They are bad because they don't show love.'

'That's one of the differences between men and eladi,' Ben noted. 'Eladi see the spirit of laws, and make decisions accordingly, where men prefer to keep to the letter, because it's easier that way, I suppose. Or maybe we're not as mature. We just don't live long enough.'

For a while they walked along in silence, while Tomas digested the new idea. Their sandals made soft scuffing sounds on the slated paths of Greystone, mixed with the quiet clunking of Ben's staff and Tomas' walking-stick. It was dark night, with the new moon riding high among the tattered, star-littered remnants of the afternoon's rain. At least the night will be cool, thought Tomas.

'So what happens,' asked Tomas, 'if someone wants to kill his whole family, for example, because he's in debt or the kchabani are coming? Or, if a man is sleeping with a married woman, and she's encouraging him? If they say they're doing it out of love, what do you do?'

'Well, in that case,' Liriel put in, 'they can't not know already, that killing the innocent, and adultery, are wrong. The man promised to protect and love his wife, and he won't; the woman promised herself to her husband, and she's broken the promise.'

Tomas felt dubious. It sounded like licence. 'I still think the human way is better. Law is the foundation of civilisation.'

'It is,' said Ben, 'but it is love which informs the Law, not the other way around. Fraternal love existed before any set of laws. Remember that "Justice is the child of Love and Truth", but Love supports the Law. That is what those images in all holy place and haildoms mean, human or eladan.'

Tomas, like most humans, had grown up with small statues or icons of some of the seven Powers in his home. The favourite was the Earth-Mother, patroness of families, child-rearing and home-keeping, who expressed love more than anything else. She was most often shown with a child in her arms, which according to the Great Myths was the son of the Rain-Father, patron of fathers, workers, farmers and judges, who loved truth more than anything else. The offspring of Truth and Love was known as the Law-Child, the spirit that inspired the Law of the Kings, in the Manhome on the other side of the world.

'And if you wish to progress in your studies,' Ben continued, 'you're going to have to think what to do in a situation not covered by the Law. Essentially, your Abilities will not grow if you don't learn to love without boundaries.'

Limlot surprised everyone, saying suddenly, 'It is not enough that you simply do no evil. You must actively do good, by forgetting yourself in favour of the "Love that kindled All."'

Tomas felt a cool breeze over his heart, but misgivings about himself. 'That is not easy.'

'Hah!' Ben laughed. 'You can sing that!' The phrase sounded funny, translated literally into Celadi. 'Even eladi need to work at it all the time,' he looked at Limlot with a grin. This was obviously a long-running argument.

Limlot looked up at the stars. 'Eladi do especially. We are bound to the earth as you are not.' He sighed, looking up at the moon. 'Our home is in the earth, with the changing seasons, the cycles of rain, the migrations of wild things, and the movements of the stones. When we die or fade away, we must return – or so it is said. But men,' Limlot looked at Tomas, 'have the gift of ultimate detachment: one brief life only, and every one of them, gifted or not, will eventually give up everything. If they are full of themselves, they will be lost with the Dark Power, for he too was full of himself, and it was not enough; if full of love and truth, they will be drawn into the homes of the Gods. It is a stark destiny, but glorious if achieved. And it can happen so quickly! They can grow old and pass on in the time it took Liriel to finish her schooling!' The others laughed, but Tomas was amazed at the implications of Liriel's age. He looked at her, to find her cool midnight gaze already on him. It seemed troubled, and Tomas wondered.

Exactly why she seemed troubled became apparent later that week. During the rest-time in the middle of the day, Liriel called Tomas in to the Healers' Room. It was a place forbidden to all but the Healers, and it was beautiful – a high-ceilinged space, cool and dim in the heat of the day. Nets misted the tall windows, allowing a cool, scented breeze in while keeping out insects (and what preyed on them). A small drinking-fountain tinkled at one end.

Liriel's face was inscrutable. Tomas had a sense of foreboding. Whatever she wanted him for, it wasn't sweet nothings. The clever comments he had planned died unsaid. Liriel gestured to a seat, eladan-low by the dark, black hearth. 'Please, O Tomas,' she said, 'make yourself comfortable.'

Tomas levered himself down on his walking-stick. Eladan furniture was much lower than that made by humans.

'Tomas,' said Liriel with an uncomfortable expression, 'I was the Healer who treated you when your comrades in the Militia brought you in from the perimeter that night.'

'I thought you must have been, Mother,' said Tomas. He thought it wise to be formal.

Liriel smiled faintly. Tomas cursed the circumstances – she certainly was beautiful. With a sympathetically amused expression, Liriel said, 'In truth I am several times the age of your mother.'

'I didn't mean that –'

'I know, I am familiar with the Southlandish usage. The Celadon word is *Mai'e*, Ma'am, which comes from the same root.'

Tomas nodded. 'I see.'

'Have you been to the Fire-Hall before, Tomas?' Liriel asked conversationally. She sat across the hearth from him. The dead, black space between them had been swept clean.

Tomas shook his head. 'I hadn't heard of it before.'

'You should go there. On the eve of each New Moon is an Open Evening, when those who have crafted new tales, songs or music share them with everyone.' Liriel's word for 'everyone' denoted 'all souls', rather than 'all eladi'.

'The last time I was there,' she continued, 'someone had a new setting of the Tale of Nunquodil the Longer.' She seemed to be watching him, 'It's a rather pathetic tale: Nunquodil was a lowly aranelado, not unlike myself, who longed (hence the name) for one above his station. He performed six tasks to impress her, each one of increasing difficulty. The last one was the killing of a lion, and he was injured and disfigured. Killing the lion made her finally notice him, and they spoke together, alone, and he professed his feelings. She gave him one last, relatively easy task to prove his love; he accomplished it, thinking she would be his; but when he returned to her, she felt nothing but contempt for him. She sent him away. Some years later, he received an invitation to her wedding.'

Tomas' insides turned to lead. He hardened his heart, saying, 'It sounds like a laughter-song.' The term referred to some humorous uses of eladon drama, to which Ben had introduced him. He looked out of one of the windows. The sun was bright on the branches outside. The crescendo laughter of a flock of babblers sounded from the trees.

Liriel said, 'It is popular among young elado males preparing for Coming-of-Age, but it's well-known as a laughter-song, yes.'

'It must have some wisdom to it, then,' Tomas said, trying to fill in the space.

Liriel rose, and Tomas levered himself back up. 'It does,' she said, 'It teaches the fickleness of young maidens, and holds –' she hesitated, seeking a word, '– a mirror to young *arani*.'

Tomas simply followed her out. There was nothing more to be said.

Outside the door, she turned and looked at him, her eyes hard and jewel-like in the light. 'If you do wish to attend an open evening, O Tomas, let me know and I should like to accompany you, to introduce you. I sometimes need to remember how the story ends.' She left.

Tomas' whole rib cage felt empty. His face burned. He was very glad to be alone... *someone above his station*. Well – he always knew it was a slim chance. As a loreman among humans, his 'station' had been middling to high, but in Greystone... Oh, rot it all. Well, he thought, it could be worse – at least she hadn't led him along until she tired of him.

His shift was just about over, thankfully. He stumped off back to the Man-camp, where he belonged.

A few weeks later at the New Year, Tomas became the Apprentice of Bethnero, with the duties of service that went with the position. He spent Midsummer's Eve in song and contemplation with other new Apprentices in the Memorial Hallows to the west of the town. It was not the way one normally spent the most social time of the year, but he found to his surprise that he quite enjoyed it. The Hallows was that same place that he had passed as a refugee in winter, in poverty and misery. Life had changed in seven months – except for the poverty, he thought.

Having discerned his Abilities, he began to take readings in Arcane Writing, Plant Sympathy and Animal Sympathy. It was rare, Ben told him, that a human should have abilities in both Artistic and Biotic spheres. He put it down to Tomas' lucky inheritance of eladon blood. In these first stages, the instruction was entirely theoretical, under Ben's guidance. Ben could teach him nothing in practice, since his abilities lay in another sphere.

Before Tomas could learn to put his Abilities into practice, he first had to cultivate Detachment, learning to cut away at the net of desire and craving all speaking beings are born with. This involved spells of seclusion in out-of-the-way parts of the forest, high up on the steep south-facing slopes of the Gildrock Mountains, under supervision with other Apprentices.

And so the New Year began, sweltering and stormy, and Tomas felt himself deepening and broadening. At times, on free evenings when things were quiet, he sat watching the sun set. Then, he felt the Light growing in him, and no language had words to express his delight and contentment.

The first month was hot and sticky. There were spectacular thunderstorms. Large spider-webs appeared in the forest, filling the under-storey between springing saplings. The activity of the kchabani and Raiders stepped up. The forces of Greystone were now heavily reinforced by Human auxiliaries.

Then there was an official visit to Greystone by a delegation from the King of the Tsuna, the dark men of the Thornlands. Tomas and

Liriel, along with Ben, Limlot and Celevrau managed to get to the official reception held on the Festival Lawn, thanks to Helder. It was late afternoon when the event took place.

The men of the Thornlands were of a different kind to the Southlanders. Their skin was dark brown, their eyes black, and their hair grew in dense curls, such as occasionally appeared amongst the Southlanders. The important men among them wore ostrich feathers in their headbands, as a sign of rank. Their clothing was very simple – leather kilts or pelt aprons around their waists, with sandals and pelt cloaks. They wore vests of hide for armour, and bore large, oval shields of wood and hide. Their weaponry was distinctive, tested by generations of use: hand-axes, hardwood maces, assegais and slingshots. They had no swords, but instead used short-shafted stabbing spears, with huge blades as long as a sword. Limlot told his companions that their iron-working techniques were very good, and their blades were just as good as those of Southlander swords.

Their culture was known to be extremely conservative, with great store set by the wisdom of elders and ancestors. They had changed little since they had first appeared in Helder's youth, in the Green Ages long before the coming of the Southlanders. Tomas knew from his own studies that their politics were fluid: any freeman who had a case could be granted a hearing with the High King. If he was unsatisfied with a judgement, he was free to leave the King's territory with his entire household and all his possessions; one king had been left with nothing but his own household that way.

The official reception was as beautiful and elegant as all eladon art-forms. Tomas could see the operation of some of the Artistic Abilities – beautiful dancers made half-imagined images and rhythms as they moved to the music of flutes and oboes, stringed instruments and hand-drums. Musicians created the light and half-imagined images explaining the music. As the sun set, the diversions came to an end, and Engolaran, Lord of Greystone, made a short welcoming speech. He finished at the Hour of the Horns, when the trees were silhouetted for a time against a luminous blue-green sky in the west. Lamps were lit, and a large table, loaded down with fine venison, cold fruit and salads was translated from the Lord's own kitchens to the centre of the Festival Lawn. The Tsuna were amazed, but tucked into the food with as much gusto as everyone else.

The following morning, the big men of the Tsuna were in chambers with Lord Engolaran and his councillors. Then in the afternoon, Bethnero and two human doctors were summoned, as the most senior people among the refugees. At the last minute, Ben asked Tomas to accompany him as well, in case extra help was needed with translation.

The conference took place in the Keep, the blocky stone tower that was the oldest building in the Old Town. It stood at the crest of the hill of Greystone, built of golden quartzite that stood stark against the blue flame of the sky. While the unworkably brittle stone walls were inelegant on the outside, the eladi had gone to great lengths to make the interior beautiful, with graceful staircases, carved red sandstone pillars, and frescoes of the remotest mythology on the walls. The topmost floor but one of the Keep was a large reception area, which could have been a throne room or a court when the oreladi first built it. Now that the ruling family lived in the nearby Great House, it was a briefing room. The walls were hung with old maps and regimental knotwork insignia.

The pace of the meetings was very slow, because everything had to be translated. Of the humans, only Tomas and one of the doctors could speak Tsuna, and only Tomas and Ben were fluent in Celadi, so Tomas' linguistic skills were stretched to their limit.

The Big Men sat down, squatting easily on the cushions and hides set about the wide, low, round table. Their wildebeest-tail flywhisks they laid in front of them, as badges of office.

Lord Engolaran and his staff sat last. Ben and Tomas sat behind the Eladon Lord, so he would hear their translation clearest. The doctor, a wiry man Tomas knew from the hospital, sat behind the Tsuna prince.

'My Lord,' Engolaran began, speaking rather high-sounding Tsuna, 'we have two translators here, so if it agrees with you, I shall speak my own language and allow translation by the doctor here,' he indicated the doctor, 'while your words will be translated for all by the *Lanula* Tomas.' Tomas was glad the Lord had not translated 'Apprentice' literally – it meant 'Unwise'.

'I thank you, Lord,' said the leader of the Tsuna. 'I have come myself, because the times demand it. There was a time, long ago, when your people befriended us, and our ancestors fought by your side when the Serpent King arose.

'My Lord, though those times have long passed, we may face something of the same again. This new leader in the Slave Coast, he is a Red King, the blood he sheds cries out to heaven.

'I have received word, my Lord, that this Kroghnash has sacked the Seven Cities, those territories in the lands of the Bafedi where the golden men, the Southlanders, live.'

The Seven Cities were in the lands named by the Southlanders the Greenstone Country, a torrid region lying below the mountains to the east of the Highlands. It had good rainfall and no frost, and should have been excellent farming country – but the hot, wet climate meant malaria, and there were wild, wooded districts where neither men not their livestock could go, for fear of the Sleeping Sickness. The Seven Cities were founded on mines of gold or precious stones. They were city-states often bickering, occasionally even at war with each other. The cities themselves were home to Southlanders, but the surrounding country was ruled by the Bafedi, a nation of dark men like the Tsuna.

'I have been told that the Prince of Greenstone was impaled on the walls of his own city.'

'This is some of the worst news,' said Lord Engolaran. 'Those cities were the treasury of the Highlands. If the Slave Coast has them, the kchabani will control the passes between there and the Greenstone Country, and the caravan routes that lead there.'

'Indeed, my Lord. The scatterlings of the Seven Cities have sought refuge amongst the Bafedi. They it was who told us. The strikes of the enemy were well planned.'

There was silence for a time, as the news was digested. Hornbills called in the distance.

'I have hoped,' said Lord Engolaran, 'that the news that came to me yesterday might have a better seat amongst us... but good news it remains: I am glad to say that our scouts report that the Western Highlands are free.'

Tomas almost missed the translation in surprise. Hunters' Wells, Sweetwaters, were *free*? In a flash, he realised he could go home; but then, that he no longer wanted to. In a rush, he translated the Lord's last words: '... one or two clans of Raiders have deserted Lord Vloch and fled to the Drylands. Our south-western frontier, while not secure, is at least not expecting an attack.'

The Big Men looked at each other with surprise. 'That is good news in truth, Lord; though you may need the extra strength. We have heard one other rumour.'

The Eladi waited, inscrutable. The Prince of the Tsuna said, 'The Mwagupwe of the Bafedi tell us that among the enemies form the east are kchabani, man-height, with skin as white as wool and able to walk under the sun.'

'Arkchabani?' asked one of the eladan leaders.

The Tsuna didn't know the word. 'We simply call them Halfmen,' said one of them.

'Arkchabani,' said Lord Engolaran. The usually impassive eladi shook their heads, and Tomas heard a muttered oath. This was bad news. If there were warriors of mixed human and kchaban stock from the Slave Coast, it meant that this war had been prepared for at least ten years. With inhuman endurance and low cunning, arkchabani gave no quarter and only took prisoners for food. 'The gems of the Greenstone Country attract evil like filth attracts flies. The kchabani have ever lusted after those lands.'

Tomas wasn't sure how to translate that. The silence grew awkward.

Lord Engolaran himself stepped in. He was tall and tawny-eyed, but more a scholar than a military leader. 'We thank you for your warning. This news is indeed heavy, and we are grateful. It grieves me that this is the mightiest assault on our lands since the last Foul War, but I see hope for all of us, if only we unite to meet it. My foresight is clouded in these days.'

The Prince of the Tsuna agreed. 'The High King has said the same thing as you, Lord, that men and eladi must unite or fall. He has sent out the call to all the clans, and many regiments are gathering at the Sandy River Bends. This Red King, he is strong beyond the count of men. It will take many spears to bring him to his knees, more than the eladi, Tsuna or Southlanders have on their own; and it will take just a few more to send him to the Abyss. But it seems to us that, despite any lingering bad feeling our ancestors may have had towards each other,' here he looked at the Southlanders, 'all our past quarrels are as nothing beside the horror of the rule of the Foul Folk.' There was sound agreement from all present. The Prince continued, 'It would be an honour to fight them alongside the Elder People, and the Southlanders too.'

Lord Engolaran's smile lit up the room. 'We are very glad to hear it! And if the different races of men can unite to fight him, the Red King would have done us all a great service.'

Hadeda ibis laughed in the distance – the afternoon was wearing on. The meeting ended on a positive note, despite the bad news.

As the humans left, Ben approached the Eladan-lord. 'May I have a private audience, my lord?' He spoke his own language, not that of Greystone.

'Of course,' Lord Engolaran smiled. Tomas noted that his hair was a strange yellow colour. 'You are Bethnero, are you not? You studied under Master Helder?'

'Yes, Lord. I am delighted you remember.'

'The years lie heavy on you, O Bethnero,' said the Eladan-lord. 'I would not have thought the time so long past, that you accompanied Helder the same way as Tomas the Lame now accompanies you.'

Tomas gave a wry smile. Is that what people were calling him, now?

Ben answered, 'It was nigh sixty years ago, lord. Most of my people grow old and die in that time.'

'Indeed' Lord Engolaran asked the other eladi to excuse them. As they left, he said to Ben, 'Of what would you speak with me?'

'My lord, I have been told by my people in the man-camp that some of the men there would return home, if it was safe. If the southern Raider clans have indeed changed sides, it could now be safe for them to go.'

'So, they would return home.' Lord Engolaran looked steadily at Ben. 'How would that affect us?' Tomas had a suspicion that the elado already had his own plans, but he wanted to hear Ben's request.

'Well, at least a third of the Human Militia hails from the western districts. They might be unhappy if they were not permitted to go home, and I have reason to believe that nearly all of them would go. If you were to allow those to go who wished to, and for them to take their arms with them, then they would be less vulnerable in their towns. They could form militia units of their own, which would give you friends beyond Greystone.'

'If I know your kind, Bethnero,' said Lord Engolaran, 'some may become bandits. I would not like that on my south-western frontier, either.'

'But if they were unarmed, they would be quite helpless against bandits and slavers already there, my lord. Those men with families will not become bandits, it is a desperate life. And, they would certainly feel great loyalty to the eladi who helped them. If the Raiders take over those lands, they have no such ties to the eladi, and who knows if they might change sides again?'

'So, what you are suggesting is that I plant friendly fields in the western Highlands, in the hope that they will distract any future incursion from that direction?' The Eladan-lord's face was inscrutable.

'Yes, my lord. Also, if those men in your Militia are not allowed to return home, then some of them might simply desert. I know you may pursue them and punish them, but surely there are more important things for your forces to do?'

Lord Engolaran gave an ironical smile. 'Indeed. As it happens, your arguments have harmonised with my thoughts. I am willing to release those men and their families who would resettle their ancestral lands.

'That is not all, however. My scouts report that there is already some strength of armed resistance in the Highlands, of humans who have escaped the ruin of their towns, but who are cut off from the Duke's forces to the east. They are in the hills above our borders, near the peak of the Highlands. I wish to make contact with them. I would offer them aid, among other reasons, against such time as we may need theirs. If you could think of any responsible human of your acquaintance, who would be willing to make contact with them, I will provide an armed escort.'

'I would be glad to go myself, my lord,' said Ben without hesitation. 'Where in the Highlands would you have me go?'

'To a place called Hunter's Wells, high on the ridge that divides the rivers. I'm told there is a Haildom there.'

Tomas pricked up his ears. Ben grinned at him. 'That was my apprentice's home town,' he said. 'If I may ask one other thing, my lord,' he hesitated. The Eladan-lord nodded, and he continued, 'I suspect that some of the eladi would leave, as your people do at times. If that should happen, would you think of leaving, too?'

'There are some who would leave, it is true: but I am not done with the Sunlands. I left the sea some time ago, and I feel the brightness and depth of this land yet. I shall not go.

'It has also been granted me to see, O Bethnero, that there will come a time when you would leave us. My heart forebodes that if you leave during this war, I will not see you again.'

Ben stood silent for some time, seemingly gazing at the floor. Eventually, he said, 'I cannot see that, Lord. I have no sense of it, one way or another. Perhaps you have seen that I may find a home among my relatives in the far south. If that were the case, that I could journey that way again, then I may well stay there. However,' he said, thumping Tomas on the shoulder, 'with an apprentice under my instruction, my duty is set for some time yet.'

Tomas suddenly had a flash of insight. With a sense of rightness and absolute confidence, he said, 'I at least shall return, lord. And it will be a day of gladness, though sorrow goes before it.'

Ben looked sharply at Tomas. The Eladon-lord arched one eyebrow. 'Your apprentice is more gifted than we thought, Bethnero!'

Tomas felt embarrassed. What on earth had possessed him to come up with nonsense like that? He saw Ben looking at him with questions twinkling in his eyes.

That evening in the man-camp, Ben asked Tomas about his prediction.

'It just burst out of me,' Tomas remembered. 'I just couldn't keep it in.' Ben nodded. 'But now, it just seems stupid! I can't think what came over me.'

'Tomas,' Ben sighed, rubbing his eyes, 'Have you ever seen a beam of sunlight shining through a gap in the clouds in the distance? You know how the light shines down on one spot, and that place is in bright sunlight, while everywhere else is in shadow? Now... that is a fair illustration of what happens at times like that. It's called a Prophecy.'

Tomas sat silent as Ben's words sunk in.

'I know the feeling quite well,' Ben went on, 'because I have had moments of enlightenment like that, too.'

'Is it related to the Abilities?'

'No. It cannot be controlled or developed, like they can. It simply comes, in a moment of pure gift; and anyone can receive it, even someone who has no abilities at all.'

There was silence for a while. The noise of the camp continued outside. Thunder rolled in the distance – the evening's rain was on the way. Finally, Tomas asked, 'A gift... doesn't that come, from maturity, or being adept in any way?'

'Far from it!' Ben chuckled. 'If so, you and I certainly wouldn't have it! In any case, that would imply that you earn it, somehow.'

Tomas looked up, suddenly intent: 'Given? By whom?'

'A good question,' Ben nodded, smiling. 'A very good question.'

CHAPTER IV

Over the course of the next week or so, Ben was often away, organising the mission to the Highlands. Tomas' studies slowed down. To add insult to injury (he thought), he was told he was not to go to Hunters Wells.

'But what am I to do?' Tomas complained. 'I'm not on the Hospital staff any more, I can't get food there.'

'I've arranged for you to eat with Limlot for the time I'll be gone,' replied Ben, 'starting next week. In return you must write for him for three hours each day. For the rest of your time,' he dropped some heavy, eladon-made, papyrus books on the table, 'these are required reading for all Apprentices.'

Tomas looked at the ponderous tomes. 'Well,' he said, 'at least I don't have to spend all day and night on the major-domo's correspondence.'

'Indeed. But, he'll be watching you, if I know him – just don't look bored or stay away from the books too long, or he'll give you one of his "brief notes" to write.'

Both laughed. Limlot's speed as a scribe was legendary, and what to him was a "brief note" could take an hour to scribe properly.

'If only Celevrau could have one of those letter-stamping machines in his house, it would be so much simpler,' said Tomas.

'Its Southlander name is a Press, a Printing Press. It's the reason, or one of the reasons, why Eladi are so much more intelligent than Men. Books here are very cheap and legible, even if a little spare in ornamentation.'

It was the end of the first month. Ben had been gone two days, and Tomas was glad to be inside, alone in the cool shade of the study in the house of Celevrau. Tomas had been wading through an ancient text, one that was cited again and again in later books. The book was printed, though the language was archaic.

There came the sound of feet outside the door, and suddenly Liriel appeared, still wearing her sun-veil. Seeing him in her own house, she jumped and squeaked. It was the most endearing, feminine thing he had ever seen her do, and also the funniest. 'Tomas!' she exclaimed, 'What are you doing here?'

Tomas levered himself up onto his feet. 'Only studying, O Liriel.' Trying to think of something witty, and said, 'I thought I found a way to conjure up dark spirits – but only found a recipe for aloe whiskey.' The Celadi phrases 'dark spirits' and 'aloe whiskey' sounded very similar.

She gave an exasperated laugh. 'If your talent for tongues only leads you to make awful puns, I wonder what on Earth Limlot has been teaching you.' She undid her sun-veil and dropped it on the desk. Looking down at the books, she asked, 'What are you reading?'

'I'm reading Orodil's Principles of Self-Focussed Thought.'

'Ah – Orodil's Idiocy.'

Tomas snickered.

'That's what we used to call it when I was an Apprentice,' Liriel explained. 'We refer to it so much, it's easier to have a nickname.'

'A clever name,' Tomas replied. And, before they knew it, they were deep in conversation. Though conscious of his ignorance and Liriel's previous warning, the flow of interest and exchange of thoughts was deeply absorbing. Before he knew it, the sky outside had bronzed with late afternoon and the Labourers' Bell had rung, announcing the end of the working day for the poor.

Liriel looked with surprise out of the window. 'Is it that late already?' The lowering sun glowed golden on the leaves outside, casting cool light over her face. Her eyes looked very dark as she looked at Tomas with a slight smirk and asked, 'So, how long did it take you to read this far into Orodil?'

'This morning,' Tomas replied.

Her knowing look evaporated. 'You read a third of that book, this morning?'

Tomas wondered what he'd missed. His eyebrows raised, he simply said, 'Yes.'

'Very funny.'

'What is?' Eladi could be maddeningly obscure, sometimes, he thought.

'Anyway,' she said, rising, 'I must be gone. *Quivae*,' she said as she left.

'*Quivae*,' said Tomas to the empty room. The smell of her perfume lingered on the cool air.

Some days later, Ben was back. In high spirits, he told Tomas it had gone well, and he now had to organise some aid for the new town. He said the original population was needed back, to get planting and running the town. For some time he was busy in the Man-camp, talking to people in groups and individually, telling them it was safe for those from Hunters Wells to return, and that there were soldiers watching the town for them. The town elders, however, were all gone, as were most of the community of the Haildom. One morning, when the sky was heavy with cloud, Ben said to Tomas, 'I need someone to run an errand. I don't want to leave it to just anyone, and I thought you'd like a break?

Just to have a quick trip out of the town?'

'Well, all right, what's to be done?' Tomas was hoping he wouldn't have to walk anywhere.

'I need some items taken to Eltorvil, an officer at the Cobra Fort, a day or so south and east from here. He paid me for them months ago, but I haven't been able to get anyone deliver them.' As a practicing magus, Master Ben made a living creating useful articles. Ben's particular gifts were in Inanimate Reflex, the technique of locking energy into inanimate articles, which could be released under certain conditions.

'That's quite close to the front.'

'It's closer, yes, but there haven't been any incursions there, yet.'

'Oh, yes, I'm not worried about that, I'm just wondering how I'm to get there?' He was eager for an excuse to get out into the bush. 'I can drive. Where do we get a wagon?'

'I'm going to borrow a cart from Master Celevrau.' Ben looked closely at Tomas. 'What's wrong? You look like someone's just spilled your beer.'

Tomas shook his head. 'Oh, nothing. When do I go?'

Ben looked at Tomas shrewdly. 'Just as soon as I can get the package together. Don't worry – Master Celevrau is a good person.'

So, before sunrise one morning in the second month, Tomas set off along the hard-packed roads of Greystone, driving a two-wheeled cart drawn by a single quaha. In the back were the artefacts altered by Master Ben, several boxes of iron-tipped wooden wands capable of detecting and purifying cursed or poisoned items.

Though he had worked in the house of Celevrau for some time, Tomas had never actually met him. On those rare occasions when the master of the house had been present, Tomas had been working for Limlot, and it would not have been proper to meet him. On this occasion however, as the designated driver, Tomas met with the Master on the evening before they left. He was gravely polite, as was fitting, and bid them a good journey.

Tomas started as the sky lightened in the east and followed the road towards the dawn, wrapped in his cloak against the early morning chill. After leaving the settled forest behind he made decent time,occasionally passing eladon patrols, some mounted, others on foot. Around mid-day he pulled off the road to a shady spot, tethered the quaha on long reins to allow her to graze, and took a nap in the cart during heat of the day, like a civilised speaking being.

He woke to find the sky crowded with fat grey clouds and the wind delightfully cool. The quaha was eager to be off, so he hitched her up again and took to the road. He made excellent time following Master Ben's written directions, sighting the fort in late afternoon just as the rain started.

Thunder rolled and rain spat down as the cart halted at the gatehouse and Tomas spoke with the guards. He reported to the commander. 'My master Bethnero sends compliments to yourself and your deputy, Ethenceldo Eltorvil, and a consignment of Magus-treated wands,' Tomas said. His Celadi had come along well.

The commander nodded, saying, 'Thank you, Apprentice. At last – we have waited too long. We have a Healer from the city here now, helping with the poisons and curses, and she may now be released to her usual duties. Are you a Healer apprentice?'

'I am not.'

'Ah, you would not be acquainted, then. I shall allocate you quarters in the Infirmary, and you may lodge there until the Healer is ready to leave.'

The following day, Tomas was at a loose end. He wandered the fort for a while until someone told him to leave a private area. That afternoon, a magus came to see him. It was burning hot, but with a heaviness in the air that promised rain to come. He was a golden-skinned elado with a merry, sun-lined face, hair bleached blonde by the sun, and bright green eyes.

'Hello, lad,' he said with no preamble, knocking at Tomas' door. 'I am Master Aravon. I am an animal magus, and I have been visiting here to help with treating injured quaha. Now that we have your Master's wands, I may return home, but like you I await the Healer's pleasure.'

Tomas rose and bowed from the waist, as was proper.

'If it pleases you,' the master went on very politely, 'I would bide with you while we wait; for since I am senior here, I may show you the fort without incurring anyone's displeasure. Would you like that?'

'Yes, O Master, thank you.' The elado's manner was easy, almost diffident; Tomas fleetingly thought the master might prefer the company of animals to speaking beings.

They walked down from the Infirmary to the main gate. Master Aravon asked, 'Are you apprenticed in your Master Ben's school?'

Tomas said, 'No master, I am to study Animal Sympathy.'

The master checked to look at Tomas. 'Ah! So you are young Tomas! Your master has spoken of you – kindly of course,' he added, with a grin. 'When the time comes, you will be joining my college.'

'Ah,' Tomas said, 'I look forward to it. Master Ben had not told me who I would go with.'

'It might have been Master Celevrau,' said Aravon, 'but he is too busy with the Lord's affairs in these days. So I have taken on many of the teaching duties in Greystone.'

Master Aravon did most of the talking, showing him the fort, the stables and rookeries where the messenger birds were kept. He greeted the bird-keeper heartily, and made introductions. There were rows of large cages, most occupied by large black birds with white breast and underparts - crows. 'These birds,' said Master Aravon, 'are just as clever as dogs, or monkeys. If you train them from the nest, and reward them consistently, they make the most reliable messengers we have, without the difficulties of homing pigeons.' He gestured towards the other side of the building, 'Though they have those too, of course.'

Tomas looked at a crow in its cage. It felt very bored. 'Hi, bird,' he said. The crow cocked its head and shuffled on its perch.

'You certainly are gifted,' said Master Aravon, watching Tomas. 'Why don't you give his head a scratch?'

As if on cue, the crow hopped to the bars and tilted his head for a scratch. Tomas did so, noting the large beak. 'Good boy,' he said, for lack of anything better.

After chatting for some time with the keeper, they walked down to ground level and made for the large clear exercise ground at the back of the fort.

It was hot there. The sun beat mercilessly down on the hard-packed red-brown earth of the exercise ground, where a detachment of mounted eladi were drilling. The bare earth shook. The mounted detachment charged, the striped forequarters of their quaha shimmering in the heat as they rolled across the field in formation. A small horn blew, and they all wheeled about, now heading towards the Tomas and Aravon. For several tense heartbeats, they came on; and then another blast sent them into another wheeling turn, stripes shifting aside for brown. Tomas could only gape: such co-ordination was simply not possible using bridled horses, at that speed. To watch these animals, with saddles and stirrups but no bridles, was an incredible sight.

Master Aravon watched with quiet pride from the shade of a line of thorn-trees at the edge of the ground. 'Is that not a fine sight? I have been trained, and trained in my turn, even as they do.'

Turning back, he led the way round the edge of the exercise ground, back along the hard-packed track to the sprawling stone pile of the Cobra Fort.

'Most of my apprentices,' the master explained, 'remain with me for only a term or two before going on to train with the cavalry. I had thought, Tomas, you were to be an officer of the militia or to join the cavalry yourself, but I see that your gifts are deep indeed. Master Ben has been lucky to find you – as you have been blessed to be found by him.'

'I know it, sir, though I doubted at first.'

On returning to the fort, the master was called away. Tomas took in the view from the walls for a moment, and then went down the stairs, smelling rain in the gathering cloud. Rain was always welcome in this heat. He remembered home, where it seldom got this hot, and set off on a wave of nostalgia and worries about his family.

His maudlin thoughts were interrupted by a strange sound: a distant shout. At first, it might have been a human voice, but as it went on, he realised it was almost like a bark: a baboon, perhaps? Baboons had not been a problem when Tomas had lived in Hunters' Wells. The vermin were never far away from settlements, and had to be controlled.

The barking was coming closer. It seemed to be echoing, somehow. Wait a minute, he thought, that's a really loud baboon! He looked around at the wooded hills, green trees dark on yellow grass. Where was it coming from? There was nothing down by the forest road; nothing up the slope, where the land mounted bare, rocky hills in the cloud-dappled, late-afternoon light. Behind him, he thought. He looked along the edge of the exercise ground. As he watched, a lone *quahastar* came galloping at speed along the road he had walked earlier. He slowed as he came up the road, but seemed unsteady inthe saddle. He swayed, and Tomas saw red all along one side of his armour. He's doomed, Tomas thought. He was torn between wanting to help and wanting to get below, out of the way of the trouble that was obviously on its way. Suddenly, someone came hurrying out of the gate below Tomas. It looked like an elada in Healer clothing, but she was alone. Tomas started down the stairs to the courtyard, unsure whether to offer help or get out of the way. Down in the courtyard, he put one hand against the golden-stone archway of the gate and looked out, to where the elada was treating the injured soldier. The quaha stood nearby, breathing heavily.

Suddenly a trumpet rang out from the tower. Fear fluttered on Tomas' heart: time to get out of sight! He wasn't even armed. As he looked out of the archway, beyond the trees on the lane, he suddenly saw what had been chasing the rider: the biggest baboon he had ever seen loped along the road at terrible speed towards the fort. At least the height of a man, with limbs like tree-trunks, and running on its knuckles, the shaggy-haired baboon was grossly oversized. Its teeth were bared in a snarl, revealing fangs longer than Tomas' hand. Instead of the usual grey colour, this monster was black, with white and grey streaks. Tomas' blood ran cold: what devilry was this? Even as he stood there in terror, several more of the monsters loped past in the same direction. They seemed to be all dogs, all males, heavy-shouldered and shaggy-furred.

It was too much for Tomas. As shouts rang out and eladi rushed to their posts, he couldn't move fast enough. He turned to go, hoping to get out of the way of the fighters, cursing his disability. Hobbling as fast as he could, he stopped short – the healer! Turning again, he looked out. She couldn't be seen from inside the gate. Tomas desperately wanted to close the gate, but where was the elada? He waited, heart hammering, for seconds that seemed like hours.

'Close that blasted gate!' came an order from the tower.

'The Healer's still outside, sir!' called an elado from the wall.

Tomas remembered the tears of the girls and women of Hunters Wells, and made his decision. Two fighters started down from the walls towards the gate, as Tomas started through the gate himself.

Suddenly, in a rush of footsteps up the stairs, the Healer was there. It was Liriel! Her face a tearful mask of terror, she cried 'Close the gate!' but it was too late.

With a buffeting of dusty fur, the massive baboon was in the doorway, right in front of Tomas. Tomas reflexively reached for the militia *equet* he no longer carried, then hefted his walking stick.

With one deft swipe of a heavy, black hand, the baboon tripped Liriel up. She crashed down to the dust with a short, sharp scream. Pinning her down by the neck with one hand, the baboon made to disembowel her with the other. In desperation, Tomas did the only thing he could think of: he whacked it with his walking-stick.

'NO! Stop!' The walking-stick clacked heavily on the thing's nose. The baboon stopped dead, seeming to only now notice Tomas. Time stood still. The baboon looked atTomas. Tomas could feel its pain and surprise: what was this?

'Let go!' said Tomas, his voice trembling.

The monster stood still. It was a Speaking Being! He had to obey. Terrible things might happen if he didn't. Tomas felt all the thoughts, as if they were his own. For a few agonised seconds, he tried to sort out which were which. The baboon sat back on its hindquarters, rearing its awful head up above man-height. It had stopped, as ordered to, but now it was confused. Why did it have to stop? Wasn't it told to go and kill as many thin-monkeys in this place as it could?

'You must not!' Tomas said out loud.

But why? The other Speaking-Being had said, they could eat

anything they found here!

'You may not eat men!' Tomas shouted.

Oh, the baboon thought. It was feeling rebellious, and was tempted to defy the Speaking-Being, but fear of pain and hunger stopped it. The memories were burned deep, and its hunger was not yet great enough to push it beyond its conditioning.

'Go – outside!' Tomas told the monster.

The baboon showed its front teeth in a subservient smile, and went down onto all fours again, showing its purple backside as it turned.

Tomas lowered his walking-stick. The baboon stopped, looking back, still a bit confused. Tomas had to make sure it left. 'Go!' he said, 'look for your friends.'

The monster was in the doorway. Liriel lay still, breathing in small, sobbing gasps, trying to be quiet. Agonisingly slowly, the monster moved into the doorway. Tomas made to reach for the end of the heavy lever that would bring the gate crashing down. As soon as it was on the threshold, he could slam it shut, kill it...

Now! Tomas grabbed the lever, but it was made of heavy ironwood, bound with metal strips. He pulled it, but the effort forced a grunt of exertion out of him as his injured hip protested. Pain shot out of his pelvic bone, and he lost concentration. Suddenly, the baboon was back, a terrible suspicion in its mind. It was Tomas' turn to panic, and he lost contact with the monster's mind.

'Stop,' came a female voice. Tomas looked behind to see Liriel, still on the ground, concentrating on the baboon. She said, 'Go out, now.' The baboon looked at her, but it had already been tricked once. It curled it lips back horribly, showing horrible fangs capable of killing a man with one bite. Suddenly, just as it started to move, there was a heavy, whipping sound and a long-shafted eladon arrow suddenly protruded from where its lefteye had been. Two more arrows hit it, in the neck and in the ribcage, and it was dead even as it crashed down in the doorway.

Tomas spun around to see two the archers at the end of the yard. 'Well met, comrades,' he said. He had never been so glad to see an animal die.

'And we thank you,' said Liriel. Her face pale, she said to Tomas in a faltering voice, 'Would you mind helping me up?'

Tomas did so, leaning heavily on his walking-stick. The *quenstari* hastened to help them. One of them said, 'Look outside – the *quahastari* have them.' Tomas saw a group of mounted eladi ride into view below the gate. They were chasing one of the giant baboons. The beast bellowed and fled, but was too heavy in the limbs for a burst of speed. Arrows came from the eladi, hitting it in the neck and ribs. In shock and pain it screamed, an unnervingly human sound. It turned to fight, and was hit by three more arrows. It stumbled and fell, coughing blood. The eladi riders reined in, circling and attacked with swords and spears until it lay still. Then, wheeling and forming up, they rode out, seeking further targets.

'That was well done,' said one of the archers.

'Indeed,' said Tomas. His hip throbbed, and he leaned heavily on his walking-stick.

Liriel was still clinging to his arm. 'I think,' she said, 'I have wrenched my –' and then a word Tomas didn't know. She pulled heavily on him, and he grabbed her under her arm. She was surprisingly light.

'I cannot walk,' she whimpered.

Tomas leaned heavily on his walking-stick. This could be difficult. The archers came to their aid, and as Master Aravon re-appeared, they helped Liriel to the Infirmary where she had been working as a Healer until mere minutes ago.

They carried her into the building, where cold lights gleamed golden, brighter than the gloomy sky. It was very like the infirmary in the City, Tomas thought.

Liriel was lowered onto a raised bed, much higher than normal eladan beds. Her eyes were closed and her face pale, as she concentrated on reducing the pain. Tomas made to leave with the archers, but Liriel said in a quavering voice, 'Tomas, would you stay by me, please?' He returned and they both answered questions from the healer. Tomas noticed a dark red stain spreading on Liriel's solar plexus – the beast had come that close to eviscerating her! Suddenly, she convulsed and vomited up a lot of blood. It spewed all over Tomas' hose and tunic, but he held her up. She then lay back on the thin mattress and grabbed Tomas' hand, as the Healer laid his hands on her. He began muttering, and Tomas caught a few phrases of Ancient Eladan. Through Liriel's hand, he felt rather than saw a hot, golden glow from the healer's hands. He closed his eyes to focus, as he did in meditation, and felt his mind drift. Another presence seemed close and familiar, and Tomas realised it must be Liriel. All at once, he felt her soul pull on him, and he braced himself to support her. The pull became a drain, but he kept himself up. He felt Liriel's presence as something bright but fractured, with her drawing strength and life from him. With a final pull that almost knocked him out, the contact was broken.

His head swam as he looked at the healer. The elado was smiling, saying, 'That was an elegant and rapid healing, O *Aranelado*. Thank you for your support of your lady-friend.'

'What happened?' Tomas slurred. He felt incredibly tired, almost drunk.

'Because our healer is not pure elada, she is too broken in soul to be healed perfectly, even though her own healings are excellent. She drew heavily on you to compensate for her weakness, and it worked. It was well it did, for she was bleeding into her stomach from that wound. I myself was unaware until she vomited blood all over you.' He pointed at the blood-stain on Liriel's abdomen, now shockingly large.

'If the healing had been incomplete, she may have died from loss of blood, perhaps before we even knew of the extent of the injury.'

Tomas heard the words, but made little sense of them. All he wanted to do was to lie down and sleep. He focused on the healer with difficulty.

'Come and sit down here,' said the healer, guiding him to a couch nearby. He called for help from the apprentices. Tomas was so tired, he didn't even see who expertly pulled his ruined clothes off, leaving him in his underwear. As he lay back, he heard the Healer again: 'You have been drained by the Healing, but your recovery will be complete: you have saved her life this day. She is now as family to you.' Someone covered him with a cool, clean sheet.

Tomas was aware enough to be vaguely amused, but fell asleep almost immediately.

The daylight woke him up. He was in a strange room, one that didn't look or even smell like the hut he shared with Master Ben. After a few seconds, he remembered and groaned. He hadn't seen that much blood, so close up before.

Soon, Master Aravon came to see him, with Liriel. 'So,' he said with a grin, 'here is our unwitting hero: that was something to see.'

'How long have I been asleep?'

'You collapsed yesterday afternoon.'

'What?' Tomas was appalled.

'I took a lot out of you, Tomas,' Liriel said with tears in her eyes. 'I cannot be too grateful. If you hadn't been there with your passion and strength, I would have died.' She bent down and embraced him.

Tomas returned the hug, though all he could reach from that position was her arm. She stood up again.

The master quietly left, leaving Tomas alone with Liriel. She sat down on the end of Tomas' couch.

'We saved each others' lives today – only you saved me twice!'

Tomas could think of no witty reply. He simply said, 'Thank you, O Liriel.'

'You are most welcome,' she knelt by his bed. 'I don't know how it is among men,' she said, 'but if you save another's life, you become as family. We are doubly so now – so,' she said with a mischievous grin, 'you are my *hanno*, my little bruv,' she punched him gently on his arm.

Tomas chuckled and levered himself up on his elbow. 'All right – *neti*, little sis!' he poked her in the ribs. They poked each other childishly a few times, then Liriel suddenly hugged Tomas again, saying, 'I remember your psychic touch during the healing. You are like me, Tomas. So like me: we are of a kind.'

'I remember feeling your presence, too. It was somehow familiar.'

'That is what is so good, Tomas. You cannot know what it is like for me. All my working life, I have either treated eladi or men, and they were always so *other*. And, because of my mixed race, my fellow Healers always felt my presence as something – lacking, or impure. And of course, because I find it so difficult to heal myself properly, I have always so feared serious injury. We,' she said with a wan smile, 'people like us, simply are not as good or whole as full-blooded eladi. But, men are such a vortex of passion and energy, and they really are not... we really have so little in common with them, either.' She sat on the bed. 'I would love to know how you came to be as you are.'

'The Healer I spoke to at your Infirmary said I was merely lucky.'

'Well, if you are that lucky, I would not want to play cards against you!'

They laughed, and Tomas noticed once again how fine her face was. He grabbed Liriel's hand, looking in her eyes. She returned the look steadily. He pushed himself up, as quickly as he could, despite the discomfort. He pulled her closer, trying to kiss her. Suddenly, she was in his mind, taking control as if he was a dumb animal. He simply let go, unable to hold her any more.

Humiliated, he flopped back down onto the bed. He ached all over. She rose to leave, and he didn't want to meet her eyes; but at the door she turned back and looked at him, smiling and pink in the face.

'Your feelings got the better of you, Tomas.'

'No,' he said, 'you did.'

She just laughed, a throaty, liquid sound. Then she disappeared from the doorway.

'This time,' he added, slightly louder. There was no answer.

CHAPTER V

'So, Tomas,' said Master Ben the morning after they returned, 'How would you like to go and live with Master Aravon?'

'I'd love to.' Tomas came out of his room drying his head. He had only just risen. 'We met at the Fort. As long as it's as an Initiate, and not an Apprentice?'

Master Ben grinned, and deliberately didn't answer. After a pregnant pause, he said, 'He's the only Master Animal Magus these days, so he's the only one you could go to.'

Tomas felt a thrill of excitement. 'I think I'm ready for it.'

'I think so, too. How long did you control that monster baboon - a minute? And you still have all your intestines!' Master Ben's eyebrows pushed wrinkles all over his forehead. 'Most animals that get that close to any baboon regret it – unless their teeth are bigger. You've more than proved yourself ready for it.'

Tomas hung up his towel and came out. 'I'm ready!'

'Very good, lad,' said Ben. 'I'm always glad when an apprentice of mine graduates to Discipleship. But first, I have a rather personal question to ask.'

Tomas looked expectantly. 'What?'

'Have you ever been with a woman?'

Tomas flushed furiously, 'Erm, no,' he mumbled.

Ben nodded. 'I didn't think so,' and went into the front room of his house. Behind him, Tomas' face deepened from red to purple. 'It's important, you see,' he explained, scooping mielie-meal into a pot from a jar, 'because your abilities require a pure spirit to grow. If you've had intercourse with a woman, even if it was only once a long time ago, your spirits have mixed: some of her spirit has – flavoured, I think the Old Eladan word means – flavoured yours, and yours hers. We don't know why, but having a mixed or impure spirit weakens your natural abilities. Get that fire going, will you?'

Tomas' heart sank. 'Does that mean I can never –'

'No, no, not at all,' Ben said. 'Once you've grown all you can, and the use of your abilities comes naturally, then you can get married.' He looked at Tomas with a carefully neutral expression. 'Once you've mingled your spirit with another's, your abilities will attenuate slightly, but it shouldn't be too marked, and you will recover nearly all of what was weakened – as long as you keep practicing, and don't marry more than one wife.' He nodded at the fireplace: 'That fire's not going to build itself, you know!'

'Sorry!' Tomas bent to scoop out the ashes. 'I'm Southlander, not

Tsuna, we don't have harems.' He cleared out the grate, stood up and said, 'What happens if you have more than one wife?'

'Never mind marrying: if you ever even lie with more than one woman, your spirit will have mixed itself too much, and your abilities will weaken permanently, and may disappear altogether – so, no cheating! If you find yourself a girl some night during your training, you might as well go back to being a Loreman.'

Tomas limped to the door, went out into the cool, clear morning and dumped the ashes by the side of the road. It was part of every house's morning routine. Every inhabited house had its own small pile of ashes outside it. Well, Tomas thought to himself, that simplifies things rather brutally. Tomas the Initiate was one thing, Tomas the Loreman was the subject of bad jokes everywhere.

'So,' Ben said as he came back in, 'No women, no money. Do you still want to do this?'

'Ha!' Tomas laughed. 'I don't have either, anyway. Can I still drink?'

'Yes,' said Master Ben, smiling. 'It's not all bad. Just don't get drunk – or at least, not regularly.'

Tomas shook his head. 'I'm seldom able to get even tipsy, unless someone else is paying for it.' He began piling sticks in the grate. 'If I've no money, what do I do for clothes and paying you board?'

'You'll be living with the Master, in his house, teaching younger initiates and doing household jobs, running errands and so on for him as payment,' said Ben. 'Master Aravon has several students, so it should be easy for you. As to clothes, the Master provides a uniform called a habit for his disciples. I seem to remember Animal Sympathy students wear hides sometimes, but it may be different here. You may have to go barefoot.'

'I can live with that,' said Tomas, sticking grass wads into the kindling and striking flint to tinder. The flame took and Tomas banked twigs around the grass. As the flames took hold, he blew on them gently. Smoke rose up the chimney as the fire grew. The water-seller's bell tinkled from the road outside. Ben took a large earthenware pitcher and went out to meet him. He returned a few minutes later with the pitcher on his shoulder (only women knew how to carry it on their heads). 'Master Aravon will be your instructor for Animal Sympathy,' he said, manoeuvring the pitcher onto the shelf. It was a clever eladan design with a tap on the bottom. 'From time to time, you'll go to other Masters for instruction in your other abilities. The arcane writers have a college in the library, I'll have to find out where the Plant Sympathy students go.'

The fire blazed merrily in the blue-and-gold light of the morning, shining through the door. Tomas said, 'I can't wait.'

Master Aravon supervised a few other students from a large, porticoed rondavel in the forest above the city of Greystone. The place had so many different animals living or visiting there, it was like a menagerie. There was a hornbill and an owl, a bushbaby and a pangolin, a couple of babblers, a big old tortoise, a three-legged ratel and a half-blind coucal who skulked in the rafters. Master Aravon kept the biggest chameleon Tomas had ever seen – as long as his forearm – and he was also the only one Tomas ever met who had a good rapport with fruit-bats.

In the fourth month, the heat abated and the rains trickled out. Tomas had been looking forward to autumn, but this warm, low-lying land had little autumn to speak of. The stinkwood and mulberry leaves bronzed and quickly showered down onto the slated roads of Greystone, without the mellowing that Tomas had expected. He simply woke up to dry winter one silvery morning.

During the fifth month, the forest streams dried up and the leaf-litter turned to tinder. Tomas wondered if there had been frost in Sweetwaters, yet. It had always been a milestone, growing up. Home seemed to be in someone else's past these days. Though touched by loss, Tomas did not mourn. Physical work and meditation stopped him from dwelling on anything; evil could not extinguish the beauty of the world, or the deepening of his consciousness.

This was the month when Master Aravon, Tomas and a senior initiate called Gentodil went to look for nocturnal animals high on the slopes of the North Gildrock range overlooking the city. It was an agonising hike for Tomas. His left hip was in pain all day, and his right arm was trembling and exhausted from the effort of supporting himself and his backpack on his walking-stick. Gentodil seemed to have little patience with him, though the master was as unperturbed as masters always were. They eventually reached their camp-site only after dark, when they should have been there around mid-day.

Tomas had tried to maintain detachment from his suffering. Over and over again that day, he had told himself 'This too will pass', or 'It will not last forever', but as he sat down on the ground in the clearing near the spring that evening, a groan escaped him, and he flopped onto his back. Gentodil looked at him sharply, his well-formed face both mystified and annoyed.

Master Aravon said to Gentodil, 'Go and collect firewood. You and I will seek wild things tonight, but Tomas can stay here and make supper.'

While the other Initiate was away, the master said to Tomas, 'I know little of your kind. Is it a weakness or a sickness that prevents you from walking properly?'

Tomas looked up at him from the ground. 'A weakness, yes, but mostly pain.'

The master looked at him levelly for a moment. 'Pain? Do you still feel the pain that you first felt when the injury took place?'

The question seemed silly at first. Then Tomas realised that the elado had never had an injury with lasting after-effects. Eladon Healing, applied to eladi, healed completely. He thought about his response, and replied, 'It is like it.'

The Master nodded slowly. 'I had no idea. I apologise if I have been unkind to you.'

'It's quite all right, Master,' Tomas gave a weak smile. What else could he say?

The Master continued, 'I have been encouraging my students to always think about the needs of others, as a means of detachment. I shall have to ensure that all know how needy you are.'

'I can manage,' Tomas said, but he was grateful, and the Master knew it.

Tomas made some root-vegetable soup by firelight while the other two walked along the mountainside, looking for bushbabies, nightjars and other night creatures. They returned some hours later followed by a jackal, and carrying a spring-hare that the jackal had helped them catch. They skinned and dressed the spring-hare, giving the offal and head to the jackal but keeping the skin for a pelt. Then they roasted the animal, adding the leg-bones to the last of the soup for the following night. As Tomas went to sleep, the jackal snuggled up behind the master, full and content. The eladi did not sleep, but lay half-awake, resting and dreaming during the cold, dark hours.

In the morning the jackal was gone. Master and initiates rose late, and spent the day relaxing and talking, since their work was only to start after dark.

That evening it was Tomas' turn, and the master walked with him along the slope to the lip of a gully, where they settled down to listen for wildlife. Eventually, as Tomas began to feel cold even in his blanket, he heard the harsh, furtive calls of nightjars in the trees.

Master Aravon said very quietly, 'You hear the birds. What do they say?'

Tomas relaxed. Listening with more than his ears, he said, 'I think they are only declaring themselves. They listen to hear who is still alive, and where.'

The master said, 'Is there anything else?'

Tomas listened more, in different directions, for about an hour. He perceived, though he could scarcely see in the starlight, a bushbaby couple higher up the gully, a young owl flying silently overhead, and a tortoise in thick bush quite close by. A serval sneaked past in the darkness, thinking himself unnoticed.

As the night grew older and most of the nocturnal animals dispersed, the master said to Tomas, 'Well done, O Tomas. Your sympathy is strong, for one so young and inexperienced. You discovered most that I could, and finding that tortoise was exceptional.'

'Why is that, master?'

'A simple being such as a reptile is less easily felt. The fact that it was asleep in the cold made it even more difficult, since its mind was dormant.'

Tomas was flattered.

'You seem to have a great natural talent. However, you failed to notice the tree-snake in the hollow trunk directly ahead of us. Given how poisonous tree-snakes are, it would be better if you could be aware of them before they are of you.'

Tomas' blood ran cold. 'There?' he pointed. He hadn't felt anything, but it was only paces away. He tried to 'feel' for the snake, but in his fright, his perception was stunted.

The master grinned. 'Yes, there. You need not be ashamed, snakes are very difficult, and it too is hibernating.'

Back at the campsite, the jackal had re-appeared. Gentodil was playing with the animal, rolling it over, tapping its nose and scratching its belly.

'Watch out for fleas,' Tomas said by way of greeting. The master laughed.

Gentodil suddenly stopped playing with the jackal. He washed his hands and started to share out supper. After they had eaten the last of the soup, they emptied the pot on a flat rock for the jackal. It greedily ate all the stock, and then made off with the last of the soup-bones.

The following day was the New Moon, and the eladi gave Tomas a head start in going home. His pack was somewhat lighter, and he was at least going downhill most of the way, so he hoped the homeward journey would be a little easier than the outward. It was not so: if anything, it was worse. The others caught up with him around mid-morning, and all went on together. Tomas found that, with others to talk to, he could think less of his pain, and it became more bearable. At noontime, when they finally reached a path, Tomas said, 'Please, do not wait for me this afternoon. Just walk on, and I shall get back in my own time.' He didn't want to be complaining and groaning for them to see and tut at him.

However, while they ate, they started a very interesting conversation about the social lives of hyenas, and when they all moved on again, between company and conversation, Tomas was able to keep up. It was near sunset when they came to the stone-paved roads. Walking along in the chill dusk, Master Aravon decided that the talk was too good to stop, and said, 'Let us go on to Ilverin's House, and we may continue in comfort. The students are all on New Moon's leave, and it would be a pity to go home and eat alone, when we could all be in company, with music playing.'

The initiates were not about to disagree. Over supper at the Free House, the conversation moved on to other things, while people came and went. Many of the customers played their own musical instruments, and others joined in the songs they sang. The music was a delight to Tomas; it was played expertly and augmented by anyone with artistic talents. Some eladi danced, and the Free House became a place of light and rhythm. The entertainment was more than just diversion - it was high art. Eladan pubs were to human ones as music is to noise, or poetry to swearing. Just being in one was a delight.

Tomas' hip-joint had taken a beating, and hurt horribly the next morning. He went to the infirmary to get it seen to. Avoiding Liriel, he went to a Healer he knew there who was familiar with humans. The Healer saw him and laid hands on his joint, the warm sensation easing out Tomas' pain. Tomas was in the infirmary until the following morning, and the Healer told him he should go slowly for the next few days as well.

Tomas spent the sixth month in the Scriptorium with Arcane Writing students. It was cold, but at least sitting down gave Tomas' lame hip a rest. It was a year since he had begun training to receive that injury. With his new-found equilibrium, he wondered at the despair and rage that had driven him to become a fighter then, when he was so unsuited to it.

The seasons turned, and the forest greened again. In mid-spring, the height of the mulberry season in the tenth month, Tomas had spent a month with the Plant Sympathy College run by Mistress Miruvire. The forest was hot, humid and muggy with spring rains, and for the first time, Tomas learned to hear the voices of trees. At the end of the tenth month, at the New Moon break, Tomas returned to the man-camp to visit Ben. There, he was introduced to a youngster called Ioseth, a refugee from the Highlands, who was Ben's new Apprentice, studying Ben's ability. Tomas was pleasantly surprised – it felt almost like having a younger brother. During a visit with Liriel, he saw large numbers of men moving towards the city. He recognised two from his days in the Militia, and spoke with them. There was a call-up, they said, but no-one knew the reason.

Later that day, he saw those same men again, in full kit, formed up in their divisions and ready to go at the Singing Gate of the City of Greystone. Armed to the teeth, they looked tense. Tomas and Liriel joined an inquisitive crowd that had gathered. As they watched, human Tinceldi marched them away, towards the east road. Everyone asked the same questions, but there were no answers. All they knew was that the entire Human Militia had gone.

Two weeks later, Tomas was in the deep forest, half a day's hike to the north-east of Greystone City with Master Aravon's college. The initiates were interacting with forest animals, supervised in small groups by qualified magi. The weather was as hot as high summer could be, and Tomas battled again with the pain in his hip. His shoulder ached from hours of work with his walking-stick, but he managed somehow, thanks to the empathy of Master Aravon.

The initiates were high up on a south-facing slope, and had a good view of the eastern end of the Green River valley, when someone noticed an odd dark cloud in the distance, on the far end of the valley. The sky was heavy with puffy white clouds and the forest stretched thick and green between them and that border. The darkness was low, just above the trees, patently wrong in the bright blue distance. The initiates asked about it, and the magi said, 'It is a cloud of magic. There, kchaban shamans cast spells, calling on the forces of evil, and the evil spirits shade themselves, hating the light of the sun.'

Tomas said, 'They are close.' He remembered that the militia had been bound for the east.

No-one said anything in reply. The filthy cloud sat like a quiet outrage at the edge of Tomas' sight, marking dire battle in the forest.

That night, Tomas lay asleep in his blanket when he was awoken by sudden unease. He sat up sharply, noticing that the eladi all about him in the tent were sitting up and looking around. There was an atmosphere, a presence around them that radiated contempt and hatred. Rising and leaving the tent, Tomas saw a sky crowded with bright, close stars, but the presence around them hated beauty and peace. The outrage was no longer quiet.

Tomas' unease blossomed into fear. There was something evil in these blessed forests. Suddenly there was a rustling in the fern and grass of the undergrowth, and everyone jumped. Master Aravon said in a quiet voice, 'Initiates, hold your ground. Magi, attend to me.' And he moved through the small ferns and wild asparagus towards the rustling. The magi converged on the sound. Suddenly, Master Aravon lunged with his ironwood staff, and something hissed. Every hair on Tomas' body stood up. Snatching it up with amazing speed, the master held it up for all to see: it was a Foul creature. In the dim moonlight, Tomas saw that the master magus held a large snake by its neck – a snake with the wings of a bat. Reaching out with his newly-developed sensitivity, he touched the thing's mind, and was shocked at what he perceived: a normal snake was a rather simple creature, and would no more bite than flee unless threatened, but this thing thirsted for hot blood. It knew the fear it inspired, but lived in permanent fear and loathing. Tomas could feel only pity for the poor reptile twisted thus. The winged serpent existed only to be flung at an enemy, to bite and kill, and then to be killed in combat or die, alone and starving.

Master Aravon said, 'No-one must sympathise with this creature. It could be dangerous for an initiate.'

Tomas broke off contact with a guilty start, but he was sure he wasn't the only one. The magi found a few other winged serpents in the next couple of hours.

The rest of the night passed uneventfully, and Tomas even slept again. The morning dawned beautifully cool and bright, but that was not the only encounter the college had with warped life that week. In the next two days, they encountered several more winged serpents, a few long-tailed rats with the heads of butcher-birds, and a handful of loathsomely vigorous, gigantic slugs which poisoned any plant they touched. The magi said that the things must have been created or summoned by the sorcery on the borders.

Back in the rondavel, the initiates discussed the warped life with the magi, and with some of the Eladan-lord's councillors. It had been the first use of such magic since the last Great War, and it indicated that there were adept magicians in the enemy's forces.

However, there was better news at the New Moon: the Greystone fighters had triumphed, and the Foul forces, despite being strengthened by arkchabani, had been pushed back. The human militia had earned great credit in the struggle. The Midsummer festival was especially joyful that year, and the men held their heads high. People even began to hope that the war would soon be over.

On Midsummer's Day itself, a new group of refugees came, and Ben was asked to be a translator where needed. Since Tomas was visiting at the time, he went to help as well. It was not the nicest way to spend Midsummer, but the human suffering Tomas saw was overwhelming and the hospital staff needed help. The refugees were well-organised, arriving in wagons escorted by eladan cavalry.

The wagons in the column carried many wounded and sick. Tomas noted that some seemed strangely wasted. Others were simply scared and staring, jumping at any loud noise or sudden movement. It was a tragedy that they should be in such condition on the greatest festival of the year, but, he thought, at least today they had come to safety. It was the best present they could get.

Tomas heard the Tinceldo of the mounted detachment speaking to the head of the hospital team. The elado was speaking too fast and low for him to catch everything, but he heard a few phrases, about kchaban slaves and people with the Darkfear. This group had been on its way to a town long occupied by the kchabani. They had been travelling by night, and the eladi had surprised them in the early morning and destroyed them.

'This is where things get interesting,' Ben said grimly to Tomas. 'Some of those poor folks, the ones that look malnourished, have goblin-spawn infection.'

Tomas felt sick. Of all the horrors of the kchabani, using living bodies as brood nests was one of the vilest. Most of the victims were men.

Detaching himself from the horror, Tomas went up with the first group of casualties. The Healer Hall was a madhouse. Refugees who were relatively able-bodied carried grey, swollen people on stretchers. He met with the human doctors in the Healer's Hall, and then went to tell the staff about the infected. He had to ask Liriel for the term in her language. Once he had passed the message on, he asked Liriel, 'What will happen to them?'

'The nurses will triage them, find out which of them is most in need. Then we shall operate: cut them open, and remove the spawn.'

'Cut them open?' Tomas was aghast.

'Yes, little one,' she said. It was the eladan equivalent of saying, "Don't be daft". 'The Surgeons use Sympathy to block the pain out. It's easier with men than animals, though, because they have souls that can trust and believe, though they do not know what we are doing.'

'Amazing,' Tomas said. 'Have you done it before?'

'Of course.'

Later that day, Tomas was still in the hospital when a man came up to him. He was obviously one of the former kchaban slaves: grey-tinged and malnourished, he wore only a scrap of cloth around his waist, and he smelled disgusting. Tomas looked at him for several heartbeats, and then recognised him. 'Tadeos?' he asked, horrified. The man just stood there, blank-faced with his hands hanging by his sides, tears flowing down his cheeks. Tomas was appalled. His friend Tadeos had been a hefty smith, always full of life and brimming with self-confidence; now he was this wreck suddenly sobbing in front of Tomas. Disregarding his fine feelings about the man's filthy state, Tomas went and hugged him. Tadeos howled like a baby, an unnerving sound.

For several seconds, Tomas stayed like that, then stood back and asked, 'Are you...?'

Tadeos shook his head. 'They got into me, Tomas! The shaman raised up a shadow, and it – it – I might have a – a thing –' he pointed to his stomach, '– the filth!' he shook his head, wailing with clenched teeth.

Tomas' own jaw clenched in sympathy. 'Well, they can help you here. Come with me.' He led Tadeos to the ward with the other spawn-infected, where human nurses were triaging people. He directed Tadeos to a pallet on the floor, since the beds were all full. He then went to Liriel, telling her, 'I've got an old friend from Hunter's Wells on a pallet near the door. He thinks he might have the Spawn.'

'Yes, Tomas, I'll see to him,' and she shooed him off.

Ben was busy at the hospital for two weeks. Tadeos had been infected, but his treatment was successful. His mental scars, however, ran deep. After working for a time as a gardener, he joined the Human Militia. Tomas had some contact with him then, and it was good to talk about old times with him, in his own language; but Tadeos would never talk about what had happened in Hunter's Wells after Tomas escaped.

CHAPTER VI

It was nearly two years after his arrival in the land of Greystone. It was Master Aravon's birthday, and his college went to Ilverin's House to celebrate. Sometime during the evening, a party of off-duty fighters came in, wearing the loose-fitting shirts that usually went under armour; as ever, they carried their swords. Tomas recognised Tenvardo, who had been with the unit that rescued Tomas nearly two years ago, and went over to chat.

'There is a call-out,' Tenvardo grumped, arranging his legs in front of him. 'All leave has been cancelled.'

Tomas' party mood suddenly felt selfish. 'Is there trouble in the Thornlands?'

'The news just came, with the scouts back from the Wide Neck. A Foul force moves out of the east, from the Greenstone Country. It is bigger than any other sent against us. They slash and burn as they go, attacking mostly at night. The Tsuna have asked for help, and quickly.' He took a swig of wine. 'So – the lancers, the heavy cavalry, are making ready to move right now. It will take them a day to get to the Wide Neck.'

'Are they all going?' Gentodil asked.

'Most of them. Half of the zebra-archers will follow in the morning; and then,' he sighed, as if already exhausted, 'the Cheetahs, that's my regiment, and the Leopards will be leaving for the Wide Neck on the day after, with the supplies. This is no longer a run and shoot in the bush, my friends. This is a Great War. I know, I was in the last one. How many does that make?' he looked blearily around.

'Four,' Tomas blurted, thinking, What kind of rotgut could make an elado tipsy?

'Dead right, Apprentice Tomas! Go to the top of the class! Oh, sorry,' he stopped, suddenly serious, 'I see you are an Initiate, now? Well done, by the way.'

'Thanks,' Tomas murmured.

Days later, Tomas received a note from Ben via Limlot: Liriel was to leave for the Wide Neck with a Healer detachment. He wrote back, but deliveries were unreliable that far out. He wondered that she would put herself close to danger again, after what happened at the Cobra Fort. The deep winter that year was tense. There was continual movement in the city.

After Midwinter, Tomas began instruction in the ways of large animals. First, he learned to control a *quaha* on his own, which he enjoyed immensely. The animals were striped like zebras on head, neck and forequarters, but bay behind. There were few things as satisfying as riding a stripe-necked beast through golden grass that grew up to your own knees, in the dusty sunlight of the dead of winter. In the saddle, he was no longer Tomas the Lame, but Tomas the *Quahastar*, the quaha-rider. He and Master Aravon requisitioned mounts from the stable house, and rode up the valley.

They made a long expedition that month, riding first to a farmstead west of Greystone called Lorelisse. It was a beautiful little arrangement of round, thatched, golden-stone buildings in parkland woods where the trees gave way to open country. There, Tomas worked with the eland and long-horned cattle that eladi used for meat, milk and hides. Tomas had a sneaking suspicion that eladi cared more for their livestock than some humans did for their own slaves.

After a week on the farm, Tomas and Master Aravon borrowed supplies and rode further west, to the empty lands high up the Green River valley, beyond the riverine forest on the drier, north-facing slopes where there was open woodland. There, they found the large wildlife: they rode among the wild relatives of the eladi livestock, as well as giraffe, kudu and bushbuck. They raced zebras, herded impala and chased hartebeest (though they never caught up with them). They sought buffalo and tsessebe, without success. Lastly, they hunted small game and guinea fowl from zebra-back, using hunting bows. In that way they stretched their food supplies for a week and a half. Tomas had never had so much fun.

Towards the end of their field-trip they stayed in camp for a few days, preparing the carcasses and hides and giving Tomas' backside time to recover from the punishment it had taken. They rested late each morning, and took their time over breakfast. Early one morning, they saw a column of dirty brown smoke beyond the mountains, slightly north of east. There was war in the Thornlands. Liriel was near there, treating the wounded. He muttered a prayer to the Hunter, the patron of soldiers and hunters, for her safety.

'If I may ask, O Tomas,' said the Master, 'why do men sleep so much?' They were lingering over their second cup of tea. It was a cool, windy morning under a huge, dark-blue sky. The grass was tall and yellow, the thorn-trees dark and bare. The shaded south faces of the Gildrock Mountains marched on in a long line north of them, their feet in the trees, ancient beyond imagining.

'Well, they get tired,' Tomas said. 'I don't understand how eladi sleep so little.'

'Eladi only sleep if they have been exposed to some sickness or suffered some injury,' said Master Aravon. 'And even then, we do not wait to fall asleep, as you do. It is something we do, not something that happens to us – as adults.'

'Perhaps men simply never grow old enough,' Tomas said. He scratched his face, now three weeks unshaven.

'That may well be,' the master nodded. 'The only man I ever knew before you was a hermit, and a truly holy man. He meditated and contemplated the One for most of the night, but I never saw him fatigued. He was a wonderful person.' The master was silent for a while, remembering. 'It was before the war, or the last war, now. He lived to be a hundred and sixty and they say that is old for your people.'

'It is,' said Tomas, 'but people in my family often reach a hundred. We are long-lived. The surgeon at the Healer Hall told me I had inherited a lot of eladan blood.'

'Well,' said the master, 'perhaps if you meditate, you too will need less sleep; or at least be more aware. There was a snake crawling over you this morning.'

'What?'

'Only joking,' the master said, chuckling. 'Snakes hibernate in winter, remember?'

'Oh,' Tomas smiled, feeling silly. Eladi never missed an opportunity for light humour. Then he asked, 'How does one sympathise with a snake?'

'It is difficult,' said the master, nodding slightly. 'And one can only do it with a big snake, an old one. Reptiles have to be old before they have enough mind to sympathise with.'

'Am I to learn about reptiles?'

The master considered. 'I could teach you. Reptiles are all difficult, though the sympathy is easy enough to maintain once begun. If I were to teach you about reptiles, we would have to find the most suitable ones, such as big old tortoises or crocodiles. The bigger the better,' he added with a sidelong grin at Tomas, 'but there are no more crocodiles between the Limtail Ravine and here, and my tortoise is sleeping at this time of year, if he's any sense. But then, I'm not sure how much you would profit from the exercise. Most magi sympathise best with certain kinds of animals, and your affinity is for birds.'

Tomas wondered what it would be like, swimming with a crocodile. Then another question occurred to him. 'What about carnivores? The big cats, especially.'

'We have not encountered any this time,' the master said,

disappointed, 'though I had hoped that a leopard at least would come after those carcasses.' He pointed to the tree where the carcasses of a springbok and an impala hung, drying in the sun.

Tomas was glad it hadn't, but would have liked to see one – from a safe distance, of course.

They took all the next day to reach Lorelisse, where they returned the items they had borrowed, and gave some of the meat to the farm household. They stayed the night there, and over supper asked for any news of the war.

'News always comes late to us here,' the farmer said, 'but we heard there was a great battle in the Thornlands.'

'We saw the smoke. How did it go?' Tomas asked.

'Very well, I believe. They captured a commander of the enemy forces.'

Tomas and the master looked at each other. 'A great kchaban?' the master asked.

'It must have been,' said the farmer.

'That is very good news,' Master Aravon said. 'Such good news, in fact, that I am now actually looking forward to going home.'

They rode home at a fair pace the next day, starting at dawn and reaching the city around noon. They went straight to the Music Hall, where the news was always written on sheets stuck up on the walls for public reading. There, Apprentices were arranging scores, playing music and improvising ballads, already commemorating the victory.

Tomas and Master Aravon read about the battle that took place on the flatlands beyond the North Gildrock range. It had raged for two nights and a day. The Fouls had been moving westwards by night, making for the Wide Neck, in a large force with a supply train that included siege engines.

The eladi and the Tsuna men had been harrying them for several weeks, raiding in the daytime when the enemy was most vulnerable. Eventually, the Fouls had encamped about an isolated hill half a days' march from the Wide Neck. If they had managed to conquer the Eladon strong place at the Wide Neck, they would have gained a considerable advantage. From the koppie they had sent out scouting parties and a few mobs of their giant black baboons, but the eladan light cavalry dealt with them well, and the enemy had less advantage from the baboons than they might have expected.

While the Fouls were still encamped, Greystone foot-soldiers had engaged their main strength on the north of the koppie in the hour before sunrise. The kchaban forces had grown into their ancient form, with hyena-handlers in the front ranks and shamans among the archers. The hyenas were a sore test of the zebras, but the cavalry mounts were trained to use their feet as weapons, and the animals ridden by the lancers were partly armoured themselves. The shamans were the worst, summoning dervishes in huge dust-storms or casting the Darkfear over people and animals, raising shadows in broad daylight. There had been few of the warped animals, perhaps because the senior magicians were dead or recovering after the first battle under the trees. With the main strength thus engaged, the Tsuna struck from behind, sneaking into the supply train and freeing all the slaves they could find, whilst firing anything they could. At the same time, a heavy infantry regiment, the Cheetahs, fired the bush on the koppie. After three months with no rain, the grass and brush burned quickly. 'That explains the smoke we saw,' Tomas said.

Then, as the kchaban commander fled the fire, he just happened to run close by some of the Cheetahs. The eladi managed to apprehend him, but his bodyguard gave chase, trying to rescue their leader. If the Tsuna had not been there, the Cheetahs may well have been decimated. As it was, they escaped with their captive, though their losses were heavy.

With their leader gone, the Fouls lost their initiative. Somebody else had taken over, but he wasn't a competent commander. At dawn, the cavalry attacked, though the rocky terrain made it very difficult. Then the King of the Tsuna and his household regiment had broken upon the horde's west flank in a wave of leather and iron, and it was all over: the huge army broke and scattered. The kchaban commander was being held at the strong place there, the notice said.

'The Cheetahs,' Tomas noted, 'that's Tenvardo's regiment. I hope he survived.'

'Indeed. Heavy casualties, they say,' the master said.

As it happened, Tenvardo had survived, and Tomas met him some time later. He had conducted himself well in the battle, been cited for bravery and promoted.

Master Aravon pointed to the bottom of the last notice. 'This is two days old,' Aravon said quietly. 'I would not be surprised if that great kchaban is now entertaining the lord's inquisitors.' He gave a calculating grin.

Tomas gave a nasty chuckle. 'In that case, may he enjoy his stay. I hope he's thinking of all sorts of interesting things to tell them.'

'As long as they are true.' The Master smiled wryly.

They left their mounts at the stable house, and went to the bath-house to clean up. Tomas decided against shaving, thinking he'd try the human style for a change. In the afternoon, they started on their long journey (at Tomas' pace) to Master Aravon's house. They had only just left the city gates when a crow, a big black bird with neck, breast and belly of pure white, landed on the road in front of them, one leg wrapped in soft hide. Looking steadily at the bird, the master said, 'Come here, old one,' and extended his arm. The crow flew up onto the arm, and Aravon removed the hide strip, saying, 'Tomas, do you have any food for her?'

'No, why do you ask?'

'Payment for the messenger. I don't have any, either. Could you take her, please?'

'Come girl, let's find you something to eat,' said Tomas, and the crow hopped onto his arm. She liked him, he was a nice speaker-thing. Tomas stroked her back.

The master read the message. 'What did I say?' He said, quietly, 'They have him in the Keep.' Seeing the crow's affection for Tomas, he said, 'Tomas Birdman, I am to go to the Keep straight away. I shall probably be there for at least another day, so you may as well take your New Moon's leave now.'

'Thank you. Shall I pay the messenger?'

'You will have to, now that you said you would.'

'I'll look for something in the man-camp.'

'Peace. See you next week.'

'Peace,' said Tomas, and carried on down the road towards the man-camp. The master started back to the city.

Master Ben was not in his hut, but Ioseth the new apprentice gave the crow some bones and gristle. Tomas asked him where the master had gone, and he said, 'He was called to the City.'

'That makes two masters called to the City,' Tomas said. 'It must be because of the prisoner.'

'What prisoner? The great kchaban?'

Tomas nodded. 'I wonder why they wanted Ben?'

Ioseth just shook his head.

The next day Tomas went to visit Limlot. The bearded old elado greeted him with a knowing smile and Tomas asked him about Liriel.

'Ah, she wrote you a letter,' the teacher said with a green glint in his eye. 'If you would help me with some correspondence I've to write, I might even let you see it.'

'Woe is me,' Tomas said theatrically, 'forced to labour for a mere note from a friend.'

'Ha!' laughed Limlot, 'not that you fool me for a heartbeat – I offer you not only the comfort of a lady's writing, but also for lunch. One does not get very much of that in these days of rationing, does one? And one living in the poverty of Discipleship must take what is offered.'

'Er, yes. Quite so.'

They sat writing Celevrau's letters for the whole day. Tomas noted that a lot of his work was meant for places with unfamiliar names, and some were for the Merchant Kobos. 'Are the caravans running to the South again?' he asked.

'They are indeed,' Limlot replied, 'now that the Resistance holds the western approaches. The good Merchant is milking the golden eland.' He saw Tomas' blank expression. 'I'm sorry, that's an old orelado saying. It means he's doing very well out of it. Very few caravans are travelling through these days, and only Kobos' goes all the way to Westerhaven.'

Tomas looked at a map of the Southlands on the wall. 'That's a long way.'

'Indeed. He is probably there by now. Rather him than me, winter in the Far South is miserable.'

'Why is that?'

'Because it rains in winter, there. Didn't they teach you anything, those men?'

Tomas had forgotten. 'Oh, yes, I remember. I never could understand that.'

'It is strange. One would think that, since it rains in winter, the trees there would shed their leaves in spring, since summer is their dry season – but it is not so.'

Tomas shook his head. Some things were mysteries. Speaking of mysteries, he thought, and asked out loud, 'Why is it that the masters have been summoned to the Keep?'

Limlot looked at him. 'Your master is a Master of Animal Sympathy, is he not? Well, his Ability extends to other minds as well.'

'What about the other masters?'

Limlot shrugged. 'All the Wise wish to know as much as they can about the enemy.'

Tomas' leave seemed to rush by that month. He arrived back at Aravon's rondavel in the forest just after sunset. The western sky was still orange as he approached the building. The door was closed, he noticed, probably against the cold – but why was the light in the window so dim? It looked like the hearth-fire was the only light inside.

Hoping that his lateness might go unnoticed, he tried the door. It was locked. He touched the ward-stone in the doorpost, but instead of opening, the lock mechanism simply clicked unlocked. Opening the door, Tomas received a nasty shock: there was a great kchaban sitting right next to the fire in the centre of the room. The thing's bald head was huge, its teeth yellow and its eyes bloodshot, reflecting red in the firelight. It had long feet, and was chained to the rafters by manacles attached to ankles and wrists. Looking up at Tomas, it sneered, 'So who are you?' It spoke Southlandish, in a voice that was smooth and dead and treacherous, like wet stone.

Tomas was disgusted. Seeing this thing in Master Aravon's house was like finding a mouse-dropping in your food. The place stank. A slop-bucket stood on the other side of the fire from Tomas. 'I live here,' he said simply. He knew the power of names.

'You a Sorcerer?'

Tomas didn't answer. This was not the time to talk semantics.

The kchaban humphed. 'You're not one of these stinkers, though you're not quite a horse-monkey, either.' It persisted. 'You a slave? A bender?' It asked with an insulting leer.

Tomas' mouth curled in disgust. The kchaban chuckled, like gravel shifting underfoot. Tomas looked around. There was no sign of the master, or of any of his students. Even the furniture was gone. It looked like everyone had moved, without telling him. What was going on?

He realised the kchaban was watching him intently. 'Your friends aren't here,' it said. 'The stinkers chained me up here, and they all left with most the stuff. Looks like they left you in the dark, my friend: I suppose slaves don't matter much.' It shook its head in mock sympathy.

Much though Tomas trusted the Master, that hurt. Tomas said, 'I know who you are, you filth.' He gave in to the temptation to gloat. Coming closer, he said, 'You're finished. Chewed up and spat out.'

The kchaban snarled, suddenly lunging at Tomas. Its expression had changed from sullen contempt to red-eyed hatred. The chain jerked taut as the thing's heavy-nailed fingers made to claw at Tomas' face. Tomas jerked back, then smirked at the captive.

'That's enough!' said a commanding voice in Celadi from the door. Both Tomas and the kchaban started. It was Master Aravon. Still in his own language, he said, 'Initiate, sink not to this thing's level!'

Tomas felt embarrassed. The master was carrying a large sack. From it he removed some food and drink packages and left them on the ground near the kchaban, where it could reach them. Then, turning to Tomas, he said, 'We are staying at the Tree House while this prisoner is here. If you had been here at the proper time, you would have been spared this contact. Come, now.'

Locking the door again, they walked the chill, dark winter pathways to the Tree House, a wooden structure built high in a clump of stinkwoods to the north of the City. It had been built for the use of magi or students who had dealings with birds or monkeys. Tomas had only ever seen it from a distance before. Inside, all the master's students were curled up in their patterned goats-wool blankets against the walls, dreaming as their kind did. The master took Tomas to an observation post, along a rope bridge to a treetop platform for a private talk. Tomas braced himself to face some music.

'Now, Tomas,' said Aravon. 'What did you say to the prisoner?'

'Well, when I came in, he wanted to know who I was, and – well, he made some insinuations.'

'Did you mention any names?'

'No.'

'Good. Carry on.'

'Well, I reacted to his suggestion that I'd been deliberately left out. I told him he was finished, and he went for me. That was when you came in.'

'Is that all?'

'Yes.'

Aravon wasn't quite satisfied. He asked Tomas to go over the conversation again in detail, recalling the exact words used. Eventually, as Tomas' teeth began to chatter, the master said, 'All right. I see no deception in you, Tomas. Let us go inside, and I shall rekindle the fire.'

With flames dancing in a large asbestos fire pot, the master said to Tomas, 'The great kchaban is Jwagga the Foot. I am keeping him in my house, because I have the ability to control him, and his masters may be searching for him, using magic. My house used to belong to a Hermit, and retains a scent of holiness that makes it impervious to magic. The kchaban's former masters will try and curse him to death before he can tell us what he knows. Though he is a great kchaban, but we haven't found any firm evidence of a parasite spirit about him – yet. He is intelligent, very manipulative... and his mind is a cesspit. His mental disease may be conditioning, rather than a parasite. He is not a Kchaban Lord, but he had ambitions, which is how he came to be leading that force.'

Aravon looked levelly at Tomas. 'Part of a manipulative personality is the judicious use of insults, which you have now encountered. As I said to the others this evening before he was brought in, lies and insults are only the edge of the blade; they weaken your peace for a stroke by darkness. Tomas, you have to remember your detachment. If you think so much of yourself that personal remarks can hurt you, it cannot last.'

'Sorry, master, I forgot myself,' said Tomas: but he felt resentful that he had to account for defending himself.

'I know it hurts to have hatred directed at you, Tomas; but once you have admitted the pain, you must forgive the one who hurt you. Otherwise, he is able to keep on hurting you, even if he is dead - and that way lies the temptation of evil.'

Tomas remembered all those wonderful meditations he had attended, as apprentice and initiate. He must have attended recently, he thought, but it felt like a long time ago, now. The theory had been wonderful, but he had failed in the practice.

'As long as you can forgive, Tomas, you will be free of that link, that evil bond. Even if he still hates your very existence, it doesn't matter; he can go on gnawing his own hatred, in the Abyss if necessary. Do you understand?'

'Yes, master.' Tomas felt tired, now. He had to think this over, to re-balance.

'Still, at least you weren't exposed to him for too long. I know you will do better next time.' The master sighed. '"The burnt hand teaches fear of fire." I shall leave you to think of that while you sleep. Remember, forgiveness allows goodness to grow in you. No-one knows why, but it does.'

Tomas slept only fitfully that night. His mind seethed with more than just the poisonous interaction with the prisoner. There was something foul in that house, and Tomas could not shake off the feeling. In the cold early light of dawn, he managed to throw off the worst of it; but the touch was there, making peace difficult to achieve.

The interrogation of Jwagga the Foot dragged on for days on end. Tomas knew that it took place in the ruins of the old city of Greystone, and the prisoner was always returned to the master's house in the evenings, where he was fed by the students.

The students' instruction lost momentum, only meditation carrying on as usual. Tomas was itching to continue his instruction after the time he'd spent in the master's company, but everyone was always crowding around him whenever he came home, and he only had time for a few words with each of them.

After several days, it was Tomas' turn to take food. In the cold of the evening, he shouldered the bag in the Tree House and walked to the rondavel where the college used to live. Inside, the prisoner was sitting in its normal sullen state. Tomas saw a flicker of recognition on its face as he entered.

'Hi, Cripple,' the kchaban said. 'Come for a bending?'

Tomas humphed. His mood, already sour, worsened. 'Dream on, dog meat.'

'Dog meat?' the kchaban snorted. 'Not by the time we're finished with you.'

Tomas wondered if there was anything in that remark. He said, 'By the time you're finished with us, you will be dog meat; and there'll be nothing left of your people but vulture guano.'

'Don't bet on it, bender. We've got arkchabani coming, and they'll squish your pretty-boys like the cockroaches they are.'

'We know about your Halfmen,' Tomas said dismissively. 'Like everything evil, they're for the dung heap, eventually.'

'You talk pretty big for a lame thing,' sneered the kchaban. 'Tell me, why do they let people like you live? I mean, you can't fight, you can't work; you must be a bender, or they're fattening you for the pot. Even if you don't know it.'

Tomas sighed and shook his head. 'That's what's wrong with your kind. Here, people aren't valued for what they can do, but for who they are. That's the reason why my culture lives and grows, while yours just sucks, like a tick.'

The kchaban gave a vile oath. 'It's the way of the strong. Look at the wild - the strong animals feed on the weak. If you're strong, you eat, and you rape, and you use, and you dominate. That's why, eventually, we will overcome you. It's started already.'

'And why do you think that, despite trying for thousands of years, your people still haven't succeeded?' Tomas interrupted, warming to a good argument. 'It's because you just take, and kill, and use, and never replace anything, never grow anything. Eventually, you all starve.'

'That's when we go hunting for you!'

'And when there's none left to kill?'

The kchaban stopped. Then he said, as if it was quite a joke, 'Why should I care? I'll be dead by then!'

Tomas nodded sarcastically. 'Then how will you prove you're strong, when there aren't any more eladi or men to rob? You people are parasites! You can't make anything or do anything new; all you can do is ruin what's already there, then bleat when it's all gone! You're just like your Black Master.'

The kchaban went quiet. His face was dark with some solemn dread. 'One day, when you're on the Other Side, you'll regret those words, mongrel.'

'I may regret some things, dirt, but that won't be one of them.'

The kchaban spat at Tomas, but Tomas was expecting it. He dodged back, saying, 'Why don't you just co-operate with the inquisitors? You're no use to your own people, in fact they want you dead. You can justify breathing our air by telling us what we want to know. If not –

you're just a waste of space: not even worth killing.'

The kchaban lunged at Tomas. Tomas didn't budge, as the kchaban jerked and tore at his chains, chafing the skin of his ankles and wrists. Judging by the strength of the reaction, Tomas thought, the interrogation must be wearing him down.

'I am power!' the kchaban spat. 'My overlord is Kroghnash the Skullbreaker, son of Smulbuggu the Bigmembered! The Dark Power will tear your soul out of you –' but his speech degenerated into incoherent rage as Tomas burst out laughing.

'Smulbuggu the *what*?' Tomas managed to say past his laughter.

The kchaban yanked his chains and roared like an animal; Tomas laughed like a hyena, but mastered himself with difficulty. This had gone far enough. He could see how the kchaban was damaging itself, and he didn't want to be responsible for that.

'All right!' he shouted over the noise. 'I'm sorry I laughed,' he failed to stifle a snigger, 'Calm down!'

The kchaban relaxed, with a sneer for Tomas' apology. He stopped for breath, his mouth flecked with foam, his wrists and ankles bloodied. He bent down to pick up an earthenware water-jug.

Tomas knew what was coming. Without even thinking, he reached out and touched the kchaban's mind, thinking mollifying, sobering impulses.

'You don't want to do that,' he said.

The kchaban lowered the jug. Reading its mind, Tomas' suspicion was confirmed. It badly wanted to kill him, and had been about to throw the jug. Tomas felt disgusted. Touching this thing's mind was the psychic equivalent of dipping into filth. How could Master Aravon stand it? Suddenly, Tomas' thoughts stopped short. Master Aravon! He had expressly forbidden initiates from making any sympathetic contact with the prisoner! If he was caught interfering...

He worked himself free, trying to break off the contact; but something strange happened. Tomas had a sense of touching something hidden in the kchaban's mind – or of being touched by something. The presence was huge, ancient and truly, deeply horrible. All at once, Tomas felt a chill, grey, dead hand on his heart. The corpse-grip was vicelike, and a consciousness as old as time opened a door in Tomas' mind – a door he never knew existed. It found memories of bondage, and of Acolyte Timaeos screaming as he died. It exulted in the horror of the memory, feeding on it. Again, it sifted Tomas' memories, and discovered the naked fear of the night Tomas was wounded in his left hip. It poked at and shuffled the memories, looking for extra horror in possibilities of what might have been: Tomas shot in the eye, Tomas hit in the groin by that spear, Tomas' jaw bludgeoned right off by an axe. His mind reeled. The presence gulped in the fear and pain of the memories, the imagination-stoked horror, savouring them graspingly; but Tomas in turn felt its hunger, its lust. It could never be satisfied, even if it glutted itself to bursting on an ocean of eladon blood and human tears.

The kchaban's appearance had changed subtly. Its eyes were strangely orange, and its face was etched with an evil beyond imagining. There was a spine-crawling darkness beyond sight about him, a horrible lack where Master Aravon was overflowing. The air was suddenly cold, and there was a whiff of sewage. A voice, as old and as despairing as the grip behind it, rattled up from the kchaban's chest. It demanded, 'What is your name?'

Tomas was in such terror, his voice came out in a strangled sob. Thoughtless of his peril, he said, 'Tom-,' and knew he was doomed.

The presence seemed to laugh. 'Now,' it said, 'you are mine.'

The corpse-grip shifted, trying to get a better hold of Tomas' being; but something slipped. All at once, Tomas felt a lessening of the deadness. The presence turned its attention to the kchaban, seeking something. The kchaban, moving jerkily like a puppet, made a grab for Tomas, but was brought up short by the chains. The kchaban sniffed the air, like one of the lesser breeds, but it didn't have the acute sense of smell that kchaban trackers had. The death-rattle voice came again, saying, 'Come closer!'

Tomas took a reflexive step forwards, but the presence had betrayed its helplessness. Tomas suddenly realised that he was free of compulsion. He loosed himself suddenly, leaving the kchaban's mind. The kchaban slumped down, exhausted. The darkness fell from Tomas' mind, and he too dropped down to his knees. What was *that*? If it was a Parasite Spirit, he was roasted! He looked around at the fire, suddenly bright in the hearth. Fire was good. There was light and life, but he had come so close to losing both!

Tomas got ready to leave, hurriedly gathering the old food litter. He wanted to go, and never come back; but at the same time his fear of discovery made him indecisive. He was tying up his bag, when he felt a prickle of fear run up his back. He spun around to look at the kchaban, pain shooting from his hip. His blood ran cold as he saw that the kchaban wore the evil face again! His flesh crawled. The Foul was kneeling near the wall, as far from the fire as it could get. It spoke, again in that voice of death: 'I see you not, Halfman, but I know you!' the voice said. '*You* are the one I seek, you disgusting mongrel! I await your sacrifice, at the Place of Dogs!'

Tomas stood, rooted to the spot. Then the darkness and chill and stink were gone, and the kchaban collapsed on the floor, sobbing and cursing, in its own voice. It pleaded, begging Tomas not to leave it alone in the dark; but Tomas had had enough. He left in haste, trembling with more than cold. He all but ran along the dark, slated pathways, careless of the pain in his hip, his fear lending gruesome shapes to the shades of the night. Something was watching! He climbed up into the Tree House, very glad of the fey light of the eladi that soothed the darkness.

He didn't sleep a wink. He lay awake with the eladi, wishing that what he saw and heard had only been his imagination. No-one said anything, but Tomas felt as though he had brought Death into the Tree House with him. He was scared of telling anyone, but he knew he would not be able to keep his indiscretion secret forever. While terrified of being discovered, he wished he was.

The next morning dawned chilly, bright and breezy. The master left early, and his students busied themselves without him. By the end of the day, Tomas had managed to half-convince himself that it would all blow over in time, and he was tired enough to sleep. Over the next few days, he kept himself busy, enough tire himself out, and within a week he had almost made himself believe it hadn't really happened, or if it had, that it didn't really matter; but still the words came back to him: *you are the one I seek*. What did the shade want with *him*, of all people?

On leave the following week, Tomas looked in at Master Ben's house, then went to look for Liriel.

She was not in the Healer Hall, and the other Healers told him she had not come in since returning from the Wide Neck. Tomas went to look for her at her father's house.

In the evening of the tail-end of winter, the old place looked like a huge, ancient rock outcrop, rather than a gracious house. The trees around it were bare and dark, the flower-gardens thick with dark-leaved winter shrubbery. The dim light seemed to hint at the gloom of Aravon's rondavel, and Tomas moved quickly, unwilling to linger in the gathering dark. Inside the house there was the smell of a certain incense used by the Healers for disturbed patients. Pleasant though the smell was, it was not a good sign. Lotu, Liriel's lourie, greeted Tomas with his customary enthusiasm, but he seemed unhappy. That was also not good. Where was everybody, anyway?

'Hello,' he called out, 'is anyone in?'

There was the sound of a door from the floor above. Tomas walked out into the courtyard, to let himself be seen, and to be able to see in turn. The first stars were peeping out. Limlot appeared on the balcony that ringed the courtyard, his tawny-bearded face sombre. 'I thought it was you,' he said, 'when I heard the bird. I don't know how you come to be here right now, but come up, she will want to see you.'

Tomas' heart sank. Was Liriel sick? How could an elada be sick, especially a Healer? He ascended the staircase, taking two steps at a time on his good leg. Never one to waste energy, Lotu rode up on his shoulder. At the top, Limlot showed Tomas to Liriel's room. He had never been invited upstairs before. It was warm in the room, with a small stone stove glowing in one corner. The incense smell was coming from there. The lourie disliked the smell, and flew back out to perch on the balcony railing. The furniture was low and comfortable. There was a bamboo screen painted with grazing gazelles along one side, shielding the bed. Limlot looked around it, and said something quietly. There was a sound of movement, and Liriel came out. Her thick, lustrous, dark hair was unbound and untidy, and she was hunched up in a shawl; but it was her eyes that Tomas noticed. No longer glorious, they were red and puffy, as if she had been crying for a long time. The sight cut him to the heart. Dropping his walking-stick, he went to embrace her, and she dissolved into helpless tears in his arms. She stayed like that for some time. Tomas' hip started to protest, but he ignored it.

'What happened?' he asked, eventually.

Limlot sighed and explained, 'She was simply over-exposed. There were so many wounded, and too many victims of the Darkfear. She has simply seen too much, for one her age.' He shook his old head slowly. 'Or of her kind – your kind.' He used the plural.

Tomas thought, surely in a hundred or more years as a Healer, she's seen it all? But then, there hadn't been a war for all that time.

'Is there anything I can do to help?' he asked finally. Liriel shook her head, and blew her nose.

'Somehow, I think you are helping already, Tomas,' said Limlot.

Liriel went to sit down on her sofa, a long, low, high-backed couch with embroidered lilies. 'Thank you, Tomas,' she said. 'I need some understanding, and you are good at understanding me. Why do you have a beard?' she asked suddenly, frowning.

Limlot said, 'I'll make some tea and bring it up to you, shall I?' He left, smiling, but didn't close the door. The old guardian was discreet, but proper.

Tomas grinned ruefully. He had been hoping for a bit of sympathy himself, but Liriel needed it more than he did. He sat down beside her, arranging his bad leg comfortably.

When Limlot returned with the tea, he found the two of them, fast asleep and hand in hand, her head on his shoulder. He put the tray down, smiled quietly to himself, and left.

The two of them woke during the night, with the stove burned low and the room cold. The tea, stewed and cold by then, was still on the table. Shivering and hungry, Tomas and Liriel went down for a late-night or early-morning supper in the kitchen, and sat talking nonsense and giggling together, trying to put worry and horrors behind them. At some stage Limlot came down to tell them to stop making a noise, but joined them in their silliness for a while. Eventually, when the night was at its darkest, he showed Tomas to the guest-room. It was a sign of progress, thought Tomas, to be allowed to stay the night. Liriel bade him goodnight, and hugged him for some time.

The next morning, when Tomas woke with winter sunlight pouring down on him through the glass of a north-facing window, he wondered where he was; then he remembered. Liriel's laughing face and lingering hands laid deliciously in his memory. Wonderful progress, indeed! Eladi always took their time over such things; Tomas supposed it was because they had so much time to spend. Nothing was ever hurried, nothing at all.

CHAPTER VII

When Tomas got back to the Tree House, he heard that the great kchaban was gone, no-one knew where. The Master was also gone.

After more than a day in which no-one had seen Master Aravon at all, a message was delivered to them saying that the master was 'indisposed'. Tomas' guilt returned in a wave. Had the Master suffered exposure to the great kchaban's parasite, one that he, Tomas, had aroused? His indirect questions at the infirmary were politely rebuffed.

Then came another message, this time from Master Helder, detailing arrangements for the initiates to be sent to study under their other masters.

So, once again, Tomas went to Mistress Miruvire to learn rapport with green and growing things – only in the dead drought of winter.

The difference this time was that Tomas was simply unable to sympathise as he had before. Mistress Miruvire thought he had been over-indulging, and sent him to help supervise her apprentices. The enforced peace and quiet of two days' meditation helped him to sleep properly again, and could almost forget the horror in the master's rondavel.

He rejoined the plant sympathy initiates in time for another punishing climb, high up on the south-facing slopes of the North Gildrock Mountains. They went to the thickest, densest, oldest parts of the forests. The trees there were old, huge, and all but talked.

Before, Tomas had learned to recognise and distinguish the 'voices' of the oldest trees, especially the ironwoods and stinkwoods, hardwood trees that were very common in Greystone. He thought he could still do it, but towards the end of his time, Mistress Miruvire asked to speak with him alone. They were at the foot of the cliffs, below the places where vultures nested. They looked up, and saw a few of the giant scavengers circling at a dizzy height.

'Do you think they see something?' the mistress asked.

Tomas tried to reach out, but could feel nothing. 'I wouldn't know, mistress,' he said. 'They are too high up. They are always on the lookout, though.'

'Your master is Master Aravon, is he not?'

Tomas nodded.

The mistress sat down on a rounded boulder, under a spreading buffalo-thorn. She arranged her long, loose trousers carefully and said, 'Do you know what is wrong with your master?'

Fear clutched at Tomas' chest. 'No,' he said, fearing and wanting the answer.

'Your master,' said the mistress, 'has suffered psychic contagion. Were you one of the students tending the prisoner?'

'No,' said Tomas, but he had been going to say Yes. Why did he say that?

'Are you lying?' The mistress' expression was flat.

'Yes – NO!'

'You weren't one of those who fed the prisoner?'

'No.' Tomas felt himself blanch. Why on earth was he lying through his teeth?

'Have you heard enough, O brother?' The mistress addressed someone behind Tomas.

Tomas whirled around, nearly falling on his bad hip. There was a golden-eyed wise behind him. Tomas gave a gasp of pain for his joint, but it came out as a snarl for the wise. What was going on?

'Yes, mistress. Three lies and a reaction to my presence: he is at least infected.'

Tomas mastered himself. 'What do you mean?'

'Turn around, Tomas,' said the wise. Tomas didn't move. He still didn't know what was going on.

'Good,' said the wise, 'It is a touch, not a hold, on his soul, I think. He was not compelled to obey me.'

'He is fortunate, then?' asked the mistress.

'Indeed.'

'Would my elders grace me with their knowledge?' Tomas asked with exaggerated politeness.

The mistress explained, 'I was surprised that your ability seemed to have atrophied, and I thought you may have been weakened by a touch of evil, perhaps by a parasite spirit. I asked about the vultures, because Animal Sympathy initiates have always been able to tell me what the birds were doing or even thinking. You could not.'

A cold hand settled on Tomas' heart. His haunted wait was over.

The wise continued. 'Now, when you return to the City, I want you to go and seek healing at one of the Sanctuaries and submit to rehabilitation. Your soul needs to recover from that exposure. I cannot compel you, but you will not recover without it.'

Tomas rubbed his forehead, 'That sounds right.' He was relieved that they didn't think he had roused the parasite that infected the master.

'It is. It was good fortune that you were not colonised by evil yourself; even so, it will take some time to recover.' He made to go. 'I shall have to go and test your fellow initiates, too. The other masters involved in the interrogation have already submitted to rehabilitation.'

Tomas said, 'What?'

'There were two other masters who may have been exposed. They have been purged, at the Sanctuary.'

Tomas swallowed. 'Purged?'

'I must tell Master Helder about you, Tomas,' said the mistress. 'He has taken the lead among the magi. You will not be permitted in any college until you are safe.'

Tomas returned through the chill evening. At the rondavel, he found only a pair of apprentices, who told him that the master had still not returned. He was relieved that they didn't know yet.

Tomas left the following morning, but instead of going to a Sanctuary, made straight for the infirmary, to see Liriel. With her people's strange foresight, she was expecting him. They went in to the healers' dining room, and after talking for a while, Liriel said, 'I have some interesting news: my father is to be part of an Embassy to the King of the South.'

'Oh,' Tomas said, thinking a little. 'That is an honour ... but a dark sign at the same time.'

'Indeed. The embassy will be led by the Magus Menelvagon, one who went to Hunters' Wells in autumn last year.'

'Ah, I remember him. I hope they will be escorted.'

'Naturally. They will meet with the Resistance leaders in your old home, and together make a combined embassy to ask the King to intervene on our behalf.'

Tomas nodded. 'The King might listen to a combined embassy, where he might not care about trouble on the Highlands.'

'Why might he not care?'

'The people of the South think little of us Highlanders, especially since the Duke's grandfather declared himself independent. Since then, the South has adopted the Awakening, while we still follow the Law of the Kings.'

Liriel sighed, 'Men are really so immature, at times.' She shook her head with an exasperated smile.

'We do make a bit of a mess of it, do we not?' Tomas said with a weak laugh. 'So when are they leaving?'

'In three days' time,' said Liriel. 'They are to travel securely, with a light-shield. They will be space-folding where possible.'

'That should amuse the men no end,' Tomas smirked. 'I would love to see their faces when they appear on top of the hill they were looking at in the distance the night before.' He scratched his new brown beard. This raised some interesting possibilities, and he wondered how he could exploit them. 'So –' he began awkwardly.

Liriel raised one eladan eyebrow, a slow smile spreading across her face. Tomas felt himself colouring. 'We might be able to see each other a bit more?'

Liriel nodded quietly. Then, she tossed cold water on him: 'You *are* an Initiate, Tomas. We have time.'

Tomas suddenly felt very tired. She didn't notice anything about him, at least.

'What's the matter? What has happened? You look terrible.'

'I have –' he began, but stopped. What was the point? The guilt and horror rose up in his mind like a wave of nausea. He lowered his face into his hands.

'Tomas?' Liriel's voice was concerned. It was so nice that she cared, he thought. No, it wasn't. She was just another elada, she didn't care about dirty little men: smelly boys with walking-sticks. She was evil.

'Tomas, look at me.'

Tomas raised his head. The bitterness, loneliness and self-pity in his soul ran rampant.

Liriel saw it. She stood up, and Tomas could see she understood. She looked at him with a strange, clinical detachment: an eladon maga in full possession of herself. She nodded, saying, 'Master Aravon.'

Tomas stood up suddenly. He had been going to stalk out in a huff, but the pain in his hip brought him back down with a bump. He gasped and sank down again, missing the low chair, hitting his coccyx against it, and then landing on the same bones on the hard floor. Pain exploded from the base of his spine, and he shouted a filthy Militia oath.

Liriel turned and called for assistance. A handful of humans and eladi appeared at the mistress' call. They helped Tomas up and Liriel ran a hand down his lower back, probing. She said to the healers and humans, 'This is Tomas, an Initiate of Master Aravon's college. He has suffered an injury to his sacrum. While his injury is minor, walking is difficult. Call a Traveller magus, and have him transported to the Hallows on the Westbourne.'

Calling a magus to act as a glorified porter was too much – and the choice of destination was strange; but it was just what was needed to get him to that Sanctuary.

Thus it was that Tomas came by the quickest means possible to the place he most needed to be. The magus transporting him barely spoke. Tomas linked arms with him, and between one instant and another they translated. Tomas gawped around in amazement. He had passed this building the previous year, as a refugee from slavery. The gardens were bare, forlorn and yellow after several months with no rain, but some of the trees showed green at the tips of their twigs. Spring had once again decided that the world should go on.

They passed through the tall, arched entrance of the Sanctuary, into the cold, domed space within. A sumptuous red-and-blue banner of the Gilyad, Lord Engolaran's family, hung solemnly above the doorway. Along the eastern side were three tall, arched windows. Opposite them was a long, low block of diorite. There, in golden runes deeply graven, were written the names of all the eladi that had fallen in combat in the third Foul War.

The only light in the building, apart from the dusty morning light through the windows, came from the sacred lamp. The central feature of all human and eladan holy places, it stood on a plinth against the western wall. It consisted of a central well of oil, from which radiated seven short golden spouts. At the end of those spouts glittered small, flat flames. It looked like a water-lily carved in fire and gold. On the wall behind it were swirling, foliated patterns, carved to focus attention on the Lamp. The other walls bore bronze reliefs of the Powers, in classical poses from eladan mythology. They were unlit, taking all their light from the One, represented by the Lamp.

The magus went to speak to the wise, leaving Tomas sitting as comfortably as possible on a low kneeling-stool. Tomas looked at the figure of Marta the Mourner, a veiled, silver-haired elada in violet with an owl perched on her chair arm. It struck Tomas again that there was more than one kind of death – the physical kind not the worst.

Tomas looked at the Lamp. It glowed contentedly, shining gratuitously on everything, good, bad and indifferent. It was impartial, excluding no-one. There was no darkness there. In fact, there was not enough darkness in all the world to put out the light of that one Lamp. Tomas felt great peace and contentment at the thought. All the darkness that plagued him was nothing more than an absence: of his ability, of love and trust, of honesty. Fearing loss, he had turned away from light; but doing so would leave him deaf to the beings of living things, crippled forever. There was really nothing more to lose.

'I am told you have been exposed to evil,' said a voice right behind him. Tomas started, turning to see a white-clad, barefooted wise. Something in him recoiled, even as he recognised the aura of goodness that beamed out of the elado.

The Traveller magus stood several paces away. 'I shall leave you now,' he said, and closed the door of the Hallows.

The wise was still looking at Tomas intently. 'You are not what you seem.'

'I am –'

'Tomas – Tomas the Lame, a Younger, a student of Master Aravon.' The elado came round and sat next to him. 'My brother told me about you yesterday. I am glad to have you here.' He pulled a chair around. 'You are a strange mixture of speaking beings,' he said. 'In all my years, I've never seen the like of you.'

This wise will be inspecting my teeth next, thought Tomas.

'You have been infected,' the wise said, looking at Tomas with that same intense stare, 'but not as you could have been. I must know everything.' Beneath his calm words, Tomas could feel a passionate interest, like a child with an interesting puzzle. 'Come with me, we can sit in the warm sunlight at least.'

Suddenly, the wise got up and went to the side door. He turned, waiting for Tomas. At once eager and reluctant,Tomas pushed himself up on his walking stick and followed, painfully.

Outside it was beautiful, the late winter morning dry and bright. The air was dusty, the land beyond the gardens still parched. Tomas followed the wise along a colonnaded walkway to a tiny, round, house-shaped building with the usual wide eladon eaves but no walls. Though the slender columns supported the roof, it was open on all sides to the air. The wise sat cross-legged on a low stool in the sun, and Tomas sat down on another near the middle, in the shade.

'I know about you, Tomas,' said the wise. His voice was somehow comforting, and Tomas' trust grew just hearing it. 'Tell me in your own words what happened.'

Tomas' heart was suddenly pounding. Unsure of where to begin, he started, 'I was a student of Master Aravon. When he was called to interrogate the prisoner, it fell to his students to take food to it every night.' The wise looked steadily at him. This much he knew already.

Tomas blundered on. 'One night when I was taking food to the prisoner, I... I was exposed to its mind. I had to control it, because it made an attempt to injure me, and... I was briefly touched by the presence in its mind.'

The elado spoke. 'You are not of the Elder. And yet, you were not instantly consumed by the shade. I am mystified: your kind is notoriously easy for Death to feed upon.'

'As you rightly discerned, I am not entirely of the Younger, either,' Tomas said.

'Are you aranelado?'

'As near as makes no difference.'

The wise made no comment, but Tomas somehow felt distaste from him. And then, he doubted himself. Did the distaste come from the wise, or himself?

Then the wise interrupted Tomas' disquiet. 'Ah, I understand, now. Death was unable to sense as much of you as it needed to.'

'Sense?'

'In order to afflict speaking beings, a parasite must perceive through one it inhabits. In this case, that one was the great kchaban. If you were merely human, it would have been enough for the spirit merely to see you, or even to know your name. However, because you are not, it needed to perceive you more. Did it try to touch you, or to smell you?'

Tomas remembered the kchaban's jerky attempt to grab hold of him; how, when the chains had brought it up short, it had sniffed the air, trying to smell Tomas past the wood smoke and goblin-stink. 'Yes,' he said, 'it tried to do both; but it was chained.'

'Then you may count yourself blessed beyond all good fortune,' said the wise. 'Master Aravon could not remain out of reach. None was there to see, but I guess that the kchaban attacked and bit him, or tasted him somehow. The parasite must perceive an elado with many senses, if it is to infect.'

Tomas did indeed count himself lucky. 'But why did it want to do that?' he asked. The air was not yet warm, and he began to shiver.

'In order to gain a foothold among the Wise of Greystone. If Master Aravon had been able to hide his affliction, as many would, his Ability would have diminished. Eventually, he may have been persuaded to make a bargain with Death, in order to regain his power and in the hope that the Shade would stop torturing his soul. If he had done that, the enemy would have known every move we made. Worse, it might have spread unknown amongst us, until we found ourselves fighting amongst ourselves, or surrendering to the Fouls.'

'But he didn't hide his affliction.'

'He may have tried to - but with the parasite on his mind, he was cut off from the contentment of the Light, and sought satisfaction elsewhere. When the girl he had begun to desire would not oblige him, he attacked her, and his affliction was revealed.'

'So we were lucky, again.'

'No,' the wise insisted. 'We were blessed. In these matters, there is seldom any luck.'

Tomas sat in silence for some time. 'I did not come, when I heard the magi had gone to the Hallows. I was afraid I might be accused of waking the parasite, and I would be, um...' he broke off into an uncomfortable silence.

'Death never sleeps in one who hosts it,' the Wise said. 'You could not have awoken it. That should be obvious. I think you see now, where your fear of condemnation came from?'

Tomas thought, and said, 'Yes. It must have been afflicting me in some way, already.'

The wise shook his head. 'It had no need to. Common fear is easy enough to arouse; and Death is a master at doing so.'

Tomas was greatly relieved. At least the wise was sympathetic.

The wise said, 'You have come here, and you have done well in that; now, there is the matter of your rehabilitation: you have touched evil, as you said. You did it of your own free will, though unknowingly. Therefore, I must inform your master, and you must take service, preferably physical, for at least a month. Do you consent?'

'I do,' Tomas said. A month seemed like a short time, compared to what he might have expected.

'Where would you be in service?'

Tomas answered instantly, 'The infirmary.'

The wise paused. 'Do you know anyone there?'

'Yes. I have worked there before.'

'Then you must not go there. You should be apart from everyone, and make a clean break. Look to the Mourner: to expiate evil, there must be a death of some kind. I think you should take service here, with me. You would be insulated from daily news and disturbance.'

Tomas knew better than to argue. 'Very well,' he said.

'The conditions are the same as for anyone undergoing purgation: you must take orders from me or any other wise serving here, you must stay within hearing of the Sanctuary, and you must attend every event in the building or around it. It is quite like being an apprentice again.' The wise smiled sympathetically.

Tomas said, 'I understand.'

'Good,' said the wise. 'You may retire to rest your injury, I shall send someone to show you where. Who is your master?'

'Since Master Aravon was struck down, Master Bethnero.'

'I see,' said the wise. 'I shall speak to you all later.'

The acolyte was a very thin, young elada who showed him to a very bare room in a low building hidden behind a screen of slender trees at one end of the gardens. She bowed him in and glided away without a word. Tomas relaxed on the bare pallet, grateful for an opportunity to rest his coccyx. If it wasn't broken, it certainly felt like it. Why was it always his hindquarters that caught it?

Though it was only late morning, he felt tired. The long restlessness of his guilty secret, the pain and the questioning of the wise had made it a long day already. Tomas lay down with a wince and a sigh; but immediately his mind began to stew. What was he doing here? He didn't belong with these people. Mindless, frothing obscenities bubbled up from him, and he wondered if he'd have been better off dying that night on the east march of Greystone. After only a few minutes on the pallet, he got up again. He was too restless, wanting to go but needing to stay. He hobbled out, almost glad of the pain that stopped him thinking too hard. He opened the door and went out. With nowhere else to go, he wandered back to the Sanctuary. As he opened the door, he saw the wise standing next to the sacred lamp.

'Ah – there you are,' he said enigmatically.

Tomas stopped, again both wanting to go in and wanting to run away.

'I was about to send for you. Come in, Tomas. I have something for you.'

As Tomas watched, the wise cupped his hands around the flame of the sacred lamp. Glancing up, he said to Tomas, 'Kneel down there, in front of the lamp.'

Still in his mental stew, Tomas was inclined to leave; but the flame on the wise's hands drew him. There was something so clean and pure and joyful about that flame. He slowly lowered himself onto the stool in front. It was very low, with just enough space under the seat for his legs, which folded beneath the seat. Sitting on it placed no strain on any of his sore bones, and he marvelled at the comfort.

He lowered his stick as the wise approached. Tomas was amazed to see the wise held fire – some of the fire from the sacred lamp. He held incandescent purity and sweetness between his hands. The light transformed him into a thing of joyful beauty.

'Behold,' the wise said in a quiet voice that shook the air, 'the Secret Fire.' He came closer, still holding the flame in front of him, burning without fuel.

Tomas gazed in dumb awe at the flame. He shook his head in denial, even as his heart leaped in him at the sight of the flame. It seemed to be burning nothing. It was alive. The wise was standing right in front of him now...

Without warning, the flame flared in Tomas' face. The fire seared his mouth, and his lungs were burned with a cold flame. That part of him that had feared the wise, the part that had fumed with obscenities while he tried to rest, screamed and withered. A shock passed through him, and the world pitched around him as he hit the floor. A wave of pure joy enveloped him, and he passed out.

It was late afternoon. That fact seemed odd for some reason. He was lying on a hard stone floor, his head pillowed by his own tulme. He looked around, blearily, and saw he was in the Sanctuary – again. Or was it still? He felt like he'd just had the best sleep in his life, but oh, he was stiff! He groaned.

There were voices nearby. He heard Master Ben and Master Helder, talking with the wise. The fear of being expelled from instruction fought past his stiff awakening. Fearing to say anything, he rolled over and righted himself. The conversation stopped and the magi all regarded him. They were smiling.

'Hello, Tomas,' said Master Ben. 'I'm told you were purged by the Secret Fire.'

'Is that what it was?' Tomas' voice sounded peaceful and strong to his own ears.

'You have been utterly cleansed of any darkness that was plaguing you. The wise took a gamble, that you would not be damaged as a man would be: proving beyond doubt your mixed heritage.'

'I am glad of it,' said Tomas, 'and grateful. I have needed nursing too much, mostly through my own fault. But what is the Secret Fire? It was so beautiful!'

'The Secret Fire is a spark of the One Light that Kindled the Stars,' said the wise. 'Only Wise men and eladi may call it forth, and only those who have had the hand-laying from one who was duly blessed in his turn.'

'What did it do?' asked Tomas.

'Darkness cannot endure the Secret Fire. The Fire will not abide it; if it encounters a Shadow in anything, that Shadow will be utterly annihilated.'

'Was that not a risk? What if it had annihilated me?'

The wise smiled. 'You are but a young thing, and have not become shadow yourself. You were quite safe.'

Master Ben helped him up. 'The wise have told us everything. You have again been trapped and injured, like when you were in the Militia, but less damage was done this time round.' He looked at the wise. 'Shall we leave him to you for rehabilitation?'

'But of course. You may visit whenever you wish, but remember he will have to take part in everything that happens here, and must not be interrupted.'

'It is good – so be it,' said Ben.

For three days, Tomas was part of the scenery around the Sanctuary. He spoke but seldom, but on the third day he began to feel the quiet satisfaction of work well done. He began to think that he might even enjoy his rehabilitation.

It was not to be.

On the night following the third day, Tomas was woken in the middle of the night by a feeling of deep dread. He had felt this way before – only then he had been in the company of Master Magi. Now, in his tiny room in the depth of the quiet night, the dread was magnified. The edge of horror reminded him of the warped life conjured by shamans.

He rose and lit his small lamp, his fingers slipping on the tinderbox. He dressed, in case he had to leave in a hurry. He peeped out of his door – the night was still and dark, with no moon. His heart skipped a beat as he saw a figure walking along the path, shadowed behind by the hedge that separated the living-quarters from the Sanctuary garden. 'Tomas?' he heard the voice of the wise.

'It's me,' Tomas answered.

'Come to the Sanctuary,' said the wise, his voice shaking slightly. 'It's safer there, and lighter. Quickly, now.'

Tomas came out. They moved as fast as Tomas' injury allowed. At the edge of the gardens they saw the little elada who had showed Tomas to his cell before, flitting through the dark toward the Sanctuary. Suddenly, she screamed and jumped. Tomas looked beyond her, and saw a rat scuttling along in his direction. There was something strange about it.

The wise said to her, 'What is it, child?'

'It looks like a rat,' Tomas chipped in, 'but –' he stopped as he realised it wasn't. Even without his Animal Sympathy, he perceived something very wrong. 'It's a warped rat. With the head of a shrike.' He lunged at the thing, brandishing his walking-stick, and it fled in another direction, towards the trees at the edge of the garden. Tomas followed it with his eyes, and saw – a boulder, or a pile of them, where there hadn't been anything before. 'There's something out there,' he whispered, pointing.

The wise looked. His eyes grew wide in terror. '*Get inside!*' he bellowed.

Frantic footfalls sounded from two different directions, as eladi bolted for the single entrance to the Sanctuary. It was too late. One of them, an apprentice known to Tomas, saw the crush around the door and hopped to a halt, then tore off across the lawn, pounding cracking through the trees as he fled.

Unable to get through the door, Tomas spun around, his left hip protesting, and looked upon a monster.

Half again his own height, covered in a bizarre mix of scales and hair, it had huge horns like those of a sheep curling out of its head and a protruding lower jaw with two huge fangs sticking out over its upper lip. Its eyes were small, close-set and glowed red in the dark. It moved on its knuckles, its arms longer than its legs. It sniffed in Tomas' direction, and swung its huge head from side to side. Tomas thought it was some new and horrible animal, but then it looked at him with its horrible glowing eyes and spoke. The words sounded like the torture of living things, the voice croaked like hinges of stone. With horrifying speed for something so huge, it reached out for him. Squirming to avoid the thing's grasp, Tomas was yanked from behind. His pelvic bones screamed pain in protest as he fell through the doorway, at the feet of the wise that had pulled him in by his tulme. The troll lunged for the door, but was too large to fit through. One tree-trunk-sized arm reached in, grabbing Tomas by the ankle. The wise shouted as the Sanctuary swirled around Tomas' head. The troll had him! Horror swamped his mind, and he screamed like a baby. Then he realised he wasn't gutted and eaten just yet: he was outside, and the troll was carrying him over its shoulder like a side of meat. He was moving through the gardens, and there was a jabber of alien voices, in the same tortuous language. On either side, visible if he turned his head, were lightly armoured, man-like figures. They numbered ten or less, straight-legged with chalky-white skin, and hideous kchaban faces. Thus did Tomas make his first acquaintance with arkchabani. It was a small raiding party, all looking at Tomas with eager interest. He heard questions, exultant shouting, but the troll said nothing.

He could see an inquisitive arkchaban close by, behind the troll. It leered at him from under its helmet. In barely-intelligible Southlandish, it said, 'You good meat, huh?' Suddenly, a grey shape appeared in the dark. Without a sound, a knife slashed the arkchaban's neck, and its body crumpled. Sudden hope surged in Tomas. That was Ranger work!

The fouls didn't seem to have noticed the death of one of their number. They seemed to be arguing about the direction to take. Tomas' hope rose still further. Suddenly, there was that familiar air-tearing sound of eladon arrows, and two of the arkchabani fell. Past his fear and pain, Tomas marvelled at the accuracy of eladon archers, shooting in the moonless dark. The troll whipped around, grunting in astonishment. Tomas wobbled and nearly fell – it was a long way to fall head-first – but the troll clamped a stony fist about his knees.

There came a bright voice from the dark: 'Arrows to melt on touch! Aim for the spine!' And suddenly the troll was hit by an arrow flashing orange as it hit with a sullen 'pop'.

The troll gave a deafening roar, and jumped around, seeking its attacker. The arrow had not hit the spine. As it moved, it was struck by several other orange-flashing arrows at once. Suddenly, its back legs went limp, and its hindquarters slumped to the ground. At least one arrow had found its mark. Then the dark gardens of the Sanctuary were filled with eladi: eladi loosing arrows with incredible speed and accuracy; eladi dancing death with their *encti* flashing. They suffered no night-blindness. The remaining arkchabani were beset by their most hated enemies. With a bestial roar, they hurled their hatred of the Fair Folk into the cold night air. No quarter was given, or expected. With the troll disabled, the arkchabani didn't last long.

One of the rangers hurled a javelin at the troll. Aimed at the thing's abdomen, it too flashed red as it hit. The troll bellowed in agony, viscera drooping from the hole in its side. Tomas half-fell, half-slid down the thing's back, flopping onto the ground and rolling away as best he could. The attack became a blood-sport. The eladi paralysed the troll, breaking its spine in several places. It still had the use one of its arms however.

'Tomas!' called the wise, running from the Sanctuary. 'That thing came looking for you!'

Breathless in his pain and relief, Tomas managed to say, 'No, father, just bad luck!'

The troll still had the use of one arm, so the leader of the rangers detailed a guard on it until sunrise, when the sunlight would turn it back into the stone from whence it came. For the rest of that awful night, the hideous, pitiful moans of that troll sounded throughout the forests of Greystone.

Tomas was battered but otherwise unhurt. Towards the end of the night, as the dawn wind began to whisper in the trees, Master Ben and Master Helder came to see him in his cell. He started to get up. 'No, Tomas,' said Master Ben, 'stay there. The wise had some thoughts on tonight's events, and we need to have a talk. Do you think the troll may have been after you?'

Tomas thought for a few heartbeats. The thing had reached into the Sanctuary for him; but he had been the last one in. 'No,' he said, 'I was simply the last one inside.'

The Masters looked at him, their faces outlined in sharp black shadows in the light of a small oil-lamp. 'Are you sure?' said Helder.

'Well – yes,' said Tomas. What were they worried about?

'There is a chance, Tomas,' Master Helder continued, 'that the shade you encountered in Master Aravon's house has... communicated in some way with a shaman. Now, I want you to think about this...' the elado paused, 'Can you think of any reason why the Shades would be looking for you?'

There was a silence that grew uneasy. Tomas said, slowly trying to remember the event he had tried so hard to forget. 'When I...' he began, 'when I took food to the kchaban that night, it spoke to me. The exchange was – not cordial, and deteriorated. In the end, the kchaban took up a container, intending to injure me, and to stop it I entered its mind, as I would a dangerous animal.'

The eyes of the magi seemed to be boring into him. He felt himself colouring. He hadn't told anyone about this, yet. 'There was a presence in the kchaban's mind, which tried to get hold of me, asked who I was. I managed to stop myself from saying my entire name,' Ben shook his head with an exasperated laugh, 'then it tried to grab me, and sniffed, but it could not touch me, physically or otherwise. Then I got free. I started to pack up, I was desperate to leave. Just as I left the kchaban spoke in its dark voice again, saying that I was the one they were looking for, and they awaited my sacrifice at the Mount of Dogs.'

'Dark voice? You mean its voice changed?'

'Yes, and it had a strange light in its eyes.'

The magi looked at each other, then back at Tomas. The silence grew again. 'Is that all?'

'It is.'

Master Helder shook his head. 'This is very dark to me. I shall have to look into it, but I have no leisure for the work.'

'I shall do it, Master,' said Master Ben. 'I have an apprentice, who could also assist.'

'Thank you, young brother,' said Helder. 'Proceed, by all means.'

Tomas remained in the sanctuary, working the gardens when there were no meditations taking place. The light-green dusting of the stinkwoods burgeoned into new leaf, and the enforced humility of a lowly position eroded the self-centredness that affected all speaking beings. Slowly, he regained peace. If he had been left to it, he may have recovered right there; but it was not to be. There came an evening, after the Song of the Sunset had been sung, when clouds had suddenly gathered, the first in many months. Thunder, unexpected and unaccustomed after winter, sang in the west, but the leering rot in the air had nothing to do with it. Tomas felt it as soon as he left the Sanctuary, and he groaned. Not again! He cast around the gloom for the cloud of darkness, but the swift dusk was upon him, and for all he knew, the darkness had come from him.

Suddenly there was a rattle of hooves on the road beyond the gardens. Between the two tall obelisks which marked the entrance rode a party of eladi on quahas, some magi with their staves, others soldiers in full armour. The leader of the party rode with his hood up, as if expecting rain, and he called out, 'Tomas!'

Tomas recognised Master Ben's voice. 'I see you,' he said in his own language.

'Where is the wise?' Master Ben answered in Celadi.

'Inside, father, the Song of the Sunset is just finished.'

'You must come with us. Events have come to a head, and you are a part of them, like it or not.'

'What?' Tomas stood, uncomprehending. Two of the magi dismounted, tied their quahas to a convenient karee tree, and entered the sanctuary. Another elado dismounted and led his quaha to Tomas. It was the wise Tomas had first met when Mistress Miruvire had revealed his infection previously. He handed the reins to him. 'Here, Tomas,' he said, 'You must take this quaha and go with your master. The enemy is indeed looking for you, or any araneladi they can find, and your presence is a danger to us all.'

Tomas stood, dumbfounded. He realised he was gaping foolishly, snapped out of it and mounted, swinging his bad leg over the saddle painfully. The armed guard left some of their members and some of the magi at the Sanctuary, as Tomas, Ben and the others returned on the road to the City.

'Master,' Tomas said to Ben, 'I believe there will be an attack by warped life on the Sanctuary, again. I felt the decay on the air.'

'We all felt it.' The Master's face was utterly invisible under his hood. 'We left the magi and knights to deal with it; its appearance simply confirmed what we have found.'

'What was that, Master?'

'They are using magic, Tomas. Caring nothing for the damage to themselves, they have some means of scanning the land from above, seeking...'

'Seeking what?'

'An aranelado.'

'Why?' An awful thought occurred to Tomas. 'What about Liriel?'

'I have warned her, too. She is gone into hiding, but it was you who were revealed, or fell into revealing, yourself. The Darkness knows you, and seeks you personally. Why, I have simply been unable to discover.'

'Thunder and lightning,' Tomas muttered to himself. As if in answer, a clap of thunder sounded, alarmingly close. The quahas started, laughing, but their riders quieted them. It was near dark under the trees, and they stopped to light covered lanterns.

'Where are we going, riding in the dark like this?' Tomas asked. They stood a good chance of ruining several animals if they weren't careful.

'Away from the Sanctuary, for now. After that, we leave the land of Greystone.'

Tomas' heart dropped down to his sandals.

'I know, son,' Master Ben said, 'But if the Darkness has marked you out for its own purposes, you are a magnet for evil; and they may have another troll, next time, and who is to say there will be a chance that someone will escape to call the rangers, as there was last time?'

Tomas nodded in the lamplight, as the quahas stepped carefully along the slated pathways of Greystone. The trees sighed in the night, and a chill, fragrant breeze announced the evening rain. A whisper of raindrops swept through the trees. In seconds, the heavy, rich smell of wet soil was all around them. 'Ah,' said Master Ben, 'I always love the first proper rain of the season.'

'Master, what am I to do? How do I leave, and where?'

'No, no, lad,' said Master Ben. 'There have been developments, and you are to come with us.'

Tomas sighed with relief. Master Ben continued, 'It happens that something has gone wrong with the eladi space-folding ability. What do you know about it?'

'Just that space-folding can only be done if the traveller has a line of clear sight to his objective – which is why there are ancient lines between notable features all over the landscape, where the bush has been cleared, or where there are artefacts lined up to follow.'

'That's right. The lines of sight in the lands between the Cedar Mountains and the coast have been cast into shadow somehow, and none of the eladi with the Ability will use them anymore, in case they are cursed, or infected as you were. The infection has to be purged by a wise. It's in Menelvagon's report. I have seen it myself.'

'How did they do that?'

Master Helder has an idea – and he says it must have cost them a lot of sacrificial blood to do it.'

Tomas had a thought. 'Does that mean that Liriel's father and his party have been trapped in the Southlands?'

'That's right. Providently, Kobos the Merchant has recently arrived, so we will join his caravan, along with a few wise-eladi, a bodyguard, and Master Helder.'

Tomas was suddenly very glad to be going. 'Master Helder? Our greatest magus is going just to help to disinfect the travel nodes?'

'Ah – no,' Master Ben replied. 'The nodes are only one of our missions.' The old man was silent for a few heartbeats.

'Come on, Master,' said Tomas in his own language, 'tell me what else.'

'I have to think where to begin,' said Master Ben, also in Southlandish. 'It's a lot to say, and no time to say it. Anyway, um...' and he changed back to Celadi, 'We are to relieve the original embassy. The King is not interested in helping his own people on the Highlands. In fact, he seems to have betrayed us. So, Master Helder, as a pure-blooded Orelado, is going to lead us on a mission to seek the aid of the king in Greenland.'

'What?' Tomas was amazed. He thought back to the large map on the wall of Limlot's study. South of the Southlands, across a stretch of ocean notorious for storms, swift currents and mountainous waves, lay a large island, uncharted by men, called Greenland. Men were forbidden there, except for a strip of territory on the north coast, where the Southlands had a colony. In the legendary past, when the Oreladi of the Sunlands had been driven from their homes by the kchabani, they had settled there, on an island that was cold, wet and densely forested. Out of the flow of history in the Southlands, their kingdom had grown strong, their people numerous, and they regarded men and the seafaring Celadi as interlopers. Seeking their help was a desperate venture, and who knew what they would demand in return for their help? Greystone, the Highlands, even the Southlands, they regarded as their own. This journey would be historic.

'You sound speechless.' Ben observed with a laugh.

Tomas admitted, 'I am!'

'I have some family down there, a practicing magus called Michellos. He can help us arrange passage to Greenland from Westerhaven.'

Tomas and Ben left their mounts at the citadel and started back to the Man-camp. The air was chill with spring rain, the stones slippery, when a cloaked and hooded figure appeared, moving quickly towards them. Tomas recognised it somehow. 'Liriel! I thought you were in hiding!'

'Mistress!' said Master Ben, 'This is most unwise.'

'I would speak with Tomas, Master,' said Liriel. Master Ben nodded, looked at Tomas with a warning on his face, then continued down the road. 'See you back at the Camp, Tomas,' he said quietly in their own language.

'Liriel, why are you here?' Tomas began.

'Tomas, hear me.' Liriel's face was shadowed, but her eyes gleamed wetly in the dark. 'I cannot let you leave, not without... without telling you some things.' She stood in the dark, her head down. 'You never came to an open evening at the Fire-Hall with me!' she accused.

Tomas was mystified. 'What?'

'I wanted you to know how the tale ended, Tomas! You remember I told you about it, but I did not tell you how it ended because...' she stopped, gesturing with her hands in frustration. 'Please, I... I want you to come back: even if I never again see my father,' her voice broke as she said it. 'But if you come not back whole, and in possession of all your natural Abilities, or with even a whiff of the Shadow about you... I will not know you.'

Tomas mastered his exasperation. This was rather melodramatic. 'Liriel, I will do what is necessary. I have begun, I am recovering. If it continues, I will be whole and free. If not, I will not even wish to return.' He had to be honest. 'Do what you must. And I shall do the same.' Struck by a sudden certainty, he added, 'If I return, you will know me, as if for the first time. If not, it would have been better had we never met.'

'You have grown, Tomas.'

'I am human. We always grow.' He turned to go.

'You are not human,' she shook her head, 'but I pray you will grow, and grow better.' She grabbed his arm, and he felt her touch on his mind as well. Even as before she had controlled him to make him let her go, now she controlled him to face her. Thus turned, she kissed him, hard and deep; then she turned and was gone.

Tomas stood, almost laughing. Who could ever understand females? Then he shook his head, and started back down the path after his master.

CHAPTER VIII

Kobos the Merchant had not made much money this time. The war, the loss of custom and stock, the extra swords he'd had to hire, the extra distance he'd had to travel to avoid hostile territory, these all had eaten into his profits; but his painted wagons still made the long journey from the Thornlands, through Greystone to the Highlands, down through the desert all the way to Westerhaven. Because there was always protection in numbers, he was happy to have extra wagons in his caravan, as long as everyone came supplied, no-one stole anything, and the men helped with guarding and unloading the stock when necessary. The people joining the caravan were a mixed bunch: there were human families hoping to join relatives in the South, a handful of magi and wise, and some eladi mercenaries. Kobos had never hired eladi mercenaries before, but seemed glad enough to have them that he didn't question their origins too deeply.

In the meantime Master Ben, with his apprentice and an initiate joined the caravan just as the final preparations were being made. The three of them were to travel in a wagon with three of the mercenaries. Tomas looked in and saw precious little room to stretch out in. 'Looks a little cramped,' he observed to Ioseth in their home language.

Master Ben happened to be behind them, and overheard. 'That's because we're also helping to carry supplies for more than a month. This is only a part of them,' he added. 'We'd better hope there's no trouble on the way, or that the Great River isn't in flood and we have to wait for the water to subside. Then we'll be wishing there was more in this wagon!'

'Ah,' Tomas said. 'Who's driving?'

'We'll take it in turns. You're going to be taking your fair share of it.'

'I can't drive a wagon!'

'Have you never driven a cart?'

'Well, yes, but –'

'It's the same thing, just bigger. And they're drawn by oxen, quaha aren't strong enough.'

'I hadn't thought of that,' said Ioseth. 'This is going to be slow.'

'Well, a fast walk anyway. We could all do with the exercise!' Master Ben's enthusiasm was infectious.

Finally, all was ready, and the caravan set out from the city gates of Greystone early in the chill of a spring morning. By mid-day, they had reached the twin obelisks beyond the Sanctuary, and Tomas again felt the recognition of the eldastones within. It was a beautiful, bright spring day, the grass springing green with recent rain. It was already hot. Tomas was looking forward to seeing the Highlands again.

The end of the day saw puffy purple clouds gathering in the southwest, and they camped on the hither, northern side of the Green River, within a short walk of the slender eladan bridge Tomas had crossed as a recently freed slave, a short eternity ago. He had walked for short spells, and how his hip was aching. He did the cooking, taking first turn, but was glad of Ioseth – apprentices should do the heavy work, after all!

The following morning, the caravan was awake at first light, and ready to go before the shadows grew short. It was hard to believe there was a war on. The cool morning breeze whispered through the grass, and long-tailed widowbirds danced over it. Sometime during the day, Master Ben got Tomas alone, and asked him, carelessly, 'How did you come to be so close with that Healer elada?'

'We talked a lot; and while you were away at Hunter's Wells, I assisted in her healing when she was attacked by a giant baboon.'

'Ah, so it was you,' Master Ben said. 'I wondered. Anyway, Do you have any idea how old she is?'

'It's impolite to ask a lady's age,' Tomas shot back impudently. 'But I know she can't be younger than a hundred or two.'

'Quite so. Do you know what that makes you, in her eyes?'

'I have thought about it.'

'You're less than a child. You may only be a pet, or an idle diversion. At worst, you could be part of a game she's playing.'

Tomas simply shook his head. 'It's not a game. In fact, it's more serious than I thought. Or it was.'

'I know it looks good for you, but...' Ben trailed off, waving his hand. 'All I'm saying is, don't get your hopes up too much.'

'I know you have my interests at heart, master,' Tomas replied.

'I've seen so many men go after eladon-maids like that, and nearly all of them ended up emotional wrecks,' Ben explained. 'You're still young, you just can't understand how great the distance is between the two of you. There is a reason why there are so few araneladi, you know: I just don't want you to find out the hard way.'

Tomas nodded. 'Of course, Master.'

'Remember, you are an Initiate. You have to give up everything – *everything* – for as long as it takes. You must not want any thing, or any one, too much, because desire can become a snare for you, and pull you down when you need to fly.' He was talking quietly now. 'If it helps at all, remember the old saw: "If you love something, set it free..." You are called to be wise, and some things may be denied you by That which calls.'

Master Ben said no more about Liriel after that. He had said all he wanted to.

The third day out of Greystone, they saw a filthy cloud on the eastern horizon as their road climbed towards the Highlands. Some stopped to look. Tomas wished the defenders of the town well, but his road lay ahead.

That afternoon, they came to the South Gildrock range, and looking back could see the Green River far to the north, and the North Gildrocks beyond that. Ahead of them, on the left shoulder of the pass, was an ancient ruin, the stump of a high tower. Ioseth asked about it.

One of the magi, a coffee-skinned orelado walking by the wagon, said, 'We built them, my people, when the first kchabani appeared in the lands of the South.'

Tomas and Ioseth looked at each other, thinking the same thing: This elado is over five thousand years old! 'If only those stones could talk,' Ioseth said.

'They speak,' said the magus. He gave an enigmatic smile. 'They speak, but the Latecomers know not how to listen.'

'Except that you were kind enough to teach some of us,' said another voice, a maga called Noromiel. 'Weren't you, Tintallon?'

Tintallon gave a sigh. 'Pure-blooded oreladi are a scattered, dwindling people. There are few now who remember the South in the Beautiful Ages, "When all the World was green".'

'Our leader is one,' offered Noromiel. 'Master Helder remembers.' But the magus would say no more.

That afternoon saw them moving in silence up a slope. As they ascended, the bush thickened about them again, but the trees were short. The road began to ascend quite steeply between slopes decked with acacias and cabbage-trees. Tomas recognised the cliff under the old tower, though he had last seen it in darkness. He said to Ben, 'Do you know, master, the last time I saw that tower, I was in a slave caravan? I just knew my enslavement was going to end quite soon. At the time, I wondered if it meant I was going to die the next day.'

'You were a slave?' the magus Tintallon asked.

'I was captured by slavers when the kchabani took the town where I lived.'

'What town was that?' Menelvagon asked.

'It was Hunter's Wells, I think we're headed for there?' he looked at Master Ben, who nodded.

Tintallon regarded Tomas thoughtfully. 'I see you have passed through much in this war. Are you hoping to find some news of your family?'

'Not family, master. They live south and east of there.' He sighed. 'Or they did, before the war.'

Around sunset, passing a steep bend in the road where water ran strong and loud far below them, they came out at the top of the pass. The trees were gone. The air was cool. For days' journey ahead, there was nothing but rolling grassland dotted with the occasional acacia tree, glowing orange in the setting sun.

A call rang out down the line. 'Circle the wagons!' And the wagons were drawn up in a wide circle, pooling firelight and relative safety under the twilight that now leaped into the sky.

CHAPTER IX

And so it happened that, in the tenth month of the year, the wagon-train made its way over the wide-open Highlands, bound for the lands of men in the South. From Greystone and the Thornlands, the caravan carried ivory, pig-iron, pharmaceuticals, gourds and animal pelts. Normally, on returning from the Cedar Mountains and the Middlesea, they hoped to have other goods, but only time would tell if the return journey was even possible. Trading was Kobos' entire life, and he could not imagine doing anything else.

For several days, the wagons followed the ancient stone-paved roads towards the Highlands. The day came when Tomas looked out on familiar, open grassland studded with dark-leaved thorny acacias and silvery sugar-bushes. Tomas felt a pang of homesickness at the familiar terrain. Sweetwaters was still a long way away, and he wished they would go just a little further east, to meet the road to Alatasdam, and maybe he could just go and look, to see... to tell them he was all right; but his path was elsewhere. Maybe one day, when the war was over... He sighed, remembering home.

Late one morning they came within sight of the high ridges that led up to Hunters' Wells, the Cliff-and-Dale country. The veld around them was all golden grass up to the animals' withers. In places they came across wide lands left fallow, and pasturelands where the grass grew tall, ungrazed. Here and there in the distance, they saw ruined, blackened buildings where men had lived - the remains of Free Farmsteads. Tomas no longer expected any kind of welcome in his destination.

That night they camped at the foot of the Goldstone Neck, which was one of the places where a paved road led over the ridge to the Highlands proper beyond. On the next morning they laboured up it, the oxen urged on by patient animal magi, ever conscious of the frowning, orange quartzite cliffs on their right. As they moved up, they felt that they were being watched, but with none of the chilling disgust caused by the proximity of kchabani. All felt that the watchers must be human, but not even the eladi could see anything in the thick, dark bushes growing on the cliffs. In the mid-afternoon, they came out at the top of the pass, only to be confronted by more hills, but gentler and less rocky. There were few trees, and the red soil was stretched thinly over golden rocks. They met no-one, nor did they see any trace of man or kchaban. The road followed a rocky outcrop obliquely up a slope. Tomas' senses, heightened by his meditations in the Sanctuary, perceived the oxen complaining about all the climbing, but this was the last ridge. Tomas recognised the skyline behind him, to the east.

At last, turning left up the slope, they crested the rise. The view behind them, to the north, was spectacular. Ahead of them was a patch of protea bushes. Under the animals' hooves, the soil was brown and sandy, where grew strange, grey-leafed shrubs that grew nowhere else. There were also tiny aloes, their spineless leaves hugging the ground. Strange, onion-like corms sprouted semi-circular fans of leaves in the short grass. Club mosses coated the rock outcrops. A cool breeze blew, rustling the leaves and the grass in the bright, thin air. It was delightful.

The caravan had stopped. Tomas pushed himself up on the driver's seat. The lead wagon had stopped, and across the road was a party of mounted men. 'That must be the guard from Hunters' Wells,' he said to Ioseth. After a few minutes, the caravan moved forward again. The road was much the worse for wear. They came to the town square of Hunters' Wells, stopping in front of the Courthouse. Among those pillars, Tomas had faced death and survived. The square behind him still bore the dark stain of the fire the kchabani had made years before, but there were stalls again – rickety constructions selling poor, scanty goods, but business nonetheless.

The caravan stayed in Hunters' Wells only a few days. Tomas met a pedlar on the point of leaving for Sweetwaters and hastily scribbled a letter to his mother, telling her about his situation. He also took Master Ben and Ioseth to see the Haildom, where he had worked. The place had been partly damaged by fire, the community of the place was gone; a lone acolyte lived there now. Tomas' memories of the place were not sweet, but he went to look in at the Scriptorium, looked around the old office. The records room had almost escaped unharmed, still full of old records no-one needed any more. There was a hole in one mullioned window, and a messy bulbul's nest graced the nearest bookshelf. The library was burned at one end, but the thatch over that end was new, which was a good sign. The Archmagister's office had been completely gutted, the *gochfeya* image hopefully burned.

On a morning of lowering cloud, the caravan moved on. The road they followed ran steadily south for another week, and as they climbed into the Littelot Hills, the weather turned wet. The hills were green and sodden, studded in places with spiky aloes. Permanent rivers were marked by the trees that grew on their banks. The wagons lumbered on, clattering up the north-facing slopes in the pouring rain. Tomas rode in a wagon with others who were old or infirm.

Around the tenth day out from Greystone they stopped in a valley in the Littelot Hills in the late afternoon. Kobos sent men out to cut fodder for the journey through the Drylands. Grass grew tall and green all around. As the grey sky darkened to black, heavy cloud gathered again, and it rained steadily all night. In the first cold, grey light of the new day, a troop of baboons appeared above their campsite, their ominous barking echoing in the hills. Fortunately, they were natural, normal-sized ones, but Tomas would never be able to ignore that sound again.

That morning, Tomas went to fetch a bucket of water. He saw a group of baboons lurking around in some shrubs just above the campsite. The big males were like massive dogs, nearly waist-high with their shaggy grey winter coats shedding. They glowered down at the campsite, kept at bay by fear of men and the smell of smoke. Tomas stopped and picked up a fist-sized rock, throwing it up the slope. 'Go on! Push off!' he growled at them. They loped off, but didn't go far.

Master Helder saw his reaction to the baboons. 'Why are you so violent towards them?' he asked.

Tomas disliked the question, when he was tired and cold and his hip was aching. He scratched his shaggy face, unshaven since leaving rehabilitation, and replied, 'I don't know. I don't think I can see them the same way again, after the Cobra Fort.'

Helder simply nodded. It was enough for him that students thought before acting. Perhaps it was just a bit unfair that real baboons should have to pay for kchaban evil on their own species, thought Tomas.

'Do you not think it would be easier,' asked Master Helder, 'not to say more effective, to control them with Sympathy?

'I have to admit, I didn't even think of it.' He sighed, emptying his bucket into a cauldron.

Master Helder said, 'Why don't you try your Ability? You have nothing to lose,' and left.

Tomas watched the master walk away, towards a fire. He looked up at the baboons, who returned his gaze warily. Sighing, Tomas cleared his mind. It was not as easy as it used to be, but it came as a relief. He reached out to the baboons. They were cold and hungry. They had had food, the leavings of camp, from caravans before, and were hoping for more. Even dumb animals could hope, Tomas thought.

Hoping to chase them away, he tried to think danger and threat into the contact between him and the shaggy, black males. While he shared their thoughts, he could introduce emotions to them; but now, he could not concentrate. He was distracted by many things: cold hands, wet sandals; a drip on his nose; the persistent ache in his hip; especially, most horrible in the quiet of his mind, the memory of that troll, and its grip of stone. The Sympathy dissolved in a mass of helpless rage. Maybe this wizardry wasn't all it was cracked up to be. Sighing again, he picked up his bucket and went for more water.

As the caravan made ready to move out, he heard the baboons

barking and screaming from the shelter of the bushes. Once, Tomas wondered if he hadn't just heard a louder, deeper bark from a baboon that was too big; but when he reached out, he felt nothing.

Later that day, they stopped at the remains of a farming hamlet, where the caravan had always taken on water in easier times. The well there was still good, but the place was deserted, the inhabitants dead or fled. The burnt-out hulks of buildings sheltered nothing but cinders and bones, some of which were human. The bones seemed to have been split and scattered among the charred stones, like the remains of a diabolical feast. They buried the bones in the grounds of the town haildom, and the human acolyte and the eladan wise held a vigil for them that night. The drizzle-laden wind moaned around the walls, singing a dreary counterpoint to their song in the night. Tomas and Ioseth joined in the vigil for some time. It was good psychic exercise, and for the rest of the journey they kept regular meditation times together.

On the eleventh day out of Greystone, when the rain had blown over, they came down from the Littelot Hills and reached the town called Acacia Fountains late in the day. From the map, Tomas knew it was a medium-sized town on the ill-defined western borders of the Duke's realm. There they found a strange thing, Highlanders and Free Raiders living together. Rebuilding was much in evidence, and the people told them that they had beaten off Raiders loyal to Lord Vloch in the past week. While Master Helder and Master Ben dealt with the men of the town, the eladi kept to themselves as much as possible, keeping their ears under their head-dresses and their mouths shut if they had to leave their wagons. Altogether, it seemed that the caravan had been extremely lucky so far. They stocked up as well as possible, and moved on two days later.

After Acacia Fountains, the road was no longer paved. The wagons simply followed a well-worn, red-brown track south through the Great Plains, those endless, rolling expanses of grass waving green and gold in the spring sunshine. The terrain was featureless, but Kobos knew his road. The sky stretched vast and blue above, edged all around by a dusty horizon; but there was no smoke of war, as yet. All were in relatively good spirits, with supplies holding out well and the going easy. Tomas now drove one of the wagons, rotating with Adaan, Kobos' lead driver.

By long stages, the caravan made its way steadily down from the Highlands. As the weeks went by, the grass gave way to sparse, open woodlands, where wary herds of small antelope grazed between the low, thorny acacias. The horses and oxen were spooked several times by inquisitive leopards, which followed the caravan at a distance or shadowed it on a parallel course. Tomas reached out for the cats when he saw them; he could tell that they were seldom hungry enough to attack, but they were curious. Jackals called at night, their crazy laughter echoing in the lonely spaces.

The weather got hot as the Highlands dried out and fell back, with days of bright skies and scattered puffy cloud, which no longer gathered for cooling summer rain. Adaan told Tomas of the life of a driver in a caravan, when the water froze in the spigots in winter, or during droughts when the sun baked the rivers dry. He told of the harassment of raiders, the perils of snow in the passes of the Cedar Mountains, and of the sea. Tomas simply could not imagine water stretching to the horizon.

Eventually, the acacia-strewn grasslands gave way to shrubland, with low, spiny bushes and thin grass. The time for spring flowers was now long past, remembered only by dry, seeding stalks. Three weeks out from Acacia Fountains, at the beginning of the eleventh month of the year, the caravan approached a wide mesa from the north, and skirted it to find a sizeable town in its shadow, called Thornspring. Kobos told Ben that it had always been a poor but generous place, but they had little to trade there but sheep and wool. The walls of the town were of brown stone, the houses of pale brown bricks, the brown-skinned people wore dusty-brown cloaks. Dust seemed to coat everything. They left after two days, having exchanged a few items of cargo for a small flock of sheep.

After Thornspring, the grass soon gave out altogether, and the water had to be rationed. The grass harvested in the Littlelots was brought out for the oxen in the evenings. Rain was a distant spring memory, and the land baked under summer sun. The caravan stopped occasionally at a muddy river where the animals could be watered. Tomas' sympathy strengthened, and he was able to drive his wagon himself, without having to rely on anyone to goad the lead animal. He didn't even need a whip. Adaan put him in charge of the lead team, and the caravan made good, steady progress with Tomas and the Magus Galbaro keeping an eye on the health of the animals.

For two and a half weeks they moved steadily south-west, through endless, flat, dry land, seeing nothing but an occasional group of nomadic shepherds, people akin to the Raiders. Bandits were seen, but the eladi mercenaries were more than able to see them off. When they met with such a group, each party was always eager for news: The shepherds for news of the war, the caravan for news of the South. It seemed that the Drylands had been little affected by the war.

The caravan moved slower now in lands with no roads, but they reached a town called Sandy Rivers in their third week in the Drylands. It was a mean, grimy place, where the children threw goat-pellets at them as they passed through. The people there spoke a strongly-accented dialect that even the men battled to understand. Water was plentiful, but the town didn't trade much.

The two rivers that met in the town only flowed for nine months of the year, but the caravan was in time for water in summer. Midsummer celebrations in Sandy Rivers were muted, though there was no shortage of mutton. Tomas wondered what the celebrations were like in Greystone, thinking of that place more often than the Highlands where he had grown up. Liriel came often to mind, and he prayed as ever for his family, wherever they happened to be.

The caravan stocked up on water and food, and left after the New Year. Showing them the map, Ben explained to Tomas and Ioseth that they were about halfway to the Cedar Mountains, and about a third of the way to the Middlesea coast. That day, he also asked Kobos if some riders could be spared for hunting parties, and the merchant agreed. As the caravan lumbered on, they brought back a steady supply of venison, for springbok and impala were common in the Drylands. Since there was no shortage of people willing to cook, a profitable division of labour developed. Such was the case for another three weeks.

At the end of those three weeks, they came suddenly to a huge, shallow valley, its opposite side lost in blue distance, where the caravan-route bent left down a short, steep slope into the wide floodplain of the Great River. Here the spiny shrubs gave way to long, green grass and tall thorn-trees, and there were birds and small game in abundance. The animals were extremely glad of the green grass, and moved slowly, grazing when they could. Kobos told Tomas that he preferred to reach this place in winter, when the water was lowest. It could flood the whole floodplain in springtime when the snow melted in the Cedar Mountains, and the river itself was too strong to cross in some summers. The caravan followed a track worn in deep, dark brown soil for most of the day. Then, with a dazzling sun dipping low and golden sunlight turning the leaves and grass to green flames, they came to a wide space by the river bank. The river stretched wide and knee-deep over beds of golden gravel, interrupted here and there by larger sandbanks where small bushes grew. Looking upstream, Tomas saw innumerable small islands and narrow channels. The channels there were narrower but deeper, the islands taller and tree-grown. This must have been chosen as the best place to cross, he thought. The water was flowing strongly and deliciously cold in the heat of the day.

Behind him, he heard a family disembarking from a wagon. A small boy asked, 'Is this the sea, mum?' Tomas smiled. It was a fair question, he thought, for a youngster. Tomas had never seen so much water in one place in all his life, so perhaps the sea wasn't too different from this. He looked past the family, downstream. The Great River continued westwards, into the setting sun. Shading his eyes, he looked down the hither bank and saw the smoke from many campfires rising from among the trees down river. He pointed it out to Ben.

'Yes, we've seen it. It may be Raiders, so we'd better be careful,' he said, squinting westward. Kobos' wagoners were already turning about in a great arc, forming a circle.

Eventually, thirty-two large and brightly-painted wagons were arranged in a wide oval, with a large, seed-laden camelthorn tree near the centre. The oxen were outspanned and picketed by the cargo-wagons, and as the sun sank low over the trees to the west, fires were lit and meals were prepared. People moved between the fires in bare feet, chatting cheerfully in the cool, green evening. Kobos sent some of his hired Tsuna guards off to investigate the campsite in the distance, since they knew how best to move quietly in this kind of country.

As the sun set in a blaze of orange, there was the sound of hooves from the west of the campsite, and there was a hurried rush for weaponry. However, when the riders appeared, they called peace to the Rider-folk in the camp. 'Hoy, comrades!' the leader called.

'We see you,' called Kobos. There were about twenty of the strange Rider-folk.

'How do you fare?' The leader asked. At least he's being polite, Tomas thought. That's a good sign.

'We are well, and yourselves?'

'We prosper,' said the leader.

Kobos seemed to consider for a moment, then said, 'Come and sit with us.'

The strangers dismounted, tying their mounts to the outside of the wagons. It was an act of hospitality to be invited to break bread with a stranger. Anyone who accepted such an offer was bound to treat the host as a relative, at least until the next sunrise. Kobos knew what to do in the Drylands.

The guards' cooking-fire was built up, tea was brewed and everyone, including Tomas and Helder and two of the magi, sat around the fire. All wore their head-dresses in the cool evening, so their ears were covered. Ioseth loitered in the background, behind Ben, placing himself to hear most of the conversation. The leader of the strange Riders was a thin, quick man named Rokko, though to Tomas they all looked so similar – dark men with short, scraggly beards, leather trousers, rough woollen or fleece tunics and mohair cloaks.

'I must ask you, sirs,' Rokko was saying, 'where do your horsemen come from? I mean the ones of the travelling people.' He was wondering why Raiders were working for a merchant.

Adaan, Kobos' chief driver answered, 'We are from the North, near Tsunaland.'

'I have seldom seen your people guarding the caravan of Kobos,' said Rokko.

Adaan simply shook his head. 'We work for Kobos.'

Kobos put in diplomatically, 'Adaan's men were obliged to disagree with a leader of their people.'

Rokko nodded sagely. 'This leader - he did not style himself Lord, perhaps?'

'Perhaps.'

Rokko nodded again, taking a sip of the strong tea. He's weighing his words carefully, thought Tomas. The silence grew uncomfortable, until Rokko offered, 'Well, now - some of those Lords make mistakes. They keep bad company. Then, they take their people where they would not wish to go.'

Adaan suddenly looked less irritated. 'Indeed! Especially when they have grudges against the Southlanders.'

Rokko's face lit up with interest. 'One of them has sent messages to my people, desiring friendship, claiming kinship and alliance. I have heard much of him, not all of it good.'

Kobos looked steadily at him. 'Lord Vloch has recently lost followers in that part of the world.'

'That's the one,' Rokko nodded emphatically. 'My people are unwilling to engage in warfare against the Highlands. We have our – differences –' he shrugged and shook his head, '– but I have heard that he is using kchabani in his war!'

Kobos butted in quickly, 'It's less a case of him using kchabani, as of them using him!'

Rokko stopped, looking intently at Kobos. 'Kroghnash the Skullbreaker?'

'That's the one,' Ben said darkly.

Rokko cursed, saying, 'The man has a head full of dung.' He drained his cup. 'I will not have my people be kchaban-food. I would help those who are against him. The next time his messengers come –' he left it hanging. Then he spoke to all the men near him, 'Vloch has fought against the eladi as well, has he not?'

'Eladi are always enemies of the kchabani,' said Ben.

'In fact,' volunteered Adaan, 'some of the people in this caravan were living with the eladi by the Green River before they came with Kobos. They had been driven there by kchabani attacking.'

Rokko seemed to remember something. 'Are there any araneladi among them?'

Ben shot Tomas a glance, and said, 'None are known to be there, now. Why do you ask?'

Rokko shrugged and grunted. 'Vloch's messengers wanted us to find any half-humans passing through our lands, and capture them for him. They were especially interested in them.' The eladi at the fire all glanced at Tomas. 'Don't know why. I think half-breeds are unnatural, anyway, though I don't know any myself; but we're on good terms with the eladi in the mountains,' he waved away south, 'and we profit from the friendship. Though they are alien, they are good and their places are wholesome. I wish no harm to them.'

The talk moved on to other things. Now that friendship had been declared, everyone relaxed. Food was brought and the evening passed pleasantly. Sometime during the night, Kobos was called away. Tomas assumed he was taking the report of the Tsuna scouts he had sent out, and returned some time later. Eventually, in the cold and smoky small hours, the visitors bedded down in their cloaks around the campfire, and their hosts could finally get to bed.

The caravan spent another day at the ford of the Great River, hunting, fishing, refilling the water-barrels, repairing tack and relaxing. Tomas heard that the scouts had reported the Riders' camp to be very large and well-organised.

On the second night, there was an incident that gave Tomas away. It was just after sunset, and the fires in the camp were burning bright and cheerful. A group of women had come from the Riders' camp, with gifts and tokens of friendship for the mothers in the caravan. It was a sign of goodwill, and a goodbye present. There was beadwork jewellery and leather clothing, sorghum beer and travel-food. Kobos, Ben and Helder held a hasty conference and organised gifts of similar value – mohair blankets, kitchen utensils and Highlands money – so that the women would not return empty-handed. While the talk and pleasantries were going on, there was a sound of horses screaming from the animals picketed at the edge of the wagon ring. Tomas had a moment of panic: all knew that only hunting predators made horses scream like that. Some tore loose from their pickets and ran blindly off into the dusk; then came the horrible whooping and cackling of hyenas over the sounds of the camp. The sound chilled the blood of all who heard it. As fast as they could, men took burning branches from the fires and jumped up onto the shafts of the wagons, looking out for the animals. The sound seemed to come from everywhere, and nowhere. Tomas took up a crooked, burning branch and pulling himself up onto a shaft using his good leg, peered into the darkness. In the flame's orange light, he clearly saw a pair of eyes, reflecting green. Tomas' blood ran cold. He called out, 'Over here!' and heard his voice crack with fear. As he waited for others to come, more pairs of eyes appeared. They all seemed to be looking at him. One hyena came up close, its huge ears framing its greeny-gold glowing eyes, behind a fearsome set of teeth. It looked straight at him, and clearly as if spoken, Tomas heard the thought, *You talk to me?*

Wide-eyed at the sight of the spotted hyena in the light, Tomas shouted, 'Get out of here!' and waved his burning branch at her.

The hyena flinched, but looked at him, whining, *I am leader here! We will fight you for the dark zebras!*

'Those are *our* horses!' Tomas waved the flame at her again. All at once, an arrow thwacked into the sod at the hyena's feet, and she danced out of the way. One of the Riders had joined Tomas on the shaft.

The hyena sniffed inquisitively at the arrow. *What kind of insect is this?*

'It is worse than a flying scorpion!' Tomas bellowed, thinking of a suitably horrible image to go with the concept.

Another hyena, probably the dominant male, slunk up to the lead female. He cackled,cringing,worried about the fire.

The lead female snarled at him, but two more arrows shot out of the dark, hitting her solidly in the neck and ribs. She gave a strangled scream and fell. The other hyenas loped off, the lead male whooping into the dark. He was calling the others away.

Tomas leaped down off the spar, but hurt his bad hip and went rolling. 'You idiot!' someone shouted, 'there might be more out there!'

'Never mind that!' Adaan was shouting, 'stamp out that fire!' Tomas' flaming branch had set fire to a clump of grass. Beating with cloaks and stamping with feet, the other men put it out before it could spread.

When the emergency was over, Adaan turned on Tomas, saying, 'What the hell did you think you were doing? Why did you jump off like that? There could have been a whole pack of those things waiting for you!'

Tomas shook his head, holding his sore left hip. 'There weren't.' He looked at the dead hyena with interest. The thing had 'sounded' female, but seemed to have male genitalia. So it was true what Master Aravon had told him about the matriarchs among hyenas. 'The other one was calling them away when he ran off.'

Adaan looked at him, wide-eyed. 'How do you know that?' The men all went deathly quiet.

Oh, stuff it, Tomas thought. He had spoken without thinking, and aroused their suspicion. He looked around at the mercenaries. They were looking at him as if he'd suddenly grown horns.

'He was talking to them, sir,' it was the bowman who had been first up on the wagon-shaft with Tomas. He was telling them they were our horses, and that the arrow was a flying scorpion.'

'I heard it, too,' said one of the wagoners.

'All right, that's enough, men!' Kobos' voice boomed out from the seat of the wagon behind them. 'This is the Initiate Tomas. He's all right.'

Tomas hobbled off towards the wagon, and a respectful space opened up for him. He didn't know what had come over him, jumping all over the place like that. Unable to climb again, he crawled under the wagon. He wondered what kind of rumours would grow out of tonight.

Master Helder was not impressed. He told Tomas not to try any more heroics, and that he should find some work to do, to keep himself out of mischief. He did think that Tomas had handled the situation well, however.

The caravan had to stay an extra day, while the horses that had fled were recaptured. Kobos fretted at the delay. He didn't want to leave the crossing too long, in case the river should rise unexpectedly. The next day, the caravan made its way across the channels between gravel bars. The sun was hot, the water delightfully cold on Tomas' feet. Because of the care needed in moving wagons over slippery cobbles, it was high noon by the time they reached the far side.

There was a cutting through the high bank, and the wagons struggled and slithered up through it one by one. While the wagons were still crossing, the eladi 'mercenaries' and Kobos' guards took up positions at strategic points on the bank, just to be on the safe side. At the top, Tomas suddenly found the horizon closer and higher than it had been for months. They had started the climb into the Cedar Mountains.

CHAPTER X

The Cedar Mountains were strange to Highland eyes. Where the Gildrock Mountains were simply vast, slanted slabs cut off at one end to form imposing cliffs, these mountains were made of folded, twisted bands of rock, carved by time and water and cold into weathered peaks. The vegetation was different: there were no more of the familiar thorny acacias; instead, there were tall, fine-leafed cedar trees growing amongst pillars and walls of stone. The low, thorny shrubs of the Drylands were replaced here by aromatic herbs and fine-leafed bushes. Their leaves were thick and waxy, or coloured grey by fine hairs. Tomas and Magus Firon, whose Abilities included Plant Sympathy, had never seen so many different kinds of plants before.

Even the weather had changed. Tomas was reminded again that the South Coast had their dry season in summer, for some obscure reason. It took three days to cross the Cedar range, the wagons first battling up the pass and then jolting down the other side, and the sun beat down on them all day long. At the top of the Westerhook Pass, on the afternoon of the second day from the Ford, Adaan told Tomas that there had been snow on the slopes above them, the last time they made this journey. Snow was something Tomas had seldom seen, and which some of the humans had never seen at all. There were ruins here too, of towers above the pass where the first Seafarers had mounted guard in one of the early Foul Wars. They stopped at the top of the pass that day, and the acolyte and the wise, man and elado, climbed up the old, rutted road to disinfect the space-folding node in the tower.

Coming down from the pass on the morning of the third day from the ford, Tomas saw the land of his remote ancestors for the first time. They had been on the road for over two months. There was some cloud that day, lapping the tops of the bleak, grey-green mountains behind. Below the cloud, swathes of aromatic herblands swept down from the heights, sunlit gold beyond the gloom. A flock of ostriches moved on the edge of sight below. By the time the caravan stopped for the midday meal, the view was almost lost behind the cedars, blowing cool in the wind. Tomas walked off into the trees with his lunch, wanting to take in the view with his meal. The cloud had thinned, and the light was bright. When he had finished his lunch, he left his bag near the rock he had been sitting on, and heaved himself up behind a large boulder, to see what he could see. Climbing with his stick was an effort, but well worth it. The view reminded him of the camps he had been on as an apprentice in the Gildrocks, two years or more before. He sat as he always did, cross-legged with his hands open in front of him, and relaxed, listening to the silence.

It must have been several minutes later when a movement below caught his eye, distracting him. He looked to one side and behind, and saw a strange sight: a large, black bird, a crow or something like, was at his lunch-bag. Its beak was massive, with a heavy, high bridge to it. Unlike a crow, the white plumage didn't cover its entire front, either, but only its neck. Not a crow then, he thought, but a raven: a mountain watcher. As he watched, the bird's heavy beak worked on the knot he had tied loosely in the draw-string. The knot was quickly untied, and the bird pulled the bag open with foot and beak. Pulling out a crust of road-bread, it flew to a low branch nearby, holding the crust in its foot as it ate. Tomas was amazed at the bird's ingenuity. Smiling, he said quietly, 'Are you enjoying that?'

The bird stopped eating and dropped the bread. It cocked its head up at him, fixing him with a beady, jet-black stare. Tomas could feel its surprise, but also its calculation – it was wary, and ready to fly. Then it did something else that surprised Tomas. In the same way that he had 'heard' the hyena at the ford on that night, he 'heard' the bird say, in feelings rather than words, *How do you talk to me?*

Tomas replied, 'It is something I can do.'

You are very strange, said the bird.

'There are few like me,' Tomas explained. 'Would you like some more food?'

The raven looked straight at Tomas, and then flew up onto his rock, landing right in front of him.

Tomas fumbled in his pocket for the paper bag of dried apricots he'd kept to nibble on. He pulled one out, took a bite, and handed it to the bird. It hopped closer, then pecked, snatching the fruit from Tomas' fingers. Tomas carefully avoided the vicious-looking, white-tipped beak.

Mother. Tomas was surprised at how familiar the bird's idea of 'mother' was.

'I am a father, not a mother,' explained Tomas.

Me too, answered the raven.

Good, thought Tomas, at least we've sorted that out. 'A bird as clever as you should have a name' he muttered.

The raven made an odd sound, a voiced sound, with a descending pitch. It sounded like 'tork'. Tomas said, 'I shall call you Tork. My name is Tomas.' He emphasised the sound by thought.

The raven cocked his head.

'Tomas,' repeated Tomas. He repeated it several times. Tork looked at him, listening. Tomas repeated his name again, and Tork mimicked him, saying 'Tomas!' Even the inflection was imitated.

Tomas was amazed. The books were right! These birds could talk! 'Very good!' He smiled.

Yes, said Tork. *More sweets?*

Tomas laughed out loud. 'You are like a young one of my kind, always wanting sweets!'

Tomas took out another apricot. Thinking with the bird to stop it pecking, Tomas made it take the fruit politely, reinforcing the action with approving thoughts. Tork took it gently this time, without pecking.

Tomas came down out of the trees with Tork sitting on his left shoulder like a patch of night. Ben looked at him with amusement and exasperation. 'Don't tell me,' he said, 'it followed you home, and you want to keep it!'

'Master Ben,' Tomas announced, 'meet Tork. He talks.'

Ben's face went blank. 'What?'

Tomas pointed at Ben, looking at Tork. 'Master Ben,' he told the bird. Then, pointing to himself, he said, 'Tomas.'

Tork made his strange sound again, then said, 'Tomas,' in Tomas' voice.

'Hey!' Ben laughed, 'He's even got your voice!'

'Do I sound like that?'

'Tomas,' said Tork, mimicking Tomas again.

'Amazing,' Ben shook his head.

Tork became the centre of attention in the caravan that day. Most people were amazed, but some were suspicious: ravens, even more than crows, had an unsavoury reputation. They were killers of lambs, stealers of sprouting crops. They were carrion-feeders, always the first at a carcass. Men said they could feel death on the air. In the inn of the village where they stopped for the night, Tomas told and re-told the tale of their meeting. Tork gladly accepted all donations of food. From what Tomas could see of his memories, life had been hard for the bird. He had been left to fend for himself at a young age, and had not managed well.

The next day at lunchtime, with Tork out looking for snacks along the caravan route, Ben called Tomas into his wagon. Master Helder was there, too, sitting against a barrel, his calloused bare feet stretched out in front of him. 'I've been wondering about your choice of pets,' Ben began. 'Why did you choose a cold-land carrion bird?'

'*I* did not choose him,' Tomas answered, 'he was simply looking for food.'

Master Helder nodded. 'Your Animal Sympathy seems to have returned. We know you have been helping Adaan with the driving. Did

Master Aravon spend any time instructing you about large mammals?'

Tomas remembered his farming and hunting expedition with Master Aravon, last winter before the great kchaban had been captured. It seemed like a lifetime ago. 'Yes, we spent time on a farm called Lorelisse, and then went hunting for a whole two weeks, it was wonderful. I have touched the oxen and horses in the caravan, but they are not of the brightest. Tork on the other hand is remarkable. He's much brighter than any dog or cat, even more so than a monkey.'

Ben sat back on the bench, sighing. He'd been walking alongside the wagons all day. 'Did Limlot ever tell you about Dircalad the Younger?'

'I don't remember the name.' Tomas thought back to the days in Greystone. Those memories were happy. Liriel's face tugged at his heart.

Helder took up the story. 'He was a sage, and a prophet. He lived in what are now the Clearmountains, even before the Bafedi came from the North. You may have heard of the ruins there, it was a city of my people; but not even I remember what it was called, any more. There are a number of his writings in Greystone.

'In one of his writings he spoke about a place called the Grey Land, and how it will be saved by elephants. I have often wondered if he referred to Greystone. It was one of the things I wanted to research in Westerhaven, or failing that, in Greenland if possible, what later sages thought it meant, or if it has come to pass already. I think it might have some bearing on our troubles. The problem is that it is quite obscure, only a handful of masters even know about it.'

'Elephants?' Tomas looked keenly at Ben. 'It seems cruel, not to mention unproductive, to push any animal into warfare.'

'There is a reward for them,' Ben explained. 'Rather like what they do with cavalry quaha. You know how they work it into the animals' status among the herds? That is why you only ever see stallions in cavalry – it's a way of earning status without kicking the stuffing out of each other.' He chuckled.

'Ah, so you think the same could be done with elephants?'

'We do indeed,' said Helder. 'There used to be elephants in Greystone, when first re-settled by the Seafarers, after the Fouls first came and we had been scattered. But as the Seafarers multiplied, and the scatterlings of the oreladi gathered together again, they needed more land to cultivate. In time, there was not enough room for both elephants and eladi, and the elephants had to go.'

'They had to go?'

'Lord Engolaran ordered Rangolo, father of Celevrau, to persuade them to leave. His intention was to send them to the Thornlands.' The

Master paused for a moment, lost in memories.

'The father of Celevrau? I never knew.'

Ben said, 'That is how Liriel's father came to live there. Unwilling to part from the animals he knew and loved, his father left with the elephants. It was unexpected. His wife, that's Liriel's grandmother, was long gone, seeking the Shining Mountain. So, as the youngest, Celevrau took the old house. As far as any know, Rangolo still wanders the bush with the elephants, somewhere in the trackless lands where no speaking-beings live.'

Tomas thought out loud, 'Perhaps that is what Dircalad was talking about: the return of – the master?'

'No Master, simply Rangolo,' Ben provided. 'It could be. But none have had contact with him at all in all this time.' He looked at Helder, who shook his head in confirmation. 'He told the Lord Engolaran that he would not return, so he must have intended it to be a permanent arrangement. Maybe he also went on the long journey, in time.'

There was a short silence. Then Tomas said, quietly, 'That's a pity.'

'Not for him,' Ben replied, also quietly. 'He loved those elephants like a family, they say. He didn't want to send them to an empty land where they wouldn't have eladi to watch over them. So, he went with them.'

All sat in silence for a while. Tomas tried to imagine what it was like in those far-off days. Ben seemed to be lost in thought, as well, until he snapped out of it, saying 'Anyway – I would like you to practice controlling large mammals, as well as birds. You seem to have a knack for birds, but we may need someone with your talent in the near future.'

Tomas raised a sore point. 'I shall need a master. I can't teach myself all from books.'

Ben sighed heavily. 'Yes. You need to resume your discipline as soon as possible. Perhaps you may find a master in Greenland? The masters should be good enough there and you would not have to wait until the war is over to find a new master.'

Tomas knew Master Ben was right. The possibility was exciting, but there was a slight problem. 'But I don't even know the language.'

'I think you will manage, all the same. We will be there for some time, and you have a natural gift for tongues, O Tomas. You should not seek a Master among men, because of the weakness of our kind. I recommend that you seek a master among the forest eladi.'

'Are there really no suitable Masters amongst the men of the South? This was where our culture came from.'

'It is. But men have the obvious weakness to their own darkness. Not only that, but people who live in comfort and plenty for many generations become distracted... they become more concerned with filling their pockets, and their stomachs, and their beds, than making a better world. As far as they're concerned, their world can't get any better. That's why this country is a great place to live in, but a bad place to make a life.'

Tomas nodded with a wry grin. 'That's a good way to put it.'

'Our fellows in the Cold South have forgotten some things they should have remembered.' Ben looked away, towards the opening at the back of the wagon. 'Ah! Here's your little friend.' Tork was perched on the gate of the wagon, cleaning his beak on the wood.

'What have you been eating?' Tomas asked him paternally.

Squashed frog, answered Tork. *Run over by the wagons.*

Ben and Helder saw the expression on Tomas' face and laughed out loud. Ben said, 'No, I don't want to know what he said.'

The caravan moved on into the Southlands, past vineyards, orchards in bloom and fields of sproutingwheat. Away from the Cedar Mountains, it was a long-settled land, where the hand of Man lay heavy. They passed blooming groves of what Tomas took to be ironwoods, but Ben told him that they were olive trees, domesticated relatives of the ironwoods. Their fruits were much bigger than those of wild trees, and were pressed for the oil that the Southlands sold to the entire world.

The sky was a blue flame, with not a cloud to be seen. Summer here was just as warm as in the Highlands. They were five days out from the Great Ford, and came to a town in the evening. There were walls around the old town in the middle, but even the new part was clean, industrious and well-organised. The caravan pitched camp outside the town, across the river in the summer fairground. They stayed there for a few days, and Kobos did some trading. The acolyte and the wise went off to cleanse the travel node at the bend of the river. Then they took the main road for Westerhaven.

They rolled steadily southwards, past neat, ordered towns and farmlands. The towns often included grand old fortresses, built of the red-tinged granite common in the region. All the castles seemed to have been purposely designed with an exquisite sense of proportion. Even the eladi admired them. The public buildings did not have the blocky, no-nonsense shapes of those in the Highlands; nor were they the graceful edifices that eladi built into, rather than on top of, the land; these were grand, elegant, sweeping structures, made by the Seafarers, both men and eladi, at the height of their power and artistry. It was common for walls to be banded with different shades of stone, and even the crenulations on the walls were tastefully moulded. Within the towns, most of which had long outgrown their elegant fortifications, all was well-organised, the people industrious and friendly. Southland speech was the same as that of the Highlands, but with a strange, gentle, sing-song accent, which made Ioseth and Tomas' speech sound flat and aggressive by comparison. The men here also preferred moustaches, where Highlanders were generally bearded.

During the course of the next two weeks they passed through or close by places where the human families from Greystone had relatives. The caravan steadily depopulated as militiamen left the caravan with their families. There was one incident, as someone tried to slip away with one of the eladon wagons by night, but a combination of Ben's diplomacy and Kobos' mercenaries settled the argument.

Thus it was with roomier wagons that they mounted the Seabergs above Westerhaven and wound their way down to the sea. Tork seemed to have decided that he was going to stay with Tomas; Tomas supposed that his feeding of the bird had something to do with it.

From the top of the pass above Westerhaven, Tomas and Tork had their first view of the sea. It was bigger than any body of water Tomas had ever imagined! He was simply astounded. It stretched dark blue to the horizon under a brilliant summer sky. The sheer size of the body of water was almost frightening. It was mid-day, with the wind whistling through the fine bush. He could see the walls of Westerhaven gleaming whitely below him in the distance. It seemed far too close to all that water for comfort.

After jolting along dusty stone roads all afternoon, the caravan of Kobos rolled into the great city. The houses were square and brown, but grander buildings were whitewashed, with pillared porticoes and red-tiled roofs. The press of people was amazing to Tomas. His first expectation of friendliness of such a large number of people together dissipated in the impersonal crowds that hurried this way and that. The people dressed similarly to Highlanders, with loose summer clothing made from simple squares of cloth, and sandaled feet. The caravan made for one of the main squares in the Old Town, where the wagons were outspanned and Kobos made ready to start business the next day.

That evening found Tomas, Ben and Ioseth in a public-house, where the Greystone humans gathered for a first night in the town. The eladi stayed in their own rooms, avoiding unwanted attention. Tork took his usual place with Tomas, where he begged shamelessly for scraps, while keeping an eye on the landlord's cat.

Tomas asked Tork, 'Don't you have any pride at all?'

What is pride? asked Tork.

Tomas didn't feel like talking morality with a bird after a cup of heavy red wine, especially not with Ben around. In any case, he thought, animals are amoral, so he left it at that.

Tomas and Ioseth had kept their regular meditation times, and Tomas maintained his Ability.

The next day, the acolyte and the wise disinfected the last space-folding node between Westerhaven and Greystone. The way was now clear for the earlier embassy to leave: all they had to do was find them and tell them about it.

Over a few days, the last of the human families all dispersed to seek long-lost family, as did the other two human leaders. Ben, Tomas and Ioseth were staying in a boarding-house. Living in Westerhaven was not cheap.

Ben and Tomas began their investigations into the whereabouts of the last embassy from Greystone. The two of them went and made discreet enquiries at the Lord Lieutenant's Chambers, but found nothing.

It was later on the second day that Ben and Ioseth heard that the King's Men were searching frantically for some mysterious fugitives. As far as they could tell, there had been some shadowy figures from the Highlands, presumed spies, who had been captured but had now escaped. The talk had it that they had escaped from the dungeons by use of dark arts; going by the descriptions on the posters that appeared on walls all over town, they had found the Embassy – and they had got themselves lost again, as hoped. The news was good, and Ben lost no time in sending a homing pigeon away with the news, though the Embassy would reach home before the message did.

However, now that one part of their mission had been successfully resolved, their main objective remained. They now had to make their way to Greenland, to make their audacious request of a king that had kept his kingdom in isolation for nearly two thousand years.

It was the first month of the new year, and Ben went looking for his cousin, the Magus Michellos, only to find that the man had left for Falmallinar in Greenland a few months before. 'All paths are converging on Greenland,' said the wise, Caranto. 'The Wind-Virgin is with us.'

By now, the money Lord Engolaran had given to Master Helder was running low, so Ben struck a deal with Kobos. The Merchant would buy some semi-precious stones or rock crystals, and Ben would use his Inanimate Reflex to turn them into eldastones for door-wards or intruder alarms; then they would split the proceeds, with Ben getting an advance on the deal. It turned out to be quite profitable, as it happened.

Once the stones had been bought, it was the work of many days for Ben to use his Ability on them. While Master Ben worked on the stones, Kobos discreetly arranged passage to Falmallinar in Greenland for Master Helder and his embassy, travelling as merchants. By the time the eldastones had been sold, the late half of summer was under way. The day the embassy left was unpleasantly hot and gusty, with low, broken cloud and a hot wind blowing from the Seabergs above Westerhaven. Masters Helder and Ben, their fellow magi, bodyguards and students made for the square where Kobos and his people had set up shop, intending to say their farewells. Tomas and Ioseth were apprehensive about travelling on a boat on that monstrous body of water, learned detachment or not. The eladi were quite excited. They chattered away in their own language, careless of the stares they attracted. Many of them had never seen the sea either. It was so hot, the eladan bodyguards wore only their studded-metal cloth armour and light cloaks, which couldn't quite hide their elegant weaponry. Tomas and Ioseth, dressed in their scruffiest clothes, led the pack horses, trying to look like hired boys.

With Tork perched on Tomas' shoulder as usual, they started into the square. They slowed down as they saw that Kobos himself was speaking to a detachment of five men, armed with pikes and short swords, and wearing leather-and-mail, with burnished helms and painted shields. They seemed too well-equipped just to be a detachment of the watch. Helder urged the party on, telling them in their own language to carry on to the harbour without stopping. He himself slowed down and approached the group, listening to what was going on. Ben did likewise. Tomas and Ioseth, unsure of whether to follow the embassy or their master, stayed behind Ben.

The leader was speaking. 'So, who did sell you these eldastones?'

'It was a wizard, I told you!' Kobos sounded nervous.

'And you say he wasn't part of a witches' circle?'

'I don't know.'

'If he wasn't, he couldn't have had a licence to make or deal in eldastones, could he?'

'I didn't know you needed a licence! I've only just come back from the Highlands.'

'Well then,' said the leader, 'Just this once, I'm going to give you the benefit of the doubt. But if you see that wizard again, I want to know. He's illegal in this country, now.'

Kobos was surprised. 'Why?'

Ben stopped. Tomas tried to look nonchalant, as if he was just passing. He started off to follow the others, but Tork hopped off, seeing something worth pilfering.

'All spellcasters have to be registered, now. The King has ordered that anyone claiming to have magical ability, without being a spellcaster, is to be held in terms of the Decree Against Charlatans and Spies.'

'What was that decree about, if you don't mind me asking?' Kobos glanced at Helder and Ben, and waved them away surreptitiously. The magi and students walked on, moving towards the main street down to the docks. Helder and Ben spoke together, quietly and urgently.

As he mentally called Tork, Tomas heard the leader saying, 'We don't allow fake witches in this country. There are some religious fanatics about, from the Highlands. They call themselves wizards, but they're spies and fakes. That's why...'

Tomas heard no more as he followed Ben, away from the square. Tork landed in his usual perch on Tomas' shoulder. The old man was swearing eloquently. When he ran out of curses, he simply muttered, 'I don't believe it. I don't believe it.'

'What is it, father?' Ioseth asked.

'The king and his Parliament have fallen out of their collective tree! Witches are legal, but Magi are not!' fumed Ben. 'It must be those Slavers. They must have the king under their influence, already.'

'How on earth,' Tomas was aghast, 'could they do that?'

'They must have been working on it for some time.'

Master Helder replied, 'Do not discount the possibility that there are real witches in high places here. I am disgusted that magicians have standing here, while magi are illegal.'

Tomas and Ioseth looked at each other. Neither spoke.

'The Slavers have done a lot of work, here,' said Master Ben. 'It's not safe for us. Let's find our ship and get out of here quickly.'

Helder said, 'I am glad the last embassy seems to have escaped.' He turned round to the students and asked quietly in Celadi, 'Got everything? Let us go.'

Finding their ship was quite easy. The pack horses were led on board by handlers, and the party found berths in short order. They occupied most of the passenger space on the boat. The order was given to cast off and Helder and Tomas were on the deck, looking out seawards. Tork was sitting on the rail, watching the crew. He felt little fear for the open sea, apparently trusting the ship. It seemed quite solid to him. He was fidgety, eager for the adventure to begin.

There were raised voices on the dock. Tomas, Ioseth, Helder and Ben turned and went to the other side of the ship to look. There was a detachment of guards on the quayside – it was the same group that had been questioning Kobos. The leader was throwing his weight around, stopping passersby and asking them questions. One of the people he spoke to pointed straight at the ship Tomas and Ben were on, and the guards made for the dock. Tomas was very relieved that the ship was a few lengths from it, already. The leader stood watching the ship. He noticed the magi and students. Then, something strange happened. A strange, dark man, very tall, dressed in black and wearing a deep-hooded black mantle over his head in all this heat, came and joined the guards by the dockside. He looked straight at Tomas, and Tomas felt a cold, urgent touch on his mind. There was a hunger and bitterness in the touch, but it seemed to slide off him, leaving a taste like the smell of a drain. Tork came and landed on Tomas' shoulder just then, and the dark man stood glaring at them. He had striking features, and might have been good-looking, except that his face looked so incredibly evil. Helder turned his piercing green gaze on the stranger; the man glowered back, looking livid. He was speaking to the guard-leader now.

'Well,' Helder said, as the ship came about, cutting off the view of the quayside, 'it seems that the stakes have been raised.' He nodded back towards the land. 'That was a High Witch, or I'm a vervet. We left just in time.'

As they cleared the Needle Cape, the hot, dry wind from the north gained strength, and they rode on a deep, gentle swell. The ship heeled over alarmingly, and Tomas felt the motion in the pit of his stomach. Fleeing below, he spent most of the day-and-a-half's crossing on his hammock hoping to die, when he wasn't leaning over the railing 'feeding the fishes'.

On the afternoon of the day after leaving Westerhaven, they came in sight of the coast, and Tomas saw why the place was called Greenland. It was covered in cool, lush forest. On the hills inland he glimpsed trees of amazing size. Master Firon guessed that the biggest yellowwoods could be thousands of years old. Humans knew very little of the place, other than that it was eladon territory, closed to them. The coastal plain on the north of the island was leased to the Kingdom, and that part was known to the Southlanders, but apart from maps of the coastline made by Southlander ships, the rest of the island was a mystery. The eladi of the Far South distrusted strangers, though they were scrupulously fair and honest in all their dealings.

Towards late afternoon on that second day, their ship came closer to the coast and the port of Falmallinar. The hot berg-wind had gone. Here were cliffs of weathered golden stone, surmounted by dense, dark-green growth. The ship found a narrow opening in the cliffs, and carefully made its way through into a sheltered lagoon. At the head of the lagoon, beneath a heavily-forested range of hills, lay the city of Falmallinar in Greenland, the main human settlement on the island. As the sun lowered over the hills in the west, they docked in the harbour. Halfway up the hill behind the town was a palace of golden stone, quite modest in comparison to the edifices of Westerhaven. There was no sign of any defensive works.

After landing, the embassy walked the crooked, narrow, winding streets, looking for a cheap place to stay. The buildings here were mostly whitewashed and timber-framed, unlike the stone or plastered brick of Westerhaven. Older buildings seemed to sag on upper storeys, giving the place a look of cheerful neglect. The people here had even more of a sing-song tone to their speech, but were less pretentious and more chatty than those in Westerhaven. Many of them had pale skin and fair hair, as well as the light eyes found all over the Southlands and Highlands. The men were all clean-shaven, as if trying to look like eladi. Once or twice, Tomas was sure he saw an elado walk by, shorter and heavier than the people of the Green River valley.

It seemed that day that there were few inns, and those were all full. By dusk, Helder's embassy was still wandering the streets. Stopping in a square, they drank from a fountain and slumped on the steps of haildom, tired and dispirited. Tork picked at some chicken-bones littering the ground nearby. Seeing him reminded Tomas of how hungry he was. 'Any good?' he asked.

Mine! Tork cawed at him.

'Obviously, you share food much more than he does,' Ben observed. The eladi laughed.

'Maybe we can get food at this haildom tonight,' Ioseth suggested. 'We're certainly among the Poor at the moment.'

'That's what I –' Ben broke off suddenly, looking across the square. 'Hey!' he called, pushing himself up. The armed eladi made reflexively for their weapons, but stayed at the last moment. 'Hey! Michellos!' Ben called, waving at a man on the other side of the square. He started over at a run.

The man turned and looked at Ben. He was wearing a dark blue tulme and a wide-brimmed hat. He broke into a smile, and started walking towards Ben. The two old men met in the square and hugged each other, pounding each other's backs, laughing like old friends. The rest got up and walked over to them, leaving Tork to pick at the old bones. Ben introduced the man, saying, 'Everyone, this is my cousin Michellos, my mother's older brother's son. He's the magus I've been looking for. Michellos, this is my old Master, Helder.'

The man's face lit up with interest, and recognition. He bowed in eladan fashion, speaking in Celadi. 'You are well come, master. Now I know indeed that great times are upon us.'

Ben introduced the other five magi, the wise, the Tinceldo and his lads, and then his fellow humans.

'Ah,' said Michellos, turning to grasp Tomas' forearm, 'I see you, two new talents! Well done, Bethnero! And human, too. No offence, but I hope you're not instructing them?'

Ben just laughed.

'Hello, father,' said Tomas and Ioseth, smiling politely.

'Well,' Ben started explaining, 'it turns out Tomas here isn't quite human – he's an odd mixture, is young Tom!' The old man's accent had suddenly broadened.

'Oh, well,' beamed Michellos. 'I think most of us have some eladi somewhere on our family tree!'

The two men turned away to talk quietly, though still within earshot. Michellos said, 'I am glad you got away from Westerhaven. Things aren't too bad here, but we are still in the king's lands, and there may be talk. We can put you all up, for as long as you need, but it will be a squeeze. How many are you?'

Ben counted on his fingers. 'The master, five magi, the wise, seven bodyguards plus leader, me and the boys, that's eighteen altogether. I don't think you'll have space for everyone!'

'We can squeeze you magi and the wise in the guestroom, but the lads and your muscle will have to sleep in the library, up in the loft,' said Michellos. 'We had a whole college of apprentices there, once before. It's not a problem.'

'That would be perfect. Thank you,' Ben said simply.

'You're meant to stay with us,' said Michellos. 'I've had a feeling you were on the way for weeks, now.'

Tomas turned and called, 'Tork!'

The raven hopped up from the gathering gloom, still carrying the bone he'd been picking at.

Tomas told him, 'Leave that thing behind, please.'

Tork flicked his head, tossing the bone away. *Food?* He asked.

'Not yet,' Tomas explained. 'Later.'

I eat this now. Tork flapped down to retrieve his bone.

'No, you won't!' Tomas snapped, wagging his finger at the bird. 'I don't want you wiping greasy mud on my shoulder.'

For a moment, Tork stood there, undecided. Then he quickly and savagely attacked the bone, pulling off a lump of gristle with some attached meat in his heavy beak, and gulped it down. Then he flapped back onto Tomas' shoulder again. *Finished,* he declared.

Tomas turned back to follow the others, only to find them quietly staring at him. 'Sorry,' he said.

'Not at all,' said Michellos. He was amazed at the interaction. 'Is he qualified?' he asked Ben.

'No,' said Master Helder, 'but Tomas is always getting ahead of himself.'

Tomas was glad his colouring was invisible in the dusk.

The group moved through the streets of Falmallinar, to a stone-paved courtyard about a small fountain. The fountain itself had an eladan look: a thin stone pillar carved around with roses in relief, standing in the middle of a deep, honey-coloured bowl filled with clear water.

The house Michellos led them to had red-brick walls and was framed by tarred black timbers. There were three storeys, not counting the windows jutting from the roof. Each storey overhung the one below it, giving the house an eerie, mushroom-like appearance to Tomas' Highlander eyes, but the windows were golden with cheery, welcoming light.

Later that evening, fed and rested in the firelit company of two elderly magus couples and a company of eladi, the talk passed to serious matters, all in Celadi for the benefit of the visitors. Helder and Bethnero told the elder magi about their mission. The human magi were dubious: the Greenland eladi were notorious for not getting involved in any human conflict. For centuries there had been a dynastic struggle among the different eladon tribes, but the oldest generation of humans had lived their lives with a united kingdom over the border. There was now a High King accepted by all Oreladi.

The magi themselves would do what they could, as long as their guests kept a low profile. They had had to leave their home in Westerhaven because of persecution, and had no wish to repeat the experience.

Tomas learned that the small community now living in the Tall House had lived in Westerhaven for over half a century, carrying on such business as it did, living quietly and simply. All had been trained by eladi, and so had maintained a detachment from the urge to power and prestige that ruined most human-trained magi. Living in their own small community, they had maintained themselves in service to ordinary people, living long as most of their profession did.

In the last year before they left, there had been a number of decrees issued by the king. Most had been aimed against those classes of people that traditionally taught the King's Law – acolytes, magi and Mythtellers. Acolytes and Mythtellers of the old school were now very rare in the Kingdom, having fled if they escaped being imprisoned.

The effect of the changes in the law on human magi had been quite sinister. The instruction of initiates had always focused on clear discernment between service that sought the good of all, and service of personal glory, which led to ruin. The foundational discipline was that of detachment, which taught a magus how to view possessions, personal satisfaction and power objectively. The Possessions Rule, stringently observed, was that that a magus should own no more than he or she could carry for a thousand paces (generally defined as up to a quarter of one's own weight), and that they should depend on charitable gifts for their maintenance, as far as was practical. There was no Ability that would not make a horror of the man or woman who used it to concentrate money, power or satisfaction, even on another's behalf.

When the magi in the lands of the king took to the Awakening, those humans who followed it threw off thousands of years of Tradition, and took any means available to increase their own power, eventually resorting to bargains with Spirits of the Shadow. Such spirits had always been regarded as evil; but once it became believed that evil spirits were misunderstood but useful, there was no reason not to seek a spirit guide. A few years before, most of the fellowships of magi that had existed for time out of mind had been replaced, forcibly or otherwise, by witches' circles, and the houses they had taken over became places of horror by night and bitter contention by day. A profession that had always been prone to attracting eccentrics, quacks and charlatans started to produce curses, hauntings and possession as well.

The Decree Against Charlatans and Spies had been issued the previous summer. Officially, it was an attempt to 'clean up' the magical professions, by making sure that anyone claiming to have Abilities had been properly trained and vetted, and had taken the oath of allegiance to the king. The only problem was that all practitioners not part of a witches' circle were deemed by the King's Law to be charlatans. Anyone denounced as a charlatan faced arrest (unless they managed to escape), and imprisonment until such time as they would join a circle, accept the 'guidance' of a spirit and take their oath of allegiance to the crown. All eladi-trained magi had fled, mostly to Falmallinar, where the ruling family was in dispute with the crown. Outside the port where the trade from Greenland was carried out, the northern strip of Greenland was a quiet, agricultural backwater, a land of foresters, farmers and loggers, and as yet the proscription against Tradition had not been strictly enforced there.

Michellos and his wife and their friends, when living in Westerhaven, had had long-standing customers; but as the Awakening took hold, those clients had either stopped coming, or had started making strange new requests: where before they had asked for eldastones, or for help with heavy lifting in construction, or with healing of a sickness that doctors could not cure, they began asking for curses against business competitors, or for love-potions, or for predictions of the future. Such things were impossible for genuine magi (and in fact it was insulting to ask them), but were the daily bread of witches. At the same time, witches' circles had begun to sow rumours about them around town, and the magi had been subject to public suspicion and faceless harassment in the market-places. They had been the victims of spells, which needed a wise to break, but wise of the Old School were becoming fewer, too. Seeing the growing power and popularity of their enemies, the magi had made arrangements to ship their precious library to Falmallinar, and had quietly left just in time.

'We left a lot of nice things in that house,' said Erolinde the maga. She was a slight lady, with white hair and dark eyes. 'But, I suppose we were getting too attached to them anyway. It almost made one feel young again, leaving to start a new life.'

Ben voiced the question that had been occurring to Tomas. 'What will you do when they start enforcing the Decree here, as well?'

'They won't,' said Iremias, Erolinde's husband. 'Part of the treaty that allows humans to live here stipulates that witchcraft is banned. The eladi won't have it. We're safe, at least until they're sure enough of themselves to violate the ban.'

'What would the Greenland eladi do if they did that?' asked Firon.

'Most think they'll ignore it, like they do everything else that goes on here,' said Iremias, 'but I doubt it.'

Arcaldo, much the oldest of the magi, had said little thus far. 'I don't know about these youngsters –' he nodded, grinning at the white-haired group around the table, '– a but I'm too tired to go gallivanting all over the place. Whatever happens, I'm not running anymore. If they come after me, I can levitate them into the sea, or something.' He thumped his knotty-knuckled hand on the arm of his chair.

'I think,' offered Iremias, 'that we should sneak off over the border to seek out the Kingdom.' He looked around the table. 'Sooner rather than later.'

'The journey is not a merry afternoon's walk,' Michellos pointed out. 'We're none of us young anymore, and the children are all gone, or fled when the troops came.' The humans around the table looked sad, remembering departed family. 'We haven't any idea where to go, or how to get there; we'd be turned back at the border.'

'I think,' Ben said, leaning his face on one hand, 'that the Southlanders may finally shake the eladi into action.' Tomas grunted agreement. 'I agree with Iremias – there could be trouble. The eladi of the south don't like men an awful lot.'

'We may be able to help you,' offered Taria, Michellos' wife. 'We know some eladi who have people in the Kingdom itself. If we can get messages to them, you might be able to get there before – well, before any trouble starts.'

'In the meantime,' Michellos put in, changing the subject, 'there is an apprentice in the house, for the first time in nearly a year.' He indicated Ioseth.

The elder magi were delighted. It was seldom in these days of the Awakening that a new apprentice should take service with a senior magus.

'Not only that,' Helder said, 'but there is an initiate as well, late of Greystone of the eladi.' He nodded at Tomas.

'What are your Abilities, Tomas?' Michellos asked.

Tomas felt self-conscious. 'Mostly Animal Sympathy, some Plant Sympathy and some Affective Writing.'

'That's quite a wide variety!' Erolinde was surprised.

'Tomas has inherited a rare proportion of eladon blood and bone,' explained Ben. 'He's almost half-and-half, apparently, though he may not look it.'

'Just a minute,' Iremias said, finger on his upper lip, 'there was a thing about araneladi, wasn't there? There was one of those new decrees, just as we were leaving... it said that "Halfmen" were to be reported to the authorities.'

Ben spluttered in indignation. 'Halfmen! How dare they change the meaning of words like that? They're entertaining ambassadors from the one place in the world where arkchabani are the lords of the land, and they call araneladi, Halfmen!' He fumed.

'But why are they looking for araneladi?' asked Tomas.

'That's one of the things I was hoping to find out here,' said Ben. 'Whenever the Fouls and the Raiders sacked a town in the Highlands, they always sought out any araneladi they could find – as if there were any living among men! There was a war band with a troll that infiltrated Greystone, and they were looking for araneladi there, as well.'

'Why on earth are they doing that?' asked Taria.

Tomas would have liked to tell them what they knew; but Ben

caught his eye and shook his head, almost as if blowing a fly away.

'Strange,' offered Iremias.

Ben continued, 'Going by history, when a large-scale kchaban mobilisation happens, it's because one strong leader has arisen among them. That, or the power behind the Shadow has taken strength somehow. It takes a lot to unite a whole race of thugs, so this Skullbreaker is unusual. In an attempt to find out why they are so interested in araneladi, I took it upon myself to search the writings. I couldn't find much in the library in Greystone to suggest why – so I thought I should come and look in yours.' He looked at Arcaldo.

'And all this time, we thought you came for our scintillating company!' Michellos laughed.

Erolinde said in Ancient Eladan, 'Our books are your books.'

'My gratitude spreads a bouquet, mother,' Ben replied in the same language.

'I appreciate the courtesy of speaking in my tongue,' said Helder, 'but your pronunciation could be better.' Everyone chuckled. 'In the meantime, the rest of us will scout around. I would like to know the lay of the land, and preferably lay hands on a new map. Then once we are familiar with the country, we shall leave the town. We should be closer to the border, and we would no longer attract any attention from eyes sympathetic to the king in Westerhaven.'

'So the boys and I must do our reading quickly,' said Ben.

Tomas went to bed that night wrapped up in a blanket under a table in the loft. It looked like a busy time ahead.

CHAPTER XI

Helder's Embassy, along with Ben's small college, stayed in the Tall House on the square. It was a squeeze. Some of the eladan bodyguards went to stay at a nearby haildom, two of them moved next door, within shouting distance of the Tall House. Another two stayed in the library with Tomas and Ioseth.

Ioseth occasionally consulted with elder magi. Old Arcaldo was a bottomless pit of anecdote and insight. Indeed, once he started talking, it was often difficult to get him to stop.

Tomas was always at work in the library, searching for references to Dircalad the Younger, and for any hints in history or prophecy as to why the kchabani sought araneladi. For all their reading, he and Ioseth found few clear references. Prophecy was notoriously obscure in the first place, and if you weren't sure what you were looking for (or why), it could be downright nonsense. Reading genuine prophecy also gave them extraordinarily vivid dreams.

With the summer now waning, it rained more often, indeed it rained a little on most nights. 'How do you think the trees grow so big here?' Ben said when Ioseth complained about the weather. Rainy days in Greenland were miserable, no matter what the season.

At first the magi travelled around, getting to know the land between Falmalinnar and the border, while Taria made contact with her people who knew local eladi. They discovered that there was one merchant family running a trade route to the Forest Kingdom through the border crossing. Their factors were the only ones licensed to trade in certain goods and naturally, they had made a fortune with it.

The trade route allowed only one border crossing: the goods were simply taken to a trading-post, unloaded and left there. No-one knew what happened to them afterwards, and indeed no-one had ever seen any wagons take the goods away. To the magi, it looked like the onward transport of the goods made use of Space-folding.

Over the following weeks the strangers were noticed, try though they might to keep a low profile. So, some twoweeks after their arrival, the eladi of the Embassy left Falmallinar, following the road to the Forest Kingdom. Ben, Ioseth and Tomas remained in the city, both to keep their eyes on the doings of the Kingdom and to be a Greystone presence in the city when required. Master Helder bought supplies for at least a week, and the eladi walked away in the evening. They were to travel mostly at night, along the trade route from Falmallinar to the heartland. Tomas wondered fleetingly that evening if he would ever see them again. It had been a cool, overcast day, as it so often was there, and rain was just starting to spit. Ben, Tomas and Ioseth saw them to the edge of town. Tomas had Tork watching for followers, but it seemed there were none. After having had the protection of fighting eladi for so many months on the road, it felt risky being without them.

Upon a mild, muggy autumn day, about a week after the eladi had left, when the stinkwoods on the side of the market square were smouldering gold, there was an incident. Tomas was in the market, on an errand for Taria. Tork was perched on top of a tent-pole out of sight of Tomas, probably watching in case someone dropped a tasty snack. A man in a deep-hooded black mantle came along slowly, looking around. All his clothes were black. He walked close by Tomas, and Tomas could see his face under the hood. He was quite good-looking, but his features were soaked in evil. With a start, Tomas recognised the man who had been with the soldiers on the dock in Westerhaven. He reeked in the warm weather – obviously, he didn't visit the bathhouse regularly. He turned a staring, bloodshot gaze on Tomas, and seemed to jump. His eyes shifted about, seeming to look for something.

'I wonder if you could help me, sir,' he said to Tomas. His voice was smooth and cultured, like one of the patricians, and Tomas instinctively distrusted it. Tomas put on what he hoped was neutral expression.

'I'm looking for a chap, quite weedy, with a Highlands accent, got a pet crow. Seen anyone like that?'

It was Tomas' turn to jump. 'Pet crow?' he hoped his tone would be taken for incredulity, rather than fright. He was painfully conscious of his Highlander beard, which stood out among the clean-shaven men in the marketplace.

'Yes. He keeps company with some suspicious wizards.'

Tomas shook his head. 'No, don't think I've seen him. There are all sorts, in the market.' He tried to imitate the sing-song local accent.

'Well, if you see someone with a crow, could you tell him his friends are looking for him?'

'I'll do that,' Tomas answered, trying to breathe in any direction other than in front of him. The man really stank.

Tomas sought Tork. The bird was not on his perch. With some unease, Tomas reached out with his mind, seeking. He was surprised to feel that the raven was very close. He moved out from the awning where he had been standing, and saw Tork hunched on a rope above him. The bird was flustered, ruffling his feathers. *Bad man,* he declared. *Disgusting, he eat filth!* Tomas' surprise at the bird's apparent moral judgement was forgotten, though – the man moved away, and in between one moment and the next, as Tomas glanced elsewhere, simply disappeared. Tomas stood, leaning on his walking-stick, his errand forgotten. An apparently solid, corporeal, rather smelly being was simply not where he had been a heartbeat ago. He returned as soon as he could. They had been discovered.

At the Tall House, Tomas told the elders about his meeting with the stranger. Ben looked worried. 'It seems it was not a physical being. If it was, he may have tried to capture or kill you, or cast a spell on you. It looks like they've caught up with us. We've stayed too long; we need to rejoin the Embassy.'

'Well, we should all go and get some protection,' said Erolinde. That evening, the whole household went to the haildom where some of their guards had worked, and were blessed individually by the acolyte. When they got home, they bolted all the doors. All stayed up late, too tense and talkative to go to bed early. Thankfully, the evening passed uneventfully.

Tomas may have thought he had escaped the attentions of evil. He had not. The next day, evil struck. It was a cool, blustery night, the coldest Tomas had seen in the South. Tomas was asleep in the library among the books he had been reading for so long, when his dreams suddenly took an evil turn.

In his sleep, he saw the Man with the Black Mantle, standing at the door of the Tall House, looking at him. Tomas quailed before the evil in his too-symmetrical, well-formed features. The stranger said, 'What is your name?'

Tomas would have answered, but in his dream, his voice had no sound.

The man in black asked again, more insistently, with anger mounting in his voice. Tomas, though frightened, remembered just then the power he sought: naming something gave you power over it.

He found his voice, and said, 'No.' His voice trembled with fear and uncertainty.

The man in black repeated through clenched teeth, 'What is your *name?*'

Tomas said nothing. He tried to move, but couldn't. The stranger came closer, and Tomas felt fear. In his own dream, he was helpless.

'I already know what you are, Halfman! You gave me not enough of your name, and I could not reach you! I suppose you think you're safe? You think you're really clever? Do you really think you can resist me?' The man's question dripped contempt.

Tomas could not lie. He said, 'No,' again, but at the same time, he realised that resistance was not necessary; he had the freedom to refuse to fight. Only remember the Light, he thought, as it came when meditating. The image of the Evening Star came to him. This was his dream, after all. His fear lessening, Tomas stood, looking the dark man in the eyes.

The stranger went red in the face. His eyes bulged as he ground his teeth. He shouted, 'It doesn't matter! You're all dead, anyway!' A massive mace suddenly materialised in his hand, and he swung it at Tomas' head. Reflexively, Tomas jerked his arm up to block the blow – and it was that movement that woke him up.

He lay in that position, with his arm above his face, for several heavy breaths. That dream had been so real! He was immensely relieved to be awake, but the feeling of leering rot that flavoured the dream did not fade. The sky was lightening to overcast outside, and he rose, shivering already in the cool, clammy air.

At the breakfast table, Tomas told the motherly Erolinde about the dream. The others came in while he was telling her. He expected some reassurance, some guarantee that he had no reason to fear; instead, he saw fearful looks all around, from everyone but Ioseth. Taria looked at him with horror on her old face.

'Please, don't tell me you had the same dream,' he said to her.

She shook her head. 'No, but we have been visited by a similar figure before. This is the first time anyone has recognised it from waking life. It shows that we are the target of a spell.'

'I think,' Michellos said, 'We need to leave town for a while. All, of us, not just the lads, Ben.'

Tomas felt his now-familiar pang of guilt, and busied himself with stacking plates.

Tomas was unable to shake the feeling of livid decay all that day. He busied himself helping Erolinde make greeting cards (a small business she ran from home) with his Arcane Writing, and with his reading as usual, but his heart was not in his work. He was plagued by a nagging guilt and fear.

That fateful afternoon, Ben went out. Ioseth went with him and returned soon after with the items that they had bought, and told Tomas that Ben would be home later. Ben had seen someone he knew, he said. However, Ben had still not returned by nightfall. In the attic, Tomas waited to hear the bell toll the sunset hour at the Palace. When he heard it, he put on a cloak and went out to look for the Master. A feeling of threat had been growing in his mind with as the slow dusk of the South descended, and he just had to do something. He left Tork inside, since the bird couldn't see well in the dark, and went out into the night.

Now that he was outside, stared at by the lambent eyes of houses, the threat took form as a dark force on his mind. Tomas relaxed himself with the ease of practice, and cleared his mind. He sniffed the sad, dank air, smelling wood smoke. The road was muddy under his sandals. He thought of Ben, his fatherly manner, and his patience and self-discipline. Tomas knew which way to go. Darkness and fear reared themselves as he started out.

Tomas made for the smarter part of town, near the Courthouse. There, in an alley between two grand houses, he saw a large, crumpled mass in a dark puddle of mud. It looked like a corpse. His heart pounded. Hoping against hope he was wrong, he went up and touched the crumpled form. It was heavy, solid, and horribly cold, lying in strangely dark mud. Bending down over his walking-stick, he turned it over. It was Ben – or it had been. His throat had been cut, his blood the source of the dark stain beneath him. Tomas stood up, feeling sick. He had seen men die in battle under trees; but he had never seen a man murdered and left for dead in a dark alley, especially such a good man as Ben. His face was bruised and bloodied. His hand and arm were cut and grazed – he had fought. Where was his staff? Tomas looked around and saw, further up the alley, a splintered and broken piece of wood. Straining his eyes in the dark, he saw another dark stain. His attackers hadn't got away unscathed.

As Tomas pushed himself up, there came from behind the wall on his right a blood-curdling, feminine shriek. Tomas froze, every hair on his body standing up. He raised his walking-stick in a combat pose, his militia training asserting itself past the pain in his hip. The scream was quickly followed by rapid, quiet footfalls: someone was running away, behind the wall. Tomas' old injury twinged painfully and he lowered his stick again. All at once, a door on the side of the house on the left side of the alley opened, and a woman's voice screamed, 'Murder! There's been a murder!'

Before Tomas knew what was happening, he was surrounded by men with torches. Many were armed, as if seeking to prevent what had already happened. There was a swirl of questions, outraged shouting and horrified faces. Tomas stood through it all, until someone said, 'He did it! I saw him standing over the corpse!'

Tomas turned to look at the speaker. It was a pretty young lady, clothed modestly but expensively. 'No, he was already –' he stammered. He didn't know what to say. His mind was still numb with shock and the fear of the day.

'Don't talk nonsense, girl,' said a crusty old man's voice. 'This body is already cold. He's been dead a long time.'

'Then who screamed like that?'

Tomas found his voice. 'It was someone behind that wall,' he said, pointing at the wall on his right. 'I heard them running away.'

'*That* house?' the crusty old man said. He looked at the wall with distaste.

Someone else said, 'The old Bentwood place.'

The gathering crowd changed its tone from a gabble to a murmur. Somebody muttered, 'That's a bad place. There's strange things go on there.'

'There's a trail of blood here,' someone had found the other dark stain. 'It's leading up...' and they fell silent. Whatever it was about the Bentwood place, it exerted a powerful influence. The shouting and muttering simply stopped.

'Can anyone tell me what's going on?' asked Tomas, shakily. No-one answered. Some of the people started to walk away, heads down.

Watchmen arrived soon afterwards. They asked questions, took notes. Tomas went over his story again and again, until they were satisfied, but again, none of them asked any questions that touched the house on the right. They sent for a stretcher and bore Ben's body away to the haildom. His face was incongruously peaceful, almost happy. Tomas hobbled to the Tall House with a man of the Watch, the distance seeming longer with each painful step. He didn't know what he was going to say to the elder magi. As he entered the small square, he felt tears pricking the corners of his eyes. It was all too much! And that revolting little... telling everyone that he'd done it! Tomas ground his teeth, all his detachment gone. Those murderers were going to pay!

Suddenly, his enraged thoughts vanished. What was that? In the darkness beside the Tall House, a dim figure was moving about. Flames kindled, spread and grew along the edge of the house, lighting up oil poured along the front of the house.

'Hey!' shouted the Watchman.

The figure rose, and came running towards them. Tomas saw a glint of steel in the firelight, but the figure remained strangely dim, as if cloaked in darkness. With his injury, running was out of the question. With the force of fear, he shouted, 'No! *Stop!*' And the strangest thing happened.

The figure halted, stumbling. Tomas could see his face. It was a thin and clean-cut, with an arrogant cast to the jaw, but the eyes were completely vacant. He was carrying a long, thin-bladed weapon of some kind.

Tomas and the Watchman looked at each other, astonished. The man was frozen in place. There was a movement on the far side of the square, where someone peeped out of a house, responding to his shout. Tomas was utterly mystified. What had happened? Looking at his attacker's face, Tomas recognised the distracted, staring look of someone who bore a parasite spirit. He had last seen it on the face of Jwagga the Foot. This person was frozen, but still bore the stiletto in his hand, raised as if to strike. The door of the Tall House opened, and Arcaldo stood there. Seeing the blade in the attacker's hand, Arcaldo made a sweeping motion with one hand, and the dark figure jerked up in the air, hanging upside-down on a level with the first-floor windows, its cloak hanging spectrally above the ground.

As he watched, Tomas felt a whoosh of air on his left ear, and an arrow embedded itself in the wall-timber next to Arcaldo's head. Tomas and the watchman turned, ducking. The old man made a shoving motion with his hand, and the suspended figure shot over Tomas into another dimly-seen shape on the far side of the fountain. There was a sickening crunch, and two voices screamed. Then Arcaldo made sweeping motions with his hands, and all the flames along the wall of the house went out. Some onlookers helped, kicking earth over the oil.

In the ensuing uproar, Ioseth came out, pale and wide-eyed. He had seen everything through the roof-window, looking out from the library. He said to Tomas, 'I saw what happened. How did you do it?'

By now, of course, the people in the Tall House wanted to know what had happened to Bethnero. In the swirl of questions and explanations, the watchman told the elder magi about Ben. It was a bitter blow: not only to them, but to the Greystone embassy. The only human ambassador was now dead, and Tomas had only narrowly avoided death himself. Then he remembered the words of the Man with the Black Mantle in his dream: *You're all dead, anyway!* The dead-eyed assassin must have been about to set fire to the house. If Tomas had not been able to return home, if the watchmen had believed that girl's accusation, the whole neighbourhood could now be in flames!

Fortunately, the watchman had witnessed everything. He had been keeping order long enough to recognise a vendetta, and drew his own conclusions.

Both assassins were dead, though only one of them had suffered a fatal injury: the one thrown by Arcaldo had suffered a broken neck. The other, though apparently uninjured, was simply dead, his face staring with naked fear at the dark sky. Their bodies no longer had that darkness about them, and they were recognised by people as well-known thugs. They had been known to hire themselves out as minders to the well-to-do in the city.

Eventually, Tomas got back to the house, where he told the full, horrible story. The elder magi were shocked, but they were still magi, and responded with grave acceptance. The whole household then went to the haildom to keep vigil for Bethnero. Around dawn Tomas and Ioseth returned to the Tall House with Iremias and Taria. Tomas could not seem to recover his detachment. The talk of the elder magi seemed fatuous. Their facile mouthings and shallow platitudes stuck in Tomas' throat. Didn't they care that Ben had *died?* The only pure-blooded human who could speak for Greystone and the Highlands in the court of the king of Greenland, was now dead! For all he knew, Tomas and Ioseth were the last of the Embassy.

In accordance with Tradition, the funeral took place as soon as possible, the following afternoon. Poor Ioseth sniffed all the way through. Although Tomas had entered the haildom in a towering rage, the ritual incantations of the funeral were beautifully calming. Tomas remembered the Light at its invocation, and felt its sympathy. Ben had been a good man, Marta the Mourner would have mercy on him.

Tomas remembered the powerful peace and beauty of those meditations he had attended in the Gildrocks, so long ago now; and he realised that, for all his rage, he was powerless. The only way to get his equilibrium back, and do the job, was to let go and to let his grief run its course.

He thought of Liriel, which usually took his mind off his problems. His heart ached. Why could they not just be together? And yet, who was to say there would be anything or anyone to return to, even if the Embassy succeeded? So much seemed to have died with his second father, he thought; and his grief broke through, and the tears came. Tork croaked mournfully from the huge tree above the graveyard. The sky was grey and he longed for the cool, dry, bright forests of Greystone. He shook his head at the bird. 'Not yet,' Tomas murmured. 'We're not finished yet. There's still work for us to do.'

Back at the Tall House, the old magi sat with Tomas and Ioseth at the parlour table. 'I know, lads, you must feel like you've been hit by an elephant,' said Michellos. 'We want you to know, as Ben's students, you are as family to us.'

Ioseth seemed to have something in his eye. Tomas said, 'We thank you...' but could think of nothing more to say. Michellos simply grabbed his upper arm and gave a sad smile.

'Now, there is trouble brewing in this land,' he said. 'We left Westerhaven when the witches gained favour with the Crown,' Iremias said, 'We always expected that sooner or later, they would start harassing us here, too. Now, Taria has spoken to the people she knows, we may be able to get over the border with a little help.'

'To go where?' Erolinde said with mild exasperation. This was an old argument, now. Even Tomas had heard all the ins and outs of it. 'The Forest People will not accept us, and the place is crawling with the biggest elephants in creation!'

'Not to mention other crawlies,' Taria shuddered. She hated the giant crickets that lived on this rainy, forested island.

'A message came while we were gone,' said Michellos. 'It was held at the shop for Ben, so I took it. I think it might be from the Embassy.' He broke the wax seal at the end of the bamboo tube and shook out a piece of paper. Michellos read it, and placed it on the table for all to read.

Contact made. Events are moving, I cannot say more. Stay where you are, do not leave the house.

H

'Could he possibly have been a little more cryptic?' asked Iremias sarcastically. 'I suppose this means we can't leave after all.'

'What do we do?' asked Erolinde. 'If we stay, the witches may try to attack again.'

'We can wait, for a day or so,' said Taria.

'All right,' said Erolinde. That gives us time to pack.'

'And I know you might not feel like it, lads,' said Michellos, 'but can you keep at the books for another night? I'd like to know we've found all we can, before we go.'

Ioseth grunted, obviously unimpressed; but Tomas saw the night stretch out before him like a long, dark, dreary corridor. He knew he wouldn't sleep, he might as well work.

That night, while Ioseth kept busy doing nothing in particular, Tomas looked for anything and everything concerning araneladi. It was a cool, rainy evening that Tomas came across a few clues in a new book by a loreman called Matteos. He had not expected to find anything there, but was simply skimming through it, since it was that rare thing, a printed book in Southlandish. The teacher wrote that eladi had a power against darkness that men had not, because of their brightness. The darkness simply hated them, and they could see through it quite easily, and were able to escape if touched; but, because they were bound to the earth spiritually as well as physically, they had no authority over the darkness, which began before space and time.

Men, on the other hand, according to Matteos, had practically no power against darkness in their natural state, because they were born with a tendency towards it ('facing towards it', the eladi said). The inclination could only be overcome by conscious, daily re-aligning. However, because their souls survived unchanged in the world beyond the grave, they had an authority over parasitic spirits that eladi simply did not possess; and if they consciously chose the Light over the Shadow at every opportunity, their power was almost divine.

Tomas wrote down the notes with interest. He remembered old Limlot saying something about the different destinies of men and eladi a long time before, in the days just before he was apprenticed to Ben. He had been walking with Limlot, Ben and Liriel along the pathways of Greystone in the cool of the evening. It seemed so very long ago. A sigh escaped him. He had lost all three of those people, one way or another, one of them forever. His motivation sagged, and he spent a while with his memories of happier times, staring out of the window at the dark, dank sky.

The following morning, Ioseth happened to see the book and the notes he had made. 'Now, that's interesting,' he said to Tomas.

'What is?'

'Eladi have strength, but not the authority; men have the authority, but not the strength.' Ioseth was gesturing, as if holding things in either hand. 'Where do you think that leaves you, as both?'

Tomas stood still. He thought for a time, and said, 'Either with neither strength nor authority, or –' he stopped, speechless.

Ioseth nodded. 'When that assassin went after you, the night Master Ben was killed, I saw everything. You told him to stop, and he did.'

Tomas' eyes widened. The possibility was staggering. 'Do you think I was commanding the taint haunting him? That could be horribly dangerous,' he said. 'I've been exposed to evil before, and they already know my name, or at least part of it. Remember I told you about that kchaban prisoner, and Master Aravon?'

'Well,' said Ioseth, 'you got away with it with the assassin.'

'That's true,' said Tomas.

Ioseth sat down on his side of the desk. 'Maybe you could protect yourself, in some way.'

Tomas said, 'It's not that simple.' Tomas got up and walked to the window. 'The Shadow almost infinitely more intelligent that I ever will be. Tricking me into choosing the wrong would be easy. If I try and control it... who knows what could happen?'

'Good point,' Ioseth admitted. 'It would find a way around you, eventually.'

'Exactly,' Tomas said. 'At least it explains what happened the other night; but I think I'd better leave well enough alone.' The possibility was intriguing, however. Tomas thought he could imagine how to do it, too.

It was the New Moon, the beginning of the second month. They were ready to leave, regardless of Master Helder's message. In the little square with its eladan-looking fountain, a small crowd had gathered under the trees on the south side of the square, looking at the notices on the door of the haildom. The doors were used as notice-boards, their wood pocked by years of nails used to hold up sheets of vellum, papyrus or paper. Tomas had seen a crowd down there occasionally, reading the news or listening while others read it who could. Taria went out that afternoon, to see what was so interesting. She came back at a jog, scattering chickens as she went. Inside, she called, 'Tomas!'

Tomas stopped peeling his carrots. 'What?' He caught the note of urgency in her voice.

'The news, on the notices - the king has made peace with the Slave Coast!'

'What? That's insane! Peace between age-old enemies?'

Peace between a kingdom where witches held sway, and the land where Halfmen walked the streets? This news could be very bad. He picked up his stick and walked out.

Under the trees, he peeped over the shoulders of two shorter people to see the notice. His first thought was, this is well done, that loreman had a sure hand. An old man standing nearby asked, 'What does it say? Who can read this?' Tomas started to read out loud for his benefit:

'King Targon X, Lord of the Men of the South, Overlord of the Highlands, Protector of
the Far Coasts, &c., Announces with Great Pleasure, the Signing of an Accord of Peace
with the Peoples of the Slave Coast. This brings to an end Centuries of
Hostility and Unfriendship, and Inaugurates a New Era of Peace, Free Trade and Pecuniary
Benefit between our Two Lands.
'In Harmony with the New Understanding, and to Provide a ready Source of Trade Goods,
the Rest Year next year is Abolished, and those currently in Bondage Will Not be freed as

is customary. They will instead be shipped to the Slave Coast. A further Decree has been
issued, that any Freeman not in continuous, day-long employment between Midwinter and
the Equinox will be deemed Unfit for Freedom. Such a man, together with all his House,
will be sold to the Slavers and his Property Revert to the Crown. There will be Other
Measures Announced in due course, to Raise the Slave Population to Acceptable Levels.'

Tomas could not help himself: 'What a load of tripe!' He exclaimed. 'Since when has he been Overlord of the Highlands, anyway?' There was a scattering of laughter from the listeners – Tomas' accent had been quite strong as he said it – but most people looked around, their faces concerned. This was a bad time to be unemployed. Tork had perched on one of the branches above, and watched with some interest. One woman raised the question everyone was wanting to ask: 'Does that apply to Greenland, as well?'

Nobody knew, but Tomas was willing to bet that it was intended to.

The second month came, and there was great tension in Falmallinar. The feeling did not come from the weather, it had been fine and warm for several days already, in a land where it seemed to rain a lot of the time. By the evening of the first day, the atmosphere felt thunderous, though the sky was clear. Men went to their beds with no idea of the storm that was about to break.

CHAPTER XII

On the second day of the second month, in the Two Thousand Seven Hundred and Sixth year since the coming of the Seafarers, the forest eladi of Greenland invaded the Southlands.

It was done with admirable efficiency: in the middle of the night, with the watch keeping only token vigilance, a column of heavy cavalry struck with unbelievable speed, isolating the only large city of the men of the south in Greenland. Simultaneously, a fleet of large, well-equipped ships, far outclassing the Southlander caravels, cut off every human port in the human-held part of the island. The fleet must have taken some time to build, but they had had time: Westerhaven and the Slave Coast had been getting closer for years.

The first Tomas knew of the invasion was when a herald rode into their little square, calling all able-bodied men to arms, and telling them to report to the Palace without delay. What arms they could bear, in a land where such were forbidden to men, Tomas never found out.

It was too late. The whole of Falmallinar was visible from the forested hills above it, and those hills were in the hands of the forest people by sunset. The city was completely without fortifications, as specified by the ancient agreement, so a siege was out of the question. From what Tomas heard later, it seemed that the eladi had made extensive use of space-folding, and small forces could literally appear anywhere without warning, especially where there were no trees to obscure the view, as in the northern strip of Greenland. On the night after the Invasion, a small band of warrior-magi simply materialised in the tower of the Governor's Palace, and took the Governor and all his family hostage. Resistance crumbled a matter of hours later. The invasion took all of three days, and there were fewer than a hundred casualties, all of them human.

On the fourth day after the invasion, on a gloriously sunny day, a grand parade was held, to which all the people of Falmallinar were bidden. Tomas, Ioseth and the elder magi watched spellbound as the strange army marched through the main road of the town, from the harbour to the castle. The eladi of the Far South of the world were deathly pale, their eyes lighter and more slanted than those of Elder from the Sunlands; they were Moreladi, Dark eladi. The Celadii, the Seafarers, had a glamour like sunlight on cool grass in the morning. The invaders did not have the same glint of blessedness about them. Their power was of a more primal nature, darker, less joyful. First came light foot soldiers, sparely armoured, armed with very long bows and short swords; then came heavy infantry, carrying long *enctii* or two-handed maces with long, elegant heads, and armoured in mail; then mounted archers, riding unbridled quaha with strange, broad, light brown stripes, which faded to brown on the neck instead of the withers; following them came a cavalry detachment wearing armour made of overlapping steel scales, bearing shields of burnished steel and long-headed lances. Their helms were high and plumed with ostrich-feathers, and covered their faces.

In the midst of some of the heavy cavalry detachments rode a group of unarmoured magi, their loose tunics and hose (or riding-dresses for the eladan-women) of strangely colourless cloth, each a slightly different shade. All wore decorated leather helms which reminded Tomas of the eladi in Greystone. Their robes seemed to blend into any background, and they bore staves of dark ironwood, each with an eldastone set in the top.

At the end of the parade came a sight that made everyone catch their breath: elephant cavalry. Tomas gaped, saying to Ioseth, 'If only Master Ben could have seen this!' It was the first time either of them had ever seen elephants in the flesh.

Each armoured elephant was driven by a heavily-armoured elado on its neck, but on its back was a mail-clad wooden box, with a heavy crossbow mounted on a stock. There were two eladi in each box, armed with lances and bows. The flanks of the huge beasts were hung with heavy canvas and hide.

Right at the back on unarmoured elephants came more magi, wearing tulmes of some rich fabric, again with the strange shifting colours. In the midst of this last group, on a gilt-edged, open-topped palanquin borne by an elephant with tusks longer than a man was tall, rode an Eladan Lord and Lady, wearing simple, dazzling white robes. The lord wore a strange crown, a high-backed circlet of polished black wood with a crest of gold attached to the back, like a fan. The lady wore a net of silver on her braided auburn hair, set with emeralds and rubies, and a necklace of lapis lazuli and large tigers eyes.

The parade wound its way to the Gatehouse of the Governor's Palace, where the governor surrendered his Badges of Office to the king, in full view of the public.

The King of Greenland then made a short speech, first in his own tongue, then in that of the Southlands. By some art of his people, his voice was audible to every man on the route of the Parade:

'My people, and men of Greenland: I greet you all in peace! I am King Arandamundon of the Tree-fern Lands, and I bear you no ill-will. However, your kin beyond the Strait of Storms have become enemies of all the Elder Children, by entering into a pact with the Foul Folk. Therefore, to prevent the threat of a Foul presence to this Island, it has become necessary to revoke the lease that has applied here for some seven centuries. Again I say, we bear you no ill will. There will be no despoiling of your settlements, nor of your property, nor will there be any punishment meted out to those who opposed my people by force of arms. However, any future threat of armed resistance will be met by all force necessary to extinguish it.

'We are aware that there are those among you who have fled from oppression and injustice. To them, we extend the hand of friendship, and offer an alliance against those who formerly oppressed you. To others, we offer the chance of taking part in the liberation of your people on the continent from the worst kind of enslavement imaginable. Aid us, and you will be rewarded. Aid us not, and we will not coerce you – but thwart us not, lest you make yourselves our enemies.'

'As of this day, the rule of the King of Seafaring Men on this island is brought to an end, forever. All free speaking peoples, man and elado, are made subjects of the Law of Greenland. Any slaves currently bound will be freed, in accordance with your Tradition, on the first day of next year. Any landlords will be relieved of their duties, with due compensation offered where merited.

'As for the townspeople, they may continue their business as normally as possible. I wish everyone peace and prosperity.'

In the silence that finished there was a loud murmur from the crowds. They had reversed the abolition! The patricians were going to get their comeuppance! There was some indignant shouting, but on the whole, the humans thought they had got off very lightly. The poor slaves were ecstatic.

The crowds dispersed, but the taverns and teahouses were very busy that day, as men wondered whether to mourn or celebrate.

The day after the show of force of the Triumph, Tomas was in the market with Taria, shopping for food supplies which had suddenly become expensive. Suddenly, a tall woman near them was accosted by a group of eladi, a magus and two soldiers. As the armed eladi seized her, she fought back, shouting in a strangely deep voice. Her veil was pulled off in the tussle, and everyone saw that it was a man in disguise. He was bundled off. Tomas and Taria walked warily after that, and the people in the marketplace muttered darkly among themselves.

Later on the way home, they saw an armed elado at the broken-down door of a house. As they watched, some people were taken out of the house, their hands bound behind them, and put on a cart in the street. Taria said, 'That's a witches' house!'

'Well, they're definitely cleaning up the neighbourhood,' said Tomas, adopting Michellos' quiet, sarcastic understatement.

As they moved on, an old man sitting on a water-butt across the street gave a wheezy cackle. Looking straight at them, he said, 'You're next, witches!'

A matter of seconds after they had closed their own door, there was a hammering on it from outside. Tomas answered it, and was confronted by a large group of eladi, all but one of them heavily armed foot soldiers. The exception was a maga with an exceptionally beautiful face, who looked at Tomas as a leopard looks at a lamb. Tomas started involuntarily. The leader of the detachment said, in heavily-accented Southlandish, 'You are all required to accompany us, for inquiries.' The accent was not nearly as elegant as that of Greystone.

Speaking in Celadi, Tomas said, 'May I ask your purpose?'

The eladi looked at him even more piercingly for a few seconds. The predatory maga said something to the officer in a dialect Tomas had never heard before, and the officer said, in Southlandish, 'Ye are wizards. We wish an account of your activities, and your Abilities.' Still in halting Southlandish, he repeated, 'You must accompany us: now.' There was no arguing with such armed insistence.

By now, the elder magi were gathered in the parlour. Tomas stood back, and Michellos stepped forward, saying, 'We shall all come, but one of us is infirm.' He indicated Arcaldo on his armchair by the fire. He had spent a great deal of time there lately.

The maga nodded, and the armed eladi pushed into the house. As the humans watched, the officer levitated the chair with a word, and two of the other eladi started to push Arcaldo out on the now floating chair. Erolinde quickly rearranged his pillows, and made the old man comfortable as was pushed outside. He said with a smile, 'Thank you, Linde. D'you know, this chap's almost as good as I am?'

Everyone collected their staves, and Tomas called Tork, who flew onto his shoulder. The couch was pushed out of the door, and everyone followed. Iremias locked the door behind them.

As the strange group moved down the narrow streets of Falmallinar, some boys came out of nearby houses, shouting and jeering:

'Hey, they've caught some more witches!'

'Kill 'em!'

'Off with their heads!'

One larger lad threw a rock at Arcaldo on his chair. Without batting an eyelid, the old man made a swatting motion, and the rock spun back in mid-air, going back the way it had come. The stone-thrower had to dance out of the rock's way, and swore at them – but there were no more taunts. The maga and the officer exchanged looks.

Tomas, watching the exchange, felt a sudden pull on his mind. Call on Something, it said, call on a Source of Power. Blast those little vermin! Tomas shook it off, but had no time to think further on it.

The party was escorted to the Sheriff's House. The sheriff was nowhere to be seen. The officer read out questions, in his halting Southlandish, about where they came from, what they did, and where they had learned their lore. Some concepts proved difficult to explain, until they used the Ancient Eladon terms, which these eladi seemed to understand. Tomas could understand the ancient language, but only barely speak it. It had only ever been an academic subject at Scribal School, and one which caused most students headaches, since it was so complex. It was extremely beautiful, however, which was one of the reasons why Tomas remembered it.

Eventually, the maga took out a dark red slate, scored with runes. Tomas recognised the runes as a very old type, but the words were in an obscure language. It turned out that the maga could speak their language after all: she said, 'I wish each of you to hold this slate between the palms of your hands,' and gave it to Erolinde. After a few heartbeats, she took the slate back, and gave it to Iremias, Linde's husband. Tomas wondered at that, since the man had no Abilities to speak of, but was a schoolteacher. After that, she gave it to each of the others in turn. Tomas was the last to take it. When he did, he felt a strange kind of lightness and tension from it. He was sure it had been scribed using some kind of Arcane Writing Ability, but there must have been some Inanimate Reflex to it as well. The reflex had a potential for violence, and he was quite glad to give it back.

The maga then said, 'You have all passed the test of the Purity Slate. With the energy this holds, no witch would have been able to hold it without giving themselves away.' Putting the slate away again, she told them 'You are all free to go. Thank you for co-operating with us. You are the first true magi we have seen thus far.' Looking somewhat less predatory than before, she sat back and asked, 'Do you have any questions?'

There was an uncomfortable pause, and then Michellos spoke up. 'What are your intentions? Why do you seek magi and witches?'

The officer said, 'No servant of the Dark can be allowed to practice their deceits on our territory. Your people have a trust broken, by allowing the crafts of evil to be practiced on your land. Your lands are – ' he stuttered as he remembered the word '– cursed.'

The maga carried on, 'For that reason, we cannot allow such evil to be practised here. But that is not all: now that your people are friends with the Fouls, it is only a matter of time until they come against us in force of war. The king has cancelled your lease, in order to make sure that when war comes, it will not be on our island.'

Michellos spoke slowly, 'The king mentioned those who have fled from persecution at home. There are many such as us. I think I speak for all of us here a –' he glanced around, to nods from everyone, '– when I say that we would like to be part of the effort to purge the darkness from the Southlands.'

Taria interrupted, 'But we have children who still live there, and we have not heard from them for some time. Even if they have gone over to the darkness, we still do not wish them to be harmed.'

'On all true magi,' the maga said, 'and on your holy men and women who have not been seduced by darkness, we lay no charge, but request your help... even though it means assisting in warfare against your own kind.' She was not unsympathetic. 'If you will not do this, you may engage in operations far from your home lands, or from the places where your kin lived. If even that is ill to you, then you may remain here, maintaining yourselves as before... though we would appreciate your help.'

'What are you doing with the witches?' asked Erolinde.

'As the Lieutenant mentioned, witches cannot be allowed; since they cannot safely be enslaved, they will have to be put to death.'

'Is that the king's word?' asked Iremias.

'It is.'

'Well, we can't say we didn't expect it,' Michellos said.

During the second month, another letter came from Master Helder. It told Master Ben to pack up, and to come with Tomas and Ioseth to the Market Square on the last day of the month. There, they would meet with Oreladi who would conduct them to the capital, the name of which translated as City-of-Ivory. They had an audience, he said, and he wanted the whole embassy to be present when he made Lord Engolaran's request of the King of Greenland. They were being accommodated at a place called Fern-Dale.

The Embassy had been gone for some time, and there was no way they could tell Master Helder what had happened to Master Ben. All they could do was to collect the reports they had begun on their research, pack what luggage they had, and take their leave. They had to go through Master Ben's things, but true to style, he didn't have much.

The elder magi made them a farewell dinner the night before they left, and gave them some small but useful gifts. They were such good old folks. As Tomas flopped into his bed that night, he looked at their luggage on the desk. 'At least,' he said to Ioseth, 'this discipleship business makes for light travelling.'

Ioseth just grunted.

The elder magi accompanied Tomas and Ioseth to the Market Square the next day, in a drizzle. Tork sat stoically on Tomas' shoulder, hunched in the rain. None knew what to expect. Tomas found a group of five eladi, three men and two women, standing in the rain near one of the fountains, all dressed in long oiled cloaks against the weather. He went up to them and asked in his own language, 'Are you the people from Ferndale?'

'Yes,' said one of the women, twitching her mantle back at the edges to look at him. 'Are you Master Bethnero?'

Tomas said, 'My Master Bethnero is dead.'

One of the male eladi said something in his own language. Tomas could pick out a few words, but make little sense of it.

The one who had spoken to him asked him, 'Who are these others?'

Tomas introduced the elder magi, saying, 'They have been like a family to us since the master was killed. They accompany us only to bid us farewell.'

The eladi greeted the magi respectfully, bowing with hand on heart. Then the translator said, 'My name is Lara. These others are Taureon, Isefiel, Haldier and Cuoron,' Tomas nodded to each in turn. 'We are all initiates. Are you students of the Spiritual Arts?'

Tomas had to think to understand the question. Ioseth asked, 'What arts?' He had never heard Abilities described that way before.

Tomas said, 'I am an initiate, though it has been some time since I sat at the feet of a master. Ioseth is an apprentice.'

'Your art, is it in sympathy with animals?' Lara asked, looking at Tork.

'Yes. This raven came to me on my travels,' Tomas said. 'He will not leave, and I do not mean to chase him away.'

'I would not ask it of you,' said Lara, smiling. 'Are you ready to go?'

'Yes,' said Tomas. Ioseth went back to the elder magi, and embraced each one in turn. Tomas did the same. Again, it was the end of an era.

Taria smiled through brimming eyes, saying, 'Look after yourselves, boys. You will let us know how you're getting on, won't you?'

'We will, mother,' Ioseth said. 'Thank you very much, for everything.'

Then they turned back to the eladi, who had moved over to a tented wagon across from the fountain. As curious passersby watched, Ioseth pulled Tomas up into the back. They waved at the elder magi, standing in the rain and mud of the market square; and that was the last time Tomas ever saw them.

Most of the eladi had only a few words of Southlandish. They had been chosen for this task by their masters only because they knew any at all. Only Lara was fluent, so Tomas and Ioseth chatted her up together. Tomas didn't tell the eladi, but he could understand some of what they said to each other. Their language was very close to the Ancient Eladan he had learned in Scribal School, though spoken much faster as a living language.

The rain cleared up as they rode past the outskirts of the town, between sodden market gardens and orchards showing the first golden leaves. For the next day and a half, they drove through the open country of the human parts of Greenland, well-settled lands for the most part with patches of forest. On the first night, they stayed in an eladan military camp, where the Initiates seemed to command some respect. They stayed in a Southlandish Haildom's hostel on the second night.

The next morning they started early, and passed through countryside increasingly wild. The trees were bigger, the overgrowth by the side of the road taller, and fewer and fewer humans were seen.

Around lunchtime on that day, the road led through the old border-post between the Southlands and Greenland, at the foot of the hills visible from Falmallinar. There stood a thick-walled construction of yellow stone, now abandoned. Beyond the gate the road was newly paved, bordered by thick, tangled undergrowth and young trees. The sun, so much weaker in the cold south of the world, shone silver and mild through fine-leafed evergreen or golden-speckled deciduous trees. Tomas was reminded of the forests of Greystone, but these were wetter, denser and darker. The birds were bigger, their colours different, some were even blue. Tork liked the woods, and often went exploring. For the rest of the day, they travelled along this Merchant's Road, as the eladi called it, spending the night at a pretty little wayside camping-ground, where the 'rooms' were simple, circular thatched huts surrounding a small, muddy field, presently deserted.

The next morning, after following the forest road for some time, they took a path off to the left. The undergrowth was tall and very thick, a secretive mat of large ferns. Occasionally they would cross a stream or small river, where the water ran cold and translucent brown under the trees. The shade under the trees was deep, and they could see no further than a few paces. The trees themselves were huge. Some of the older yellow-woods, all hung with old-mans-beard, had massive trunks wider than Ioseth and Tomas' outstretched arms together. Despite their size, Tomas could 'hear' little of their hearts. They were only conifers.

Occasionally they heard a strange, guttural, hissing caw from the branches, but they seldom saw the animal that made them. Tomas asked in his halting Ancient Eladan what they were, and one of the magi said, 'A *luri*,' a turaco. The word was exactly the same as in Celadi. The birds themselves were quite different to those in Greystone, though – where the Green River birds were grey, these were bright green, with brilliant red flashes on their wings. Unless they flew, they were not easy to see. However, they shared the grey lourie's tittle-tattling: they shadowed the wagon for some distance, making a racket that no animal would be able to miss. 'I wonder if they're warning animals about us,' Ioseth snorted, 'or trying to warn us about animals?'

As the day progressed, the road deteriorated and narrowed. They stopped for lunch under a graceful stand of stinkwoods with buttress roots big enough to sit on, their leaves shining wet in the wan sunlight. In the afternoon, the road ascended a steep slope, making a series of sharp bends. That evening, when the path had levelled out, they slept in a wayside stone structure with a slate-tiled roof. It stood in a clearing as if it had been there since the world was made. It was also circular, and was heavily overgrown with moss on the south side.

Just before sunrise the following morning, they were awoken by a loud, ponderous cracking. Tork was screaming from his perch in the rafters above them. Tomas jerked awake to see a massive, strangely hairy elephant pushing its way through the trees. Ioseth jumped up, but the eladi motioned him to stay still. The elephant looked at them for several seconds, as Tomas' heart hammered at his rib cage. The elephant was a bull, and in a bad mood. Tomas could feel his irritation at the spindly, slow-moving monkeys, but also his reverence: he had respect for eladi, or at least at the moment. After a long, tense moment, the elephant moved away. Heaving a sigh of relief, Ioseth said quietly, 'I wonder what he would have done if there were no eladi here?'

Tork came down from his roost, making concerned 'tok' noises. *Beast surprised me, too!*

To Tomas, the eladi seemed a bit put out by the visit of the elephant, as if they should have expected it. They rolled on south-westwards through the dense forest, a nearly trackless region where men were unwelcome intruders, and even eladi had to negotiate. Fern and tree-ferns were everywhere, and the trees were huge and varied. Apart from the big old yellow-woods, there were hardwoods: two kinds of stinkwood, blackwoods, red and white alders, hard-pears and ironwoods like those in Greystone. They found tracks of duikers, leopards and bushpigs; a few times, they saw shaggy grey monkeys.

At mid-day, they stopped at the base of a slim, gracious waterfall, green and graced with tree-ferns, sparkling cold. After lunch, Taureon, who seemed to be in charge, stood up in front of everyone and said, 'We leave wagon here. Now, we go there,' he pointed up the waterfall. Tomas looked up, horrified. The cliff was at least five storeys tall! He was about to protest, when the elado said, 'We move you,' and grinned. The other eladi all looked amused at Tomas' expression.

As they watched, the Initiate stood at the base of the cliff. Holding his arms out horizontally, he lifted straight up in the air. Tomas saw concentration knotted on his forehead, and his arms shook slightly as he took off, as they supported his weight. Moving slowly at first, he moved up the cliff, then forward to the edge; then he was out of sight.

'Inanimate lifting,' noted Ioseth.

'Speak for yourself,' Tomas grinned.

After a moment, Taureon called down in his own language, and one of the other initiates beckoned to Tomas. 'There,' she ordered, indicating the spot from which Taureon had ascended.

Tomas said to Tork, 'You can fly, I'll see you up there.' Tork sat on a rock, his head cocked up at Tomas in mystification. Tomas did as he was directed, holding out his arms. Wearing his backpack and carrying his walking-stick, he wondered how heavy he would be. All of a sudden, his arms felt like they were being pushed up, and he tensed his shoulders. He rose steadily, until he was halfway up the cliff. Looking down, he saw four eladon faces and one human face gazing up at him. Just as well I changed my underwear yesterday, he thought, chuckling.

Tomas felt a jolt, and heart skipped a beat. He stopped laughing abruptly. His sense of being lifted had suddenly been replaced by one of being pulled up. Tork flew around him, making surprised '*Cor!*' sounds. The raven was almost laughing, something that Tomas had never seen before. He was now level with the top of the cliff, and was being drawn towards Taureon. He got closer, until his feet brushed the ferns, and he felt himself lowered lightly. Then the lift under his arms was no longer there, and he landed softly on the rocky soil.

'Hey! That was great!' he grinned.

Tork landed in a nearby tree. *Men fly!* He said.

'They can't! It was the elado here that made me.'

Taureon ignored him, and called down again. In short order, Ioseth was levitated up, followed by three of the initiates. The last one, Isefiel, walked back a bit, until she could see the others on the cliff edge. Then she vanished, to appear abruptly standing right next to them. Tomas had never seen such brazenly confident space-folding.

'And these are initiates?' He murmured to Ioseth.

The view from the top of the cliff was spectacular. They looked back north, towards the sun and warmer lands. The treetops were still above their level, and the foreground of their view was all waving green. The colours were many: greeny-grey of ironwoods, silvery green of yellowwoods, the gold-spangled stinkwoods, and here and there a dead, black snag from some forgotten forest fire. Beyond that, the land swept down in a graceful concave slope, its contours hidden by old-growth forest, for at least half the distance to the coast. The rest was the open, green country that had belonged to men, until recently. Five days' journey in that direction was the Tall House, and the dear old elder magi who had become a family to Ben's students. Far beyond was the sea, and a shining horizon on the edge of sight. Again, Tomas thought about a land very much further away, where (if the Powers had preserved her) an aranelada with beautiful deep blue eyes lived yet. He sighed. The others were waving at the wagon, as its driver turned about and headed back to the border-post.

Turning about, they faced into yet more trees, and followed the course of the stream that plunged down the cliff behind them. Tomas followed the rest with difficulty, hoping he would not have to walk far. Fortunately, here was another wagon waiting for them in a small way station well back from the cliff. Though it had only 2 very large wheels and was unlike any other transport Tomas had ever seen, it was comfortable and spacious enough for all. Tomas and Ioseth marvelled at the workmanship.The wheels were sprung on metal bands, and the whole thing was drawn by two pale grey quaha, the stripes on their necks pale grey.

For the rest of that day they followed a paved road southwards, until they stopped for the night at an eladan town. Tomas and Ioseth had lived in Greystone, so they knew what to expect, but the first sight of a flourishing eladon settlement was always surprising. Everything was neat, ordered and moulded into the landscape, looking as if it had always been there. There were no middens by the houses, no filth in the streets; there were the chickens, pigs, dogs and cats that were expected; but also tame ibis and louries, some kind of serval, a lynx or two and even a few bushbabies in the evening. The houses were mostly thatched, but in this climate the thatch grew moss, giving the houses a wild, shaggy appearance. All was living, growing, with the touch of the Fair Folk on every stone and beam.

They stayed the night in a house where there were a lot of other travellers, even a few of Ioseth's own species. The men there were talkative, as were the eladi, and they sat up late, engrossed in polyglot conversations. Everyone seemed to want news of the invasion. They eventually got to bed, and it was very good to sleep in proper beds for a change.

They awoke later than usual the following morning, and enjoyed a big eladan breakfast, which consisted mostly of fruit. They were on the road again soon afterwards, the party eager to get to Ferndale. Around noon that day, they came to an open stretch, where the trees seemed to be losing their hold on the landscape. After an all too brief stop for lunch, they crested a rise and came within sight of a marvel: a city of purest white, gleaming in the afternoon sun like a scattering of pearls, filling a large part of the horizon to the south.

'See!' said one of the initiates. 'The Ivory City!'

Tomas just drank it in. Ioseth gaped in wonder, saying, 'By all the gods!' under his breath. They were dazzled at the City of the Elephant Throne. It still seemed so far away, Tomas thought, but it was so huge! There were towers, turrets, steeples and bell-towers, domed roofs and curled gables, all in gleaming, creamy white. Between the buildings tall trees raised their heads. The structures were actually quite far apart, but there were *so many* of them! Even Tork sat still for a change, looking at the place.

As they moved through the townlands, they saw pastures where herds of strange, white cattle or golden-dusted ostrich moved. The orchards were wide, planted with a variety of trees all growing together.

Their entrance to the city was quiet and unhurried. The city walls were only lightly manned, by eladi in strangely ceremonial uniforms. If Tomas and Ioseth had first entered Greystone gawping, this time they were speechless. The size and beauty of the buildings, and the numbers and beauty of the eladi living there, amazed them. He and Ioseth in turn attracted stares, from eladi who had never seen men before. The gazes turned towards him were fascinated and amused in equal parts.

They came to a tall, graceful set of buildings, arranged around ornamental gardens of many-greened trees. All of seven storeys high at its central point, the main building was crowned by a white dome. The buildings in the Ivory City had none of the wide eaves that Greystone had. The walls of these buildings were smooth and white, with ornamental details picked out in muted shades of blue, yellow, green, or orange. Figures of animals on the pillars, pediments and roof-edges were painted in lifelike colours. Escorted through the tall, arched doors in travel-stained clothing, smelling like primates, the students were acutely conscious of their own meanness and ignorance. The main atrium was an echoing space, roofed above by a fretted dome of translucent aragonite tiles. It was surrounded by five floors of balconies, all supported by eight pairs of massive pillars. Tork took off, flying around just for the sake of seeing the place. The floor was patterned with stones of different colours, worn smooth by centuries of eladi feet, the harder stone standing out above the softer. There they were told to wait, while their guides consulted with some eladi in long grey robes.

Then the initiates wished them well and left, and the grey eladi showed them through the building, out onto a wide lawn patrolled by ibis and strange, long-tailed birds. Tomas so wanted to stop and rest under one of the trees, but they kept on, across the close-mown grass to what seemed to be a patch of forest. Summer seemed to linger in this garden, with only a few of the trees showing gold. Among the trees were circular houses of stone, and they were shown to one of the larger dwellings. They entered. There, waiting to meet them, were Master Helder and the ambassadors.

'Tomas and Ioseth,' the master said, smiling, 'you are welcome. Where is the master?'

'Master,' Tomas said, bowing, 'We are the only ones left. Master Ben was killed...' he stuttered and trailed off.

Master Helder stood, solemn-faced. He looked just the same as he always had back in Greystone, except he was wearing soft hide shoes now, where he had never worn them in the Sunlands. He indicated a table and chairs, long-legged in human style, indicating they should sit. 'Tell us everything,' he said.

Tomas and Ioseth sat down, and someone poured them some of those eladon cordials, tingling with vitality. It had been made by someone with a Healing Ability, Tomas thought. The drink washed away his joint pain, but his weariness remained, for it went deeper than his physical self. He told the story, leaving nothing out. Ioseth took over when he forgot, or lost the train.

At the end, Master Helder said, 'This day has brought woeful news, as I thought it would in the beginning. How apt that it should come from a man with a raven.' He sighed heavily. Bethnero had been his student. 'At least you two have survived. If you both achieve half of what Bethnero did, you will bring great hope to us all. There will be some human blood at least when we make our petition to King Arandamundon.

'We have been granted Ambassadorial status,' he replied to Tomas' expression of surprise 'and our audience is day after tomorrow. I had hoped that we could have a genuine human master in the party, to make the point that humans are not as much a pestilence as kchabani; as it is, I shall need the two of you in plain view throughout the proceedings.

'For now, the One has favoured you, and you are here just in time. The elder magi, as you term them, deserve our heartfelt gratitude.'

'They showed us every kindness, Master,' Ioseth said.

'If we had had the means, I would have left them something in return,' said Tomas, 'But we have nothing.'

'Nor would they expect you to have, as students,' Master Helder said. 'We shall make it up to them as best we can, when we can. For now, you may share Master Bethnero's living-space. We leave for the Ivory City tomorrow morning.'

Ioseth later found out that the place where they were staying was a college guest house. The living conditions were spare, but comfortable. Around mid-morning the following day, the embassy and their bodyguards took a comfortable, four-wheeled coach drawn by two pairs of quaha, and drove along the main highway towards the City. Riding in comfort, Tomas could appreciate the scale of the place. What had seemed like a vast pile of white stone the day before was really a family of smaller towns, each nestling in extensive gardens and parkland. Green space was a part of all eladon settlements.

Around noon, they reached the Water-Lily Palace. The entrance to the main complex was a slender, white bridge over a wide, shallow pond with patches of water-lilies. As they passed over, Tomas saw a vast complex of marble and limestone structures, combining minutely-carved detail with giant scale. The complex occupied an entire hill of the city. The coach was left at the gatehouse, and they continued on foot, following a guide who had waited for them. For once, they moved at a slow enough pace for Tomas to keep up. Even the eladi wanted to go slowly, just to appreciate the scale of the place. They walked and walked, taking the long way around to the Ambassadors' Reception, around several of the numerous courtyards. In those open spaces grew gardens, or perhaps they had been left wild when the place was built. Some of the courtyards they passed harboured fountains. The buildings around them had gracious, sweeping lines, which made even the grand forts of Westerhaven look second-rate.

They came to their suite, thickly carpeted and well-lit by skylights and tall windows. There were few solid walls, most partitions being wood-and-fabric screens that could be moved to let in the daylight and air. After so much travelling, Tomas could have quite cheerfully slept on that carpet, but he and Ioseth had proper beds in a room of their own next door to Master Helder's. Tomas could easily get used to living here

– as long as certain people could join him, he thought with a smile.

They were told to present themselves in the Throne Room at the stroke of the fifth hour of daylight of the following day, to make their petition. In the meantime, they were to be joined for dinner by a Lord Dragelion, the head of the Beastmasters' Hall.

That evening, scrubbed and changed, they sat around a table bearing silver and fine crystal, the furniture higher above the ground than the Greystone eladi were used to. Lord Dragelion could speak their language, since he had been a student of a master among the eladi in the Cedar Mountains, several centuries before. He was accompanied by his wife and seven children, whose ages ranged from under a hundred to three centuries. After some time, there was a flapping from the window, and Tork hopped in to the room. Tomas had tried to lock the bird in, but the light, airy architecture had allowed the raven to find his human. He flew onto the back of Tomas' chair, and said, 'Yummy!' in Tomas' voice. He clacked his heavy beak. It was his way of asking for a snack.

Tomas was embarrassed. He didn't want to be responsible for bird fouling in this decorated chamber. 'I thought I told you to stay!' He fumed at the bird. 'I was going to bring you some!'

Hungry, said the raven, *too dark to find food. Big owl outside, dangerous.*

Tomas didn't know what to do. He couldn't just up and leave to feed the bird. He looked around, to see everyone staring at him.

The lord's youngest child, a golden-skinned eladan-girl of only about eighty, was grinning broadly. Her name was Telie. She said something in her own language, which Tomas only barely understood. She picked up a piece of ostrich meat in her fingers, and offered it to Tork. The bird cocked his head, but didn't move.

'You can take it,' Tomas said in his own language, 'she won't hurt you.'

Tork hopped onto the table, but he wasn't sure. As everyone watched, he edged towards the girl and snatched the meat from her fingers, swallowing it quickly.

Lord Dragelion said, 'I see we have an Initiate here who is of the Younger. What is your name, O Man?'

'I am Tomas, your lordship,' Tomas said, rising and bowing. He noticed the elado had strange tawny eyes, almost yellow in a face that was pale. He had long, black hair, held back with a thick brass band. The combination was striking.

'Did you raise that raven from the egg?' he asked.

'No, My Lord,' answered Tomas. 'He came to me in the Cedar

Mountains, and has been with me ever since.'

The elado looked surprised. 'The Cedar Mountains? Is that so?' He looked thoughtful, as if remembering something. 'Do you know, I used to know a raven, when I was an Initiate there. The whole tribe was on good terms with the people there. They were excellent watchers.'

'So is he, lord.'

'He might even be descended from the ones I knew... wonderful! Do you have an Ability in Animal Sympathy?'

'Yes, Lord. I was studying to be a magus when I came.'

'You say you were? Did you abandon the study?'

'My master...' Tomas began, but Helder butted in.

'His master suffered exposure to the darkness. He had been interrogating a Foul. There was no time to find anyone to take his place before we left.'

'I thought the Greystone Valley was where Master Rangolo lived?' Lord Dragelion asked.

'He left a long time ago,' said Magus Noromen, shaking his head. 'He went with the elephants.'

Dragelion nodded. 'I see. There is a tale to tell here, I think, but perhaps not at the moment. Well, this initiate seems to be quite gifted. If he has already bonded with an animal, I would take that as a sign of his maturity, perhaps even mastery in due course.'

Talking of his Ability reminded Tomas of his training. Master Ben had thought he might find a Master in the south. Taking a gamble, he decided to risk asking. It could be the best, perhaps the only chance he would get. 'My lord,' he blurted, 'Since you mention it, I wondered if there might be some place for me as a student in the Beastmaster's Hall?'

Masters and magi stopped dead. It was an audacious request.

'Well,' Lord Dragelion was quite surprised, 'I think there may be...' his expression slowly changed from surprised to thoughtful.

Master Helder stepped in suddenly. 'This initiate is very anxious to resume his instruction, lord. He would not find a master among men, and his people are in Greystone.'

Tomas noted the master's attribution of his origins.

Lord Dragelion noted it, too. He said, 'His people? Are there men in the Green River Valley, too?'

'No, My lord,' said Helder. 'Tomas is of mixed heritage. Though he may not look it, he has a rare balance of blood. Many of his ancestors were of our people.'

Tomas was grateful to the master – but Lord Dragelion's expression briefly showed some distaste, before being politely controlled.

He looked thoughtfully at Helder, saying, 'It would be a sign of faith in each other, would it not, if one of your initiates took his final tests with us?' Master Helder nodded.

'Yes, my lord,' Tomas replied. 'I greatly desire to be a magus, and to help clear the Fouls from my homeland. I have wanted that for years, now. Your college is my best hope.'

Caranto the wise made a pointed observation: 'Of course, he also wants to return to a certain aranelada in Greystone!'

Everyone laughed, and Tomas blushed. Lord Dragelion said, 'Truly, that motivation is better than most! Now I know he will succeed,' and laughed heartily. It was not a sound often heard from eladi.

'Well, O Tomas,' said the lord, 'If you would like to join the college for a few moons, to fit in, and get to know the language and so on, then I can find a place for you on the trials in the spring. Are you willing to commit to that?'

Tomas' jaw dropped. He stuttered, 'Yes! Except, um, I haven't meditated very much lately.'

'That doesn't seem to be a problem, does it? Your Ability is still strong enough for you to interact with a highly intelligent bird.'

Tomas could not believe his luck. Mixed with his apprehension was a deep feeling of rightness, as if this was exactly what he was meant to do.

'I should mention that payment for the instruction is seven years' working for the King's Charity. The Charity is a group of skilled people from all walks of life, who work for the Royal Exchange, doing work for the poor, or the Crown, for free. It's the way they pay the Crown back for supporting them through their studies.'

'I should still be grateful for the chance, lord,' said Tomas. Seven years?

'I don't think you will have to do seven years, though, since you would only be with me for six months. I can give you a warrant for short service. I believe a year is some time to you people.'

Tomas was extremely grateful. Suddenly, he was on top of the world. Ioseth smiled, muttering to him in their language, 'You lucky swine! You've really landed in the butter, now!' To cap it all, Tomas became the centre of attention for the rest of the evening, as Tork shamelessly begged scraps from everyone. Towards the end of the evening, with the wine flowing and the musical instruments out, Tork started playing around: he picked up the long condiment spoons and dropped them on people's hands, sticky end first. Tomas laid the bird on his back, scratching his belly feathers, making Telie shriek with laughter. Later on, Tork played 'find the pea' with her, even getting it right most times.

That bird is really clever, Tomas thought.

As he consumed more alcohol, Tomas found himself less able to communicate with Tork; the situation only became worse when Telie gave Tork some of her wine. Strangely enough, as Tomas became less able to communicate with the bird, he was sure he understood Telie more and more.

Eventually, even the eladi started talking very loudly, and Tomas decided he had had enough. He stood up and excused himself, holding his arm out for Tork. Tork hopped very unsteadily along the table, and toppled right off the edge. Luckily for him, a chair broke his fall. There were hoots of laughter from all present, and even Master Helder was laughing out loud. Tomas bundled up the raven and took him back to his room. Ioseth stayed a little longer, but followed soon after.

It was probably because of intoxication that the sun had been up for quite a while when Tork came in, sitting and cawing on the end of Tomas' bed. Tomas got up and went to look out of his window, into the courtyard. The shadow on the sundial below showed just short of the fifth hour! They were due in Court within minutes!

'Ioseth!' Tomas shouted, slapping the man's feet as he passed his bed, 'Get up! Now! We're late!'

Ioseth sat up, blinking owlishly. 'What time is it?'

'Nearly the fifth hour. Eleven hours of the clock, in our reckoning. We have to be in the Throne Room, almost immediately!'

Ioseth cursed colourfully and got up. 'It's strange,' he noted as he came out of the garderobe, 'I'm not much hung over.'

'That eladon wine is good stuff,' Tomas said, combing his hair. 'Very fine, no impurities.'

Ioseth frantically washed his face. 'Just as well we don't have to shave.'

'Yes,' laughed Tomas. 'We've been getting steadily shaggier since we left the Highlands. Come, Tork!' The raven flapped onto Tomas' shoulder.

They dressed in the grey togas that had been left out for them the previous night. Then, slamming the door shut behind them, they made their way down the red-granite staircase, sandals slapping and Tomas' walking-stick clacking. Eladi passed them by, looking disdainfully at their bearded faces and haste. 'Carry on,' Tomas told Ioseth, 'I'll catch up. Try and slow things down.'

Ioseth hurried on ahead.

Tomas heard a bell beginning to toll the hours just as he came in sight of the mighty, gilded, yellowwood doors of the Throne Room, which they had passed the day before. He was now late! Breaking into an agonising run, he saw the doors opening as if on command, and the Greystone magi swept solemnly in, all in green-grey togas. Ioseth and Caranto hung back slightly, giving him a sliver of time to catch up. Beyond them, a vast, honey-coloured, echoing space beckoned, coloured by polished stone and mosaics, lit by numerous tall windows. It was fabulous. Tomas stopped running, his left hip in agony, as he first glimpsed the Elephant Throne. Twice, three times a speaking being's height it stood, a vast gilt statue of an elephant's head, with a tall-backed, yellowwood throne nestled in front of the trunk. Huge tusks of mother-of-pearl swept down from the elephant's face on either side of the throne. Seated on that throne was the same inscrutable elado that Tomas had last seen on that huge grandfather elephant, the day after the eladi had taken back Falmallinar. He wore plain white, as usual, and his beautiful, ageless face watched the embassy as they entered. Forcing himself to a last, hopefully-unnoticed burst of speed, Tomas managed to reach the doors just as they had opened to their farthest extent.

'Thanks,' Tomas said quietly, speaking out of the corner of his mouth. He thought, Heavens, but this hurts! He leaned heavily on his stick. One of the magi glanced back, his eyes ordering silence. Tomas fought to keep moving at the same sweeping pace as the rest of the embassy, saying to himself, 'They need this back home, they're counting on us; Liriel's counting on me; Ben would have wanted it.' The pain and memories made his eyes smart.

At last, they reached a golden line of stone set in the floor. The assembled host of courtiers watched, a fey garden of muted colour and light under tall greenstone pillars. The steward made the introductions, and Tomas caught the phrase, 'Tomas the Lame, an Initiate of Greystone.' He genuflected on his bad leg at the appropriate moment, then levered himself up again.

After the introductions, the king said 'Make your –' and a word which Tomas didn't know.

Master Helder spoke in his own dialect, announcing who he was and where he came from, his ancestry and his profession. What Tomas could understand of it sounded quite grand. Then he said something else which Tomas could not quite catch; and to Tomas' lasting shock, turned to him and said in an undertone, in Southlandish, 'I want you to read this. You are both man and elado, and it is fitting that we should make our petition in the name of both our species. Read the passage on the other side, it's in your own language. I shall translate.'

Tomas felt like ice was growing on his face. His mouth suddenly dry as winter, he took the piece of paper from the master, and moved forward. He recognised the writing. It was Ben's.

If Tomas had been on time, if he had been physically able, he might have sounded dignified and restrained. However, his exertion and the resultant pain, combined with the memories that loaded the handwriting, coloured his presentation. He found himself reading Lord Engolaran's message with energy and hurt and sorrow in his voice – and he could feel the reaction of the assembled eladi to his message, as Master Helder translated every passionate phrase.

> Lord Engolaran of the High House of Gilyad, to the Ruler of the Elder Children in Greenland, greetings and blessings in the name of the One.
>
> The territory of Greystone is home to many of the Elder Race, as Your Majesty knows. Here between the Highlands and the Thornlands dwell many who are descended from the Seafaring Elders of old. Here, too, are many who in these later days are called Oreladi, or who count them as kin.
>
> Although we have maintained our lands in peace for many ages, war is now aflame such as has not been known for many centuries in the Wide-Sky Lands. A monstrous assault is upon us, and our foes, the warped ones, are stronger and more dire than ever we have faced. In times gone by, the Foul Folk have been contained by ourselves with the aid of the peoples of men with whom we have friendship. Alas, the assault of evil has fallen earlier and harder upon them in these times, and their realms have been laid low. We have called for help from Westerhaven across the water from your lands, but these have betrayed us, being deceived by the arts and stratagems of the enemy.
>
> My lord, I fear for the existence of the Speaking Peoples in the South of the World in the current crisis. If there is any entreaty I can make for your timely and mighty intervention, I would make it most fervently. In a short space of time, perhaps less than a cycle or two of seasons, there may be no strength of the Elder or Younger between the spreading cancer of the Foul Folk and your own lands. For though by folly some men have allied themselves with the Enemy, they too will be consumed in due course.
>
> Should you respond favourably to this entreaty,

my people and those men allied to us will be truly grateful, especially in those territories which we have heretofore been under the care of the Men of the South.

  We await your answer with keen anticipation.

  Yours humbly

    Engolaran, Lord Argilyado

  As the last translated phrase slid gracefully off Master Helder's tongue, there came a silence. Tomas was keenly aware of many gazes, both long and deep. He felt a wave of solidarity from the assembled courtiers, so intense that it brought a lump to his throat.

  Like a trumpet into the silence, the king said something in his own language. It sounded like a rhetorical question. Then, he said something of which Tomas could make some sense: he said, resolutely and with feeling, 'Yes! We shall aid our people in the North.'

  Master Helder murmured, 'We have succeeded, brothers. Let us give thanks.' He went down on one knee, and the entire embassy followed suit, their ironwood staves standing like the bare branches of a burnt forest. There was a murmur from the Court, which swelled to a muted roar. The embassy rose as Master Helder said to Tomas, 'Well done, O Tomas. Your passion spoke louder than words.'

CHAPTER XIII

In the ancient, tree-clad lands of the Far South of the world, war was planned against the Foul presence in the hot north. The Embassy saw preparations already begun: indeed, they must have begun more than a year previously. As the armament proceeded, and ships were built, and fighters mustered, the Elephant Throne turned its gaze on the coasts of the Swift Rivers country, where the kings of men had little influence. If there was a chance of getting past the Evil Alliance, it was in that torrid country, where the tribes of men were ancient and stubbornly independent. It was the greatest preparation for war that Greenland had ever seen, even in a thousand years of simmering tribal warfare. Events moved, but for Tomas it meant a resumption of his training, and perhaps a chance to return to those he had left behind. For the present, he bid farewell to Ioseth, who would continue his apprenticeship with Master Helder.

At Midwinter, the sixth month of the year, when the Ivory City was a gleam of pearl under heavy grey cloud, Tomas went to live with the initiates in the Beastmasters' College. Suddenly, he was immersed in the culture of Greenland eladi. If not for regular contact with Master Helder, and without Celadi-speaking students from the mainland, he would have suffered serious culture shock. Fortunately, he remembered some Ancient Eladi, so his Moreladon came on quite well: he soon found out that his nickname *Ovanmar* meant 'ugly bloke'.

Tomas' Ability in Animal Sympathy was stretched to its limit in his time there. He often went to bed physically exhausted, but he had seldom had so much fun working with animals. He attracted interest and sometimes suspicion from the other students in the first few days, so he shaved off his long-standing beard, so as to look less alien. Lord Dragelion's support had been made known somehow. He was welcomed in word and deed by the other initiates, but never befriended. His studies were completely unencumbered by any social activity. It was not as hard as it seemed.

Tomas found out that there were several different nations of oreladi represented at the College, each with its own dialect, but everyone was obliged to converse in Old Eladon at all times. Ethnic differences were set aside, the discipline of detachment preventing strife.

Tomas was more welcomed by Galdie and Henvaro, a couple who had met in the College and planned to marry when they had qualified. They were part of a rather egg-headed group of friends. Their arguments were long and interesting, and Tomas even started to contribute as he mastered the language, though he was sometimes ignored.

For their part, Galdie and Henvaro were fascinated by someone so young who seemed so mature. They saw him as some kind of savant, and told everyone so.

Tomas' time at the college was at times a personal trial, despite the triumph of learning so much, so fast. Living with suspicion and lack of human contact, on a bad day his thoughts turned to darkness in the night: while eladi were socialising to all hours, he tried to rest, but could not forget what Ioseth had said: *Where do you think that leaves you, as both?* Time and again, he wondered if he could control evil like that in the assassin, and get away with it. By the time the seasons turned again, the temptation was a nightly event, conquered only by conscious detachment.

Eventually, as the seasons turned and alders greened again in the bright southern sunlight, the time for Testing came round. Those judged ready were invited to take the Ordeal for the degree of magus. Among them were Tomas and the Galdie-and-Henvaro crowd. The young couple promptly got married very quietly: the others only found out when they arrived at the breakfast table one morning wearing their new jewellery. Everyone congratulated them.

Over his time in the College, Tomas had been told about the Ordeal. It took place a few day's journey from the Ivory City, on the eastern plains in the island's interior. Most of the plains were limestone terrain, where the soil was thin and there were many caves. Along the southern edge of the plains ran the Blackfoot River.

The test for Animal Sympathy students was simple: to make your way across the plain, from the volcano called Eradero on the western end to the coast at Ardcalen, in ten days or less. Apart from the fact that it was impossible to do it on foot in that time, there was the small complication that the student was only allowed to take a small tinderbox, a bag for food and a water-bottle, one blanket and a specially-crafted long knife, which would be theirs if they finished. No other equipment was permitted. Even clothing had to be kept to the bare minimum, and the journey had to be made barefoot.

Prospective animal magi made their way across the plain to a rock formation on the eastern end, an ancient volcanic plug called the Devil's Thumb. There, they would be given one decent meal and the robes they had chosen to graduate in. Once fed and dressed, they were to make their way through the settled country by any means they liked to Ardcalen. If they had made it the journey in time, they were accepted into the convocation of magi immediately, and the party with their friends and relatives began right away; if not – well, there was always next year.

The timing of the test was important: the rocky, forested region where the Devil's Thumb stood was a favourite place for herds of large herbivores such as the white oxen to spend the winter. The big animals in Greenland were somewhat different to those on the continent.At the end of summer, they moved into the woodlands of the east or the forests around Eradero, to shelter from the snows of the plain. After the calves had been born in the spring, they migrated in herds back to the plains, where there was more grazing and open space to roam. It was those moving herds that the hopeful candidates were to use to help them cross.

This year, rainy weather had persisted into the tenth month, so the students put off their tests as long as possible. Then, at the end of the month, the weather turned dry, and there was a rush of applications from the candidates. Twenty-one students (an abnormally large number) all had to do the Ordeal quickly. It was decided that, instead of letting two candidates go each day as usual, they would be sent off at two hour intervals between sunrise and sunset.

Tomas went to the departure point straight after a large breakfast, wearing the graduation robe Master Helder had obtained for him, and barefoot as specified in the rules. The weather was cool and overcast. There, he was met by one of the magi conducting the test. When he went into the prep building, there was another student, sitting barefoot in front of a maga at a desk. She was to leave before him. She was calm, but poker-faced. She looked at him with a mixture of disgust and apprehension, as if he was one of the predators she would have to evade in the next few days. Tomas' thought lingered on Liriel again. One more step, he thought; one more week, and a lot closer.

The elada went off to get ready while the magus read Tomas the rules. He had already heard them at least once. Tomas' grasp of the language was such that he could understand the eladi better than he was understood.

As his last instructions were being read out, he heard a small bell ring, faint but clear. A few minutes later, the maga came in to the room carrying the elada's bundle, and said, 'She is away.'

The magus nodded, and said to Tomas, 'Do you have any questions?'

'Yes,' Tomas said, holding up his walking-stick. 'Can I take this?'

'No,' the magus said immediately.

'But I need it to walk with,' Tomas said.

'Why?' The magus gave a quizzical look.

'I had an arrow-injury to my hip, less than three years ago. The healing was... incomplete, and I still feel the pain when I walk. If I don't have the stick, I can only walk slowly. I cannot run either, unless in the gravest emergency.'

The magus sat in thought for some time. Then he took out a small book and started paging through it. He spoke with the maga for some time, and Tomas saw the looks of distaste on their faces, probably at his mixed ancestry, he thought. Finally, the magus said to Tomas, 'I am sorry, young brother, but the rules are quite strict. You could still use this stick as a weapon, to kill a rabbit or some bird for food; the object of the test is to have animals feed you, and to forage yourself. In any case, if you wish to cross the plain in time, you should use your own legs as little as possible.'

It was the answer Tomas had expected. He thought he might manage without the stick for some time anyway, and it would be better to prove himself against the odds; but he had to try. And, if it came to that, walking-sticks grew far and wide.

They made small talk for a while, until the next candidate arrived. Tomas and the magus went out to the changing-room. Tomas undressed and folded up his robe neatly, changed into the rough homespun trousers and tunic that would be his only clothing for the next week, then went through a door to a stall at the back of the building. He was shivering with more than the cold. The walls were waist-high, and there was a shelf on the outside wall of it, where the magus was standing. He took Tomas' bundle from him, and Tomas gave up his walking-stick. He tested his weight on his left hip, and was quite pleased to feel only a light twinge. 'Maybe it's time to do without it anyway,' he muttered to himself.

'Right,' said the magus, 'I must tell you a few more things, but first you have to hold out your arms and turn a full circle.'

Tomas did so, feeling even sillier than before.

'I must check for concealed items,' said the magus, patting him down. 'Candidates have been known to try smuggling weapons or food. Now, here,' he pulled a satchel out from under the shelf, 'are your supplies for the week.' The satchel looked woefully small. The magus unpacked it, saying 'Your blanket, some dried fruit, some biltong – the food will last one day at the most, so if it is all gone tonight, you are a fool or unlucky – and a tinderbox. This tinderbox will only be good for about a week: replace the tinder all you need, but the flint will not last, it is but a silly little thing. This, on the other hand –' he took out a long-bladed knife in a plain leather sheath '– is good for ever. Should you pass the test, it will be yours for life; if not, it will be taken from you at the other side, and kept for your next attempt. Use it well, and lose it not!'

Tomas drew the knife. The blade was quite broad, leaf-form, like nothing he had ever seen before, and half again the length of his hand. It was double-edged, and so perfectly balanced, it seemed to weigh next to nothing.

'It is a beautiful blade,' said the magus. 'The smith-magus who made it must have foreseen warfare for you.'

Tomas somehow knew he spoke the truth. 'Indeed,' he said. He slid the beautiful blade back in its sheath. Someday it should have a nice scabbard, he thought.

'Right,' said the magus, 'pack up, and I shall ring the bell when your time comes. You have no belt, but most people attach their knife to the strap of their satchel.' He smiled, saying 'You are about to embark on a great adventure. Remember to enjoy yourself, and go in the sight of the One.'

'Thank you,' Tomas replied with what must have been a nervous grin. 'Stay well,' he remembered the polite Moreladi term for farewell.

Tomas stood in the midmorning gloom. The magus stood behind the stall, near the hourglass. Tomas fiddled with his pack, attaching the sheath to the strap. He was still fastening it when the bell rang, cold and clear. He jumped and fumbled, standing up to go even as he finished fastening the strap back. He was halfway down the slope when he finally flung the thing over his head, and across from one shoulder.

Tomas' walk down into the trees soon turned into a limp. By the time he was out of sight of the starting-point, he could feel every movement in his left hip. By the time he reached the closed canopy of forest, he was having second thoughts. By the time he reached the golden-brown stream that ran out onto the plain, he was starting to think this was a bad idea. By the time he reached open space again, he was in serious pain.

It was no good; he had to stop. Picking up a hefty stick that was more or less straight, he saw a large, grey limestone boulder and hobbled towards it, trying to take the weight off his left hip. He thought it would be a good place to sit down and get his bearings, but when he got there, he saw the rock was scored with hard lines of flint, making sharp little blades on the surface. As he stood looking at it, his hip gave a stab of pain, and he caught himself on the rock; he found a patch that was slightly smoother than the rest, and sat down on it gingerly.

The overcast was breaking up into silver and blue as he sat his rock like a baboon, looking around. The plain stretched eastwards, all wavy green grass with patches of shrubs and cabbage trees. Here and there, mighty forest trees raised their solemn heads, marking underground watercourses and cave entrances in the soluble bedrock below.

Tomas sighed and thought, right when I need them, the animals are all gone. There wasn't a furred or horned head in sight, and he couldn't go looking for one. For upwards of half an hour he sat there, rubbing his left hip absently. More than once he wished he could call for Tork, but the raven was in the Ivory City with Magus Galbaro; and in any case, calling him might be cheating. Then, he caught movement out of the corner of his eye; there, strutting solemnly through the grass, was an ostrich. It was a cock, with brilliant white wing-feathers, but the rest of its plumage had strange bronze-tinted tips, where mainland birds were all black.

Tomas stayed as still as he could; ostriches were notoriously stupid, and could deliver a lethal kick with their huge toenails; but they were also some of the fastest runners on the plains. He had heard of ostriches being ridden, in fact it was the deciding factor in one of the First Foul War battles he'd read about, but he had never seen it done, only read about it. He decided it was worth the risk.

He reached out and felt the bird's mind. As usual, he found the avian mind elegantly simple to the touch, compared to that of a mammal. This species, however, was more simple than elegant, a real bird-brain. Finding a memory of a hen, he got the bird to come to him. It came within easy sight, and Tomas could feel its surprise at finding this huge, pallid, hairless monkey on a rock: where was the hen?

Tomas concentrated, taking complete control of the ostrich for a time. He quashed all natural reactions, putting the bird into a trance. It was the technique used to prepare animals for slaughter or castration, but he had another purpose in mind. No-one could keep such control for long, he had to do this right first time. He got the bird to stand close to the rock, its rear towards him; then, keeping his satchel behind him, he swung his bad leg over the bird's hindquarters, and plonked himself down, grabbing the nearest convenient handhold: the wings. Just as he did that, he lost his tight control of the ostrich's mind, and it reacted instinctively to the weight on its back – it ran!

Using only two legs, it could make amazing acceleration. Tomas hung on as hard as he could, as he jogged along. The two-legged gait was very uncomfortable, but Tomas was glad that he was moving along at speed, on legs at least half again as long as his own.

Tomas rode the ostrich for upwards of an hour, directing it eastwards. As he rode, he adjusted his position, but it was a great strain on the arms. He had to take regular breaks. Sometimes he rode at a run, others at a walk. When he felt the bird beginning to tire, he made it slow down and allowed it to forage while he got off and massaged his aching arms and hands. Unlike a zebra, the ostrich didn't have the sense to get used to having a rider, so he had to control it for the whole time. In that way, he made good time eastwards for that whole day. He managed to convince it that he wasn't a threat, so the bird stayed with him that night, and he rode it again the next day.

It was the evening of Tomas' second day on the plain that he experienced a setback. The sun was sinking behind Eradero in a swathe of pink and powder blue, when he directed the bird to a patch of forest around a tumbled mass of wrinkled grey boulders. Tomas thought it looked like a safe place to spend the night, but he was wrong. He forgot the first rule of a Beastmaster alone in the wild: to think like a herbivore. His negligence could have been excused as fatigue and hunger, having finished his food supply that morning; as it was, he simply left the bird to fend for itself while he sought a secure sleeping-place in the huge branches of what looked like a big bushwillow, a tree with several trunks sprouting from a central point. All of a sudden, he heard a spine-chilling sound: a deep-throated snarl, and the crashing sound of something heavy running through trees. Tomas' blood froze. He reached out, looking for life, detecting only two large beings: a bird and a lone feline. Creeping to the edge of the trees, he saw in the dying red evening light, his ostrich running for its life, a magnificent black panther close behind! The chase continued out of sight, and beyond Tomas' perception.
    As his heartbeat slowed, Tomas started swearing under his breath. That had been too close! He was glad it was the ostrich that had run into the cat, and not himself; but now how was he to travel?
    For the rest of the night, he slept fitfully and uncomfortably in his tree. If the panther felt hungry again and started searching for aranelado, he needed to be alert.

He awoke cold and hungry again. It was the darkest, coldest hour before dawn. The ever-present Greenland cloud had cleared, and the stars spread themselves across the heavens in a brilliant cloud, low in the sky in this far country. There would be no animals abroad at this time, or at least none on which he could hitch a ride. He sat on his branch, shivering in his blanket, watching the eastern horizon slowly lighten. He made use of the time to do some meditation. As the sky brightened to green, the Light warmed him, and he was no longer shivering. The casual miracle was heartening.

The eastern sky turned orange, and Tomas' thought turned to travel, and to food. He had seldom given much thought to how much food the average person needed, since coming to lands where there was no war. How was he going to continue his journey, hungry as he was?

As daylight broadened, Tomas grew worried. The panther, now resting well-fed in a thicket among the boulders, was only part of the reason. Without his stick, he couldn't walk any distance.

He swung out of his tree and moved around, supporting himself on low branches. He found a bush with small pink berries on it which he recognised. The ripe berries he could find were good, but they were only enough for a snack. If transport didn't turn up soon, there would be trouble.

The sun rose higher, the day became warm. Sitting still under his tree, Tomas saw or perceived several small beasts: some small grazing animals, a kind of bushpig, some large baboons in the distance; nothing big enough to carry him. Hunger gnawed at his innards. Hunt or look for transport – which should he do?

It was getting warm, close to midday. Tomas had moved a little distance, towards a water-course. He had a headache from hunger and thirst. He couldn't move fast enough to catch anything, and he'd already wasted a few good throwing-sticks trying to down birds. What good would it do him, to be all good and virtuous, if he ended up failing the test, or starving to death out here?

The sun rose to its zenith. Tomas had managed to get to the river, a cold, brown stream. The water was too muddy to drink. It was warm and still, and Tomas had difficulty maintaining his detachment. There were no animals, everything was resting in the middle of the day, even here in the cool south. The panther had gone, or at least Tomas could no longer perceive it. Failure stared him in the face. What if he could not qualify? He would never see Liriel again. At least on this island, he might be safe from the ruin of the continent: safe, impotent and alone. He fumed at the sheer unfairness of it all, and his detachment broke and splintered. There was no help from the heavens. They were as indifferent as ever. The lesser gods were not helping, and the One could not care less. He thought back to Ioseth's words: *You told him to stop, and he did.* What if...?

Tomas imagined what it would be like to call on the Shade. He remembered its touch from Jwagga the Foot, the cold, dead caress that felt like something rotten. Unbidden came the thought: the power was his to command. No-one could tell him what to do. No-one would ever know. Finishing the test, becoming a magus, even being with Liriel again, was no longer important. Now, he had to survive. He would take whatever measures were necessary, because no-one else was going to help him.

He took a deep breath. Somehow, he knew what he had to do: it needed blood – just a little. He didn't even wonder how he knew, maybe he read it somewhere. He took out the beautiful knife, and the sight of it gave him pause. It would be such a shame, to lose... But would he really lose anything? All he wanted was to call on another source of power, one which would do his bidding, one which would come when he called. He would deal with consequences as and when they came; but his resolve faltered. The early afternoon sun, so soft in this cool country, shone down benignly, bringing out the beauty of the plains below the thicket. It was mild, calm, and peaceful. The wind was pleasant in his hair, the trees and grass were so green, bare soil grey under branches in the shade. It was sublime.

All this will fade and die, if you do this.

Tomas' heart skipped a beat. 'Who said that?' he asked out loud.

You have known Me. I know you. Do not ruin yourself like this! The Voice was aggrieved.

Tomas' heart broke. That Voice was the distillation of all his meditations, the background to all the consolations he had ever felt. He knew full well What it was. 'I'm sorry,' he said with a lump suddenly in his throat, 'but I'm in trouble. I need help!'

I will help you. Stop listening to your own fear and darkness. Listen to me.

Tomas was tempted to say, 'No, I won't.' For all he knew, he was expected to die out here; but even death in that Presence was no bad thing. It was a naked choice, with no certainty either way, other than the promise: *I will help you.* Taking a deep breath, he said, 'All right. I am listening.'

There was no reply. The breeze blew, rustling the leaves of a hundred plants. Tomas heard no more of the Voice, though he tried, listening so hard that he heard the blood in his ears. Eventually he gave up, but his black mood did not return. He couldn't stay in this tree, it was uncomfortable. He climbed down from where he'd been perched. Looking around, he found a dead branch with a convenient bend, which could serve as a crutch for the present. He moved away from the tree, keeping his senses open to life. He heard small birds in the trees.

After a few minutes, his hip was feeling a bit sore again, and he stopped under an ancient cabbage-tree, just like the ones in the Highlands, only much larger. He stood leaning against one of its thick trunks, and heard a blessed sound: trickling water. Behind one of the trunks was a tiny spring, where water welled up from under some grey stones, trickling down into a mossy watercourse. A tree fern shaded the spring. Tomas drank all he could of the clean, cold water. It was wonderful. As he raised his head, he saw something that made him start: there, just a short distance away, was one of those grey Greenland quaha!

'Well, well, well,' he murmured to himself, 'It's amazing what you find when you get up off your backside.'

Convincing the animal to come and have a drink, and then allowing him to climb up on its back was the work of minutes for Tomas, and then he was away. Thanking the Voice, he rode east for a few hours, until the mid-afternoon.

Just as the heat of the day was dissipating, Tomas saw birds of some kind circling over a point in the south-east, and turned in that direction. The birds were not like vultures that he knew from the continent: they were more like bearded vultures or gryphons, and there were ravens as well, of the same white-necked, heavy-beaked kind as Tork. As the sun sank low behind him, he came to a doline, a wide, round depression in the landscape where an underground cave had collapsed, and water had gathered into a shallow lake. Tomas brought his mount to the edge of a cliff, some two or three times his own height. Looking down, he saw what the scavengers were after: there at the bottom was a dead rhino. It was strangely hairy. It must have fallen down the cliff, he thought. By the size of its horn, it had been quite old. Perhaps it had lost its way in the dark and fallen off the edge.

The gryphons and ravens were perched on the carcass or in nearby trees. The carcass was still intact, the hide unbroken. Lacking the strength to tear the thick hide, the birds were waiting for something with sharp teeth and claws; or in this case, Tomas thought, a sharp knife.

He rode around the lip of the doline until he found a way down. Once at the bottom, he dismounted and let the quaha loose to graze. He warned it not to go where the grass was very thick, in case the ground was treacherous.

Then, using his makeshift walking-stick, he picked his painful way through the dense undergrowth to the foot of the cliff, waving his arms to shoo the birds away. They simply drifted off to nearby trees. Tomas counted himself lucky that there wasn't any competition for the meat so far – something had to be first – but he was willing to bet he hadn't been the only carnivore to see the birds circling. It was only a matter of time until something bigger and stronger than he came to investigate, and when that happened, he had to be away. He watched with more than his eyes, as he approached the carcass and investigated. The hairy rhino had died with grass still in its mouth. So it had died suddenly, he thought; must have broken its neck.

Pulling out his knife, he went to cut open the carcass. 'This could get messy,' he muttered to himself. The beast had been lying in the sun all day, and might be ripening by now. At least it wasn't bloated, so the meat should still be safe, as long as he cooked it well. As the gryphons jostled each other in the trees and hissed, Tomas held his breath and plunged the knife into its side. There was no sound of gas, but it smelled pretty foul, all the same.

As the ravens croaked around him, Tomas got to work. It took some time to cut away the hide – it was so thick, it was like armour – and then he started carving some meat off the hip joint. The gryphons floated over him on their heavy-feathered wings. They were hungry. He felt further out, realising that he hadn't been keeping proper watch, and perceived a large feline some distance away. He jumped, almost dropping the meat. He looked around wildly. Which direction was it? It was behind the cliff, and getting closer... time to go. He limped away with the products of his scavenging, looking forward to getting it cooked. He had never tasted rhino before.

He found a convenient spot among some tumbled rocks, out of the doline and on the opposite side from the approaching carnivore. It was getting dark, and his quaha would alert him if it smelled that big cat, so he decided it was time to settle down here for the night. He spent a comfortable night by the fire, well-fed and wrapped up in his blanket.

The following morning dawned overcast and close, promising rain. Tomas washed in a stream and made ready to go. He called his zebra and mounted with the help of a tree. He was on his way east when he saw a large, heavy-bodied antelope with short, spiral-patterned horns, an eland, making its way in the same direction, with someone on its back.

'Hi!' Tomas shouted. The figure started, and waved. Tomas rode closer, and saw it was the elada who had left just before him, the one who had given him the dirty look. She wore a short shift of the same material as Tomas' trews. It was only knee-length, exposing a lot of leg.

'Hello,' she said, 'how are you doing?'

'Not bad,' said Tomas. 'I had rhino for supper last night.'

'Rhino?' she asked. Tomas noticed how drawn her face looked. She must have been going hungry, he thought. 'I suppose it's all gone by now?' She looked so desperate, Tomas' heart went out to her.

'I doubt it,' Tomas said, 'but there was a great cat in the area last night.'

'Is it still there?'

'I haven't checked.' She looked helpless. Tomas said, 'You haven't been eating well, have you?'

'No, I had to walk for two days, at the beginning. I've had to make up time. I found this eland after I saw the birds circling, but I couldn't get here before dark last night.'

Tomas decided to do her a favour. 'My name is Tomas,' he said. 'I can give you get some meat, but we shall have to hurry. I don't want to be in that hole when the rain starts to fall.'

Her eyes showed tears as she said, 'Thank you. I am Iscie.'

They returned to his campsite, keeping their senses open for large animals. The cat had been and gone from the carcase during the night.

Tomas cut out about half his leftovers, gave Iscie her bag back, and picked up his stick. They were moving back to their animals in spitting rain when they both perceived the same feline presence behind them. They whipped round to face the cliff, but the cat was nowhere in sight. They knew it could see them, however. Tomas could feel the brooding, watching presence of a hungry thing. He turned back to call his quaha, but Iscie was in front of him: pulling herself up on the quaha's back with an agility Tomas could only dream of, she urged it away and was galloping for the slope down which she had come while he shouted, 'Hey! Come back, you stupid cow!'

The rain started to fall. Fuming, he picked up his bag. The bitch! It was suddenly empty.He cast around for Iscie's eland. The huge beast was on the far side of the lake, and in danger of wandering into the boggy ground. He called it as Iscie rode his quaha up out of the doline and out of sight. Tomas fought to keep enough detachment to encourage the eland to come to him, and to keep his senses open to the cat. He hobbled along, away from the hungry cat, using his improvised walking-stick, as the eland reluctantly came towards him. Hoping that the wind wouldn't change and the eland suddenly smell the cat, Tomas hauled himself up onto the animal's sloping back. Few animals had backs as level or as broad as that of an equine. He put his now wet blanket over his shoulders and lay flat. The eland appreciated the warm covering, and made its way up out of the doline. Eland seldom put on any speed unless in great danger, so there was no way Tomas could catch up with Iscie. He fumed some more, anger oozing past his detachment.

He shook off the vicious circle in his thoughts and scanned the area, looking for any danger. He felt something off to the north-east, several somethings: they were moving away. They didn't have the dark, acid tang of felines, nor the dusty, pungent smack of mustelids; that ruled out great cats and hyenas, thought Tomas, but the light, savoury smell reminded him of domestic dogs. Hunting dogs were less dangerous to him, but were still a threat to the eland. He was glad they were moving away. He wondered briefly if they were chasing Iscie on the quaha, but he couldn't do anything even if they were. In any case, a quaha had a good chance of getting away, as long as it smelt them in time. The thought was enough for him to let go of his resentment.

By evening, Tomas was in luck, of a kind. Ravenous again, he found his way to a mixed herd of game: wild, white-haired cattle, grey quaha and a kind of black hartebeest. The animals were like and yet unlike those on the continent. He rode the eland to a small pond where he guddled for fish, catching them with his bare hands. It was dark before he had one, but well worth it, even if the fish did taste a bit muddy. At least he went to sleep with something in his stomach.

The following day he hitched a ride on another quaha which took him into the middle of the plain. Looking back westwards, he saw the wide, symmetrical cone of Eradero in the blue distance; but looking forward, he could see nothing that resembled a thumb sticking up out of the ground. It was the fifth day out from the start of the Ordeal, and he didn't even seem to be halfway, yet.

Around midday the herd crossed a small river, and Tomas literally dropped off to have a swim and a drink. He found some berries growing along the bank of the river, and ate as much as he could. It was delicious. He filled up his water-bottle and took up with a southern buffalo, the bearded type with the horns pointing backward, on the other side. As evening came, the quaha slowed to a stop and stood side by side, facing in opposite directions, settling down for the night. Tomas found a low-slung tree and made himself as comfortable as he could in the branches. The moon rose very bright in the small hours of the morning, and the great beasts were restless. He found a huge white cow and climbed on, in case they should start moving without him. He dozed as he rode, following the rising sun. The beast moved at a slow, steady pace, its conveniently level back wide and stable.

He spent the day riding east, but his water-supply gave out quite quickly. Late in the afternoon, he directed his cow to a low hill where he found a small spring. It was amazing how much water there was in this country, he thought. Looking for a convenient place to spend the night, he found a large hole in the earth under a leathery-leafed bush. He sniffed at the hole: there was a strange stink. He cleared his mind and looked: whatever it was, it was a warm-blooded thing, and deeply asleep. Tomas could tell it wasn't an aardvark or a ratel. With his stomach clamouring its hunger at him, he decided it was a good enough chance at supper. He sneaked around to the entrance.

As the sun shone horizontally under the clouds in the west, he drew his dagger and banged the stick on the ground above the hole. There was a squeal, and a boar with large tusks charged out, but Tomas was ready. Lunging reflexively, Tomas brought his beautiful blade down on the animal's neck. The pig screamed as it died, but Tomas exulted. 'Thank you, Hunter!' he laughed up to the heavens, and whooped for joy!

The boar was a huge, old beast. When he hoisted the carcass, it was a dead weight on his hip. He roasted it over a fire that night, keeping some by for later. He overcooked the meat, as one should when cooking pig.

When he rose the next morning, he thought he could see the Devil's Thumb in the east from the top of his koppie. It didn't look particularly thumb-ish from where he was: but he had been told that there was no other similar rock formation in that direction. After a breakfast of water and cold roast pork, he called another cow from the last night's herd, and rode east all day. By afternoon, he was at a small patch of marshland, where he guddled for fish again. He was more practised at it this time, however, and he grilled two over a fire, leaving others to smoke over the embers. He had an all-meat supper and slept in his blanket by the fire as usual.

The next day was the sixth. He called a quaha and resumed his journey east. He felt a wild kind of freedom, travelling towards recognition and status, watching the Devil's Thumb growing steadily with each passing hour.

He ate the last of his smoked fish that afternoon, while his quaha rested in the shade of a tree. The afternoon passed uneventfully, until the quaha herd became skittish at the sound of some awful howling in the distance. Mounting up, Tomas allowed his quaha to get away, moving at a canter and a gallop slightly north of east. As they did so, the rock formation in the distance took on a very thumb-ish look.

By evening, they had reached the end of the plains. Finding a patch of more open country, Tomas camped in the branches of a tree again. He had run out of food, and spent a hungry night.

The seventh day dawned, cloudless blue, and Tomas found some early wild apricots, the bitter fruit that grows on vines over rocks. There were some gooseberries as well, the small golden fruit growing in their own little leafy packets. If he could only reach the Devil's Thumb by that evening, there would be enough there to keep him going.

He cantered and galloped through parkland woods all morning. All was delightfully cool and green. He rode at a good pace, and reached the foot of the rock formation just as the setting sun peeped through the trunks of the trees. The quaha needed some persuasion to keep going in the wooded country at sundown. At the foot of the tor were several round, thatched huts. When he saw them, Tomas gave a whoop of delight. He had made it! An elado with a book noted Tomas' name and gave him his graduation robes, which had been sent on from the starting point. Tomas went and had a bath in the waterfall behind the huts and dressed like a civilised being for the first time in more than a week. After a meal of salted meat, raisin-bread and sweet, new wine, he slept on the floor of the hut, leaving his quaha to fend for itself.

The next morning, Tomas found the animal had strayed. However, while looking for it, he found another Greenland ostrich eating the crops sprouting in someone's field, and lost no time in mounting up. He rode at a spanking pace several times during the day, travelling through farmlands. The farmlands in this cool, wet country looked wild. He followed the steadily widening road eastwards, and around lunchtime came across a strange herd of hoofed animals, ridden by several of his classmates. Some were already too late, and were just riding along in their rough-woven, single-piece garments for the sake of company, already looking forward to next year's attempt. Others were eager for the graduation ceremony to be over, and the party to start. Among the party were the newlyweds, Galdie and Henvaro. Everyone laughed at Tomas on his ostrich, but he wasn't the only one riding uncomfortably: many were mounted on hartebeest or other slope-backed antelope, and were balanced very uncomfortably on their mounts' backs, trying to stay on as the party trotted along. Around noon they caught up with a wagon, heavily laden with firewood, driven by a merry-eyed eladon farmer. Several eladi rode on top of his heap of firewood.

The people riding on their animals took a break in the afternoon, and the wagon carried on. Later, they overtook the eladi who had been riding on the wagon, now walking on foot. Then they saw the gate-dolmen of Ardcalen, and the ride became a race.

Tomas' ostrich easily outpaced the heavy mammals at first, but it became nervous in the city, where eladi crowded round to gawk at the bearded human on the ostrich. By the time he had reassured the bird, and asked amused passers-by for directions to the Beastmasters' Hall, the others had almost caught up with him.

'Hey, cactus-face!' Henvaro shouted, referring to Tomas' stubble, 'Which way do we go?'

Grinning from ear to ear, Tomas simply urged his bird forward. 'I'm not going to tell you!' He jeered as he bumped along down the road, in the direction he'd been told, towards the edge of the town.

As the bird hurtled down the muddy street, he heard Henvaro's bellow: 'Follow that ostrich!'

Tomas turned to look behind him, and saw a wall of hide, hooves and horns bearing down on him. The faces of the eladi behind them were bright with laughter. It was a sight Tomas would never forget. The ostrich looked back briefly, too, and almost panicked; Tomas had to keep tight hold of the bird's mind.

As they ran, a long, low drystone wall appeared on their left, with a wide pasture behind it – the lands around the Beastmasters' Hall. The tree-lined facade of the Hall itself soon appeared, with a wide, cobbled track leaving the main road and passing through one wing of the golden-stone building. Tomas directed the ostrich through it, but had to hold on tight as the two-legged change of direction almost unseated him. Through the wide, arched gate he charged, and out onto a flag-stoned track through thick, short green grass, and a marquee pitched under a huge, old deciduous tree. There, he hopped and skidded to a stop, as eladi came out of the marquee, applauding the laughing stampede. Lord Dragelion himself was one of them. He called out to Tomas, 'Well done, O Tomas of the Double Heritage! You have justified my faith in you, and brought credit to the peoples of the continent!'

'Thank you, my lord!' Tomas said, bowing from the neck.

'Some of your friends are waiting for you in the Hall,' said the Beastmaster, waving back towards the building.

'Do I have to dismount here?' Tomas asked. His temporary walking-stick had gone missing in the charge from the dolmen.

'You are to ride at a walk,' said a steward, 'from here to the staircase at the Masters' Entrance.' He pointed to a low, wide staircase on another wing of the Hall. 'You are to wait there, until told to dismount.'

Tomas did so, while Lord Dragelion spoke to the other magi-elect. He greeted them all by name, and congratulated them, even those who were too late to qualify. As Tomas sat in front of the steps, Magus Galbaro came out to meet him, Tork perched on his shoulder. Tork flew onto Tomas' outstretched arm, ignoring the suspicious look the ostrich gave him.

'Hello, father,' said Tomas, 'and hello, Tork! It's good to see you.'

'Hello, Tomas,' said Galbaro. 'How did you manage without this?' He handed Tomas his walking-stick.

'I didn't, really,' said Tomas, accepting it. 'I had a few rough sticks I picked up in the bush, but I lost my last one in the stampede. Thank you very much for bringing this.'

'Not at all,' said Galbaro. 'You may not even need it, now that you are to receive a staff.'

Tomas' heart thumped like a Tsuna drum. He had made it! If only, he thought with a pang of sadness, his family, or Ben, or Aravon could have been here; or still better, Liriel. He wondered how Ioseth's studies were going.

When the magi-elect were all assembled on the animals they had ridden into town, they were allowed to dismount, setting their animals free to roam the pasture. They were allowed to go and refresh themselves in the Hall's Bathhouses, and then waited in the marquee for those on foot. In the late afternoon, the candidates on foot finally arrived. Iscie was not among them. After they had been welcomed and refreshed, all the candidates lined up in front of the wide staircase, and their relatives and friends came out and sat on the stairs. Tomas spotted Caranto the Wise when he passed Tork back to Galbaro, and waved. The Greystone eladi were the closest to family that Tomas had there.

As the sun set, Lord Dragelion made a speech congratulating the successful candidates. The only part of it Tomas remembered later was, 'Some of you may be willing to join the military, or to take some other part in the liberation of the continent. For those of you willing to undergo the training, the rewards will probably be substantial; but if there is one thing I wish you to take away with you tonight, it is this: there are no old, bold warrior-magi. The wisdom you have gained through your apprenticeship and discipline is sorely needed in His Majesty's forces.Use it well. Use it to make sure there are eladi to accept the rewards offered by the people there.'

Tomas wondered fleetingly if Lord Engolaran's offer of land to the Oreladi had not been too generous; but any eladon rule was preferable to that of the Foul Folk.

Finally, the magi-elect were called forward to receive their badges of office: the ironwood staves. Where staves of Greystone magi were only rough sticks, those given in Greenland were sanded and polished, though otherwise unworked. The Greenland staves also had a single, polished, semiprecious eldastone in a knot or a specially cut setting at the top. Like most eldastones, they were reservoirs of energy, which was released in response to a physical event, such as a touch or a word. These stones, however, had been treated by those with the Ability for four days and three nights. The super-treating made them abnormally efficient energy stores, such that instead of going cloudy, losing their crystal structure and becoming useless after a few decades, they retained their quality for centuries. It was thought that used only sparingly, they could last up to a thousand years.

When Lord Dragelion called out, 'Tomas of Greystone!' Tomas made his way forwards, supporting himself on his walking-stick. As his hands closed on the smooth wood of a staff with an amethyst set in the top, he had a profound sense of something clicking into a place made for it. He was *meant* to bear this staff!

He returned to his place among the candidates, strangely free of any ache in his left hip. Riding must have helped to take the weight off, he thought. When everyone had been given their staves, they faced west, the setting sun in their eyes, and went down on one knee to take the Oath:

> 'I promise to love all, as the sun shines, as the rain falls, as the trees shade, as the earth feeds;
> I shall oppose the Wicked and reprove the Erring; I shall support the Helpless and make whole the Broken;
> May no being find me a cause of stumbling, may no-one find my work wanting, may no-one want for my protection and nurturing, insofar as I can give it; and may curses on me rebound on their originators;
> I respectfully call on the Powers to witness this, in the Name of the One Light which kindled the All: these things are promised by me – Tomas of Greystone.'

As he rose, Tomas noticed that he no longer had to lever himself up. He put his whole weight on his left hip, and was amazed to feel not the slightest twinge. He was as delighted as he was puzzled. As Galbaro and Caranto came over to congratulate him, and Tork settled on his shoulder, he said, 'I can stand on my hip again!'

Comprehension dawned on their fair faces, and Caranto said, 'Is your joint now healed?'

'I think so,' Tomas said. He was grinning all over his face, almost laughing.

Galbaro was sceptical. He asked, 'Can you stand without any help at all?'

Tomas paused, and handed over his new staff. As he did so, some of the pain returned to his hip, and he winced. It was improved, but only slightly. Galbaro returned the staff, saying in Celadi, 'It is as I thought: the eldastone is helping you, but you have to maintain contact. It may heal you in time; but you should treat the joint carefully if you wish the healing to occur. Put it under no strain.' He added in a low voice, 'That is why we of Greystone do not use such aids. A magus' staff should not become a crutch.'

Tomas and Caranto had leant close to hear what he was saying. They now stood up, nodding slowly. Caranto said, 'A pity.'

Tomas said, 'Well, I for one am glad of it. Any improvement is welcome.'

'Of course it is,' said Caranto, slapping him affectionately in the face. It was the same gesture given by Timaeos the acolyte a short lifetime ago, just before the Archmagister had come out and put an end to Tomas' life among men. Tomas now had a whole new life: it had begun or been conceived that terrible day, and had now been born into something altogether new and wonderful. Caranto said, 'Well met, Magus Tomas.'

'Yes,' said Galbaro, 'Well met, magus.' He held up his hand, palm out. Tomas matched the gesture, and their palms met with a faint clap. He had never done it before: it was a fraternal greeting amongst magi.

'I thank you, fathers,' Tomas said, simply. It meant a lot to him.

'I think, Tomas, since you are no longer in training,' said Galbaro, 'you may call us brother.'

'Or even cousin,' quipped Caranto, 'since the relationship is somewhat distant?'

'First cousin?' offered Galbaro. The Celadon term was a single word.

'Once removed?' suggested Tomas.

'Not too far, I hope,' said Caranto, smiling.

'Come, now, lads,' said Galbaro with a mock-serious expression, 'this is getting silly!'

'Who's silly?' Lord Dragelion said, sneaking up behind them.

'Oh, hello, my lord,' said Galbaro, 'we were just talking about you!' The two had obviously become close, thought Tomas after his initial shock had receded.

'It's all fibs, I tell you,' said Lord Dragelion. 'I just need a drink! Now, if you have quite finished trading barbed compliments amongst yourselves, we may proceed to the Hall, where I'm told there is a feast of some magnificence prepared against our arrival.'

'Ah,' Tomas breathed, 'proper food!'

'Yummy!' said Tork, clacking his beak. Tomas laughed out loud.

CHAPTER XIV

That night in the Beasthall, Tomas slept heavily and comfortably, well-fed for the first time in more than a week: no more patiently waiting for fish to come within reach, no more hoping to find an unmolested carcass, no more searching for sort-of-ripe berries – it was sheer luxury. He had a new appreciation of the benefits of civilisation.

Sometime during the night, he looked out in a dream, northwards to the continent. Black clouds gathered there, darkening the horizon. Lightning stalked the land, trees writhed in a storm. As he looked, a spark of light flared in the gloom, tiny in the distance. It brightened, and he heard a voice calling over a vast distance: 'Tomas! Where are you?' Then the spark faded. It was Liriel's voice, and the sound cut him to the heart.

He awoke, acutely conscious of the gap in his heart. He had tarried far too long in the South. He had to go back through a wall of rock and steel and flame and blood, and there was only one way to do so. As the daylight lightened Greenland's soggy clouds, Tomas decided on the service of arms for the second time in his life. It was the seventh day of the eleventh month.

At breakfast, he asked Galbaro and Caranto if it would be possible to join the forces sent to the continent. He didn't surprise anyone.

Caranto said, 'Somehow, I doubt that you hope for a gift of land, as so many of the Greenlanders do.'

Tomas weighed his words. 'I dreamed I was called, last night.'

'And have you meditated on this dream?' Galbaro asked. 'You told us you were visited by darkness once, in your sleep.'

Tomas hadn't thought of that. 'I was. You are right, discernment is needed.' He explained further, 'The voice was of someone I know.'

Both of the eladi nodded, understanding. Caranto said, 'Then I shall consider the question on your behalf, too; but you are still a part of our embassy, and under the command of Lord Engolaran. Remember that.'

They stayed in Ardcalen for a few days, while the last of the magi-elect came in, graduated, and partied. Lord Dragelion clearly enjoyed himself.

The day of their departure dawned clear and bright, and they took ship in the harbour and sailed up the river towards the cataract at Falgalath, where they would take to the road again towards the Ivory City. Tomas was very glad not be sailing on the sea, after his last experience.

At the end of the first day of travelling, Caranto asked Tomas, 'Do you still wish to join the invasion forces?'

'I do,' Tomas said. 'I have tested my thought in the light of the Secret Fire. I should go with the forces, though not as a fighter. I wasn't a very good soldier before.'

'I didn't think you would be,' grinned Caranto. 'Also, you are still a part of the Greystone Embassy, regardless of the studies you have undertaken here. You have brought credit to your fathers among men, by passing the Ordeal, and that with a disability. Between you and me, Ioseth is doing well under Magus Herendo, also. I would prefer it if you kept your position among us.'

Tomas leaned on the ship's rail. Tork hopped towards him along it. 'Perhaps I could do both,' he said. 'Surely there should be someone from the embassy in the head of the forces, to communicate with the Highlanders, and with Greystone? When we eventually get there, that is?'

'Master Helder is going to do that,' said Caranto. 'But, he has to be here for the present. Politics can be delicate. Perhaps sending you would be a good idea.The fact that you speak all three languages would be a great advantage.' The elado stared out over the north bank, watching the dense, green countryside pass by. 'I think you should go, too; we shall speak to the master when we return to the Water-Lily Palace.'

Back in the Ivory City, the Greystone embassy had been moved to luxurious apartments. All other magi were out, leaving the bodyguards sitting around playing cards. Tomas stopped to chat with them. They were bored. He went looking for Ioseth, and found him in a small but well-appointed office, writing out correspondence. As he entered, Ioseth looked up with a smile, saying, 'Tomas!' Then, seeing Tomas' ironwood staff, he stopped and stood up, saying, 'Sorry, I mean: Hello, father.'

Tomas laughed, waving the formality aside. 'Save the titles for official use,' he said in their own language, 'you will always be my brother.'

Ioseth smiled sadly. 'Thank you. It's a pity Master Ben didn't live to see you with a staff.'

Tomas sighed. 'It is. You know, when I was in hospital recovering from this injury –' he patted his left hip '– he said I could support myself with a staff when I got one. At the time, I thought he was off his wagon; but he was right all along.' Tomas sat down heavily on another chair, which was long-legged like human furniture. Tork hopped off his shoulder and went snooping around. There was a lot to play with in offices. Tomas looked at Ioseth's desk, a mass of paper, ink wells and brushes. 'I see they're keeping you busy,' he noted.

Ioseth grunted. 'I haven't had time to think, lately. I only get to meditate late at night. I haven't been able to read anything for days. Not that that's easy, of course, their alphabet is a nightmare. I can at least speak the language, now – well, as long as I keep my notes to hand – but writing it takes so long, because I have to look up our letters in a list of seventy-two glyphs.'

'I worked it out in the Beastmasters' Hall this winter,' said Tomas. 'I could write out a comparative alphabet for you; and a rune-row as well, maybe, that'll be useful. Then you can look it all up at once.'

'Oh, I've done that already,' said Ioseth, pulling out a thin, whitish sheet. 'I wrote it on a sheet of this paper. The paper here is very fine, it makes light books.'

'I've used enough of it,' Tomas said.

It burns like kindling, so they have these special book-lamps,' Ioseth pointed to a pot-bellied, brass oil-lamp, its wick encased in a glass vase.

'Yes I've seen those,' said Tomas. 'In the Hall where we had the graduation feast, they had whole chandeliers of those glass lamps - really pretty. They reminded me of a Sacred Lamp.'

Ioseth's face lit up, as if he'd been reminded of something. 'Speaking of which,' he said, 'I heard something about araneladi a few weeks ago, which I thought you might like to hear.'

Tomas shifted in his chair, and retrieved an ink-bottle that Tork was eyeing. 'Go on,' he said.

Ioseth gave the raven an empty bottle to play with. 'There was a wise who came to visit with Caranto. I was serving in the bar at the time, which is dead easy here, people pour their own drinks, and you just have to keep the bottles full and the goblets clean. Anyway, they were talking comparative theology, but they were talking nice and slowly, because Caranto doesn't speak Moreladan too well. The wise was saying that he had read some things about araneladi, from someone who had visited from the continent a long time ago.'

'Which to him, was probably two thousand years,' Tomas interrupted. He shot a reflexive glance over his shoulder, but there wasn't any point: there was no-one to hear, let alone understand the human language. 'Anyway, go on.'

'Right, anyway: this wise said that araneladi could either be a great blessing, or a great curse. He'd heard through the creepers that you were a strange mixture, and said you should be watched closely. He said that, araneladi had both the strength of the Elder and the authority of the Younger.'

'Well, we read that, didn't we?' said Tomas. 'In Falmallinar that time...' His spine crawled with the memory of the night of the assassination, when he had stopped that killer with a single word. A dreadful temptation to power reared in his mind. He thought resolutely of the sun on the grass, that beautiful day on the plain when he had been tempted to call on that power. The Voice had been so different, and so beautiful: *All will fade, if you do this...*

'Are you all right?' Ioseth asked. 'You're looking strange.'

Tomas clung to the memory of the Voice, and the temptation faded. He said to Ioseth, 'Yes, I, um... I was just remembering.'

Ioseth grinned. 'You looked like you were wandering mossy glades, or something.'

Tomas chuckled and shook his head.

'Anyway,' Ioseth continued, 'he said that this visitor had said that araneladi could command a parasite spirit, without making a bargain with it, which raises the stakes you now gamble on.'

Tomas nodded, his face solemn.

'But,' Ioseth went on, 'and it's a big but: each time they do so, the spirit finds out something new about them. If they try and control the evil more than two or three times, it comes to know them well enough to gain control of them. There have been two araneladi on the continent, who thought they could control the Darkness forever: but they were both taken over, enslaved. The first, more than a thousand years ago, was held and eventually cured, but the desire for that power, and the visions of the evil trying to drag him back, drove him mad. He became a blithering idiot, and had to be chained to a post in a shed. Eventually, no-one would take him food, because he was so violent. He only became peaceful and sane as he lay starving to death.

'The second one, who lived just before the last Foul War, was never found out by the acolytes, and he left, alone, and went to kchaban territory in what is now the Greenstone Country. There, he became the Serpent King.'

'The Serpent King was aranelado?' Tomas asked, aghast.

'That's what the wise said,' Ioseth said.

Tomas sat in silence, digesting the information. The terror of the Serpent King's reign was legendary, even among kchabani. It was the Serpent King that had begun the Third Foul War, with the express intention of enslaving all Speaking Beings in his reach. He had conducted every magical ritual he could find in an effort to prevent his own death, and made daily sacrifices of the heart of any being, human, eladon or kchaban. His cruelty was the stuff of nightmare: he liked to dress in the skins of his victims, he ate unborn babies, and he ate the brains of prisoners while they were still alive. He amused himself in the most unspeakable ways. 'I needed to know that,' Tomas said. 'I read in the library at Greystone, that the way he died was also quite horrible.'

'What happened?' Ioseth asked.

'When the Allies sacked his city at the end of the war – you know, the Haunted Ruins place in the Greenstone Country – he ran for it, all alone; but he was caught by some kchabani on the way to the Slave Coast. There, they tortured him for a whole year, before disposing of him. It seems he taught them too well. They really weren't impressed that he had taken them into a war that they ended up losing, after becoming as much of a scourge to them as he was to us.'

Ioseth nodded. 'It gets worse, then,' he said, 'Caranto's visitor said that, because the Serpent King had taken so many measures to make himself immortal, he couldn't die, even when he wanted to. That might be why they were able to torture him for so long. After his body was wrecked, his soul would probably have drifted about, with nowhere to go. It will probably still be drifting when the whole earth crumbles to dust.

'But, I think we should change the subject.'

'Definitely,' Tomas agreed. He resolutely avoided thinking of how close he'd come to becoming another Serpent King. If it hadn't been for that Voice... What was it? Did the Starkindler speak to people?

Tomas had no time to consider esoteric questions in the days following his return. Events had moved along while he was in the Hall. His volunteering as communicator was eagerly accepted, and he accompanied Master Helder on his hectic schedule for twelve days, learning diplomacy and proper form from a master. Helder was able to wring concessions from the most unlikely people: with diligent effort, he managed to convince the Greenland eladi leaders that they were on a rescue mission to the people of Greystone; but he made as few promises as he could about what the oreladi would get in return. Tomas knew he would have to live a lot longer to become as good as Master Helder, but since his position among the armed forces concerned communications between the forces and the embassy and nothing else, he was required only to follow directions.

In the second half of the eleventh month, Tomas took ship for the continent. He travelled with a detachment of warrior-magi on a two-masted transport ship, one of several in an invasion fleet. This time he had his sea-legs, and wasn't quite as miserable as he'd been on the outward trip. They were to join the staff of Lord Randacano, commander in the Spearhead, the vanguard of His Majesty's Forces in the Swift Rivers, but for the crossing he was travelling with a unit of warrior-magi.

The first sight of the Swift Rivers coast came at dawn one morning. It was unlike any land that Tomas had ever seen: a beach of brilliant, pale gold, backed by steep slopes where grew elephant-ear palms. It was a world away from the rainy South. They moved close to the shore, out of the strong, warm current that flowed south-westwards along the coast, and Tomas could see the shore quite clearly. Every now and then they would pass an inlet or lagoon, where dense, lush vegetation cloaked the sides a deep-cloven valley. As the day grew older and warmer, the wind followed, driving them ever farther up the coast.

At night they dropped anchor in shallow water, within earshot of the thundering surf on those steeply-sloping beaches. They weighed anchor again at first light, and followed the heat north-eastwards. In the late afternoon, they came to a place where the shore was less steep, the beach broad. The ships ahead of them had stopped and were ferrying personnel to shore in longboats. Tomas' group of warrior-magi went ashore last. By then the brief subtropical dusk had fallen, silhouetting the palms black on a turquoise backdrop. It was cool in the summer night, but not nearly as cold as it had been in Greenland. Tork was glad to be heading to dry land again, and flew off while Tomas was boarding the boat. The longboat rode the surf to shore, grinding to a halt where the shallow waves broke. The warrior-magi piled off into the water, kit on their backs, and pushed the boat back off the sand. The sailors waved and wished them luck, then rowed back to the ship. Wading up to the beach, the magi were directed to a lantern-lit desk under the palm trees, where an officer took their names and affiliations down, and they received a tiny wooden tablet with their information painted upon it. It was amazing how the Moreladan glyphs allowed so much information to be written in such a small space, Tomas thought.

There was a long queue for supper, but there was a great amount of it. Taking their heaped bowls, they found a comfortable place with some other magi around a fire a way along the beach. There was a relaxed atmosphere among the fires, with bawdy songs and laughter audible all up and down the beach. Tomas hoped someone was keeping watch, in case the natives hadn't yet been told that they were friends. For the moment, the warrior-magi enjoyed the break from supervision. Tomas had made a few friends in the company, and one of them, a Maga Varië, was to join the same unit as Tomas. She was a Lifter, a maga with a lifting and moving Ability. Tomas found it easier to get along with this group than he had in the Beastmasters' Hall. His race was obvious to anyone hearing his accent and seeing him shave in the morning. Perhaps, he thought, not all oreladi were so suspicious of humans.

The following morning Tomas awoke with the sun in his eyes. Tork was making raucous noises in the bush above him. The sun traced an incandescent silver path straight out to sea. Tomas sat up to savour the sight: such a cool, mellow morning, the sand cold outside his little sleeping-hole, the sky a defiantly burning blue, promising heat. He wondered if breakfast had been organised anywhere. Stripping down to his underwear, he took himself off down the beach for a wash, passing the washed-out holes where eladi had slept. He chuckled at the thought of the rude awakening they might have had.

As he stood in the surf, scrubbing himself with rough sand, he saw a longboat being rowed to shore. Instead of stopping in the shallows like the others had the night before, the rowers got out and pushed the boat up onto the dry sand. A handful of well-dressed eladi got out. 'That must be the General Staff,' Tomas muttered to himself.

'General Staff?' asked a voice. 'Where?'

Tomas turned round to see Varië, a loose shift plastered very attractively to her body, keeping her balance in the swell. She was putting her arm through one sleeve, as if she'd been washing herself underneath it. Tomas said, 'What are you doing here?'

'What are *you* doing here?' Varië shot back. 'I was here first.'

'Oh. In any case, I was thinking about that group over there, who were pulled all the way up the beach. The sailors did not make that much effort for us.'

'Ah,' said Varië. 'It would seem the holiday excursion is over.'

Tomas smiled ruefully. 'We are back in the war again, today.'

They were right. That day, the troops set up camp just inland, in a wide swath of tough grass beside a river. The river that flowed along one side of it was deep, and the ships bearing the war-animals could navigate it, one at a time. That whole day, they watched as the huge, strangely hairy, small-eared elephants and grey quaha were put ashore from their ships. It was an awesome sight.

In the afternoon a column of dark-skinned humans appeared, escorted by mounted scouts. Tomas thought they looked similar to Tsuna, physically; but their shields were tall, and made of hide only, with no wood backing. For clothing, they wore only pelt aprons, without the leather vests that the Tsuna wore as armour. Tomas spoke to some of them in Tsuna, but they replied in an impossible language which included bizarre click sounds. It was amazing to hear, but Tomas could make nothing of it at all. Tomas heard that there was a Tsuna with the leaders, who was presumably the interpreter. He would have liked to meet the man, but circumstances prevented it, and he wasn't called for.

That evening, as the leaders of the men conferred with the Generals, some local men joined the eladi on the beach for supper, as a show of hospitality. The men in turn shared some of their supplies, and it was quite a sociable evening, even with the language barrier. None of them knew more than a few phrases in Southlandish, though a few of the Greenland men from among the Human Volunteers asked around. All they could establish were a few names (replete with impossible clicks), and the name of their tribe: the Xagandu. At least that had only one click, Tomas thought.

The following day, as the foot-soldiers and the mounted companies moved inland, the elephant cavalry made ready to leave. Tomas and Varië were assigned to an elephant driven by Handler Vagorion. Like all elephant handlers, Vagorion was a lifelong companion to his animal: elephants were intelligent and nervous, and were not readily co-operative. They quickly became dangerous if their handlers changed. With Tomas the interpreter for this column, his animal was the first to leave after that of the Lord Randacano.

They left in the afternoon, after the hottest part of the day, moving northwards behind the lancers and scouts. The animals raised huge clouds of dust as they moved. The foot soldiers, mostly eladi and Xagandu, marched ahead and behind, following the gentle slopes picked out by the elephants. It was a massive movement of people, with the armed forces only part of the migration. Behind them came a vast baggage train, carrying everything from spare sandals to portable forges for the repair of arms and armour. The Invasion of the Sunlands had begun.

It took them only a day or so to leave the palm-lined beaches and lagoons of the coastlands behind. Beyond the salt spray of the coast, the land was covered in golden grass, so like that of Tomas' home, but dotted with spreading, thorny acacias, tall enough to shade an elephant. Along the courses of rivers grew dense, broad-leafed forest. For a few weeks, they followed the Xagandu warriors along carefully-scouted routes through the wooded grasslands to the Spear Fence, the mighty range that divided the Swift Rivers from the Highlands beyond. By then it was the twelfth month of the year, and full summer. The massifs in the blue distance were sometimes obscured by thunderous grey clouds.

They were making for the south of the Elephant Land, where the mountains between the Swift Rivers and the Highlands were lower, and the elephants could walk with relative ease. Since elephants cannot climb, the routes they followed across valleys could be tortuous. Tomas knew from briefings that they were making for the Vulture Pass. It was a route for the Fouls from the Slave Coast, as well: but if they were to fight on the Highlands, they must gain that pass. It was there that the hand of the Elephant Throne would fall heaviest.

Tomas had forgotten how bright it was on the Continent. The cool of the morning was long gone, though the sun was only halfway up the sky. It was the end of the twelfth month, and the sky was cloudless and dusty. He rode in a cab on the back of an elephant, through grass that grew as tall as a man. The column passed among large, flat-topped thorn trees, surrounded by cool, green shadows. Elegant white egrets stalked alongside, looking for a snack in the beasts' wake.

Off to Tomas' left, about a bowshot away, rode the Red Buffaloes, a company of lancers. Their high helms glittered in the sun, their red ostrich-feather plumes fluttering in the light breeze.

To his right marched a regiment of Xagandu men, their patterned shields moving like a line of upright beetles. Tomas could only admire their stamina: they could jog along like that for more than an hour. Then they would walk at a slow pace for some time, before starting another run. When they had the breath, they would sing a stirring song in their deep-toned voices.

Behind and in front of Tomas stretched the line of elephants, ten in total. Most had the war-towers on their backs, where a pair of eladi magi or archers sat, while the armoured handler rode on the beast's neck. The archer towers also had a mounted crossbow attached to the front, the bolts of which could punch through plate-mail. At the head of the column rode the Lord Randacano and his aides, also seated in war-towers.

From time to time, Tork would fly out with a message to magi in the other columns, now out of sight behind. He was always paid in snacks by the recipient, so he had taken to holding his foot out to Tomas for a message if he wanted food.

It was after midday, someweeks after the landing on the beach. The column was resting in whatever shade they could find, when a grey kite flew to the commander's tower. Moments later, the lead elephant spoke, in deep rumbles that were scarcely heard by men or eladi. Tomas could hear the tension in the animal's voice. Vagorion suddenly started up from his daydream under a spreading thorn-tree, put on his helmet, and announced, 'The scouts have spotted Fouls! All to stand by.' He climbed up on his elephant's neck with the ease of long practice.

'Are we moving?' Varië asked.

'Not yet,' said the handler. 'It seems to be a gang of kchabani hiding out of the sun for the day.'

A messenger from Lord Randacano jogged off towards a patch of acacias where the Red Buffaloes were resting. In short order, the cavalry had mounted, formed up and set off at a canter, raising a cloud of red-brown dust. As the rest of the column watched, they crested a rise and disappeared. The column suddenly seemed vulnerable without the heavy cavalry.

After a few minutes, Tomas felt uneasy. The silence was just too deep. Tork sensed his mood and gave a few anxious croaks, provoking similar responses from the other two messenger birds in the column. The men looked at them with suspicious eyes; great, black birds could not help sounding like bad omens. Tork took off, saying, *I go look.* He caught a thermal and started to ascend, circling like a vulture.

Tomas called out, 'Watch out for hawks!' Some of the raven's natural enemies might be working for the enemy.

Tork had not been soaring long before he came down again, plummeting like a piece of black-and-white rag. Tomas could feel the bird's fear, but he wasn't fearful on his own account. Reaching out, he asked, 'What do you see?'

Tork's frantic cawing translated to anyone with even a touch of Animal Sympathy: *Baboons! Baboons! Baboons!*

'Giant baboons!' Tomas shouted. 'It's a trap!'

One of the Volunteers called out in Southlandish, 'What's happening?'

'Giant baboons!' Tomas shouted, in the same language.

The commander's elephant gave another subterranean rumble, and the great beasts moved, forming a great U. The men moved into the space inside the formation, breaking into defensive groups of three just as the first deep-toned barks were heard. The eladi on their elephants cranked and loaded their heavy crossbows.

When the huge black baboons came running up the slope, they checked briefly at the sight of the elephants. The Commander boomed, 'Fire!' and six heavy bolts sailed towards the baboons – but the monsters came on too fast, barking their challenge. Not one of the bolts hit. They came round and went for the side of the U that was higher on the slope. Six of them jumped up onto the nearest two elephants, clawing and biting. Another six ran around the outside of the formation, making mock-charges and threatening, trying to panic the elephants. Another two attacked the men in the middle.

The elephants under attack shook their heads and trumpeted, while the eladi in their war-towers and on their necks tried to beat the monsters off with long spears and arrows.

Tomas looked for the leader of the monsters: it would be one of the biggest, meanest-looking baboons. Unfortunately, they all looked extremely large and violent, with the fur on their heads and necks puffed out, and their lips turned inside out, exposing those massive fangs. He focussed on a scarred beast attacking the outermost elephant. As Tomas watched, it pulled the handler off the elephant's neck into the long grass.

'Hey, you!' Tomas bellowed at it. The monster stopped, fixing Tomas (or the elephant he rode) with a baleful, red-eyed stare for just long enough: the elephant swung his huge head, smacking the baboon smartly in the head with one tusk. It staggered sideways, and Tomas could feel its pain and confusion. Tomas concentrated on fear and dizziness, trying to keep it off-balance for long enough for the handler to get away. The handler, however, did not rise. His elephant circled and trumpeted, trying to protect him, while the eladi on his back tried to get a clear shot from the moving beast.

Tomas looked around in exasperation, and took up a bow from a rack in the cab. He pulled an arrow out of the seat quiver, maintaining his contact with the dazed baboon. Thanks to his Militia training, he hardly had to concentrate on nocking and aiming the arrow. As he let fly, the baboon broke free of his control, but it was too late: the arrow cracked into its skull, right above one eye. The monster staggered and fell. 'Got him,' Tomas said, breathing heavily.

Tomas looked to see if the others had noticed their leader falling, but it seemed they didn't. As he watched, the nearer elephant went down. Two baboons had succeeded in disembowelling the animal, and it fell screaming, its blood splashing the golden grass. The eladi in its war-tower jumped out as it fell, running to join the Volunteers. The baboons danced back, screaming and hooting, and went for the next elephant in line. Varië made a chopping motion with her hands, and one of the baboons fell as if hit by a tree-trunk. The first elephant had lost its war-tower and was fleeing, while the remaining two baboons jumped on the fallen tower and thumped it. Tomas could not see the eladi that had been inside.

Two of the other elephants, carefully managed by their handlers, moved towards their comrades. They waved their trunks, flapping their ears and trumpeting. It was a magnificent sight, and Tomas was glad not to be on the receiving end of it. The mighty animals charged at the baboons, but the monstrous monkeys were canny: they scattered and regrouped, surrounding the elephants that threatened them. The situation looked grim.

Tomas looked around for another leader baboon. Troops were sometimes led by pairs of dominant males, and the death of one of them would make no difference in a fight. If he could get the other one, the balance of the fight might shift in their favour. He saw that three of the baboons that had been threatening were now dead, one of them ruined by a heavy crossbow bolt. Another was being trampled by the other magi's elephant. Suddenly, there was a shout of triumph from the men – they had succeeded in killing one of the baboons! The other, suddenly finding himself alone, flailed about wildly, felling two men. It ran away and went to join its fellows attacking the fallen war-tower. Varië tripped it up and rolled it around in the grass; but she could not kill it simply by moving it. She picked it up and dropped it, trying to injure it somehow.

Tomas looked at the monsters around the fallen war-tower, and saw another scarred face. Extending his thought, he shouted, 'Come here, you ugly animal!' but he allowed his emotions to seep into the contact, and lost it. He gained more attention than he bargained for. The dominant baboon gave up trying to crush the war-tower and came charging towards Tomas' elephant, quickly followed by the other two. Tomas' fear at the sight of three sets of fur and fangs barrelling towards him swept aside any attempt at concentration. Two of the monsters jumped up at the head of Tomas' elephant. Vagorion hacked at one of them with his glaive, and it jumped off with a scream. Tomas looked for another arrow, but Varië had one ready. She shot the dominant baboon in its arm. With his head free, the elephant was able to attack. He scooped the lead monster up on his tusks and tossed it. Then, charging forward, he trampled the baboon that Vagorion had wounded, and lifted the one he had tossed, holding it by one leg. Tomas felt the elephant's red rage as he skewered the monster on one tusk. Blood gushed out onto the grass as the elephant shook his huge head, tossing the wreckage into the air. Tomas felt nausea and triumph in equal measure.

He looked around, seeking other targets, but there were none. Two baboons were loping away, but the rest were being butchered by the men and eladi on foot.

It had been a bad day. One elephant dead, another wounded and unable to fight, and half the men in their column were badly injured or dead. Tomas wondered what had happened to the Red Buffaloes.

That evening, as the sun silhouetted the trees against a blue-green sky, the column following caught up with them, guided by an owl. They came with Healers in three wagons to tend the wounded. As the campfires were lit and the animals relaxed, a handful of Red Buffaloes rode into camp. The company had been caught in an ambush by arkchabani. Although they had broken the ambush, the unit had been scattered. Their captain was dead. During the night, more of the Red Buffaloes came riding in, in groups of two or three. Scarcely three score had returned, from a total of about a hundred.

Their column was held up for a day while the hurts of ambushes were tended, and the dead were buried. The lead column was not the only one to suffer attacks that day, but had been the hardest hit. From then on, the columns moved within long sight of each other.

For another week or so, the Greenland forces moved steadily north-eastwards. They suffered continual harassment, mostly by kchabani striking at night. The giant baboons were a frequent threat, but after the first attack, Lord Randacano had learnt the lesson. He sent small groups of zebra-archers out on sweeps, to find and report, but not necessarily engage, any threat before it found them. The men also sent scouting parties to probe ahead. If baboons were found, they were dealt with by heavy cavalry. The tactics proved effective.

Sometime during the long skirmishes, Midsummer came and went. Tomas, as part of Lord Randacano's staff, accompanied him and a few other leaders to the Place of the Elephant, the Xagandu capital, for a courtesy call on the High King of the Xagandu.

The delegation rode on the Command Elephants, Lord Randacano's personal elephant cavalry detachment. As they crested a grassy slope, Tomas saw a large settlement of men, the like of which had remained much the same since before the kchabani came.

A stockade of unshaped wooden branches crowned a low ridge, which had been raised around a large town of round, beehive-shaped structures, made entirely of the one material easiest to hand – grass. Unlike the Tsuna or Bafedi, the people of the Swift Rivers country did not build in stone. Some of the more important beehive-buildings were surprisingly large.

As they approached the city, Tomas saw large crowds gathered outside the gates. Right in the middle of the gate, surrounded by warriors resplendent in royal ostrich-feather plumes, stood a man of surprising size. Not only was he a full head taller than anyone else, but he showed considerable middle-aged spread, as well.

Tomas accompanied Lord Randacano as translator, as the eladi dismounted and approached the King. Tomas looked for his opposite number: there would have to be someone to translate Southlandish into Xagandu. He saw a short, old man of mixed Southlander and Swift Rivers ancestry standing by, and nodded; there was someone else to translate.

For several minutes, Tomas and the old man translated pleasantries under the hot sun. Then a praise-singer bellowed something in his own language, and the crowd erupted in song. In a dancing procession, the eladi and men passed in to the town, where the Midsummer festivities got under way.

The celebrations were alien, and the circumstances not joyful, but men and eladi made every effort to enjoy themselves. For many of them, it was the last Midsummer they would ever see. For many, the 'never-again' phase of their hangover had an ominous undertone.

After the festival, the column moved northward, through countryside that changed as they climbed. There were a lot of dykes – rocky ridges crossing the land, crowned by spiky aloes. The trees became more bushy than flat-topped, and the country was more open, making ambushes less likely. After the third week, they came to the lands near the territory of the Slave Coast. These were empty of human habitation, though oreladon ruins were common. Game became sparse, with wary herds of small grazers taking over from the bigger animals. Their course now took them west and northwards, up the long slopes towards the Spear Fence, where distant cliffs sparkled with running water.

As they approached the Vulture Pass, the special forces of Greenland caught up with them: companies of mixed infantry and archers, all guarding Animal Magi who handled great cats. Most common were lion-handlers, but there were groups of cheetahs and leopard scouts, as well: lions for power, cheetahs for speed, leopards for stealth. Naturally, they had to march away from the cavalry, though elephants were less perturbed. It was these divisions that were to meet the threat of the hyena-handlers, the shamans and the giant baboons among the enemy forces. Tomas briefly regretted that he hadn't had the opportunity to join the leopard-handlers, as he saw the beautiful cats moving like liquid, golden violence through the dark, windy afternoon before a thunderstorm in the foothills; but he knew that the cat-handlers were a breed apart. Their training was every bit as exclusive as that of elephant-handlers.

With the approach of other units came more mundane work for Tomas. He took his first despatches from Master Helder as Greystone Communications Officer (the title was all one word in Moreladan), and sent replies by way of courier birds. For two days, the Greenland forces mustered within distant sight of the Fence, and the Vulture Pass that was their objective. Then, rested and provisioned, they moved on.

As they passed through lands under the hand of evil, Tomas' heart became troubled again. One evening, he sat apart on a rock under a tree, watching the activity in the camp. He was not on kitchen duty, and he decided to take his ease while he could, before someone appeared with some work for him to do. Tork had found a perch in a thorn tree above him, and was settling down for the night. Tomas looked west, towards the mountains. Though lower and easier than further south, they loomed black, mounting step-sided in the distance, closer now that the climb had begun. A cactus-like aloe taller than himself reared its spiky head close by to the left, silhouetted against the apricot clouds of sunset. The scene was at once imposing and beautiful. Tomas relaxed his senses, trying to meditate and clean his mind. He had just relaxed when a memory flashed unbidden in his mind: an elephant falling, mortally wounded, and monstrous baboons dancing and screaming around it. Though tempted by rage Tomas relaxed his hold and let it slide. It was evil, and evil fed upon its own consequences. He had the choice to drop it; he did so, sighed, and relaxed again.

When the sky was all but dark, Varië stepped up very quietly, and sat down wordlessly beside him. She looked in the same direction as Tomas. The light in the west was dim. Night came fast in the north of the world. The cooking fires of the warrior-magi were bright and cheerful, and the beautiful voices of the Elder folk floated out in the warm night.

'This land is beautiful,' Varië observed quietly. 'Harsh and hot, but so beautiful.'

Tomas smiled. This kind of countryside was almost familiar to him. 'When we get over the Pass, it will be less hot. It is more open, the scenery less interesting... but cooler.'

'First we have to get there.'

'Are you having second thoughts? Do you want to go home?'

The warrior-maga sighed. 'No. How else is a girl to see the world?'

'Seeing the world is not as exciting as it might seem at first,' said Tomas with a sigh. 'When the world is trying to chop you to bits, it becomes too exciting. I want to get back home.'

'Where is home?' Varië asked. 'I don't think I've ever asked you, before.'

Tomas looked up at the mountains. 'Home is a wide valley, far beyond those mountains. You go onto the Highlands, and travel north and west until you go downhill again. There is a forested valley, full of tall trees, where eladi live.'

'Eladi? The people of Lord Engolaran?'

'People of his tribe, yes; but also many of your race. They are called oreladi, there. There are others, too, of the Younger.'

'Your people?'

Tomas had to think about that. 'My people, yes. But I am of mixed race.'

'So the Elder and the Younger intermarry there?'

'Not often.'

'So you are a rare beast,' she smiled.

'We are,' he said, smiling back. 'Though there are no animal magi to concern themselves with us.'

'Is it your father or your mother that is Younger?'

'It is complicated,' Tomas said. 'They are – were – both Younger, but they themselves had many Elder ancestors.'

'Have they died?' Her voice was quiet.

'I don't know. I left home years ago now, and I was living in another town when the kchabani came. I found myself in Greystone, but I never heard anything about what happened to my family.'

'So you don't come from Greystone after all? Why do you call it home?'

Tomas smiled. 'I served in the human militia there, and later started my Discipline there. Also, a very special person lives there.' He smiled, but sadly.

Varië nodded. 'I see. Everyone misses someone, in the military.'

They sat there for quite a while, savouring the peace of the night. It was cold. Looking to one side, Tomas saw people lining up for food, and he nudged Varië. He realised she had been meditating, and said, 'It's supper-time.'

She unfolded her legs and stood up. 'It is strange. I just cannot imagine what my life will be like after the war.'

'Well,' Tomas said with a shrug, 'neither can I.'

'There must be some reason I can see no further,' Varië said, 'but I'm quite sure your life will be very different.'

'You are?' Tomas asked, surprised. They went to their packs for their eating utensils.

'Yes,' she said, 'it is strange. Most of the time I see my own future better than others'; but it seems yours is important. I know the wise are concerned about araneladi, since they may go bad so horribly. I hope that you do not. I might have to be the one to stop you.'

Tomas tried to smile, but failed. He remembered that night of dread in Master Aravon's house, and the great kchaban's parasite: *I await your sacrifice*. He said, 'I know the risk I face very well – better than you might think.'

The look Varië shot at him was deeply suspicious. They didn't talk about it anymore that night, but Tomas at least knew from then on, why he found it so difficult to make friends amongst the Greenlanders.

The Spearhead had gained strength as it moved north-eastwards, after the losses it had suffered in its push through the Swift Rivers country. Lord Randacano's elephant column was back to full strength, and Tomas joined another, consisting of the remains of his own, plus those of several others. The foot soldiers had been joined by large groups of Xagandu warriors, as well as others from the kindred Naicweru nation, who had joined them en route. Tomas' division was now at the back of the Spearhead. Each elephant cavalry company was accompanied as usual by one detachment of lancers and another of foot, a company or an impi of men.

A few nights later, they were camped on a north-facing slope, within striking distance of the Vulture Pass. It was the middle of the first month, and a warm, wet wind was blowing down from the mountains. The warrior-magi were briefed after supper, in a lamp-lit space between two overhanging buffalo-thorn trees. If they were to meet serious opposition before the Highlands, it would be at the pass. If the Fouls seemed not to have taken them seriously thus far, that only meant that there were some nasty surprises being prepared. According to the leopard-scouts and the mounted scouts, there was a strong-flowing river to cross before they got to the Vulture Pass. At the foot of the pass was a ford, the only place where the banks were not too steep for the elephants. Overlooking the ford was an isolated, round-topped hill, an ideal place for the kchabani to site artillery pieces, catapults and ballistae. By the reports of the scouts and their spy-birds, there was great strength already on the far side of the ford, and probably some artillery on the hill, though it had not been there when the intelligence was gathered. That was as much as could be seen, since all the slopes were patchily forested with thick bush, as was the floodplain of the river. Though the trees hindered the scouts' vision, they would also afford the foot-soldiers of the Spearhead some cover.

The next day, the eladan wise invoked the protection of the Powers in front of each company as the sun rose. The level of tension was eased slightly, butbreakfast was still a quick and nervous affair. If anyone told a joke, it was greeted with oddly strident laughter. The sky was a deep, bright blue, but there were flat-bottomed, grey clouds suggesting weather on the way, and any shade was good news for night-eyed kchabani. Lord Randacano gave a speech, which Tomas knew was inspiring, but only because he read it later: at the time, though he listened, he remembered nothing.

One last equipment check, another hurry-up-and-wait to form up, and they were away, leaving a detachment of guards with the supply train and the Healer wagons. Maga Varië was extremely nervous, as they made their long trek to meet history. Tomas tried to comfort her, but it wasn't comfort she wanted: it was action.

The front of the Spearhead was some distance ahead, close to the ford at the foot of the pass, but the rear was to deal with the artillery. During the afternoon break, Tomas saw the birds that gave the Vulture Pass its name: circling high, they floated like specks of death against the ominous purple clouds in the distance. He reached out, and felt their interest. They had seen battles before, and looked forward to having the field to themselves. Tomas laughed with bitter irony. Varië looked at him with an odd, pinched look in her eyes. 'Why are you laughing?'

Tomas pointed at the vultures. 'No matter who wins today, they will be glad.'

Varië looked up at the birds with disgust.

A coucal flew down to the elephant of Lieutenant Darebor, the leader of Tomas' column. At once, the orders came, relayed by runners and birds: the main companies of the Spearhead were to engage the arkchabani holding the ford, and the rear elephant company, together with the lancers and heavy infantry that marched with them, were to deal with the kchaban artillery on the hill. The column moved accordingly.

Tomas told Tork to hide himself in the rear of the cab. The bird was quite willing to obey, since the weather had turned gusty by the time they reached the round hill. Tomas hoped that the heavy clouds would not gather or build. Any bright light was welcome when dealing with Foul Folk. Unless they were arkchabani, he thought.

As they steadily ascended the rounded hill in the gathering storm, the lancers scouted a path up the south side of the slope, which would bring them out right on top of the artillery. As they rode away, the rain started falling in fat, cold drops.

The lancers were just out of sight when a shower of arrows and slung stones rained down on the men and eladi on foot. The foot soldiers were prepared, however, and their advance barely slowed. Visible in the swirling rain were about a hundred kchabani, just within bowshot. The Commander called out an order, the elephants rumbled, and the archers in the war-towers made ready. Tomas wondered briefly if the crossbows would work in the rain, when the heavy bolts went whistling through the air. Obviously they did, he thought. The damage they inflicted was quite substantial, where they hit. The kchabani shot an ineffective volley at the elephants, and then ran, back up and along the slope. With a roar like thunder, the Xagandu and Naicweru warriors gave chase. The eladi foot soldiers, showing greater discipline, carried on their steady course. They outnumbered the kchabani. It was transparently a trap. The elephants continued on their gently ascending course to bring them out on a level with the artillery.

The rain was thinning out, when Tomas saw frighteningly large objects flying ahead, from up the slope on the left, towards the ford below on the right: with a sinking feeling, he realised that they were boulders flung by the catapults towards the ford. The bombardment of their friends had begun, but they could not strike the artillery yet; and elephants do not run uphill. Hopefully the cavalry would reach them soon. Maga Varië was saying, 'Just a little closer, come on!' Vagorion could not urge his elephant any faster. The maga was still too far away to use her Ability.

All at once, he heard wild cackling and whooping up ahead. It was from hyenas in a heavily-armed company of foot-kchabani. The trap had been well and truly sprung. As if to confirm his thought, he saw heavy ballista-bolts arcing toward them from the other side of the hill. He felt out for the hyenas, trying to isolate leaders.

Tomas looked across the valley. The air between him and the far side of the valley was thick with falling rain. Mobs of black figures were charging down to the ford. As he watched, a big brown boulder went hurtling down towards the hither side of the ford, which was hidden by trees. As it travelled, it seemed to slow down in mid-air! A Lifter in the Spearhead must have caught it. The boulder fell heavily, well short of its target, but there were many more where that came from. He focused on a hyena running towards the eladi foot soldiers: he imagined nausea and disorientation, and the beast's run faltered. The animal was hit by at least two arrows.

Tomas looked right, down the grassy slopes, to where companies of mounted archers, heavy infantry and impis brought up the rear of the Spearhead. The men and eladi on foot ran down towards the ford, but the zebra-archers turned and made up the slope towards him. 'Here comes the cavalry!' he called to Varië.

She wasn't listening. Her fine face scowling with concentration, she made a pulling motion with her hands. The cab rocked with the reaction, as a heavy boulder launched from the hill above suddenly changed direction and fell down among the kchaban archers.

'Well done!' Tomas said.

'Thanks,' she said, panting. 'Now it's your turn!'

The hyenas were running among the foot soldiers. Men and eladi were hard put to defend themselves against the carnivores as well as the kchabani. Tomas saw a big hyena mauling an elado on the ground. He reached out, imagining a threat behind the animal, and shouted, 'Look out behind you!' It worked. The hyena turned and attacked one of its fellows. It was a male. Darn it, he thought, we need the leader.

Tomas looked about. There she was! The lead hyena was attacking the leader of the *enctostari*. He was cut off from his men and surrounded. It was only a matter of time until he was pulled down. Tomas reached out again, touching the hyena's mind – it was very different to a wild one. Wild hyenas attacked for food and status, but this one had all it needed. It had been warped by the kchabani into a thing that fed on pain and fear.

Seeing that she was feeling some fatigue, Tomas seized on the feeling and magnified it. Why don't you just stop, he thought. This is too much hard work, it's not as though you'll be allowed to eat him afterwards.

The hyena stopped briefly to catch her breath. It was all the Captain needed. He brought his long sword whistling down on the beast's head, and it fell with a groan.

Tomas carefully amplified the fear in every hyena he could reach; the elephants trumpeted and mock-charged, adding to the carnivores' panic. That was the breaking point. There was a sudden loss of momentum in the hyenas' attack. Running in all directions, they attacked anyone in their way, even kchabani.

At the same time, the artillery fire ceased altogether. Looking up the slope, he saw the lancers among the kchabani and their machines, their beautiful glaives flashing in the cloudy green light as they hacked and slashed. The Fouls on this hill were all but finished.

Tomas and Varië looked at each other, grinning. They had made it! They were still alive! But the battle still raged on. Tomas saw a Xagandu man running from a pair of hyenas. Tomas turned to control the animals, and had distracted one of them when he heard a loud whooshing sound over his head, coupled with a startled exclamation from Varië. Tork screamed and took off into the rain. Ducking reflexively, Tomas turned around to face the maga; but she was no longer there. Instead, there was a wide splash of brilliant red on the side of the cab. He gaped in astonishment.

Vagorion was looking back towards Tomas, his fine face pure white, a mask of horror. He gave a moan, of horror or sickness.

Before Tomas could think, the elephant in front of him was struck by a monstrous spear, fully as long as Tomas was tall, thick as a young tree. The animal fell with a scream, throwing its war-tower down in ruin. Tomas looked ahead; another group of kchaban artillery had appeared on the slope! They must have sneaked up behind the hyena infantry. Their ballistae were firing more of those huge bolts, making the same lethal whooshing sound that Tomas had heard just before... At the same time, the catapults in the new group had resumed the bombardment of the ford. What had happened to Varië? They needed her now! Rushing to the other side of the cab to look for her on the ground, Tomas looked over the side. For the rest of his life, he wished he had not. What remained of her was scattered in the red-spattered, yellow grass. Tomas' blood ran cold and he gagged. All detachment left him.

The elephant Tomas rode on trumpeted and shook his head, confused and frightened. He didn't know what to do, and his handler was in no state to tell him. Tomas fought nausea, and the elephant, in a panic, turned to run.

'Handler Vagorion!' Tomas shouted. The elado turned to face him with his terrible, haunted look. He must have seen it happen, Tomas thought, I'm glad I didn't. 'Control your charge!' he ordered. The elado seemed to welcome the order, as if it gave him something to focus on. 'Take us out of here,' Tomas told him. 'There's nothing more we can do, now.' They started moving away, and another of the elephants did likewise. Then there came a rumbled command from the lead elephant, and all stopped. Lieutenant Darebor was turning everyone around, directing them to attack! The elephants turned back to face the siege engines. Over the racket of war, Tomas heard the Lieutenant bellowing, 'Ready bows!'

The archers in the war-towers turned their monster crossbows towards the kchaban artillery. They just had to fight back for long enough for the lancers to get there. Tomas heard the rattling of the crossbows being drawn as the elephants, trumpeting in rage, charged the kchaban artillery head-on.

'Fire!'

Heavy crossbow-fire raked the kchaban artillery, several seconds before the Lancers overran them. The arm-length crossbow bolts thudded into machinery and operators, shredding wood and bone. Only one ballista-bolt was fired, narrowly missing the lead elephant. Then the lancers, regrouped, were there, and the elephant cavalry turned its fire on the remains of the kchaban forces, until the light cavalry and the foot soldiers could deal with them. It was all over within half an hour. As the last Foul resistance crumbled, the Lieutenant sent a detachment down the back of the hill to check for any other nasty surprises. Tomas looked east, along a straight stretch of the river below, just visible through the rain. In the middle of a straight reach he saw the ford: there was a thick clot of darkness under the cloud down there, as if something had arisen that shrouded itself in shadow; but as he watched, the darkness dissipated, and an elephant strolled onto the gravel drift of the ford. It trumpeted, and Tomas could feel its triumph over the distance between them.

Vagorion was looking in the same direction. Turning around, he shouted, 'They've taken the ford!'

'We've won!' Tomas cried out. The news was taken up among eladi, men, elephants, quaha and birds. Tork came swooping in to land on Tomas' shoulder, cawing with triumph. Amid the scattered cheers and the songs of the men, Tomas looked again at the red spatter of blood on the cab wall. Shock hit him again, and he wept aloud. Varië had helped with this victory. The last time he'd seen her alive, she had been tired but smiling. Now, she would never smile again.

Through his shock, Tomas heard how the Fouls had lost the Battle of Vulture Pass: there had been kchabani held in reserve above the ford, ready to attack when the allies were fully committed in the water; but they, eager for the fight and lacking discipline, had charged down before the whole of the Spearhead was engaged. The men and eladi on foot had outflanked them, coming down from the steep part of the bank to the east of the ford, and raked them with arrows and slung stones from the cover of thick bush on the river bank. By the time the shamans had summoned their wind-devils, the great cats were on them. The Fouls had played their hand too soon, and paid the price: outflanked, fighting in water with the dervishes unable to attack the great cats, they had been beaten down.

Most of the Foul leaders had escaped, but for now at least, the Fair Folk and their allies controlled the bottom of the Vulture Pass. Now, they had to deal with what was at the other end.

CHAPTER XV

The green-robed Wise sang, his voice rising and falling in smoothly controlled passion. Tomas followed the song after the first line, with all the other survivors. It was the General Vigil for the fallen, and Tomas kept Varië in his heart, wishing her rest and consolation. Everyone mourned, but there wasn't a tear in sight. The 'green wood', the people who had joined up at the same time as Tomas, had all been blooded. All now had that same penetrating stare, the closed doors behind their eyes, since the passage through the Swift Rivers Country and the Vulture Pass. He assumed he had a similar look, though he seldom saw his own reflection these days. He hadn't shaved for a week.

Although the Moreladi had never fought kchabani in Greenland, there had been a very long dynastic struggle which had forever altered the oreladi there. Never again would they flee warfare, and their long, bitter experience now bore fruit in any struggle against less disciplined opponents.

Just before sunrise on the morning after the battle, Tomas was sent in a small detachment of mounted scouts and magus cavalry to the top of the Vulture Pass. They were to contact any humans they might meet there, and report back by means of his raven. They had already started, when Tomas recognised the leader of the scouting party – it was Lord Randacano himself! He was dressed as a common quahastar, however, so Tomas thought it better not to say anything. Eladon leaders often did their own reconnaissance. It had definite advantages.

The path was a gentle incline, but very long, and it switched back on itself again and again and again. It was late afternoon after a long day's riding before they saw the top of the Vulture Pass, and Tomas looked on the Highlands for the first time in more than six months. The top of the pass was a sudden emptiness after the stepped, grassy slopes below. The path ran out between two huge buttresses of golden sandstone, standing like the posts of some colossal gate. Beyond them, the eastern Highlands rolled away into the distance, leagues upon leagues of lush, green grass. The forests and thorny woodlands were all gone. But, the grass near at hand in the pass was strange: tall, thick stalks of the stuff, most of which the quaha would not eat. 'It's sour-veld,' The second-in-command said, 'Grass will have to be cut for the cavalry down below, and brought up.'

Tomas nodded. 'Such a waste.Grass everywhere, and not a bite to eat for the animals.'

'There should be more suitable grass in the watercourses, and elephants at least can snack from the trees,' said Lord Randacano.

Apart from the forage problem, something else nagged at Tomas' mind. There was a sad, resentful air about the place. He commented on it to one of the magi, who said, 'I feel it, too. Perhaps the Fouls did evil here. The land would remember.'

'Perhaps,' said the sergeant. 'In which case, time under us will cleanse it.'

Another of the Scouts had a peregrine falcon. He sent her out on a long, wide sweep while they went investigating. If there was any sign of Foul activity, the bird would have seen it. They were satisfied that the area was clear at present.

There was a small river that curled cold and grey through the huge gateway. There they found their spot, and set up camp. Tomas drew the straw for first watch. In the chill night, after the eladi were all wrapped up and dreaming, Tomas stood up and strolled away from the fire, toward the pass. He wanted to see the full moon rising behind the buttresses, and to keep his feet warm. Once away from the fire, however, he paced back and forth. The depressing mood of the place was a constant ache. He was able to detach from the worst of it; but it deepened with the night, until it took on overtones of dread.

As the moon came up behind the left buttress, the land was bathed in a beautiful, silvery glow. Tomas looked straight at the moon, wondering at the sight. However, the dread he felt in the air deepened to horror. He thought of returning to the watch-fire.

Then he saw it.

A figure, not quite human-shaped, was crouching on the top of the left-hand buttress, tiny in the height and distance, silhouetted against the full moon. Tomas stood, still as a stone. How long had they been watched? The horror multiplied in the night, and his detachment came under assault from gibbering fear. He looked back towards the campfire, where the light from the embers threw the leaves of the sheltering trees into relief.

Trying to move quietly, he returned to the fire. Maybe the Thing, whatever it was, hadn't seen them yet. Why was there so much fear here? Was that the reason why the kchabani were not present here? As he came back to the fire, all the eladi rose instantly. 'What's wrong?' asked the sergeant.

'There's... there's a Thing out there,' Tomas waved his hand behind him. His eyes were wild and staring. 'It was on top of the rock wall on the left,' he said, his voice breaking despite himself.

'What is it?' the Sergeant prompted.

'I don't know,' said Tomas. 'It's man-like, or man-shaped at least, and –' he broke off. There was a sound in the distance. It was a kind of raucous cough, a lot like a leopard's call, only subtly, horribly different. At that sound, every hair on Tomas' body stood up on end. The quaha started and reared, and would have bolted but for the efforts of the animal magi. Their high-pitched, laughing calls rang out in the night, as the eladi rushed for their weapons. Somebody kicked sand over the coals, and everything went silver and cold in the moonlight. The magi soothed the animals with the ease of long practice, but they took Tomas' mood, and would not settle.

'*Magus!*' barked the sergeant. 'Pull yourself together, you disgusting little rodent!'

The insult and tone of voice got through to Tomas. He snapped out of it, his Militia training taking over. The quaha calmed down.

Lord Randacano said, 'It affects you more than it does us.' In an undertone, he added, 'Which worries me.' He said out loud, peremptorily, 'You stay and mind the quaha.'

Tomas was ashamed and relieved in equal measure. He went to the pickets and stood there, trying to calm down. The scouts and magi moved off, on foot and in complete silence.

Tomas stood, fingering his knife-hilt. He calmed down enough to feel guilty. He had given in to fear, and now his mates had to face that horror, whatever it was, without him. The horrible barking cough came again, jangling his nerves. What was it about that sound that made him so frightened? Then with a chill of terror, it came to him – it was a sound straight out of Southlander folklore, out of cold winter nights when the wind moaned and hissed in the dead grass, and the moon was full: tales of the leopardman. The call had connected with something deep inside him, with the ancestral memories he carried within: how a terrible creature, a mixture of man and beast, lived in lonely places, haunting isolated hills overlooking the plains. It preyed on men, and on their animals.Dogs were its favourite snack. By day, it was a blond-haired, tawny-eyed man, but by moonlight a leopard of awesome strength and cunning; any human badly injured by it would become a leopardman themselves; and it could not be killed, save by weapons edged with gold.

They didn't stand a chance. It meant disobeying orders, but he had to warn the scouts: if the leopardman was real, so was the magic protecting it. At least they weren't Southlanders, who would think him off his head for raving about a mythical creature. He felt out, locating the others. Like good scouts, they had left with no physical trace, but they were scared: they were moving closer together than they should.

Tomas was in shoulder-high grass, concentrating on following the scouts and magi, when he heard a sound to his left. All at once, he was confronted by a large cat, its spots in groups of five clearly visible in the moonlight. Tomas felt the cat's surprise past his own: he was not what it had expected. Suddenly, with a snarl and a thrashing of grass, a *second* leopard bounded through the grass from the opposite side, and leaped at something *behind him*! The first leopard dodged around Tomas, and bounded towards the same place. Drawing his long knife with a steely ring, he spun round, blade and staff at the ready,, and saw the cat-fight in the long grass.

The two leopards were circling a strangely long-legged, catlike form, slightly larger than themselves. The pattern on its pelt was that of a leopard, but through his Sympathy Tomas knew it was not. *How had he not felt it?* Terror reared up in him, but now he knew its name, and mastered it with some difficulty. He let the fear run through him and around him, while he stood, a rock in the stream.

The leopardman snarled and spat as it fended off the leopards. Fear and loathing radiated from them, in waves anyone could sense. The thing slashed out, first at one cat and then at the other. The enraged animals bounded back, circling at bay. Leopards seldom if ever hunted together, and didn't work together unless they were young siblings, or mates. Suddenly, a leopard-scout appeared to the left of the fighting cats, loosing an arrow at the leopardman. The arrow hit, but stopped suddenly as if hitting mud. The leopardman turned to face the elado, and Tomas had to act fast. Waving both knife and staff in the air, he gave an unintelligible cry. At the same time, he reached out for the leopardman's mind: it was a mass of rage, with just enough clarity for a horrible, calculating intelligence. The leopardman turned towards him, as the two leopards attacked again, trying to defend the eladi. The were-creature slashed out left and right, and the cats fell back, one of them wounded. The obstructions out of the way, the leopardman turned its attention to Tomas and leaped at him.

Tomas brought his staff up to meet the thing, and something happened that was completely unexpected. In later years this event had whole a field of study devoted to it: the amethyst in the top vibrated so hard that it hummed in its setting, as the energy it held became part of Tomas. With the augmented power of the stone, Tomas pierced the monster's fury, just as it hit the foot of his staff. There was a flash of amethyst-purple, and the leopardman fell back, gagging: Tomas had hit it in the neck. He drew aside the thing's rage like a curtain, uncovering the fear and horror and madness that were its foundation. Speaking words that were not his own, he bellowed '*Be Still!*' even as Timaeos the acolyte had ruined the sorcerer in Hunter's Wells a lifetime before.

The leopardman cowered and cringed, laid low by turmoil within.

Deep within its mind, Tomas perceived a knot of darkness, lying at the root of insanity. Tomas feared to touch it. Who knew what could happen? Instead, he bound it up tightly, muffling it with calm and forgetfulness and acceptance, as one gentled any large animal. As the leopardman moaned and sank to the ground, Tomas became aware of the scouts, the magi, and others: leopard-scouts and other, lightly-armed fighters newly arrived from below the Pass.

Tomas looked around. The eladi were thunderstruck. For a long moment they stood, watching Tomas standing over the gentled cat-thing. The uninjured leopard stood, tense and ready to spring.

'What did you do?' the sergeant asked. Some of the scouts' arrows were aimed at Tomas.

'I have gentled it, for now,' Tomas said quietly. He thought, If I could untie that knot of darkness... 'It's under a spell of some kind. Is there a wise here?'

'Yes,' came a surprised voice. An eladon wise stepped forward, robed in green in the fashion of Greenland clerics. 'I had an intuition that I would be needed here before sunrise, so I requested a fast escort and climbed all night.'

'You were called indeed, father,' Tomas said with relief. 'I have seen the heart of darkness in this creature. Would you please give me your blessing, as protection and strength against evil?' He sank to his knees, and the arrows aimed at him were lowered.

The wise came up to him and placed his hand just above Tomas' head, almost touching. 'I will give you what I can,' he said. He murmured, and Tomas felt warmth wash from his scalp to his sandals. There was a delight, and a power in the benediction. Tomas felt like laughing for sheer joy.

Then the wise moved away. Tomas took up his staff and knife together, and the crystal began to hum and vibrate again as he turned back to the leopardman. Tomas closed his eyes. Delving once more into the creature's mind, he soothed the fear and hatred that had grown since his last touch. Finding the mad knot and sweeping away what remained of its muffling, Tomas concentrated the love and joy and power of his blessing into a narrow beam, and shot it straight at the heart of darkness.

The knot vanished like smoke. Tomas was dimly aware of the leopardman convulsing, but he was concentrating too hard to move. He soothed flat the places where the knot had been attached, and made the creature's mind calm. Tomas was astonished at how complex it was: a mixture of hominid and feline. Casting around one last time for any other warping or darkness, he was glad to find nothing obvious. He broke off the Sympathetic contact, to see the long-limbed cat lying face-down on the ground in the silver light. As he looked, the leopard gave a deep-throated moan. Then its shape shifted, the patterned fur thinned to fine golden hair, and the feline face became human. Tomas closed his mouth, which had dropped open in amazement: in place of the leopard was a furry, blonde woman, her hair filthy and matted, sobbing naked in the moonlit grass.

For some time the human-like figure lay prone and weeping into the grass. The sound took Tomas back to the worst time in his life, to his slavery after the kchaban attack on Hunters' Wells. Sinking to his knees, he smoothed the figure's matted hair, wanting to comfort her, to do anything to stop the crying. The eladi stood around in amazement, until Lord Randacano took charge. Sending the scouts back to the campsite, he directed others to help the leopard scout with his wounded cat. Tomas took off his cloak and covered the leopardwoman with it. She looked at him with an expression of worshipful adoration in her tawny eyes.

'What language do you speak?' Tomas asked her in his mother-tongue.

'The common tongue of the South,' she said, with a strange accent. 'It's been so long since I said anything.'

'Were you –' Tomas looked for a diplomatic way to phrase the question '– were you born human?'

She nodded, and sobbed again. She looked at her hairy limbs and torso, felt her face. 'Is it over?' she asked. 'Am I still...'

Tomas shook his head. 'It's over.' There was a long, horrible story there; but the telling would have to wait.

Back at the campsite, Tomas was questioned by the lord and the wise. Then the leopardwoman was examined by the Beastmasters, who concluded what Tomas already knew: that she was unnatural, a magical combination of beast and speaking being, though there was no trace of darkness about her any more, other than the pain of suddenly returned reason. The horror that had driven the real leopards wild was gone, and even the sad atmosphere of the place had lessened. The eladi didn't know what to think of her, but Tomas could not hate her for what she could not help. She was no longer a killing fiend, or she was at least unlikely to become one without warning. Her name, she said, was Taliga.

When he finally got to sleep that night, the leopardwoman snuggled up to him, still wearing his cloak. She smelled quite ripe, and Tomas was sure she was the reason he was suddenly itching; but she trusted him utterly, and Tomas was too soft-hearted to shoo her away. At least someone didn't mind getting close to him, he thought.

The next morning, Tomas was woken by the activity of the camp. He rose, grumpy and sandy-eyed, and left Taliga sleeping while he went to the stream for his ablutions. It was a cool, bright morning. On the way back, Lord Randacano called him.

'What are you going to do about your, um... captive?'

'She seems safe. I don't want to send her away, in case something happens to turn her savage again.'

'The wise thinks her unsafe.'

'If she were to meet a kchaban shaman, I don't know what it could do to her; but as long as she remains with me, she can't change back again. I would like to take charge of her, personally.'

The eladon lord nodded. 'Very well,' he said, 'until I am informed otherwise, you may keep her by you. Just don't let her out of your sight.'

'Yes, my lord.' Tomas was glad not to have to argue for now.

Tomas returned to his tent, and woke the leopardwoman. 'Master!' she said with that unnerving expression of worship on her face. 'So it wasn't all a dream, after all!'

'No, it wasn't,' said Tomas, shaking his head. 'Listen carefully, Taliga. You must stay with me all the time, all right?' She nodded. 'Don't go wandering off without telling me, because someone might think you were still mad.'

She nodded again, her fuzzy face concerned. 'But the leopards know I'm not.'

'That's good,' Tomas said, thinking, *she's sympathetic to the leopards*? 'But it's not the leopards that you have to worry about. There will be many eladi coming up from the lowlands this evening or tomorrow – very, very many of them, all armed and dangerous, and some with other animals. Just stay with me, and I'll look after you, all right?'

She nodded again, solemnly, like a young child. 'I like you to look after me, master.'

'And you don't have to call me that,' Tomas said. 'Just call me... Tomas.' He thought it safe to give his own name, now.

As the first detachments came up the Vulture Pass, Taliga stayed obediently by Tomas. She watched in amazement as the beautiful army came through the sandstone gateway. Time wore on, and she asked for food politely. She could at least feed herself. That evening, as the sun set over the Highlands in swathes of pink and orange, Tomas cut

Taliga's matted and infested hair, using a borrowed pair of barber's scissors. It was a messy job, and she looked a bit ragged, but she sat quietly through it. Tomas told her to take a bath, but she simply refused: she didn't like the water, or at least not in the cold and dark. 'Maybe when it's daylight again,' she said.

The movement of the Spearhead up the Vulture Pass took several days. In the meantime, the scouts located a shallow valley nearby where the soil was different and grass more palatable.

In that time, Tomas finally got Taliga to take a bath, and she found she liked it. Tomas took that as a good sign: if the cat's dislike of water was reduced, perhaps the human part of her was becoming stronger. He managed to get some military-issue maga's robes for her from the quartermaster. They were the only clothes suitable for women that he could find.

As the Spearhead ascended the Vulture Pass, the main body of His Majesty's forces was making its way through the Swift Rivers country. Kchaban forces continued to make raids, but there were no major incidents before the rearguard secured the Vulture Pass. By that time, the eladon forces had camped in the thick forests around the pass, and were practically invisible. There was one more battle some time later, when a force coming from the kchaban-controlled Highlands to re-take the pass was utterly defeated by the rearguard.

However, Tomas never saw the main body of His Majesty's forces coming to the Highlands. A week's journey down the infant Great River brought them to a place where the stream was joined by another from the north. The river from the north was polluted, probably by kchabani upstream, but the Great River was clean. The confluence was easily defended, and made a good staging site.

Taliga adopted Tomas as family, and seldom let him out of her sight. There were distractions for the leopardwoman, however: when some leopard cubs were born on the journey, Taliga assisted at the births, and became a day-mother to them. Her empathy with the cats was very strong, and the mother leopards trusted her completely. The cat nursery was useful to the leopardscouts, since it freed the mothers for work or hunting.

One evening in the campsite at the confluence of the two rivers, Taliga was sitting surrounded by golden, fluffy, spotted cubs, some sleeping, others bumbling around, chewing toys made from strips of old riding tack. Tork had settled down for the evening. Tomas was playing with the cubs, when a messenger came.

'O magus,' he said, 'The Lord Randacano wishes to see you, now.'

Tomas heaved himself up and retrieved his staff. He wondered if His Lordship wanted to question him about Taliga. Tomas hoped he wouldn't have to argue too much. He followed the messenger, not to the command pavilion as expected, but to the messenger's depot, near the ford of the Great River. He went in to the tent to find Lord Randacano, Lieutenant Darebor and a few other high-ranking eladi, all sitting around a portable table. Tomas' heart lightened to see who else was there: standing in front of them was a human, in the uniform of the Dukesmen. He was in his thirties, stocky rather than fat, with muddy-blonde hair and weather-beaten crinkles just appearing around his eyes. He had a ready smile, but had the smooth, dangerous confidence of thelifelong soldier, wearing leather and mail with no rank insignia.

'Ah, Magus Tomas,' said Lord Randacano. The High Commander was darker-skinned, almost brown, with eyes as grey as a summer cloud. He was of the same nation as Lord Dragelion, the High Beastmaster. Like most men of his tribe, he wore his black hair long, tied at the back with a band of gold. 'This Younger has just arrived, and we have need of your linguistic skills.'

'Very good, my lord,' said Tomas.

'Please ask him his name and designation, and what his message is.'

'A pleasure, sir,' said Tomas, grinning. As courtesy dictated, he began by asking after the other's health. 'I see you. How are you?'

The messenger was surprised to hear his own language. Tomas was clean-shaven again and wore a Greenland mantle, so the man had not been able to see his ears. He replied 'I am well, and yourself?'

The man had a West Highlands accent. It was so good to hear your own accent, thought Tomas. 'I am well,' he replied. 'I am Magus Tomas of Greystone, but I was born in Sweetwaters, in the west. I have studied with these people, and know their language, but there are very few here who speak Southlandish.'

'You're a wizard?' The messenger's face was clouded by some doubt.

'I studied under eladon masters,' Tomas explained. Now was not the time for this argument. 'I am not a spellcaster.'

'Oh, I see,' said the messenger. Tomas was relieved that he accepted the distinction. 'I am Iohan, son of Ioseth, of the Duke's Victor Commando. I have with me a message from the Duke himself.'

Translating the man's words to the eladi, Tomas took the bamboo tube he offered. It was a message-tube like this that had begun it all, he thought.

A green-robed wise was sitting there, and he rose to take the tube. He turned it over, looked at it, sniffed it, and passed it back to the commander. He said, 'It appears to be safe, my lord.'

'Open it and read it to us,' said Lord Randacano.

Tomas broke the wax seal, and pulled out a sheet of papyrus. The message was written in court hand, and Tomas translated as he read.

> "To the commander of the eladan forces, greetings from the Duke of the Highlands.
>
> "I and my general staff congratulate you on your taking of the Vulture Pass. We praise you for your heavy strokes against the Fouls, and would like to assure you of our support and good will. We would offer you such aid as is possible for us to give, but we could give it more effectively if we knew Your Eminence's plans for the future.
>
> "Our forces consist of several Commandos in the field, including those elements of our people resisting still in the north-west, near the Green River valley.
>
> "Some four-fifths of our territory is now occupied by the kchabani, who in the past several months have been much engaged in the war against Greystone, where some of your fellows lived. We have recently heard from our people in the west that their chief city has fallen, and its people are scattered in the forest and the western Highlands."

Tomas stopped. Greystone had fallen? His heart grew hollow, and he stopped reading.

Lord Randacano prompted him, 'Is that all, magus?'

Tomas swallowed his emotion. 'No, my lord. I shall continue.'

> "Though the Fouls used monsters and magic in their conquest of Greystone, I am told that they have paid dearly for it. My city of Tor Arfarass, alone among our chief cities, stands yet unconquered. However, with our people few and the enemy outflanking us, I fear we have little time left before our final stand.
>
> "If you have indeed come to purge the kchabani from the north, we urge you on with all due speed, and wish to assure you of our co-operation. Should you wish any assistance from us at all, it shall be given insofar as is

possible."

"Yours faithfully,

"Iosef, Duke Aradorion"

The eladi sat still for some time. Then Lord Randacano said to Tomas, 'Ask him if he knows anything about the Lord of Greystone.'

The answer came back, 'He doesn't know himself, my lord; but the city has fallen, and nothing has been heard of him.'

'When did it happen?'

Another round of translation: 'Four weeks ago – the kchabani fired the forest.' The hollow feeling deepened inside Tomas. He remembered the trees, their delightful shade. Had it all come to nothing?

Lord Randacano considered. 'It seems we are too late for Greystone. If the Lord Engolaran is dead, any promises or bargains made by him are moot.' Speaking to Tomas, he said, 'Ask him if he knows where the enemy's hand is heaviest now.'

'Do you know where the main kchaban forces are, or where the Skullbreaker is?' Tomas said in Southlandish.

'The latest information is that the Skullbreaker is with his forces in the east of the Greystone territory, or near Alatasdam in the north of the Highlands.'

Tomas translated, and Lieutenant Darebor unrolled a copy of the map that had been made from the one that Master Helder's embassy had brought to the South. All pored over it for some time, asking the messenger for any other facts he knew. It was late at night before the meeting broke up.

Tomas spoke with Iohan for some time afterward, asking him more about the war, and what had happened in Greystone. The Fouls had new and terrible sorcery, such as had not been encountered before: they could conjure up spiders as large as dogs, which could drive men and horses berserk with fear. Though their venom was seldom lethal, it caused madness. Tomas had already encountered the giant baboons, and the winged serpents he hoped not to see again. These new horrors, said Iohan, were in addition to the dust-devils, the magical lightning and the Darkfear and Despair that they had always used before.

The night passed, and Tomas took Iohan for some food, and then made space for him in his own tent. Taliga was all wrapped up and asleep, the slumbering cubs curled up around her. Her face was invisible, but she was snoring gently. Tork was roosting in the tent's roof-tree, his beak buried in the white feathers of his neck. Iohan just flopped down and fell asleep almost instantly, his head on his saddle-bags. He was an experienced soldier.

Tomas woke with the wakening wind of a rain shower moving the canvas of his tent. The others were all asleep. His heart was horribly cold and empty. If Greystone no longer stood, what was he here for? Liriel could be dead, or worse; but many eladi had escaped, Iohan had said. The may-be's and the what-if's chased themselves around Tomas' head for some time, until he wearied of them. With the strength of long discipline, he simplified it for himself: he was doing all he could in the war, whether they won or not – and he could choose to hope, or not to. Deciding on hope, his mind calmed, and he slept again.

He was woken in the cold morning by something nibbling at his hand with very sharp little teeth: it was one of the leopard-cubs. He rolled it over and scratched its little round belly. Other furry little creatures were bumbling around the circular tent. One of them was padding over towards Iohan, who lay snoring by the tent-flap. Taliga was gone. The grass rustled in the wind outside, and the cubs were mewling for their mothers. Scooping the stray cubs together on Taliga's blanket, Tomas left the tent.

Some time later, he went to fetch Iohan to show him to the mess tent. He found him awake and alone in the tent, with a strange expression on his face.

'Who is that bearded lady?' he asked after the customary pleasantries.

Tomas thought that was a more flattering label for Taliga than the truth. He said, 'Her name is Taliga. She is... a very... rare person.'

'Is she also a Beastmaster?'

'Not really,' Tomas said, searching for tactful ways to avoid saying too much. 'She is very gifted, though. She might make a maga, in time.'

'I was woken up by one of those leopard cubs licking my face,' Iohan said. 'Then, its mother came in, and I thought I was finished.' He chuckled.

Tomas smiled ruefully. 'I'm sorry I wasn't there. I should have warned you.'

The man waved the apology away. 'Anyway,' he went on, 'I went for my sword, but the girl came in, and she just made some kind of sound to the leopardess. She picked out some of the cubs, and they just followed their mother, like kittens! I just couldn't believe it! Why do the eladi keep leopards?'

'Leopards are natural scouts,' Tomas explained. 'They move very quietly, are very inquisitive and are loners, unless they're a breeding pair. An eladon leopard scout is a beastmaster with a natural affinity for the cats, who has complementary personal qualities to leopards. His training diverges from that of a normal animal magus quite early on, and once they have completed it, they're a leopard magus for life. They adopt a leopard-cub once it's weaned, and they form a family bond with at least one cat. The cubs Taliga minds are badly needed, since some of the mature cats died when we took the Vulture Pass.'

'That's amazing,' said Iohan. 'Can only eladi do that?'

'Anyone with the Ability can do it; but men find it difficult to get the training – most humans with Abilities go bad, unless they're trained properly.'

'You mean like spell-casters?'

'Yes.'

'I see,' Iohan nodded. 'So, is Taliga being trained?'

'No, not yet,' Tomas said.

'Is she your ...?'

Tomas gave a rueful laugh. 'If I kept concubines, I couldn't be a magus.'

'Oh, I see,' Iohan looked somehow relieved. 'It's not allowed.'

'No,' Tomas explained, 'using another for personal pleasure is –' he cast about for a loose translation of the Celadon term '– unloving. My spirit's integrity can only be maintained if I make a gift of self.'

Iohan nodded sagely, obviously having not a clue what Tomas was talking about. He said, 'I wondered, since she speaks very highly of you.'

Tomas smiled. 'She has adopted me as family. I – helped her when she was suffering.'

Iohan looked Tomas straight in the eye. 'You know, when she came in – I know it sounds stupid – I could have sworn she was a leopardman.'

Tomas returned the man's gaze. Something deep burned behind those eyes, and Tomas suddenly knew that there was more to Commando Iohan than met the eye. He was no common soldier. With the certainty of prophecy, he knew the man had to know. He said, slowly and quietly, 'She was. I healed her.'

Iohan's face was still as stone. He said, 'I believe you. I've seen enough of old tales come true in the past week: eladi, on elephants, with great cats walking among them; and wizards; and now a werecreature.' He looked intensely at Tomas, as he said, 'Are you absolutely sure she's healed?'

Suddenly it made sense: here was something that involved Tomas only briefly, but importantly. Tomas said, 'As long as she stays out of the clutches of the kchabani and their shamans, I'm quite sure.'

'Right.' Iohan may have been waiting for more information, but Tomas didn't say any more.

They went to the mess tent, where they breakfasted. Later that day, the Dukesman rode away, bearing communications to the leaders of men in the Highlands. Tomas was not told what they contained. Taliga watched him go, and asked Tomas, 'Will he come back?'

'I'm sure he will, Taliga.'

'He is a special person,' she said.

Tomas smiled. 'He thinks you are, too.' *What* had happened that morning? And *how*?

Taliga's face lit up briefly, but then fell again. 'Does he know about –' she touched the downy, golden hair on her face. Tomas wondered if it wasn't a little thinner than it had been.

'Yes,' Tomas said, 'I explained to him.'

'And what did he say?'

'Nothing,' said Tomas. 'He only asked, and I told him you were no longer cursed. He wanted to be sure you were healed.'

Taliga said nothing, but Tomas had not seen her so relaxed. She was in great humour for the rest of the day.

The Spearhead packed up and moved west the day after, and Tomas reported the first contact with the Highlanders to Master Helder in Greenland. He sent the message with a special courier, knowing that any reply would probably be a long time coming.

The middle of the third month found Tomas with the Spearhead in Rhino Spring, a small town in the East Highlands. They were welcomed by the humans, who weren't sure whether to be fascinated or afraid of the strange eladi. Children stood watching the eladi on watch for hours on end, and when their parents came to fetch them, some of them stopped to stare, too.

Tomas decided to go to town, just for the pleasure of being among humans again. After getting leave from his Commander, he walked out of the camp, his eldastone staff in one hand and Tork perched on his shoulder like a patch of night. He wore the Southland head-dress which draped down over the shoulders, instead of the Greenland mantle that was part of the military uniform. As he walked into the town centre, a small crowd tailed him, mostly inquisitive children. He went to the town square, where people went about their everyday business. He spoke with a few shopkeepers he met. They were a little apprehensive, but he told them all how well-organised the eladi were, and how they really hated kchabani. Tork accepted any snacks that were offered. A group of them gathered as he started to make his way back to camp, and asked him if he was a wizard. He said, 'I have studied with the eladi of Greystone and of Greenland, and it was they who trained me to become a magus. I was with the embassy of Greystone when they asked King Arandamundon for help in the war, and he has come to help us. You must not fear them, for they hate the kchabani even more than we do.'

Then he left, allowing the natural rumour machine to get working on what he had said.

The next day it was said around the camp that they would be moving again soon, to meet the humans' leaders. Sure enough, the order to break camp came the next day. They were to take the high road to Tor Arfarass, for a meeting with the Duke and his commanders at the Red Pan, a wide, shallow, seasonal lake on the road to the capital.

After the first contact with humans, Tomas was withdrawn from the elephant cavalry. He was now attached to Lord Randacano's general staff, and rode with the commanders, so that he was readily available when his services were needed. Since the commanders seldom spoke with him, it was not exciting, or even sociable, but at least now he was privy to most of the news.

The Spearhead passed over the wide, golden plains of the Eastern Highlands, dotted with Free Farmsteads and small villages. The kchabani were a constant threat here, with roving war-bands probing the humans' defences. The weather had cooled. The only exception to all that wavy, golden openness was a single, lonely butte, marking the horizon to the north. It was dark, and hazy-blue in the distance, a conical hill surmounted by a tower of hard rock that glowed bloody red in the sunset. Something about it reminded Tomas somehow of the *gochfeya* statue in the Archmagister's office, a lifetime ago.

The lonely butte drew Tomas' eyes as a magnet draws a nail. Riding in train with the Commanders, he watched it for a few days as it drew nearer. He asked around for the name of the butte, but none of the Greenland eladi knew. His diplomatic correspondence took up some time, and he was expecting to be very busy at the summit conference at the Red Pan in a few days' time; but the lonely butte had a singularly fateful look to it, which only increased as the distance between it and the Spearhead decreased.

CHAPTER XVI

The weather at the tail-end of that summer was much like any other. Tomas rode with the general staff in golden, dusty sunlight, relaxed and confident that the war would eventually be won, and no matter what happened thereafter, he wanted to go back to Greystone. Even in the heartbreaking case that Liriel was dead, he could think of no better place to live. They would need animal magi there, he thought, when people came back to the valley. Perhaps he could make a life for himself there. Perhaps, if he could find his family, they could come too? At times, the world seemed just too big.

Tomas had no idea that history was rushing to meet him like a flash flood.

The first surprise came three days out from Red Pan. A courier bird arrived, a peregrine falcon no less, bearing a message to Tomas from Master Helder. It said that he and Caranto the Wise were about a week behind them, in the main body of the forces from Greenland. Lord Acetaliun, King Arandamundon's great-uncle, was leading a force larger than the Spearhead, dubbed the Brazen Hand. They would catch up with the Spearhead at the meeting of the captains, and Tomas was to keep a careful record of what happened until then, and brief them fully when they arrived.

The second surprise was bad news. That same day, some scouts rode into camp in the evening, closely followed by a handful of humans. Both eladi and men bore similar messages: a huge Foul force, numbering up to ten thousands, was approaching from the north-east, from subject territories in the Highlands. They must have mustered all the kchaban hordes they had. They were plainly hoping to cut the Greenland forces off from the Southlanders, to prevent any united resistance from forming.

Mobilising to meet them was a force of seven Southland Commandos, more than two thousand men, already on its way from Tor Arfarass. They could meet the Fouls together, the communication said, and send them to the Abyss before their plans came together. If they could just hold the Fouls until the Brazen Hand arrived, they could still win.

Lord Randacano gave the Spearhead only a few hours to rest that night. In the small hours of the morning, when the air was cold and a layer of thin mist draped the ground, the elephant cavalry, the cat-handler detachments and all the foot soldiers struck camp. By the time the sun was up, they had already been marching for an hour.

Sometime during the morning, when the marching divisions had stopped for a break and a bite, the mounted troops caught up. At sunset, after a whole day on the march, they halted on the featureless plain, setting up a wide perimeter watch with the humans in the middle of the camp: no-one expected men to be any good at night fighting.

In the gathering evening, they were hailed by the Southland Commandos. The eladi welcomed the men into the camp, and Tomas was on hand to translate. When he saw who the Commandant was, his jaw dropped.

'Iohan!' said Tomas, to the shock of the other humans. Tomas, though a magus, had no obvious rank. 'I just knew you weren't a regular soldier!'

'You weren't the only one, Tomas,' said Iohan with a fatherly grin. It made him look a lot younger. 'I couldn't keep the pretence for very long, but His Grace needed to know what was going on, and he needed someone senior to do it. So, I volunteered. And it was a good thing, too – where's your beautiful little girl gone?'

Tomas shook his head, smiling. Some things were just incredible. 'She's minding the cubs again. I'll tell her you're asking for her.'

'I'll send for you after the meeting, if you don't mind,' Iohan said, and hurried away to meet with the Commanders.

Late that night, with a quarter moon low in the sky, Iohan came to see Tomas and Taliga. The former leopardwoman had gone to great lengths to make herself look good, and had even scrounged some make-up from someone. With her short, blonde hair and tawny eyes, she looked almost eladan. She was quite pretty under that golden fur, Tomas realised. Was the fur thinning?

When the Commandant came in, he brought a surprise. He had a small pendant for Taliga and a candle for Tomas.

'What's this?' Tomas asked.

'It's a sitting-up candle,' answered Iohan.

Tomas laughed out loud. A sitting-up candle was used by a girl's father to time the length of her boyfriend's visit. They could sit up at night, for just as long as the candle lasted: when the candle went out, the suitor had to leave. It was a custom observed among country people, on Free Farmsteads. This candle was not a short one. By giving Tomas the candle, Iohan had publicly acknowledged him as her guardian: but in turn, he had declared his interest in Taliga, and Tomas was expected to give the couple space, for as long as the candle lasted.

Tomas didn't know what to say. He just said, 'Oh. All right, I suppose,' and looked at Taliga. She was smiling quietly at him, obviously expecting him to leave. Unfortunately, there was only one room in a tent.

With a theatrical sigh, Tomas said, 'Come on, Tork, wake up. We'll leave the young people alone,' which was quite ironic, since Commandant Iohan was some ten years older than Tomas. Tomas thought he should make the point, and said quietly to Iohan, 'I don't think, sir, I need to remind you of the importance of propriety in a diplomatic mission, for a man in your position?'

Iohan simply said, 'I shall be a jealous guardian of her virtue, sir.' He said it in the most aristocratic accent Tomas had ever heard. It was a bit more courtly than Tomas was accustomed to. He simply bowed, and held out his arm. Tork obediently hopped onto it, and they left. Tomas went to the sentinels' fire. Those who were on duty for the night, but whose shifts had not yet begun, were sitting up still, keeping each other company in the cold night.

It was past midnight when Tomas returned to his tent, having dozed uncomfortably by the fire for longer than he had intended. The candle was long out, and Iohan was leaving. They bid each other good night, and Tomas crashed on his pallet, leaving Tork in the rooftree. As he reached to darken the lamp, he noticed that Taliga's eyes were shining strangely.

He asked, 'Are you all right, Taliga?'

'Yes,' she said, with a smile that lit up the tent. Her tears flowed freely now, smudging her makeup.

'Are you sure?' Tomas asked. 'He didn't hurt you, or anything?' Tomas would have been surprised if he had.A man who brought his own sitting-up candle was obviously one who did things honourably.

'No,' Taliga shook her head vigorously. 'I'm not sad, at all.'

Tomas didn't need to Sympathise with her to see that. If anything, he thought, she looked deliriously happy.

The next morning dawned tense and bright. Tomas was now certain that Taliga's facial hair had thinned, but he had no time to think about it. The tension before the Battle of Vulture Pass was nothing compared to this morning: there were no jokes, except among the imperturbable magi, and people spoke little. The breakfast queues in the camp were sullen, and scuffles broke out.

The combined Greenland and Highland host struck camp and continued their march north-west, now headed in the direction of that lone butte in the plain. It was directly in front of Tomas, and he could not take his eyes off it. Tork seemed interested in it still, and Tomas said, 'Maybe you could go and look at it, after all this is over.'

'To look at what?' asked Lieutenant Darebor.

'Your pardon, sir. I was talking to the raven about that lonely butte.'

'That,' said the Lieutenant, 'is the Place of Dogs. I wouldn't go there. It was a place of sacrifice when the kchabani infested this land. I remember my father telling me about it.' He shook his head in disgust.

Tomas gaped. His doom had approached in plain sight.

Around noon that day, the army stopped for a break. It was mild and dry, and the animals were taken to a nearby river for a drink. Watering the beasts gave the foot soldiers some time to rest.

The afternoon wore on, and the first reports came in from birds and riders: the huge Foul force was approaching from the northeast as expected, with as yet no sign of activity from any other quarter. About a long, low ridge the leaders of divisions made speeches to their troops, rallying their spirits. Tomas translated for the Greenland Volunteers, but remembered little.

The Allied commanders positioned themselves in a pavilion on one low ridge, a wave of golden quartzite in a sea of grass. Beyond it, just out of bowshot to the north-west, was another low ridge, where four companies of various foot-troops took position. Behind those foot-troops waited two companies of Greenland archers, and one of lancers. On either side and in front of the ridge, on flatter ground, elephant cavalry took their positions, accompanied by their supporting divisions of mounted and foot troops. Another squadron of elephants was held in reserve, out of sightto the southwest, behind the low ridge.

It was mid-afternoon, and clouds were building, when the first Foul companies appeared in the blue distance: hordes of kchabani on foot, and in front of them, a group of companies that looked like hyena-handlers, and perhaps shaman-and-foot divisions. It looked like the central formation with the shaman standards was driving straight at the massed Allied foot soldiers. Kchaban tactics tended to be brutally simple. With any luck, they would show little imagination, and try to punch through the line at the Allied commanders, allowing the elephant-backed forces to come round and encircle them. However, the enemy force was so huge that they could probably engage every Allied position and still have strength to spare.

The day was bright and cloudless, with a stillness that spoke of autumn. Tomas could tell when battle had been joined by the darkness that grew in the air to the northwest. There, spells were woven, summoning the unnatural creatures that assailed the foot-troops before the main Foul onslaught. Strangely, there were no baboons: perhaps they had been used up, or had turned against their masters.

It was a departure from custom for shaman detachments to be in the front of the army. It showed two things: the enemy had a lot of spellcasters, and its commander was an innovator. Lord Randacano all but rubbed his hands in anticipation. He sent wise to as many infantry detachments as could be reached, to break any curses or spells while they were being cast, and preferably ruin the spell-casters in the process. If the shamans weren't stopped, the front of the enemy might just punch through the foot soldiers before the elephants could cut them off.

After a small eternity waiting, the trumpeters blew a coded signal, and the forward foot divisions charged down the slope. At the same time, a lion-infantry company called the Reavers engaged the kchaban hyena-infantry, while the Blue Dogs, a company of eladan spearmen, engaged the arkchabani in front of the Shamans. A company of human Greenland volunteers made for another hyena detachment, covered by eladan archers, the Golden Ratels.

For some time the sounds of fighting drifted back from the spellcasters' darkness ahead. Then suddenly a tall, smoky shadow appeared, fouling the late-afternoon sky with its presence. Growing a vaguely human shape, it emitted a roar before blowing away on the breeze. It was a signal: within seconds, the entire Foul force charged, and the foot soldiers of the Greenland-Southland Alliance were going to be swamped. The pincer formation was needed, and quickly. Lord Randacano gave an order, and the trumpeters blew another coded sequence. In response, the elephants and support companies charged, making for the shaman-cored horde; but they were going to have to fight through masses of kchaban foot, some with hyenas. Their best advantage was daylight, and that would only last another two to three hours – less if the clouds grew to form rain. Going to the aid of the foot soldiers already engaged, the remaining foot-divisions on the low ridge charged as well: more Greenland archers and the Volunteers, mostly men from Falmallinar. The Turquoise Eagles, a lancer detachment, rode to fight the shamans. The shadows rose to greet them.

As the afternoon wore on, messenger birds came in, flying low as the clouds built up. It was going to rain, perhaps for the last time this summer. There were crows and ravens and falcons and kites and coucals. Some didn't go back again: their magi were dead. Others left, but did not return. In the centre of the mêlée, where the tall Shade had arisen, there was a tight knot of dark activity, but the darkness was smaller than it had been. A lot of the shamans must have been destroyed.

The welcome news got better: from the reports received, and from what Tork could see, the arkchaban infantry and the hyena company guarding the shamans had been thoroughly thrashed by quaha charges; but Alliance losses had been heavy. There was no word from the Reavers, and the Blue Dogs and the Golden Ratels had been engaged for too long. The Volunteers could no longer be seen.

Suddenly there appeared on the ridge in front of Tomas' position a company of Raiders. As Southlanders and Oreladon zebra-archers charged them from the shallow dip in front of the commanders, another group of arkchaban infantry, their pasty-white faces visible at the distance, appeared behind them. The enemy had breached the line. Another Southlander commando charged down into the dip to meet them. The commanders released their lancer detachment to assist.

Again, a coded trumpet-signal went out, and the elephants and support held in reserve to the southwest advanced, creating their own dust-trail, golden in an afternoon sun that peeked through angry purple cloud. The Greenland infantry, archers and elephants of the commanders' company moved to positions around the commanders. Commandant Iohan's personal commando stayed close by.

The raiders and arkchabani on the ridge were all but defeated, when there appeared on the ridge something new and shocking: arkchabani mounted on horses! Such a thing had never been seen before. Heavily armoured but undisciplined, they spread out along the stony ridge. With amazing discipline, the lightly-armed, highly mobile commandos of the Southlands wheeled and charged, flanking the rocky ridge, loosing arrows before closing with the enemy using side-arms. They were followed by more heavily-armed Greenland lancers. The zebra-archers fanned out on the slope below, providing covering fire.

Dreadful battle was joined on the ridge. Tomas said to Tork, 'Go up and see if there are any of our people left beyond the ridge.'

The raven flew up again. After a while Tomas heard him again. *Many horses and quaha come.*

'Are there any people on foot?'

Some enemies on foot. Else, just lots of dead. Enemies beyond, big herd, still coming.

Tomas swore. It was looking bad. The forces were too unevenly matched. In the glowering sun, the kchabani were facing south and away from the dying light, gaining strength and confidence. 'The Fouls coming, are they on horses?'

No. I see many coming on horses, but they are men and eladi.

'My Lord!' Tomas called to Lord Randacano, 'There are more kchabani on foot coming over the ridge to the north. It looks like all our foot soldiers are defeated!'

The High Commander nodded grimly. 'The reserves are moving. At least they will be able to meet the force behind. The cavalry and commandos will have to hold the ridge, until we can get there.'

Lord Randacano ordered a signal, and the zebra-archers directly in front of him moved to meet the approaching kchabani. As the Fouls appeared on the ridge, they were suddenly overtaken from behind by the lancers and Southlanders returning from the defeat of the advance enemy companies. The Alliance still held the field, but the setting sun was gone behind black cloud, and thunder mumbled in the distance. Healer teams moved in to tend the wounded, even as the last of the kchabani were slain or scattered.

Shading his eyes against the setting sun, Tomas watched the reserves advancing. Elephant cavalry could be painfully slow at times. Turning slightly and looking northwest, Tomas could just see the Foul command companies advancing. Among them were machines, moving painfully slowly. They had artillery. Behind the machines were a few tall structures surrounded by banners, probably the palanquins and sedan chairs of the enemy commanders. They moved among massed foot-troops and wagons.

'I think I recognise that device,' said Commandant Iohan unexpectedly. He stood close to Tomas, with the eladan commanders standing nearby. 'You see those banners, coloured like dried blood with a grey death's head? That's a senior commander. It was he who led the attack on Greystone.'

Tomas nodded, keeping his cool. It would be so very satisfying to ride off and join the attack. These might be the Fouls that killed Liriel. He bit down on his anger, channelling it into resolve. They would pay in time. He was on the winning side.

As the setting sun glanced under the cloud, covering the veld with blood, the enemy commanders came within striking distance of the ridge. The mounted companies that had come late to the ridge joined with the men and eladi already there, and wheeled, striking at the Raiders and arkchabani in front of the enemy commanders. The fighting time of the men was running out with the daylight, but the same applied to the arkchabani. The elephant cavalry with their support were still moving along the western flank. They would close with the command divisions as the sun set, with the light at their backs.

The forward elephant cavalry was within long bowshot of the Fouls, when Tork drew Tomas' attention. Circling about the commanders, he told Tomas, *There are men and eladi coming, from the dark-side.*

Tomas looked northeast, and saw ragged men and eladi running, some unarmed, some scared, straggling towards them. He looked to the northeast, and saw no elephants. There was wreckage of battle for sure, but who were the victors? He couldn't see at that distance, in the low-angled light. He asked Tork, 'Can you see kchabani? Which way are they moving?'

Yes. They come.

Bad news, Tomas thought. 'Can you see any elephants?'

Some, many on ground. Others move away.

Tomas relayed the information to Lord Randacano, who didn't seem surprised.

'I suspected so. We haven't heard from them for too long. Do you know how many there are?'

Tomas had another cryptic exchange with Tork. 'There are three large groups, my lord: and many hyenas.'

All at once, there was a message from the elephant cavalry. There was another Foul force coming out of the sun, from the west! It was at least as large as the remainder of the force ahead, and the kchabani would be getting stronger as darkness fell. As the sun dipped in glory, a filthy, sorcerous cloud erupted in front of it: there were shamans in the new force as well.

With the forward elephant divisions engaged, and the mounted companies gone from the ridge ahead, the only course of action was to divert the reserves. Messages were sent, but the western divisions needed no prompting: they wheeled into the setting sun to meet the new attack. As the zebras, horses and elephants turned to meet the threat, Tomas felt fear. They could very well lose this battle in the night. As if in confirmation of his fear, hyena calls drifted down the breeze from the northeast, quickly drowned out by thunder, now closer. Tork landed on his shoulder, adding his ominous croak to the dying day.

In the dim, swift dusk of the north of the world, Tomas saw flames light up the northwest. The artillery was burning. The bloody banner must have been overthrown. With the hyenas' whooping and cackling coming ever closer, Lord Randacano decided on a gamble. He sent the commanders' archers and spearmen to the aid of the elephants in the west. That would leave him with only his own elephant division, and Commandant Iohan's personal commando.

When the order went out, the elado foot soldiers cheered. They were tired of waiting for action. Forming up in quick time, they ran at full speed down the slope towards their comrades, singing a bloody song as they went. The western sky still had some blue light in it, beyond the shamans' stain.

Suddenly, Iohan grabbed Tomas' arm. 'They'll never get there in time! Listen, Tomas, my horses can't face hyenas. Tell your lord that I'm taking my own commando to deal with those shamans.' And he turned to go.

'Wait!' Tomas said, 'I can't just tell him like that! You have to –' but the man turned back, cutting him short.

'Where's Taliga?' he demanded.

'I'm right here,' said Taliga in a small voice. She was standing behind Tomas, ever the faithful shadow.

'You must come with me,' said the Commandant.

Taliga looked at Tomas. 'You don't mind, do you, Tomas?'

'No,' said Tomas, sighing. 'You might just be safer with him. We're going to be in the thick of it very soon.'

Iohan all but dragged her away, bellowing orders to his men. Taliga didn't even look back.

Lieutenant Darebor appeared at Tomas' left. 'Good,' he said, 'The High Commander wanted them to leave. Men's horses would be no good against the vermin.'

'He took Taliga with him,' Tomas said.

'You did the right thing, O magus,' said the Lieutenant. 'We can't watch out for refugees. Now come with me. We're mounting up, and I want you with me to deal with hyenas.'

Tossing his staff up ahead of him, Tomas climbed into the Lieutenant's cab. Tomas thought the staff wasn't a lot of help with walking these days. In fact, it seemed to have lost its magical effect on his hip since the night he'd tamed Taliga. He looked at the amethyst in the top: it was cloudy. As the command elephants formed up among the crossbow-bearing animals, Tomas said to the Lieutenant, 'That's it for my crystal, I think; I must have drained it on Taliga.'

Lieutenant Darebor barely looked. 'I hope you can still control beasts without it.'

Tomas just nodded. He saw now the wisdom of not having an aid in your staff, as the Greystone magi did.

The elephants were nervous at the sound of the carnivores, but they would not panic. In the great scheme of things, hyenas do not pose much of a threat to a full-grown bull elephant. The great animals turned to face the oncoming threat, and Tomas, facing left from the cab, found himself looking straight at the Place of Dogs black in the distance, visible on the horizon as lightning flickered in the sky. Where it had always looked like a warning before, now it seemed to breathe threat at Tomas. It was late in the third month, and for some reason that was significant; but exactly why was lost in the urgency of the moment.

The trumpeter sounded an alarm, and an answering trumpet called from the northwest, where the fires from the dying artillery had fired the grass. The surviving Alliance forces were on their way, but the command elephants would have to deal with the hyenas on their own in the meantime. The reserve eladon foot soldiers were still running westwards, night-eyed in the long grass.

All the light was gone from the sky when there was a stirring in the east. Tomas felt the chill disgust caused by the proximity of kchabani, and the stink of hyenas drifted down on their laughter. Tomas fought down the fear of elephants and men that drifted up to meet it.

'Ready bows!' Lord Randacano sang out. The heavy crossbows around Tomas rattled and creaked. In the dim, black-and-white vision of flashes of lightning, Tomas saw a wide, muddled mass of kchabani in front of him. Behind them was a tight mob of kchaban archers, still out of range. There were more archers among the hyenas. Tomas put Tork down on the floor of the cab, out of sight. The bird couldn't see well in the dark.

Lord Randacano bellowed, 'Fire!' Heavy bolts thudded from the crossbows into the night, aimed by Fair eyes. Some of the elephants trumpeted, and the note of the hyenas' laughter changed. They had been upwind, and had not smelled the elephants.

Rain fell. Battle was joined, and the hyenas were loosed, charging with the kchabani. Right in front was a strange figure, horribly thin and dark. He waved a staff and screamed orders around him, but didn't seem to be armed.

'It looks like they're led by a shaman,' observed Lieutenant Darebor.

Suddenly, on the ridge that had been the focus of so much slaughter that day, there appeared mounted men and eladi. With the humans' yodelling war-cries, they fell on the kchaban archers beyond the hyenas. The kchabani showered them with arrows, and many of the lancers and Southlanders fell, but the momentum of the charge could not be stopped. Within a few breaths, they were among the Fouls, laying the lightly-armoured figures low with starlit steel. As the shrieks of the archers drifted over the hyenas' calls, a new sound came from the crest of the ridge: the awful moaning of lions, and the snarls of lesser cats. The hyenas whooped their challenge into the night. Through his sympathy, Tomas felt their confidence: there were very many of them, they were led by the Half-Witch, and they would feast on lions this night! Tomas thought, What on earth is a Half-Witch?

Tomas looked around for the lead hyena, but there was no obvious candidate. He saw other animals behaving strangely in the rain and lightning, as the Beastmasters confused them, and decided that he should watch out for the hyenas he could see for the present. The heavy-shouldered mustelids were right among the elephants, and kchabani archers ran among them, aiming their arrows at the elephants' eyes. Tomas reached out to a hyena, and knew himself watched by magic. The spell was coming from someone... he looked around, and his eyes rested on the strange, thin, dark creature, apparently wearing

Tsuna-style clothing, a kilt made of strips of pelts, hide vest and sandals with an antelope-skin cloak over all.

The figure looked back at Tomas, and Tomas felt some kind of recognition from it. As he looked, the kchaban, or whatever it was, ran closer, moving incredibly fast. In the ear-splitting thunder that closely followed a lightning flash, it came closer, and Tomas' mind recoiled. It was human-shaped, but it was only half a person! Its right side was invisible, if it had one: it had only one leg, one arm, its torso was cut in half, and its half-head had only half a face. With diabolical agility, the half-man leaped clean over a tight knot of kchaban archers, and landed looking straight at Tomas from the ground, within bowshot. Pausing only briefly, it executed another fantastic leap, and landed in the cab, between Tomas and the Lieutenant. Tomas drew his knife, the one he had carried since graduating in Greenland, and the Lieutenant looked at him.

'What are you doing?' the Lieutenant asked, looking straight through the invisible side of the half-man. He couldn't see it!

Tomas slashed with his knife, but the half-man, again with unbelievable dexterity, grabbed his knife-hand and twisted. Tomas screamed in pain, dropping his knife and his staff. Lieutenant Darebor suddenly perceived the half-man, and swept out his sword, but Tomas never saw the blow land. The half-man gave a malicious cackle, and Tomas' world went black, zipping past him as the being folded space. He had lost his staff and his knife.

When Tomas' senses came together again, he seemed to be on the stony ridge, across from the commanders' elephants. He briefly saw the slaughter inflicted on the Foul archers, as well as the elephant cavalry and foot soldiers still on their way from the burning wreckage of the artillery. They might yet win!

Thoughts of victory were driven from his mind, however, as the half-being folded space again. When they stopped, Tomas' senses reeled to see the fateful butte filling the sky in front of him. Surrounding him on all sides in the darkness were masses of black goat-hide tents, with pasty-white arkchabani moving in amongst them.

CHAPTER XVII

Tomas was too shocked even to move. He was in the camp of the enemy! The half-being cuffed him on the back of the head, sending him stumbling. It pointed at Tomas with its own staff. '*Wagga!*' it said, kicking his backside for good measure.

The kick forced Tomas' stupefied limbs to move. As they moved down the slope into the camp, pasty-white arkchabani came out of their dusty-black hide tents to stare. They were incredibly ugly, with lumpy features that looked somehow unformed. They were all taller than men, but moved clumsily, as if their lumpishness was more than skin deep. They were all interested in what was going on, but were plainly too afraid of the half-being to come closer.

Without his staff, Tomas walked painfully. It was only thanks to the prolonged exposure to healing of the eldastone that he was able to walk at all.

The half-being pushed Tomas through the camp in the dark, going up beside a small stream flowing down from the butte, choked with filth. The darkness of the camp, Tomas saw, was not only due to the darkness of a sky with a sickle moon: the grass had been deliberately burnt, so that the tents were the same colour as the land.

They left the watercourse and followed the path up the bottom of the butte slope. Not far above stood a large pavilion, of canvas instead of hide. It was painted with garish, abstract designs in the most lurid colours Tomas had ever seen. In daylight, Tomas thought absently, it must look revolting. A pair of tall stands held bowls of burning oil on either side of the entrance. As they approached, Tomas noticed a pair of human guards standing by the lamps. They were the only humans Tomas had seen in the camp, and wore good-quality arms and armour, though of a style Tomas had never seen. One of them spoke at the tent-flap, and it was whipped aside. There, backlit by a brazier, stood what looked like a very tall human. Clad head to foot in black armour and cloak, Tomas recognised him instantly. It was the Man with the Black Mantle. He alone seemed unafraid of the half-being.

To Tomas' surprise, he spoke to it in Tsuna: 'I see you! Is that the last one?'

'There may be others,' said the half-being, 'but your forces are finished. I could not get close to any others. I had to lead the last of your stupid, shrieking apes on a suicidal attack, just to get close to this one. It was with the Shining Ones' commanders.'

The tall man swore eloquently. 'The one we seek has to be among them, Thakadekha! The Equinox is tomorrow!'

The half-being spoke with callous indifference. 'That is little concern of mine. You, as you are so fond of pointing out, are the Chosen One – O Kroghnash the Skullbreaker.'

The tall being snorted. 'I don't make mistakes. My destiny was written before the world was made,' he said. 'I have no doubt that you have played the part set for you.' He turned to one of the guards. 'You,' he said in the Raiders' dialect, 'chain this one round the back, with the rest.'

The guard brought some heavy manacles and a chain out from a box at his feet, and Tomas was chained for the third time in his life. Though his situation had even less hope now than the first time, the weight of fear was less. Whether that was due to detachment or to shock, he was in no state to tell.

As the sour-faced guard pulled Tomas round the tent, Tomas felt the Skullbreaker's eyes boring into his back. The black-hooded leader watched while Tomas was chained to a post, along with seven eladan magi, their faces invisible in the dark. The rings for the chains were set high on the pole, just high enough to prevent them from sitting down.

As the guard locked Tomas' chain, Tomas felt a prickle on his mind, as if the kchaban king was looking with more than just his eyes. Tomas remembered the last time he had seen that smoothly evil face: in a grim dream, that night in Falmallinar before old Ben was killed. Thinking back to that time, his emotions roiled. He had difficulty controlling a mad desire for power. The temptation to Control became a lust.

The Skullbreaker's face wrinkled into a grin. 'I think,' he said in Southlandish, 'this may just be the one I seek.'

Tomas stomped on his emotion. He had to pretend he hadn't understood the human tongue.

Just then, the Thakadekha soared over the top of the Skullbreaker's tent, landing behind him with a thud. The King jumped as the half-being said in Tsuna, 'I remain to be paid.'

Kroghnash tried to smile, but it turned into a guilty grimace. 'But of course.'

The half-being grinned a mirthless half-smile, and followed the kchaban king into the warm-lit interior of the tent, walking without hopping. So, Tomas thought, maybe he has two legs after all.

Tomas looked around at the other prisoners. All were Greenland eladi, as far as he could see. Their mantles were down over their eyes, and they stood silent in the dark. They seemed sadder than Tomas had ever seen Elders.

'What's up?' he asked. 'Is anyone hurt?'

The nearest magus addressed him bitterly. 'Don't be stupid,' he spat,

'Just shut up and die!'

Tomas was taken aback. 'Sorry, I only...'

'Shut up, will you?' sobbed another magus. 'Just shut up!'

The magi all stood stood, heads down, their faces downcast, their hands suspended at head-height. They were more than just weary with long standing. Tomas could think of only one thing that could cause such sadness: a spell of despair.

Tomas was thinking clearly enough to realise that being caught with a group of magi was good news, if only they were of sound mind. He searched his memory for something to counteract the spell. He remembered Timaeos the Acolyte, muttering quietly as the witch in the Archmagister's office was ruined by his own spell. What had he said? It was like a chant of some kind, an invocation. They were recited at events in haildoms, but right now Tomas could remember none. That'll teach me to pay more attention in gatherings, he thought wryly. The dreadful night deepened around him as he gleaned some fragments of chants from his memories of his life in the Scribal School, before his old world had ended. He started chanting under his voice, cobbling odd lines together. The words were soothing.

Suddenly, there was a roar from inside the tent. Kroghnash the Skullbreaker stomped out, carrying a shambok, a short, rigid rawhide whip. He came straight at Tomas, and laid about his head and shoulders with it, screaming obscenities all the time. The magi only looked on, perhaps less numbly than before.

Past the white sting of hysterical blows, Tomas saw the Thakadekha standing at the entrance to the tent and beside it a short, shaggy, fat creature that breathed decay. It had the long, matted dreadlocks of a shaman, silhouetted against the brazier-light. He had no time to consider them, as he tried to avoid the shambok-blows that came whistling down onto his unprotected head, arms and shoulders.

When the Skullbreaker had exhausted himself, panting and literally foaming at the mouth, Tomas was in agony. Bleeding from cuts, with his arms white-hot with pain, his detachment splintered. The shaman raised its arms and chanted in its own vile tongue. Tomas felt a thick, fetid blanket of despair settle onto everything, as the Skullbreaker returned to his tent. Thus began a night of deepest misery.

The pain and the dark and the cold stretched for an eternity. Tomas had thought for nothing but his own pain, physical and spiritual. Eventually, as the sun rose beyond all hope in the east, the spell was broken, and the eladi looked around, as beings newly freed. Tomas felt the weight of horror ease, and it almost made up for the pain of his own whipped hide. His arms were covered in welts, and he tasted his own crusted blood on his mouth.

A hunchbacked kchaban came to give them breakfast: hot water, bowls of thin sorghum porridge and shreds of some kind of dried, smoked meat to eat. The meat was given with such a gloating look that none of the magi ate it. For all they knew, it could be eladan or human flesh. Instead of being disappointed at their refusal, the kchaban simply took out his own breakfast – green cheese, maize bread, and more smoked meat – and ate it in front of them, making sure he visibly enjoyed every mouthful. If he hadn't been so hungry, Tomas thought, the display would have been pathetic.

After the hunchback had gone, the magi muttered among themselves, exchanging news and introductions. The spell that had affected them the night before was completely broken. Tomas told them as much about the end of the battle as he knew, to their great satisfaction.

One of the magi said, 'What is that half-thing?'

'It is the Thakadekha,' said Tomas. 'There are old stories of it among the Tsuna and Bafedi, but I had always thought them merely folk-tales. By what they said, it must have cost Kroghnash a lot of money to hire the thing. I imagine it was the only thing that could do the job: it has natural Abilities, and can do magic at the same time.'

'It looks like all he wanted was male animal magi. The maga next to me wasn't touched,' said someone else.

'It's as if he was looking for someone,' observed another.

'It's probably me,' Tomas said

The magi looked at him blankly.

'I am half-eladan,' he added.

The magi understood. Their race's suspicion of men was now fully justified.

Tomas' head cleared in the awkward silence, and he suddenly remembered the date, and its significance. He was almost past caring, but not quite. In spite, or even because of everything, he was now in the right place at the wrong time; or maybe it was the other way around.

'Well, if it's just looking for you, what will become of us?' a magus asked.

Just then came the voice none of them wanted to hear. Speaking in Southlandish, the Skullbreaker bellowed at them from the tent, 'Belt up, you useless shower!' The tall being came out, shading his eyes from the light. 'It's such a pity the despair is broken by sunlight. Otherwise I could have a whole day of peace.' He came walking around the captives. When he came to Tomas, he stopped. 'Ah-ha! I suspected so – this one is human, more or less.' He pulled Tomas' face towards him by means of his ear. He wrinkled another smile as he said, 'It's our chanting little friend from last night. No limp-wristed elado would be growing stubble at this time of the morning!' He pulled off Tomas' mantle. 'The ears prove it. Right, little maggot,' he let go of Tomas' ear. 'I'll bet you understand every word I'm saying, don't you?'

Affecting the sing-song Greenland accent, Tomas said 'Yes, I understand.'

'Good,' said the Skullbreaker. 'Then maybe you can translate for your little boyfriends, here.' He cuffed Tomas on the back of the head and stood back. 'Pay attention, filth-wipes! Today will be the last day of your regrettable lives.' He looked at Tomas: 'Translate, catamite!'

Sullenly, Tomas said, in Moreladan, 'He says we all die tonight.' Even here I'm the translator, he thought.

The Skullbreaker continued, with Tomas translating each sentence. 'All of you, except for one. One of you is destined to be the first of many sacrifices in the New Age which will dawn tomorrow. That one Halfman has been followed in all its travels from the Far South. I will know the one I seek; I know he is of mixed blood, for the hand of the Soul-eater has guided him to us; the shamans have his scent, and it revealed his presence in the little rabble sent against us. I am sure you will all be devastated to know that your forces have been pounded into the dust, and that the head of your former commander will soon grace my table.'

'Or so he wishes,' Tomas added in translation.

'That one Halfman,' continued the Skullbreaker, 'is to remain. The rest of you are to be set free.' He waited for effect. 'Free to go, to walk out through the camp, where kchabani of all breeds are waiting, licking their lips and fingering their tools in anticipation. You might be interested to know that there are spells in force around you for the time being, which alert me to any magic you will might attempt. The selection of the victim will be done this afternoon. After that, the rest of you will be released into the loving arms of my little friends at the bottom of the hill. Until then, I have a lot to do. Have a good day.' He then swept back into the tent.

After a short silence, one of the magi said, 'Well, if he is to turn us loose, he won't mind if we leave early.'

The others looked at him keenly. 'Did you achieve a contact?' asked another, cryptically.

'I did,' said the magus with a mischievous grin. His name was Finduro. 'In case the rest of you wonder what we are talking about, I have made contact with two of the crows that come for the carrion in the camp. When the camp settles down after lunch, I will send them in to look for the keys to this lock.'

'Why bother?' said another, named Galmio. 'I am a lifter, but I move small objects best. I worked this lock out, this morning.' As the others looked on in amazement, he unlocked his chains with a look and quickly locked them again. 'I can do the same for each of us, and we shall all be free in the time it takes that idiot to pass water.'

'Why did you not you say anything before?' Finduro asked.

'There was no before,' said Galmio. 'I could do nothing, last night.'

'You may be right about him passing water,' observed another magus. 'By the smell of him, he has galloping venereal disease. Urination must be really painful to him.'

Tomas laughed with the others until his face cracked.

'Brothers,' said another magus whose name Tomas couldn't remember, 'one does not simply walk out of a camp of Arkchabani after lunch.'

'Well,' said Finduro, 'I doubt we will get very far. But I will not stand still, waiting for doom to fall. I wish to go to the Mourner with my hands dripping kchaban blood.'

There was general agreement on that.

'What does the spell do, which the shaman was talking about?' Tomas asked.

'I believe it listens for sound of some kind,' said a magus called Heriago. 'Or it alerts when it hears a spirit being invoked. These sorcerers insist our arts are just another kind of magic.'

The captive magi waited, meditating and praying as best they could. Sometime in mid-morning, a crow brought news of the location of the Raiders' horses.

'They are at the edge of the camp, that way' Finduro said, indicating the direction with a nod. 'We must run past many tents. It looks like a very poor chance.'

'I care not,' said Galmio, 'I shall take it.' Nobody disagreed.

The morning dragged on. It grew warm in the sun. The daily activity of the Foul camp continued. Below the Skullbreaker's tent, human slaves moved along the paths between the black hide tents, on the way to their labours. Companies of bone-white arkchabani marched from camp to daily posts. Few dared to look up at the High Commander's pavilion, towards the post where the magi stood chained, hour upon hour in the bright sunlight. Towards late morning, a great kchaban arrived, resplendent in rhino-hide armour and crocodile-skin shield, an ornate steel helm on his huge head. He was followed by a retinue of ten hulking kchabani in matching sets of plate-mail. The great kchaban went into the tent alone, and his retinue slouched around on the dust outside, chatting amongst themselves and gawking at the prisoners.

Tomas' left hip was throbbing. He had seldom had to stand still for so long. He even tried to take some weight on his wrists, but he couldn't do so for long. The pain made it harder and harder to maintain any detachment. Using his Ability once free was going to be difficult. The eladi seemed unperturbed, as if being chained to a pole was just something they had to do sometimes.

Tomas noticed a change in the note of the conversation of the kchabani down the slope. Suddenly, tempers flared and machetes were drawn. Within seconds, there was a bloody skirmish in front of the Skullbreaker's pavilion, as ten heavily-armed kchabani laid into each other. Kroghnash's human guards tried to break up the fight, but were cut down in short order. As more human guards arrived from a post below, Kroghnash himself came out with the great kchaban. Kroghnash showed why he was called the Skullbreaker as he personally stove in the heads, helmets and all, of two of the kchabani with the biggest mace Tomas had ever seen. The Kchaban King was immensely strong. The great kchaban decapitated another, and order was quickly restored. By the time the Great kchaban left again, his bodyguard had been reduced from ten to three.

As the order went out for slaves to come and clear up the mess, Tomas noticed two of the magi shaking with suppressed laughter. 'Did you enjoy yourselves?' he asked quietly.

The eladi burst out in sniggers. One of them said, 'Why, yes thank you, we did.'

The other magus, called Teloron said, 'It was so easy. It is hard to believe anything could demand so much respect. You'd think they were little godlings, the way they carry on!'

'It makes fomenting trouble easier for you,' said Galmio.

'Perhaps we can obtain some weaponry,' said Tomas, nodding towards the cleaner-slaves, kchabani this time, who were gathering round the bodies below.

The two magi who had caused the fight concentrated on the slaves for a while. The magi managed to get one of them to bring the machetes up and hide them among some barrels nearby, but that was the best they could do in the time they had.

The day wore on. Eventually, the camp became as quiet as it would get during the afternoon rest. The human guards below changed shifts, but the magi fortunately did not have to pass them to escape. Finduro said, 'It is time,' and Galmio unlocked everybody's chains. The magi went to collect the machetes, and Finduro said, 'Spread out, but keep in sight of each other. If someone goes down, don't stop, just get to those horses.' Turning to Tomas, he offered him a machete.

Tomas refused it. His arms were in agony with swollen welts, especially now that blood was flowing into them again. He knew he probably couldn't escape. He said, 'I cannot run on this leg, brother. You run, and I shall try to distract them. I know it's me they want, anyway.'

Finduro looked painfully undecided, but said, 'Tomas, I shall send a horse for you when I get one. Just follow as best you can.'

Tomas nodded. 'When you escape, flee south by east. The main Greenland force will be coming from that direction.'

'Thank you, O Tomas,' said Finduro. 'May the Hunter be with you.' So saying, he hurried after the last of the magi, running fast and light between the black hide tents towards the paddocks.

Tomas limped down the slope. He stopped for a while, breathing deeply and calming his mind to detach himself from suffering. When he had done so, he carried on, trying to ignore the pain. The magi were gone, and he followed as best he could. He felt out, looking for his mates. They were all very excited, and none were yet aware of any pursuit. Tomas picked out a path among the back ends of the tents, trying to move quietly. He had gone some distance when he heard shouting from up ahead – the first of the magi had escaped. He started moving a bit faster, and got careless. He tripped on a tent-stake, and fell on the next tent. There was a roar from inside, and Tomas got up quickly and tried to sneak off; but the occupant, a particularly wide and ugly arkchaban, came running around the tent, sword drawn, looking for what had fallen on him. For a moment, he stood in dumb shock. Tomas opened the Foul's mind, seeing murder there. He quickly modified it to a thought of reward for an escaped prisoner. Suddenly, arkchabani crowded round, looking for the cause of the noise. In the racket that followed, he tried to get them into a fight with each other, but lost concentration while being pushed around. One of them twisted his arm behind him and frog-marched him up the road, back towards the Skullbreaker's pavilion. The pain and noise, on top of his fatigue and fear, suffocated his attempt at detachment. On the way, Tomas saw a horse trotting smartly up the path towards them. The sight lifted Tomas' heart: it seemed that the magi had got to the horses, at least. Finduro had been as good as his word, bless him, but that horse may as well have been on the moon.

The human guards saw them coming, and ran. They didn't want to be present when Kroghnash reacted to the news of the escape. As it turned out, running didn't do them any good. When the kchaban king came out, he sent some of the arkchabani to arrest them. He also sent others to get two stakes. Tomas shuddered to think what awaited them. The arkchabani cackled with glee.

Tomas was bound up hand and foot, with a chain linking his head and ankles. It was so short, there was no way he could stand up. He was gagged, and a smelly cloth bag was tied over his head. The arkchabani then dumped him on the stony ground behind the tent again. Sometime later, he heard two other bundles being dropped nearby. A human voice said, 'At least we caught two of the rubbish. We can save some of our reputation. I always thought these buggers were too dangerous to keep, but it's more than my brains are worth to say so.'

'What about the one that was shot?' asked another voice, as they moved off.

'That's not our problem,' said the first.

Tomas heard no sound from the other prisoners. Tomas thought they must be bound up as he was. The afternoon grew older, and Tomas was grateful for one thing: being bound up in a crouch took the weight off your feet.

He was awoken by an awful sound: the two human guards were being impaled. Their crying and screaming burned into Tomas' heart. Not being able to see what was happening, with only the horrible sounds to go by, Tomas lost all equilibrium, and cried into his gag, praying for it to stop. It carried on for so long. The arkchabani cheered and hooted, and cackled each time one of the men made a sound, imitating them and mocking them in their own Foul language.

Eventually, the sounds of pain died down and Tomas fell into a nightmare-laden sleep, exhausted. He awoke feeling cold, very stiff and dry, with a headache that would fell a buffalo. A chilly autumn evening had come on. There was movement, and the bag was taken off his head. It was almost dark, and the human guard moved from him to the other captives. After their head-coverings had been removed, Tomas saw who they were: Galmio and Teloron. The guard turned them all around to face the rear entrance to the pavilion, where the Skullbreaker stood with the grossly fat shaman. He stank of stale sweat and bodily odours, even from this distance. Tomas wondered how Kroghnash could stand it. Shifting its ponderous weight, the shaman began an incantation. Tomas expected a spell of despair, but the suffocating, clammy blanket never fell. Instead, he felt his mind tickled and poked by a strange presence. The sensation didn't last long, and when it was over, the shaman pointed straight at Tomas. The Skullbreaker then picked up his huge, two-handed mace and strode over to the magi. He killed the eladi with one sickening blow each. Tomas averted his eyes.

The Skullbreaker spoke to the human guard. 'Call some slaves out to take the meat away. Make sure you hood this one again, first,' he pointed at Tomas. 'When that's done, let him stand up, and bring him in to me. This is the one I want.'

The guard saluted, and Tomas had the bag put over his head again. Sometime later, the guard was back and Tomas was made to stand up, as best he could. The guard led him into the pavilion by the chain around his neck.

Inside, it was warm and bright. The decor was Foul. The guard left him on the floor, and called out. A short, fat kchaban came in, looked at Tomas, and beckoned to the guard. The guard led Tomas into another room, all lamps and cushions. On one pile of cushions sat the fat shaman, fetid and rank in the small, enclosed space. On a low chair in the corner, behind a long, low, eladan-style desk, sat Kroghnash the Skullbreaker. His black mantle was off, exposing pitch-black hair, which was oiled and swept back, cut short at the sides and back.

'Well, Tomas of Greystone,' said the kchaban king, 'we meet at last. You have proved elusive. I suppose you thought you could avoid your fate forever?' Kroghnash's voice was smooth and deep.

Tomas' throat was too dry to speak properly. He started to say, 'I don't know what you're talking about,' but all that came out was a dry croak.

'Hm, we can't have that,' said the Skullbreaker. 'You might as well be fed, before your journey to the Abyss.' He turned and spoke in the Foul language to the short kchaban, who scuttled off. It soon returned with a large flagon of water, which it gave to Tomas to drink. Tomas gulped it down gratefully.

'Now, Tomas,' the kchaban king said, 'You may be wondering about all this. You see, the Lord of Death is to be released from the bounds which have been set about him. The process is legal, he has the right to return if he is worshipped as he once was, in this place of sacrifice. Unfortunately, the only place still surviving with the original blood-mark still in place is near the top of this butte, the Place of Dogs. Every other place, in the Greenstone country, in the Gildrock Mountains, in the Highlands, has been desecrated by your ancestors, of both breeds. Quite often, they built their own holy places on the sites of ours, just to make sure the mark was gone.

'I don't know how much of this you know already,' he went on, 'but it scarcely matters. The sacrifice has to be at the Place of Dogs, so there had to be a war to get possession of the site. Of course,' he said with a wrinkled grin, 'while we were about it, we might as well butcher as many of you weakling under-beings as possible. The time was right for it.

'According to my learned friend here,' he indicated the shaman, 'the sacrifice has to be one who represents both the Elder and the Younger species. You are a particularly good candidate, since the two bloodlines are so intimately interwoven. You leave a wide trail in the spiritual world.'

The Skullbreaker paused for thought, and then said, 'I would really love to know how you managed to get past my spells. I already know that you could not possibly be a stronger magician. Unlike most witches, I know it's not your strength, but the depth of commitment to Death that counts; and no-one can be more committed than me. Besides, then we'd be on the same side. So – how did you do it?'

Tomas' dehydration-induced headache had not abated, but he could at least talk. He said, 'Our Abilities are not magic. We don't command anything. We were born with the talent, and when we use them, we are being obedient of our own free will. We aren't trying to force our own will on others.'

'Whom are you obeying?'

'The Light That Kindled The All.'

The Shaman snarled and spat, muttering in its own language.

The Skullbreaker said, 'So, instead of ruling over lesser beings, you force someone else's will on them? Don't you see what a slave that makes you? Don't you ever wonder what it would be like to be free, to do what you want, instead of what you are told? Your master is judgmental. He thinks he's holier than anyone else. He hates people to act freely. His followers are the most pathetic of the lot. Or perhaps,' he said, 'he gives you power in exchange for obedience. If so, there's no difference between your magic and mine.'

Tomas sighed. He was in no shape for a theological argument. 'I do it for love; you don't. You think you're free, but your freedom is only licence. Your desires rule you.'

The Skullbreaker stared at Tomas for some time. The Shaman suddenly came alert and muttered something at him. The Skullbreaker fiddled with a knife on his desk for a moment, and then said, 'Shall I tell you how your precious little light-godling will reward you for all your loyal service, hm? You don't want to know, but I'm going to tell you: in the morning, you and I and High Shaman Machmool here,' he indicated the shaman, 'are taking a little walk to the top of this mountain, and there we will cut open your ribcage, cutting through the nipple. After breaking a rib or two, we will be able to reach your heart. Then, we will cut out your heart, and cook it on a fire. We will then eat it. You, in the meantime, will be on your way to the Abyss, where the Lord of Death will doubtless be delighted to see you.

'Now, does that sound like a just reward?' The Skullbreaker's voice became strident. 'All that abstinence, that fasting, that chastity, that self-denial, for what? Is your long search for power worth it, now? If it is, please tell me, I could do with a laugh. You will have the rest of all time to consider the waste you have made of your life, giving your best to a spirit that doesn't even care how you or your friends die!'

Tomas sat passively. Apart from the fact that he couldn't talk properly with his sore head and throat, he'd thought of all these arguments before. Though they hurt, they didn't change anything. Kroghnash quietened down and called the short kchaban, and gave it some orders. Tomas was taken back outside, where he was given more water and a bowl of maize-meal, sweetened with honey. It was a feast fit for an Eladan-king, as far as Tomas was concerned. The short kchaban also gave him some dried figs, which Tomas pocketed. Shortly afterwards, the guard came and escorted Tomas to the stream, where he relieved himself. The guard then chained Tomas in a crouch again, but didn't replace his hood. The shaman came, and cast another spell. This one didn't sink Tomas into despair; apparently, he was supposed to have despaired already. This spell simply turned all his muscles to water. Tomas was then dumped outside for the rest of the night. It was the longest night of his life.

The Skullbreaker's words had burned deep into Tomas. In an attempt to regain some sanity, he tried to meditate, crouched with his head on the ground and his sore arms above his head, wrapped in his tulme. He became less concerned about what was going to happen in the morning. His mind was occupied solely with the present. He knew, or at least had faith, that the darkness was an inveterate liar, and what Kroghnash had said about him going to the Abyss was nonsense. As long as Tomas didn't give in and panic or despair, trying to take control again, he would soon see Ben and Varië again; perhaps even Liriel. He would be free of the war, free of the pain of his body, free from the dreams of violence that woke him in the night, free from the guilt of having survived when so many others had not. All he had to do was put up with a little more pain. Such thoughts gave him a stark, purified peace. Sometime during that long night, he dozed off again, in a resignation that was almost hope.

Tomas woke shivering in the cold pre-dawn, and watched the eastern sky turn from inky black to dull grey. The spell seemed to have worn off. Under their filthy hide tents with their horned-skull standards, the Foul host of the Skullbreaker stirred. Pasty white arkchabani lit fires to begin the day on the near side of the butte. The place stank in the small hours, with the smoke and refuse smell trapped in a layer of cold air close to the ground.

To Tomas, dawn was the messenger of death. It stank, and it was the last he would ever see; just one last agony to pass through and it would all be over. His reflections stopped when a kchaban appeared, its ugly face both eager and fearful in the dark. Tomas tried to look into its mind, but couldn't maintain the contact. Something had made the kchaban's mind closed to him. The Foul loosed the chains that kept Tomas in a crouch, replaced them with the lighter, longer ones, and took Tomas to the Skullbreaker again.

The Halfman's evilly handsome face radiated triumph as he said, 'Well, Sacrifice! It's time! Today, thanks to you, the King of the World will be given his rightful place. By the time that filthy sun shows its face, your sad excuse for a Power will have all its pathetic sentimentality revealed for what it is –' and he brought his face close to Tomas' '– weakness!' He stood back again, saying 'There is no-one to save you, Halfman. Even if your friends cared, you're out of their reach, now.'

Tomas' eyes smarted at the implied desertion; but he knew it was said just to break him down. For sheer spite, he refused to despair.

The High Shaman stirred like a heaving pile of garbage. He didn't seem to have moved since the night before. He mumbled something and gave a rasping laugh. Tomas thought he saw an awful image, of the Shaman with bloody holes where his eyes should be. It lasted only a moment, but Tomas' heart leapt with a shock of new hope.

Taking the end of Tomas' chains in one hand and a single torch in the other, the Skullbreaker led Tomas and the High Shaman to a cart, drawn by raddled, naked kchaban slaves. Halfway up the slope of the Place of Dogs, the cart could go no further, and its occupants hopped out. While the Skullbreaker led Tomas with the torch, the night-eyed Shaman carried a load of dry wood for the sacrifice.

Tomas' head and joints still ached with hunger and dehydration. He stumbled on in growing misery. As the Skullbreaker's torch guttered and died, the eastern horizon lightened. They came to the foot of the cliff, and took an ancient staircase, carved for just such a purpose as theirs in the Dead Years before the Seafarers came. The Skullbreaker and the High Shaman had been there recently; but other than that, the staircase had probably remained untrodden in all that age of the world.

The sky had brightened noticeably by the time they got to the top of the stairs. In the growing light, Tomas remembered the chant he'd heard from the wise before the battle, a few days before. He recalled it, caressing each sovereign phrase. With his fear eased, he looked east, where Light kindled the horizon. There was a stunted thorn-tree sprouting from the edge of the cliff on the north-eastern side. Perched in its branches was a large, black bird. As Tomas watched, it flicked its wings in a familiar fashion, and gave a portentous croak. Tomas heard it over the distance, but the Fouls were talking to each other, and didn't even notice. They had no way of knowing the white-necked raven, but Tomas did. Daring to hope, he reached out and recognised Tork. Communication was possible, but there was nothing the bird could do for the moment, other than be there to comfort Tomas.

They came to an ancient altar, a more or less flat-topped lump of quartzite with dark stains still fouling its sides after at least two millennia. It was right on the edge of the cliff, with a sickeningly sheer drop of some ten storeys on the far side. The cliff on the side with the staircase had been somewhat shallower, and steeply sloped, rather than vertical. The High Shaman pulled out a horrible, hook-bladed knife and started whetting it with a long, rounded stone. It hardly seemed necessary, but Tomas knew the steel was shown and the sound made purely for his torment. With his equilibrium now restored by the presence of his friend the raven, the attempt at intimidation suddenly seemed overdone, and it appealed to his sense of the ridiculous. If he had suffered less in the past days, he might have laughed; as it was, he was unmoved. If Tork could be there, against all expectations, perhaps there were other pleasant surprises in store. He kept his face inscrutable, remembering the fleeting image. He knew what to do. While the shaman amused himself trying to scare Tomas, the kchaban king took the shaman's bundle of wood and set it alight with a short incantation. It blazed brightly in the darkness below the stone.

The High Shaman, getting no reaction from Tomas, stopped its sharpening and said something in its own language to the King.

The Skullbreaker broke Tomas' chains and hauled him to the stone. He shoved Tomas to his knees. He was incredibly strong. Then he used a knife of his own to cut Tomas' tulme and tunic open down the front. The shaman stood up on the stone itself, head thrown back and arms stretched out. It began an incantation, in a dialect that made Tomas' skin crawl. It was now or never, Tomas thought. Immediately, the temptation to power reared like a monster in Tomas' mind. He remembered the assassin in Falmallinar. It would be so easy to command this Foul to throw himself off the edge! Making his choice in the blink of an eye, Tomas detached himself from the lust for power, and called to the raven: *Tork! Assist! Attack the Foul One! Blind it!*

For three tense breaths, the shaman's obscenities continued uninterrupted, and the air became even colder. It looked as if there could be no help from the bird; but as Tomas watched, Tork flew from the right, black on the orange sky of dawn, and fixed himself on the shaman's head, flapping to stay in place. Clawing with his feet, the raven's heavy, deep beak pecked savagely, once, twice! Flesh flicked and splattered as he flew. Then he was gone.

The shaman screamed in its own language, clutching at its suddenly empty eye sockets. He dropped the knife, which rang as it bounced off the stone, landing right at the edge of the cliff. He looked exactly as Tomas had seen in the fleeting image. The Foul stepped in the wrong direction, tottered and fell, shrieking as it dropped into empty space.

Kroghnash the Skullbreaker swept out a short sword, but Tork was long gone, flying high in the lightening sky, cawing in ugly triumph. The Foul leader was beside himself with fury. He raged at Tomas in his own language, frothing at the mouth. He raised his sword, and Tomas cowered, unable to avoid the blow – but it wasn't meant to kill. Tomas' senses reeled as he was struck on the head by the flat of the blade. With awful strength, the Skullbreaker hauled him up by neck and crotch, and threw him onto his back on the stone. 'You're still dying, you dung!' Kroghnash snarled.

Holding the end of the chain, he went round the stone to retrieve the sacrificial knife dropped by the shaman. It was right on the edge of the cliff. Through his pain, Tomas felt the chain under his back tighten as the Skullbreaker pulled it reflexively, trying to keep his balance. Without even thinking, Tomas shifted his weight, and the chain slipped free from under him, rattling on the stone. The Skullbreaker gave a wail of terror as he toppled off the edge. The hook-bladed knife clanged and spun glittering off into space, following the High Shaman. The kchaban king's black cloak went over his head as he fell, head first. Tomas gave a shout of triumph, hoarse with pain – but then he saw where the kchaban king was: caught by his head between two weathered tablets of rock on the edge of the cliff. Moving with frantic haste, Tomas swung his legs over the edge, and kicked down hard on the hooded head as the hands scrabbled madly on the crumbling edge. Kroghnash bellowed and screamed in pain, and suddenly came loose. Clawing at gravel, he slid out and away – but he didn't fall far.

Under the growing dawn, an ominous darkness suddenly billowed and coalesced into a shadow, deep as Death itself. It caught the Skullbreaker and lifted him, gibbering with fear, back towards the top of the cliff. The sacrificial knife suddenly reappeared in his hand.

Tomas knew the Darkness. It had haunted all his nightmares for years. It had taunted him in Jwagga the Foot, attacked him in his dreams in Falmallinar, tempted him with revenge and desperation ever since, fed on his horror and pain in the war. Had it come to earth anyway? Was his mere presence in this place of sacrifice enough to summon it? He knew he should be scared – but he wasn't.

Even as the Darkness grew in defiance of the dawn, Tomas' heart lightened with an invincible delight. A joy welled up in him, as the Source of all the goodness he had ever known blossomed and sprouted, growing until tears of sheer happiness and relief flowed freely from his eyes. A delightful tension, born of the space between indescribable longing and its complete and profound satisfaction, grew all around him. Kneeling on the altar-stone, Tomas raised his arms, his head thrown back in childlike delight. He was vaguely conscious that his posture imitated that of the High Shaman, but where the Foul had been summoning something, Tomas was responding to a summons. He emptied his heart into the new Presence, and an incredible Light shone around him, dimming the dawn.

The Darkness was blown back, like smoke on the wind. With its protective shadow gone, the Thing in the dark was revealed: a vast, loathsome shape, most like a vast, bloated spider with the head of a baboon. If Tomas had seen the thing in everyday life, he would have shrieked in terror; as it was, the Joy enfolding him annihilated all fear, and the Thing cowered in the presence of the Light. It wished to flee, but was held from doing so.

The Light dimmed itself, allowing the Thing to gather some shade around itself. Then, responding to an irresistible command, Tomas spoke: 'You have not been permitted here.'

The Thing looked at him, an unbearable weight of time and loss behind its small, red, close-set eyes. Tomas was safe behind the Presence, and stared straight back.

'I have the right!' the Thing said, in a voice of rushing water and stone. 'Look at all the suffering I have caused! Your creations have despaired, you have failed them! Admit it, I have the right!'

Responding again to an order, Tomas stretched out his right hand and made a grabbing motion, pulling back with his whole arm. The Thing somehow unravelled and was pulled out of itself, before winding back up again and adopting its original shape. It bellowed and writhed in pain.

Tomas said, 'Silence! The suffering you have caused is no more than a Rest Year's worth of payment for their own evil, against My goodness and against each other. You call yourself a Soul-eater, but you have had *none*! As for the living, I shall console them for seven times as long as you have been allowed to afflict them!'

'NO!' the Thing bellowed. 'You have no right to take my prey from me!' Tomas could see to its heart, so easily: it lusted for pain and sorrow, despair and shock, harvested from weaker beings; but it could never be satisfied, no matter how much it imbibed. What it truly needed, could only be provided by Light; but the Thing had determined long ago that it would be its own Light, and had thus become Darkness.

'This one has not despaired,' said Tomas in a voice calm and still. 'Because of everything you have done, he stands in place of both his peoples: you said so yourself. Because he has not lost hope, and especially because you have transgressed your bounds, it is you who have lost.'

The horrible shape blubbered and howled in impotent rage. It tried to leave, but was again held from doing so.

Tomas spoke, again in obedience: 'Furthermore, it is I who grant all rights.' There was a suggestion of truly dreadful anger behind his voice. 'If I say you have none, it is so. Be gone.' He waved his left hand, and the Darkness dispersed. The Thing vanished.

Kroghnash the Skullbreaker dropped like a piece of raw meat onto the stony ground far below. In the merest instant before the kchaban king hit the ground, Tomas saw with more than his eyes a vast, black space open up beneath the plummeting figure. There clumps of orange burned, pained and dull in remote depths. Kroghnash vanished, becoming one with the Void. Then the vision was gone.

The sun rose in a blaze of glory, and the Presence turned its attention to Tomas. Tomas felt shame and longing, in equal measure. The Light was so good, so true, and so beautiful: he knew that he was a mean, petty, dirty thing, but he desired the Light so very much. All around, in refracted shades of the One Light, he could discern the seven Powers: there was the Earth-Mother, the Rain-Father, the Fire-Youth, the Wind-Virgin, the Craftsman, the Hunter and the Mourner. The figures retreated into the background, and Tomas heard the Voice in his head again, as he had during his Ordeal: *My child,* the Voice said, *You have done well.*

Tomas bowed with gratitude. There was nothing he could say.

Your work is not yet done, however.

Tomas sighed in exhaustion. What had he to do *now*?

The Voice seemed to laugh. *There is someone waiting for you, someone you love very much. The rest of your life's work is with her; as is a great deal of rest, and happiness, and satisfaction, and good works that will endure.*

'Does she really feel that way, Master?' Tomas asked.

You will have to ask her that, yourself the Voice said with a paternal smile, and was gone. The memory of that smile never left Tomas, though his days were long.

In the glorious morning sunlight that only imitated the Light that had gone, Tomas sat down on the stone. It was warm, he was tired, and he needed to rest for a bit. He noticed that the ancient Foul altar had cracked neatly down the middle. There were other, welcome changes: the welts from Kroghnash's shambok were suddenly and inexplicably gone from his arms, his head was fine and – most remarkably – his hip had not the slightest twinge. He felt in the pocket of his ruined and indecent clothes, and was glad to find the dried figs from the night before. As he sat chewing contentedly, Tork flew around and landed on the rock next to him. The bird stood waiting expectantly.

'Do you mind?' Tomas said. 'I haven't eaten since last night.'

Tork cocked his head at him. 'Yummy!' he said, in Tomas' voice. Tomas just laughed weakly. 'Oh, all right then, here,' he said, and gave the raven his last half-fig.

Tomas looked out, shading his eyes against the morning sun. It would do no good for him to be stuck here, with several hordes of Fouls at the foot of the cliff. Had they seen the light and the shadow? If so, what would they do?

He looked to the north, where the kchabani were camped. The place was strangely quiet. Tomas knew kchabani were nocturnal, but the few dark figures he could see were all lying still on the ground. Nothing moved. Was the whole camp dead?

Tomas looked to the south, towards the arkchaban camp, where the Kchaban King had had his pavilion. In contrast to the north-side camp, the south-side one was teeming with violence. There were several full-scale battles in progress, and fires burned out of control among the tents. However, it seemed that most of the arkchabani were either fleeing in small groups, with varying degrees of discipline, or looting others' tents. The Raiders were simply gone, along with their horses.

Tomas waited for some time, while the fighting died down in the arkchaban camp and the fires spread. Anything not burned was being looted by the survivors of the battles, who then fled towards the east. Tork went down to look for food in the camp, and came back some time later. He simply cleaned his beak on some grass, and Tomas decided against asking him what he'd found to eat. 'Are there any people in the camp, Tork?' he asked.

No, said the raven. *All gone or dead.*

'Good,' said Tomas, hopping off the rock. How nice to be able to jump off something! 'I hope I can find some food there, too.'

I can show you where there is human-food, said the raven. *I had some, too.*

'Oh, good,' said Tomas. It was great having a bird like this around.

Tomas and Tork finally got back down in the bright morning, to find the camp mostly charred wreckage. In the Raiders' section, guided by Tork, Tomas found some stores. Tomas had a fair-sized lunch there, and took enough food for a day or two, all that was left. There was even some water, but not much. Packing it all together with some clothes in a saddle-bag, Tomas left with Tork after noon. On the way out, he took a look at the north-side camp, and every kchaban he could see was dead. All had died where they stood or sat or lay. The place was unnerving, and not even Tork wanted to stay and look around. Both he and Tomas wanted to be well away from the place by sunset. Tomas had not the heart to look for the wreckage of the Skullbreaker.

After walking south-eastwards for some time, without even the slightest pain from his hip, Tomas saw a straying horse. It wore Raider tack. Tomas called the horse to him. It was a gelding, short but strong, and Tomas liked the beast immediately. Freeing him from bridle and bit, he rode the horse onwards until sunset, in the direction of the eladan forces.

That night, Tomas slept under a Raider's blanket, inside a Raider's tent, with a Raider's horse tethered to a thorn-tree nearby. In the cold of sunrise, he awoke to the anxiety of his horse. The animal had scented a great cat on the dawn wind. Tomas perceived it quite close, no more than twice the distance of a sprint. As he calmed the horse, he sent Tork out on a wide sweep to look for the predator. The raven took off in the chill morning air, a shred of night on an achingly dark-blue sky. 'Do you see anything, Tork?' He asked. Even when thinking over a distance, it was easier to frame his questions in speech.

Yes, came the reply. *Elado with leopard, and...*

The bird's thought became seriously distracted. Tork was simply not interested in Tomas any more. Going by the flavour of the distraction, Tork had encountered a hen of his species in season. Charming, Tomas thought, so much for my scout. At least he knew that the leopard had an elado.

Tomas saddled his horse, and mounted up. It was such a pleasure, he thought, to be able to mount a horse without any pain. He stood up in the saddle and waved the Raider headscarf, trying to get the attention of the leopard-scout. He could see the two ravens circling each other, but the elado and the leopard were invisible. Tomas dropped back and urged the horse away from his campsite, reassuring him that the leopard was not hungry.

Thus did Tomas of Greystone come on the remains of the Spearhead, the vanguard of the Greenland invasion force, at the end of the third month. As Tomas had suspected, Lord Randacano was not dead, but his army could no longer be called one. The foot-troops had been worse than decimated, and the cavalry and elephant-cavalry outnumbered them. The supply-train had caught up with them, however, and near where the army had taken its stand four days before, there was now a stockade with an earthen wall and stony rampart around it. It looked almost like a small town, except the largest stands were given over to a field hospital. There, the human and eladon wounded were still being treated, with the remarkable Healing Abilities of the Fair Folk.

Tomas made his report to the High Commander and his staff, including a green-robed wise, after the wise had examined Tomas' mind for traces of tampering. He knew that something was wrong, however, and that his briefing was not well-received. The magi that had escaped, if their escape had succeeded, had not come to the Spearhead, and Tomas could only hope they had found the Brazen Hand which followed, now only a day or two away. As Tomas finished his statement, the leaders simply sat and stared at him, which was unnerving.

Eventually, the wise spoke. 'Tomas,' he said, 'I find your statement – interesting, but,' and he paused, referring to some questions he had written down, 'I know for a fact that when you were captured, you had a staff. What has become of it?'

'Oh, yes,' said Tomas, 'I lost it in the Lieutenant's cabin. I dropped it when the Thakadekha attacked me.'

'Indeed. And perhaps you can tell us why you no longer need it?'

Tomas didn't understand the question. 'I do still need it. It's my badge of office.'

Lieutenant Darebor said, 'When you climbed into the cab with me that night, you said something about your staff. Can you remember what it was?'

Tomas was incensed. 'Do you doubt me?' It was a grossly impertinent question, but at the moment, Tomas couldn't care. He had suffered too much, for too long, to bandy frivolous questions with anyone, no matter how high-born.

'Not quite yet,' answered the Lieutenant, mildly. 'But unless I receive answers to my questions, I shall.'

Tomas cast his mind back to that fateful night. It seemed years ago. 'I said that it hadn't been helping my hip lately, and the crystal was fogged. I thought it had happened when I gentled the wereleopard.'

Lord Randacano nodded slowly. 'How is it that you no longer need the support of your staff?' He asked, quietly.

'That was one of the things that happened, when the Light left me. I found all my injuries healed.'

'So what you're telling us,' said the Wise with growing impatience 'is that the Sunkindler himself was on that mountain, with *you*, on that morning?'

'Yes,' said Tomas. He was at a loss as to what else to say.

'And I suppose,' said the wise, 'that it was the One that turned your hair white?'

'What?' Tomas was thunderstruck. He felt for his hair, but it was still short and he couldn't see its colour. He felt his face, feeling the three days' stubble that grew there. He stuck his tongue in his cheek, the better to see. His heart skipped a beat as he saw it: it was silver.

CHAPTER XVIII

Tomas didn't understand. He was confined to quarters for a day and a half, until Master Helder arrived. Officially, it was to allow the Healers to observe him and make sure he was all right – but Tomas knew he was being kept out of sight. While confined to his tent, Tomas sent Tork out to see what was going on. He would sit inside the entrance to his tent like some white-haired Raider patriarch, while the raven brought him news.

On the day after his arrival, Taliga came to see him. As she approached, Tomas noticed that the golden, feline hair on her face had thinned to a fine, downy fuzz. She regarded Tomas closely as she approached. Tomas patiently sat his place.

Taliga asked hesitantly, 'Father? Is that really you? It's so good you're alive!'

Tomas stood up, rejoicing in his pain-free hip. 'It is I, O Taliga,' he said. 'Please, come in, since I can't come out.' He nodded towards a very bored eladi guard standing nearby.

Taliga came in, and Tomas looked closely at her. 'You're losing your fur!'

Taliga smiled. She really was quite pretty, Tomas thought. 'It's nearly gone,' she said.

'I wonder how that happened. And why?' Tomas said.

'If you don't know, father,' she said, 'no-one does.'

Tomas smiled. He'd never been addressed as that kind of 'father' before. 'I would not be surprised if it has something to do with love,' he said. 'Caranto would say so. As far as he's concerned, love is the answer to all questions. So,' he sat, affecting a paternal air, 'How is your young gentleman? I hear he conducted himself well.'

Taliga told Tomas about the battle, giving him a depth of detail that left his head spinning. Tomas was impressed. Iohan was a gentleman and a great soldier. In his limited experience, the most dangerous humans tended to be the least civilised. After her account of the battle, Taliga asked Tomas what had happened to him. Tomas was telling her an abbreviated version of what he had said to the commanders, when a messenger-boy came and called her away to help with some cubs. She did not come back.

When the Brazen Hand, the main force from Greenland, arrived the next day, the High Commander was received with due ceremony, and the Greystone ambassador was informed of the developments surrounding one of his staff. Master Helder took personal responsibility for Tomas. At the debriefing in the master's tent, Tomas gave his version of the story. Helder and Caranto heard him out, asking for details, especially about the Thakadekha and the Skullbreaker. The Thakadekha was known to the Greystone eladi, but the kchaban king was not.

Master Helder asked, 'What kind was the kchaban king?'

'He seemed to be human,' Tomas answered, 'except that he was head and shoulders above any of us, with that very odd, pale skin, and straight black hair. He may have been partly kchaban.'

'Or he could have been of mixed ancestry, to the same extent as you are eladan,' Helder said.

'I would not have thought that possible,' said Tomas.

Master Helder said, 'Your testimony harmonises with that of Finduro and his two companions. They came to us on the day before yesterday. You have revealed what happened to the others. May they rest in peace.' Helder sighed. 'For the sake of clarity, Tomas, I would like you to write down your recollections of the event, in as much detail as possible. Not only for clarity, but for posterity.'

'Yes, master,' Tomas said. 'I have already begun the work. Could you tell me what you saw, if anything, that morning?'

'I can indeed,' said the master. 'We saw a very bright light on the top of the mountain in the distance. It looked like a very bright star. It must have been visible from here, I cannot understand why they haven't accepted your account.'

'I think I can shine some light on that, master,' said Caranto, 'as far as my knowledge goes: the intervention of the One on the mountain that morning conflicts with what the Moreladon wise know of him. They do not believe that he concerns himself with events in the physical universe, leaving the governance of the world to the seven Powers. What to us makes sense is to them dubious. In time, the Moreladi may even forget what they saw. I doubt very much that Tomas' words will ever be accepted by the wise among them.'

'The truth will always come out,' said the master, shaking his head. 'It always does.'

'It is out already,' said Caranto, 'but as long as that wise sits at Randacano's right hand, it will not be given a hearing amongst the great.'

Tomas rubbed his forehead. Theology had been the bane of his life. 'So,' he said after a silence, 'what is to happen with me?'

'The officers commanding here have requested your replacement,' said Master Helder. 'They fear you might be a spy of some kind, sent to infiltrate their counsels.'

'Simply because I said something that doesn't agree with their view of the universe?' Tomas was aghast.

'Tomas,' said Helder, holding up his hand, 'you must see it from their seats. You come back, inexplicably healed in mind and body from your ordeal, with hair bleached white, less your staff; you sit at the entrance to your tent for hours, obtaining news from a familiar raven, which I might add is a bird of ill omen to them; you are araneladon, which they already hold an ill mixture, and you tell them that their wise have been less than wise for centuries in their teaching. How would you react in their place?'

'I would expect more wisdom,' Tomas said, 'though you have put a darker vision before me, than the one I thought I walked in.'

'Wisdom is not common, O Tomas,' said Caranto with an ironic smile. 'If it was, there would be no place for such as us in the world.'

'For the sake of the Alliance,' Master Helder continued, 'I have decided to relieve you of your duties. In any event, now that I am here myself, I no longer need a deputy. I mean no dishonour, at all: you have done excellent service, and have earned honour from us all. And, you have been privileged witness, even the agent, of an event of unimaginable significance: a theophany! Once the lands are safer, someone should go to the Green River valley, to see if any of our people yet dwell in Greystone City.'

Tomas said, 'I was hoping to do that.'

'I would be grateful, brother. After lunch, I would like to speak with Taliga. Such a thing as healing of a werecreature has never been done before, to my knowledge.'

Later, while they were waiting for Taliga, Tomas asked after the others. They were in Greenland still, Helder said, and Ioseth had begun his Discipleship, in Metal and Water Divination. He was studying under a master who had been a friend of the elder magi in Falmallinar, who sent their regards. There had naturally been no contact from Greystone.

When Taliga arrived, Tomas sat next to her for moral support. He translated for Caranto, and reassured her when they wished to examine her mind. They were interested to hear about her involvement with the Commandant, and laughed when Tomas told them how he had designated himself as her suitor.

As the shadows became long in the afternoon, Tomas remembered Taliga's unexpected talent. In Celadan, he said to the master, 'Since Taliga came to live with me, she has shown some unusual sympathy with the cats of the scouting regiments. She acts as a day-mother for cubs, especially the leopards.'

'I wondered about that,' said the master. 'She certainly has potential.'

'Do you think she should receive instruction?' Tomas asked.

Caranto said, 'I think instruction would be a kindness to her. Her heart has been so deeply wounded by evil, any exercise in detachment would be a blessing.'

Changing to Southlandish, Tomas asked Taliga, 'What do you think about taking instruction in becoming a maga?'

'Do you mean, like you?' Taliga said. 'What would I have to do?'

'You will have to study, learn to meditate, and so on,' Tomas said. 'After spending some time with a mentor, you will go to serve a master like Master Helder, who will guide you further.'

'How long will it take?'

'I don't know; anything up to six years.'

Taliga hesitated. 'I shall have to think about it.'

The master and the wise were disappointed, but accepted Taliga's answer.

Later in the evening, Tomas realised why Taliga had declined. When they were alone in his tent, he said, 'You want to marry Iohan, don't you?'

She coloured slightly and said, 'Yes: as soon as this war is over and his obligations are fulfilled. That's why I don't think I can become a maga.'

'I'm surprised he wasn't married already.'

'He was. His sons are in the army, but his wife and daughter were killed in the war. They were in Alatasdam.'

'I'm sorry to hear that,' Tomas said. 'So, you probably won't have time for the maga training.' Discipline required long separations and extended celibacy, which was simply wrong for a married couple. It might be asked of eladi, who had all the time they wished; but human couples had only a handful of years, and time would not wait.

'No,' said Taliga, 'I won't; but our children will inherit my talent, wouldn't they?'

'Most probably,' said Tomas, 'especially if Iohan has some talent of his own, even a little.'

'Well,' said Taliga, 'when they're old enough, I want you to teach them all.'

Tomas smiled. He said, 'It would be an honour, though they will have to come to Greystone, since I am settling there. You are very generous to want it for them; but discuss it with your husband first.'

She nodded, with one of those luminous smiles.

Master Helder took over as the representative of Greystone and Tomas disappearedinto the background. At first, he was secretary to

Helder, but the Moreladi objected. Their mistrust was not much changed even when the mounted scouts sent to the Place of Dogs returned. The scouts brought news of two camps, one burned, the other rotting without even any scavengers to pick the bones. With autumn begun, the corpses would probably desiccate over the next several months, leaving a grisly memorial at the place someone had already referred to as the Tomasberg. One good result of Tomas' vindication was that his staff and knife were suddenly 'discovered', and returned to him through Master Helder. The staff was without its clouded amethyst.

By the time Tork returned with his new best friend, the rumours about Tomas had already begun to circulate, especially among the humans: how Magus Tomas, using his strange, araneladon powers had summoned wereleopards in the night, which had killed all the Fouls; or how the kchaban king had summoned a dark spirit, and a Power had come from Heaven to blast it, killing everyone including Tomas (who was then brought back to life, in some versions); others said Tomas called on the Power himself. Most arguments centred on whether Tomas really was who he said he was, or not.

With the death of the Skullbreaker, the different Foul forces were left at the mercy of their own commanders. The horde besieging Tor Arfarass dispersed suddenly, overnight, and all over the Highlands, other armies lost heart or fell to fighting amongst themselves in the absence of the Skullbreaker's unifying reign of terror. In the north of the Duke's territory, however, and in the Seven Cities, history took a different turn: there were Foul leaders strong enough to control the shamans and rich enough to pay human traders to supply their people. For the Seven Cities, the kchaban presence did not cease with the end of the Fourth Foul War.

After discussions between Lord Acetaliun and Duke Iosef, the Moreladi encamped in the east of the Highlands, to stage their operations against the Fouls to the north, in the Greenstone Country. As Master Helder expected, they were less interested in the Highlands than in the Seven Cities. The Greenstone Country had been a heartland of their people, thousands of years before; and even now there were many Moreladi who still hoped to return there.

The Greenland army moved to Tor Voldimar, a small town east of Tor Arfarass. It was a stage in the push for Alatasdam in the north, the next military objective of the Southlands and Greenland. While the preparations for the move were being made, the Greystone embassy was given a large old house in the town by the Duke. Somehow, with his formidable skill as a negotiator, Master Helder was able to keep Greystone in the game, while the Elephant Throne pursued its own ambitions on the continent.

Sometime during that sad, empty autumn, a party of five humans appeared in the camp. Purely by chance, Tomas happened to see them being brought into town under arrest. They were demanding loudly to see Tomas the Seer! He went to the guardroom and announced himself, saying he would speak to the humans and see them on their way. He was shown into the small room where they were held, and introduced himself. He was astounded at the greeting they gave him: they bowed low, as if he was royalty. Their leader, an acolyte in a plain red-brown robe, said 'O Prophet, we have longed to see you!'

'What?'

'You have heard the Voice of the One,' said the acolyte. 'Please, tell us what He said.'

'I have written an account of the event,' Tomas said, 'and when copies are made, they will be distributed to anyone who wants to read them. Most of what the Voice said only applied to the moment.'

The acolyte knew what he wanted: 'But the One said that we were to be rewarded for opposing the Fouls, did he not?'

Tomas sighed. 'Please,' he prayed under his breath, 'give me the right words for these people'. Aloud he said, 'The Voice said, and I'm paraphrasing, that we will have good times for seven times as long as the war has lasted, because we have not given up hope.'

The men were ecstatic. They hung on his every word, desperate for good news. Tomas thought the conversation was over, when one of them said, 'Please, master, tell us if the rains will be good next summer.'

Tomas gave an exasperated laugh. 'I can tell you what any weather-wise farmer will tell you: watch for rain and snow. If there's rain in winter, the summer will be dry and hot.'

They seemed disappointed at that. Another asked, 'Please, master, tell me if my son still lives.'

The man's question was touching, and Tomas felt for him. Tomas shook his head, about to say, There's no way I can possibly know that, when he knew: the man's son was dead. He stopped, thinking, Where did that come from? He wanted to say nothing, but it hurt: his brain burned in his head. Either he would answer the question, or he would never speak until he had. Faltering with bewilderment, he said, 'Your son is dead, sir. He fell with honour in the siege of Tor Tanderlad, giving his life to save many.'

The old man went pale, but he held his head up. 'Thank you, master,' he said simply.

Tomas turned away, his hand over his mouth. What was he saying? Another man, quite sour-faced asked, 'If you know so much, tell me how much money my business has lost this year.'

Again, Tomas wanted to decline and leave, but he knew the answer. 'You've lost more than a thousand crowns, including assets.'

The man stared at him, his face a mask of astonishment, even fear. Tomas went on, obeying the prompting in his heart. 'But you can get it back, if you start business again as soon as possible. All your drivers are still alive, and they're hoping to get their old jobs back now your town is free. Just make sure you give some money to the helpless, this time,' he added, 'it has been granted you for a purpose.'

The man reached out for the wall, as if not trusting his feet. 'Yes, master,' he said.

Tomas fled. This was not supposed to be happening. The next day, the guards sent him some food and clothing that the men had brought as payment for the Prophet. Tomas gave them away to some destitute people he'd met in the town. He felt he really did not deserve them.

Unfortunately, it was only the beginning. For the rest of his life, Tomas would be known as TheSeer. To those for whom he had an answer, he was never wrong.

It didn't take long for Helder and Caranto to hear about Tomas' new-found reputation. That night, Caranto said, 'I'm not surprised that people have come to you. The truth is out, no matter what the Moreladi think. But I am surprised that you had answers for them, and still more so that they were accepted.'

Tomas gave a wry grin. 'So am I.'

Helder said, 'This will be very unwelcome to Randacano and Acetaliun. I'm afraid, Tomas, that you can't stay here.'

Tomas sighed. 'You're right. I can't.' He rubbed his forehead. 'Well,' he said, 'you did want someone to go and make contact with home, with Greystone – maybe now is the time.'

'A good idea. It is time,' said Helder.

'By your leave, O master,' Tomas said, 'I know nothing of what happened to my family in Sweetwaters. I would like to go there and find out what has happened to them, before I do anything else.'

'Of course,' said Master Helder. 'I would do the same, in your place. I will arrange a mount and provisions for you.'

'Thank you very much, master. I don't think I should take Taliga with me, yet. The lands are unsafe and lawless still.'

'I shall watch over her,' said Caranto. 'When I go back to Greystone, I shall bring her with me.'

'Are you going, too?'

'As soon as I see your report on the situation, I wish to go there. The sooner you send it, the sooner I may return home.'

It was a glorious, crisp morning of blue sky and golden grass on the leading edge of winter, the fifth month. Master Helder, barefoot again, walked down to the messengers' depot, where several grey quaha stood picketed in lines. The air was heavy with dust and the smell of equines. Flies buzzed lazily.

Seeing the master approach, an apprentice came out from under his awning and bowed, saying, 'A message, master?'

Helder smiled, 'Not today, Curaldo. I wish to speak with the magus who came for a mount.'

The morelado's face fell. 'Oh, the um... *mortelion*. He's there.' and he pointed towards the trough, where a thin figure in leather riding pants, a tulme and Highlands headdress was watering a quaha.

Master Helder nodded and strode down towards the figure. 'Tomas!' he called.

Tomas turned towards the master and smiled. 'Hello again, Master Helder – and fare well.'

'Yes, hello and peace it is. I am sorry it had to come to this, that you have to quietly get out of the way, after all you've been through. But, think what would have been, had everyone believed you.'

'It has occurred to me,' said Tomas, 'and I think I shall enjoy some anonymity.'

'Enjoy it while you may,' Helder said. 'It will not be yours for long.'

Tomas nodded with a lopsided smile. 'I shall consider that a warning.' He led the quaha out of the paddock, to where a pack animal was already waiting, loaded with supplies. Helder saw Tomas' staff standing up against the fence. Tomas led the animal to the fence and began checking the saddle, adjusting stirrups. He said, 'I think I shall enjoy getting away from everything for some time. Thank you again for arranging these for me.' He gestured to the pack quaha.

'Not at all,' Helder smiled. 'We need to know how the western Highlands are faring, and you wish to go there. Once you are gone, I can build up trust with the Greenlanders again. They will have to be watched for some time.'

Tomas nodded. 'I wish I could be here to help. I just hope we haven't exchanged a Foul invasion for a Fair one.'

'If that were to happen, even the humans may be happier,' Helder laughed. 'But that is not our way. Of course, Moreladi are always different. If there is to be an extended invasion, it will fall heaviest in the Greenstone Country. That was my heartland in the Green Years. In those days, we thought the Highlands cold and barren, good only for summer grazing; and the world is cooler and drier now than it was then.'

Tomas shook his head and smiled. 'The age of the oreladi always amazes me.' He mounted up.

'So, you go to your home town first?' the master asked.

'Yes – before I do anything else. From there I shall go to Hunter's Wells. The journey should allow me to see a good part of the western districts. Then to Greystone. Nearly all I hold dear is still there. I shall send word to you from there, as circumstances permit.'

Helder nodded. 'Even as we agreed. By the time you get there, one or two of our Embassy to Greenland should have reached the Green River valley. It is my hope that there is someone in authority there.' The master paused, looking straight at Tomas. 'You are going to many places on this journey, Tomas. You may find much news that is hard to bear.'

'I may,' answered Tomas, 'but I have to hear it, regardless of how bad it is.'

Helder nodded. 'If I have learned one thing in my time, it is the importance of truth: no matter how unpleasant.'

Tomas gave a world-weary smile. 'If I have learned anything in mine, it is the importance of hope.' He waved and trotted away, west into the golden morning.

Helder smiled, too. 'It's a start,' he murmured to himself.

EPILOGUE

Tomas had sent word that he would be arriving in Greystone just before the Winter Solstice. There had been a small trading caravan leaving for Greystone, and he had asked, was there a healer there called Liriel?

'Well, sir,' said the lead driver, 'there is *a* Liriel, a Mother Liriel. She's the new ruler, or at least very senior among the eladi. Someone said she did eladi healings, but I haven't seen it.'

'What does she look like? Are her eyes a funny colour?'

'Yes, sir! That's the one. Her eyes are blue, not a human colour at all.'

Tomas had smiled. 'I thought so. I knew her in the old days.' How old those days seemed now, Tomas had thought. 'Could you give her a private message for me? Here's a quarter-shield for your trouble.' He handed over a scroll in a bamboo tube, along with the small silver coin.

'Well, thank you kindly, sir!' said the driver. He took the coin, unthinkingly giving it a trial scratch with his fingernail. 'Who shall I say it's from?'

'My name is Tomas.'

Then the man took in Tomas' white hair and staff. 'You are Tomas the Seer?' His face grew pale under his tan.

'There are those who call me that,' Tomas had said. This was getting a bit tiresome.

Tomas' message had run as follows:

> My Dear Liriel
>
> I have finished my work with the Oreladi, and am visiting Greystone, where I would love to see you. I remember your words to me at our last meeting, but I realize things may have changed between us since then. If you have a place in your heart for me yet, leave a light in your window on the eve of the Solstice.
>
> With love,
>
> Tomas

Since sending the letter, Tomas had returned to his old home in Sweetwaters. His brothers were gone, one to Tor Arfarass, the other dead in a kchaban raid. His father had died during the war, and his sister now lived with his mother, both earning a meagre living as seamstresses.

With the last of his money from the King of Greenland's Army, he bought an old wagon and some supplies, hitched his two animals to it and loaded his family and all they had left onto it, and started for the Green River valley.

It was evening where Greystone had been. Large tracts of the forest had been burned, the black stumps of once beautiful trees standing like silent screams in the chill grey evening. It was a desperately sad place. Tomas' throat ached to see it all. But, the Celadi were quietly replanting, even as they eked out a living from the depleted soil.

Tomas had left his family in a small, rude Celadon village, while he rode ahead. He had heard Mother Liriel lived in a new village on a hill, where there had been no burning. He had a date to keep, but whether he lived to regret it remained to be seen.

Cresting a low rise, his quaha walking slowly in the dark, he came in sight of a roughly-built town wall, one that had obviously been built in a hurry. A single elado sat sentry on top of a squat tower by the gate, his bow discreetly by his side. From his own experience, Tomas knew it already had an arrow nocked, and the sentry would be able to put an arrow through his eye in the pitch dark.

'Hail, stranger,' said the elado in his own language. 'What would you be doing on the road after dark?'

'I had hoped to be here earlier,' Tomas replied in the same language. 'I ask shelter for the night.'

'That you may have,' said the sentry. 'We never turn our own away, especially in these days. If you have the means, Mother Liriel keeps an inn, and if you have not, the Hallows is ever open.' He disappeared, and soon his voice came from behind the insubstantial, rough-hewn wood of the gate, 'Dismount and lead your animal through.' The bar inside was thrown, and one side of the gate opened. It was not a very good gate, Tomas thought.

Tomas removed his hood. The sentry was taken aback at his white hair and beard. 'May I ask your name, sir?'

'My name is Tomas.'

The elado's face lit up the dark. 'Well, father – follow the light.'

That was a bit cryptic, thought Tomas as he led his mount along the street. The town was little more than a dusty camp, with houses no more than wattle-and-daub shacks roofed with thatch. The smells of settled places were heavy in the cold, still air: wood smoke, refuse, pigs and chickens.

Follow the light, the sentry had said. There was light ahead, so he made for it. Turning a corner he saw a big old house, wide-eaved in the dark – and light blazing from every window.

GLOSSARY

Archmagister: Chief religious and legal authority in a Southland town; often the head of a Haildom, a community of clerics.

Arkchabani: Foul folk bred with some human blood; large, strong, able to fight in daylight, with chalk-white skin.

Bulbul: short-billed bird with a yellow rump, about thrush size.

Celadi: 'Lamp Light-People', new or latecoming eladi who appeared after the Green Years in mighty ships; settled in parts of the South that had been abandoned by the Oreladi in the Foul Wars; also their language.

Coucal: Large, long-tailed bird, related to cuckoos but without their breeding habits; brown above and cream below, with a black cap; its long, low, liquid coo sounds a little like running water, and its call is said to herald rain.

Eladi: 'The Light People', the Fair Folk, wisest, eldest and most beautiful of all speaking beings, distinguished by small, leaf-shaped ears.

Ethenceldo: In Celadi usage, a centurion, or 'leader-of-120'.

Haildom: a place where cultural memories are preserved and propagated; always includes a sacred space (The Haildom).

Hallows: Celadi version of a human Haildom.

Kchabani: ('ch' as in Scots 'Loch') – the Foul Folk, made from primate stock in mockery of the Eladi in the Beginning of Days by the First Liar.

Lourie: (Loo'-ree) a turaco, an omnivorous bird with long tail quills and a crest, about the size of a crow; clumsy flier, often seen moving through the trees of a forest; appearance differs by latitude.

Moreladi: 'Dark Light People', another word for Oreladi, but mostly refers to those of Greenland; their language.

Oreladi: 'Old Light People', a distinct race of the Fair Folk, the original inhabitants of the Sunlands and all the South of the World; characterised by coffee-coloured skin, black to brown hair that bleaches gold in the sun, and green, hazel or tawny eyes.

Quaha: A large, domesticated species of equine related to zebras, having stripes only on its head, neck and forequarters. The hindquarters are chestnut. Animals from the island of Greenland are grey on the hindquarters.

Ratel: (Rah'-tel) a honey-badger.

Tinceldo: In Celadi usage, a Decurion, or 'leader-of-12'.

Printed in Great Britain
by Amazon